Things Unborn

Things Unborn

EUGENE BYRNE

EARTHLIGHT

LONDON · SYDNEY · NEW YORK · TOKYO · SINGAPORE · TORONTO

www.earthlight.co.uk

First published in Great Britain by Earthlight, 2001
An imprint of Simon & Schuster UK Ltd
A Viacom Company

Simon & Schuster UK Ltd
Africa House
64-78 Kingsway
London
WC2B 6AH

Simon & Schuster Australia
Sydney

A CIP catalogue record for this book is available
from the British Library

ISBN 0-743-40911-6

1 3 5 7 9 10 8 6 4 2

Typeset in 10/12.5pt Melior by
SX Composing DTP, Rayleigh, Essex

Printed and bound in Great Britain by
Omnia Books Ltd, Glasgow

For Monique

Even such is Time, which takes in trust
Our youth, our joys, our all we have,
And pays us but with earth and dust;
Who in the dark and silent grave,
When we have wandered all our ways,
Shuts up the story of our days.

But from this earth, this grave, this dust,
My God shall raise me up, I trust.

Sir Walter Raleigh, adding the last two lines on
the eve of his execution, October 29 1618.

SUNDAY, 17 AUGUST 2008

PILOT OFFICER GUY BOSWELL

My new family are a very rum lot, though very friendly. Sir Digby Lovejoy is a publisher and scholar from the seventeenth century, while Lady Lovejoy is a formidable old Victorian bird who does a lot of charity work. Their daughter Arabella was born here.

I was told at the reception centre that keeping a journal helps one get settled in, though I'd probably have done it anyway. It might help me organize my thoughts and feelings, and it'll keep me out of trouble. I need as many distractions as possible to stop me from brooding too much on those I have lost (those who have lost me?).

I have my own room at Sir Digby's handsome villa in Hampstead, a large attic job with two dormer windows, a very comfortable bed, a table and chair, a wardrobe and the loan of one of these transistor-radios upon which I have just listened to Sir Henry Purcell's new oratorio. We are all welcome to watch the television in the drawing-room downstairs if we wish. Sir D. is a big fan of the television, though Lady Lovejoy thinks it a destroyer of the conversational arts and damaging to the morals of the common people.

It is a large household – a cook, two maids, a butler, all of them related to the Lovejoys as far as I can tell.

Then Sir D., Lady L., Arabella, Arabella's companion Miss Constance Bright, and eight or nine assorted hangers-on and relatives like myself. We are, the expression goes, of Sir Digby's affinity, a big extended family of ancestors and descendants.

I get the impression that Sir D. would be happier without his affinity (and without Lady Lovejoy, for that matter), but he is a seventeenth-century gentleman and considers it his duty to look after us because he can afford to. He was reborn twenty-two years ago and made his money in publishing comics for semi-literate retreads about personal and public hygiene. Apparently you can still die of the bubonic plague here. There was a major outbreak in Manchester only two years ago in which fifty people died.

I find the idea of death here very queer indeed. As a retread myself, and having already died once only to find myself back among the living sixty-eight years later, I can only wonder what happens to you when you die here. Do you wake up in yet another world? No one here can answer that question with any authority, although plenty of folks claim they can.

I won't impose upon Sir D.'s hospitality any longer than necessary (though he appears to have rather taken a shine to me) and will find myself a flat in town as soon as I've found my footing.

Tomorrow evening I start my new job as an apprentice of detective police at the Bow Street station. Sir Digby was quite impressed that I am to be a thief-taker. At lunch today (very pleasant, informal meal which went on for most of the afternoon – the weather is hot, so *some twenty of us sat down to eat and drink on trestle-tables in the garden), he had me sit by him and told me how the modern police use a lot of advanced scientific techniques to solve crimes. They have vast card-indexes, huge records of fingerprints, and can tell an enormous amount from the tiniest scrap of evidence using microscopes. Each officer, he says, carries a portable radio telephone and an automatic pistol. I didn't have the heart to tell the old boy that the police used most of the methods he described back in my day, though they never carried guns then, of course.*

He is something of a scientific dabbler; he was among the earliest members of the Royal Society back in the 1600s and tells some very funny stories about Sir Isaac Newton, whom he considers an imbecile. Newton, he noted with some relief, lived to a ripe old age, and so is unlikely to reappear in this world. The iron rule seems to be that only people who died before their time, of accidents, disease, war, murder etc., reappear as retreads.

Lady Lovejoy was horrified to learn I am to be a Bow Street Runner and told me so in no uncertain manner. 'Mr Boswell,' she said imperiously (one has to be here a few months before you're on first name terms), 'you are a man of breeding and education. The police force is our great defence against crime and anarchy and is a noble calling for men and women of good character from the labouring classes. But you are a gentleman, and it is not a fitting occupation for you. Now what about the Church? Or the Civil Service? Or politics, even?' (Politics a fitting occupation for a gentleman? Ha!)

She didn't mention the Army or the Air Force. There is an air force here, apparently. She probably assumed I didn't much fancy getting into an aircraft again. She might have a point there.

Lady L. has been very kind to me, but she really is a frightful old snob. As a Victorian retread from the upper middle classes, she carries on like the most peppery Indian Burra Memsahib. She trotted us all off to Divine Service this morning, herding us all into our pews at the front of what I imagine is the most fashionable place of high Anglican worship in Hampstead (though I don't know the area at all). Naturally she led the entire Lovejoy affinity in the singing, intoning 'Now thank we all our God' in a trilling falsetto that set everyone's teeth on edge.

Her daughter and Miss Bright, who were seated to either side of me and who appear to have taken it upon themselves to make my stay here as pleasant as possible, found the old girl's singing mighty amusing. More amusing still is Lady L.'s pet charity, which the Vicar, the Reverend Perkins-Holdsworth DD, singled out for especial praise during a mercifully brief sermon on the virtues of Christian charity. One suspects he was buttering up the old girl in the hope of a hefty donation towards the price of a new organ, or something.

Lady L., it seems, is chairwoman and secretary of the Hampstead and District Ladies' Trouser Redemption Circle. The minute the Rev mentioned this, the girls made snorting noises, desperately trying to suppress their mirth. One can see why. What my hostess and her society ladies do is trawl around pawn-shops redeeming the trousers of working men who have hocked their garments in order to buy drink or, in some cases, opium, 'bhang' (hashish) or morphine. The ladies carry their prizes to one or another of their drawing-rooms and then pass a few convivial hours in gossip while, with scissors and sewing-machine, they modify the garments to fit small boys. They then visit the hovels of these indigents and present the trousers to their sons, on the infallible assumption that a man who pawns his own clothes for drink or drugs is unlikely to set aside much of his wage to clothe his children.

Arabella – Miss Lovejoy – and Constance – Miss Bright – explained to me afterwards that Lady L. is a little behind the times; these days few fathers who are alcoholics or drug addicts live with their families any more, and that the state has an elaborate system of outdoor relief to keep the poor in food, and indeed trousers. There is little unemployment here, though, and very few people are that deprived, unless it be by choice. Most retreads wake up here and think they've gone to Heaven.

Consider my own circumstances; I have been here just over a week and have been treated with the utmost humanity and kindness. I awoke, naked in a field, almost certainly on the spot where I died. I wandered around feeling mighty chilly for a while before a kindly farmer found me and loaned me a horse-blanket and took me to his kitchen. There I was fed some excellent stew and bread by his wife while he went off to fetch the people from the reception centre. They arrived half an hour later in a large white van not unlike an ambulance and took me away. They have these reception centres all over the country, many of them actually attached to

5

hospitals, and they appear to be run by a combination of private charity and municipal funds.

I was given a sedative and over the next few days they explained what had happened to me, and then found me some family; Sir Digby is an ancestor on my mother's side. In fact, I do vaguely remember that Ma owns (owned?) a book he wrote back in the seventeenth century on how make a better type of gunpowder or something.

The reception centre people telephoned Sir D. to see if he'd take me in for a while; this is very common. Passing new retreads over to their kinfolk gives them an instant circle of family and friends, even if only for the first few weeks they're here, and it saves the local council and charities a great deal of money. I was given a suit of formal clothes, some casual clothes, two pairs of shoes, a sum of money to tide me over, and a rail warrant to Waterloo Station. The reception centre also arranged my new job for me.

At Waterloo last night I was met by the Misses Lovejoy and Bright and taken here in a motor-cab, all the time having to tell them every last little detail about myself. On arrival here I was fed and then given a sound thrashing at tennis (Sir Digby has his own court in the back garden) by both of them in turn.

Arabella and Constance are smashing girls. Arabella is a shapely and, I suspect, rather sensual blonde with a terrific sense of fun. What I can't quite work out is why the very proper Lady L. allows me, a young full-of-beans chap with all the usual appetites, to consort so freely with her daughter. At the reception centre they told me that there are fairly strict laws of consanguinity which forbid one from marrying blood relatives within a number of degrees and generations. I cannot see, however, what would prevent marriage between Arabella and myself (not that any such thing is on my mind, or hers I am sure). Our kinship is very distant; Lady L. is no relation of mine and Arabella is not a retread. She was born to Sir Digby and Lady L. here some twenty years ago and is their only child. I can only assume that either Arabella is betrothed to some other chap (good luck to him!) or that relations between the sexes here are radically different from my time. Back in the 1930s, before what they here call the Hitler War, young men and women of our class had very elaborate courtship conventions, and certainly they wouldn't be left alone without a chaperone for very long.

It's possible, of course, that the old girl wants romance between Arabella and me, though I can't see why. Especially since I am to be a common policeman, and so would not be a suitable match at all.

Actually, if I had to choose between the two, I think I would opt for Constance. She is more serious and frankly more intelligent than her friend. Not a blue-stocking, but well read (we were quoting Seneca and Catullus at one another this morning), and with a splendid sense of sardonic humour. Unlike Arabella, Constance is a retread, having originally perished as a small girl in the influenza epidemic after the Great War. When she showed up here she was adopted by an ancestor of hers, an eighteenth-century gent who has now made his fortune here as a brewer in Islington. She lives with her adoptive father most of the time, but spends weeks on end here because she and Arabella cannot bear to be separated. Constance has beautiful curly black hair and lovely brown eyes and a tall, willowy body which . . .

No! No! No! This is all wrong!

I have been taken in by these kindly people, have the run of a beautiful house with an excellent library. I have a comfortable room, the weather is lovely and I am starting what should be a fascinating new job tomorrow evening. I also have the attention of two very attractive young women. I should be extremely happy, but . . .

Well, when I first found myself here in Arcadia (I've also heard it referred to as Toyland, Heaven, Utopia and Purgatory – but never Hell, which I suppose is heartening), but . . .

Oh, I don't know. I have just re-read what I have written so far. I can see that my sense of humour is intact, but I feel a great weight crushing me. It's the people I left behind, the disorientation of time and all sorts of things which might be clear to anyone else, but which gnaw at my innards during my every waking moment. Here I am eating and drinking and having intellectual conversations with Sir D. and flirting with these two very beautiful girls while back in another world, another time, my poor parents are grieving for their only child. And P. I miss her desperately. Perhaps in time I will get used to it.

Of course my parents are actually both dead by now. The reception centre people checked the records for me. They both passed away before the Atom War of 1962, and were both fairly old, so there is no chance they'll reappear. I didn't ask about P. Perhaps she was killed in the Hitler War, or the Atom War, or in the Feudal Wars of the 1970s.

One day I shall go to the Public Record Office and find out what befell her. But for now I don't think I could stand knowing.

LATER ...

Now I feel even worse. Just as I finished writing the above and was getting ready to turn in, who should knock on the door but Lady L.? She came in and sat on the bed and had a long chat about my previous life. She told me about how hard she found it when she was reborn and promised me that one does get over it. 'Human beings find it far easier to adapt to changed circumstances than you think,' she said, and gave me a glass of laudanum to help me sleep. I was sure she was then going to lecture me about the infinite mercy of the Almighty, but she did nothing of the sort. I take back all the beastly things I wrote about her earlier.

The only problem is that her kindness has left me feeling even more guilty and confused. Roll on the new job, I say. Anything to take my mind off all this.

Lord, I am tired! (Must be the laudanum.)

FREQUENTLY ASKED QUESTIONS

Should the resurrectee be aged over sixteen years, literate and of twentieth-century provenance, reception centre staff may expedite Preliminary Acclimatization Procedures by giving him or her these sheets to read when he or she reaches full consciousness. They are not recommended for subjects from earlier eras.

Where am I?

You are at . . . . reception centre in the county of . . . . The date is . . . . 2 . . . You are not in Heaven or Hell. You have died, but now you have been returned to life on Earth, some years in the future.

Why do I feel strange?

You may feel odd because you have been given a sedative. You may remember waking up naked, in a field, in a street, or even someone's private house. Perhaps you were found wandering in the fields or streets in a state of confusion. Medical assistance would have been summoned and a small and harmless dose of calming drugs may have been administered to you in accordance with the assessment of the attending officer.

What of the disease or injuries which killed me?

You are no longer affected by the illness or injury which killed you. Your body is the same age it was when you

10

died and over the coming days you will find that all your memories of your previous life are intact. Many of the ailments from which you suffered in your previous existence, such as bad teeth, deafness, poor eyesight, etc., will have been healed.

How did I get here?

Many who died prematurely in the past – of disease, in childbirth, of suicide, judicial execution, murder, etc. – have been resurrected. Few people aged over fifty-five years have returned. There are more resurrectees from recent centuries than from earlier times. This is because the population of the country was larger in recent centuries.

There is no pattern to the order or numbers in which resurrectees arrive. Currently about 600 new resurrectees appear each day in England, Wales, Scotland and Northern Ireland combined. At some point the number of possible individuals who can be resurrected must be exhausted. This may happen soon, or may not happen for several decades yet.

Usually, resurrectees materialize close to the place where they died. Although your physical appearance is exactly the same as in your previous life, you are no longer made of the same physical matter. Those who have witnessed a resurrectee's arrival describe the phenomenon as being attended by a small whirlwind, which appears to gather up dust, or soil, or even stone or furniture.

The reception centre is legally obliged to make available on demand a wide range of books and pamphlets outlining all the known current theories explaining the phenomenon of resurrection. Scientific explanations include those concerning particle resonance and cross-dimensional matter displacement. Many people, however, feel that their return is the work of God, who is giving them an opportunity to live more righteously than hitherto. A common popular expression for a resurrectee is a 'retread'; the word can be taken to mean one who is once again walking the earth, or as a cynical adaptation of a twentieth-century word meaning a restored motor vehicle tyre.

When did people start returning from the dead?
Probably in 1962. In that year a catastrophic war was fought between an alliance led by Great Britain and the United States of America and one led by the Soviet Union (Communist Russia). This, the so-called Atom War, culminated in the use of extremely powerful weapons which caused severe destruction throughout Europe and Russia, in Great Britain, and on the eastern side of the United States. Invisible rays released by the bombs continued to kill and cause sickness for many years following their actual use.

In many areas, including Great Britain, a complete breakdown of civil order followed. During this time, the first reappearances of the dead occurred in areas affected by the War. Some people claim that the 'collective unconscious' of mankind is summoning forth the spirits of other dead to replace those lost in the War. This theory has no formal scientific basis, but is attractive to many who can no longer believe in a God who would permit the cruelties of the Atom War, or have any confidence in the science which created the weapons used in the War. In general, people tend to resurrect in areas within a 400-mile radius of places where atomic weapons were detonated. There have been resurrectees in North America, all over Europe and the Middle East, in the former Soviet Union and in parts of the Far East. Very few people have returned from the dead in Africa, India, Central and South America and Australasia.

What has happened in Britain since the Atom War?
Three-quarters of the native population died within ten years. Some died at once, others died later of hunger, of violence in the breakdown in civil order which occurred, and from what is now called the 'radiation plague', a sickness caused by the rays from the bombs. The population now is still less than half of what it was before the War. The government collapsed and for some years the country was divided into small fiefdoms ruled by local warlords. As the more aggressive of these conquered others, a form of government similar to the medieval feudal system developed.

By the mid-1970s, several small wars were being fought in various parts of the country. These eventually crystallized into a single struggle between two forces; the Nationalists or 'Roundheads', and the Coalition. The Nationalists were for the most part Protestants and supporters of the Duke of Monmouth's claim to the throne. The Coalition was an alliance of many different forces and creeds, including Catholics and Protestants as well as Socialists, Liberals and democrats.

By the end of the 1970s, the Coalition had been completely victorious, much of its success due to the support of the United States, whose President sustained it with materials, modern weapons and military advisers, even though his own country had also been grievously harmed in the Atom War.

The final act of the Feudal Wars was the entry into London of Coalition forces and the implementation of what was known as the Liberal Settlement, which includes an Act of Toleration, by which the state recognizes the legitimacy of all Christian denominations. Since this time, order has been restored throughout the country and most of the physical damage caused by the wars has been repaired.

By the Liberal Settlement, Britain is ruled by the King in Parliament, though in effect King Richard III has no real power. Parliaments – the House of Commons and the Senate – are elected every five years by all men and women over twenty-one years of age who can read and write. The majority of MPs belong to political parties with which you may be familiar – Conservatives (Tories), Liberals and Socialists (Labour). The minority parties include the Radicals, the Communists and religious parties such as the Fifth Monarchy Men and the Essenes. Other religious parties refuse to stand for Parliament as they do not recognize the Liberal Settlement. Although it is over thirty years since the Feudal Wars ended, some ill-feeling remains.

Much of this ill-feeling is, however, blunted by the fact that after years of stability, Britain can now offer its citizens a higher material standard of living than that experienced by most people in their previous lives. The Government, through taxes raised, pays for several services, including the reception centre in which you find yourself at the moment.

Are there others like me?

At the moment, about a third of the population of Great Britain have come back from previous lives. About half of the remainder are those who survived the Atom War (and their children); there are large numbers of these in remote parts of Wales, Scotland or south west England, but they can also be found in the cities. The rest of the population are the children, many now grown to adulthood, of resurrectees.

Will I encounter any language difficulties?

Any educated person knows that the English language has changed a great deal down the centuries. Because people from different times and different regions of the country speak differently, the British Broadcasting Corporation is trying to encourage the use of a Standard Form of English through its radio and television programming (see below). The Standard Form is also used on all government documents (including this one) and communications, and it tends also to be the language of business and newspapers, although there are many papers and magazines written in more archaic forms which are read by resurrectees from particular periods. The Government does not wish to eliminate archaic or regional forms of English; it is in fact most anxious that these are preserved. For the efficient conduct of business and government, however, it is necessary that everyone is also able to speak and understand a language which can be used throughout the country. Individuals from the late nineteenth or twentieth centuries will encounter little difficulty with the Standard Form, sometimes also known as 'Standard' or 'BBC'.

Might any of my kinfolk and friends be here?
If they died prematurely, they might be here, or they might arrive in years to come. Using public records, we will ascertain whether any of your close relatives are here. You are not obliged to contact them if you do not wish to do so.

Should your spouse be here, the law regards you as no longer under any obligation to each other. This is because one of you may have arrived here several years ago, and it would be unfair to expect people to await the arrival of a spouse who, given the random nature of resurrection, may never arrive at all. Should you wish to remarry, you must undergo a civic or religious ceremony.

Will I be able to have children?
If you were capable of siring or bearing children in your last life, you will almost certainly be capable of doing so here. There are also some children who have been resurrected and who are available for adoption. Very few babies and infants return, which has led some scientists to conclude that a certain level of sentience is necessary before one can be resurrected.

Has anyone who has died prematurely since the Atom War come back?
As far as is known, nobody who has died since 1962 has been resurrected.

If I die prematurely again, will I wake up alive in another world?
Nobody in this world can answer that question with any certainty.

MONDAY, 18 AUGUST 2008

The past is a foreign country; they do things differently there.
– L.P. Hartley, *The Go-Between*

Matteradamn that there was a heatwave on, Detective Inspector Scipio Africanus never started the evening shift without a cup of coffee. His own personal kettle and mug had gone AWOL in the chaos wrought by the workmen, so he had had to content himself with some stuff in a plastic cup from the coin-operated hot slop machine in the reception area.

It was scalding his fingers. If only he could reach his desk . . .

Half a dozen people competed for his attention.

'Inspector,' shouted Constable Waverley, his hand cupped over the mouthpiece of his telephone, 'we've got a murder.'

'Don't you mean a *suspected* murder, Waverley?' said Scipio.

'Oh no, sir. Nothing suspected about it. Unless he managed to dash his own brains out with a spade.'

'Stranger things have happened,' said Scipio sourly, spilling a good quarter of his coffee on to the abundantly stained and cigarette-singed linoleum. 'Radio Sergeant O'Rourke and tell him to take a shufti.'

'Very good, Inspector,' said Waverley.

Bow Street police station had not been big enough for

the amount and variety of crime in this part of London for three decades or so. Most of the original building had been demolished by one of the three bombs which had pulverized much of the old city during the Atom War in 1962. The station had been rebuilt back in the 1980s, but it was just too small. This was, after all, the middle of Rumville, the Great Wen, a very magnet for people of daring and enterprise seeking their fortunes.

Now, at last, the wretched builders were in. Or rather, they were not. They had gone home for the evening, leaving planks, sacks of cement, stacks of bricks, bags of tools and lengths of electric cable lying all over the shop. These, and a fine covering of brick and plaster dust on everything. Scipio and the rest of the CID had had to leave their regular quarters. They and their desks were now temporarily camped in the front office, sharing the space with a dozen harassed-looking woodentops who were failing to cope with the Herculean workload that high summer always brought.

'Thee dost'nt wanna drink coffee, blackamoor,' shouted King Edward II, who was handcuffed to a radiator in reception. ''Tis the devil's brew, 'tis unwhole-some, an' gives you the piles summat wicked . . .'

Scipio ignored him, reached the sanctuary of his desk, and put down the cup. He looked at the mountain of paper that he had brought from his office and groaned. You could forget most of this when it was neatly concealed in filing cabinets.

And so to work, he thought, and took the bottom half from each pile of bumf, and dropped it into his waste-paper basket. It was more certain than income tax that someone somewhere would have five copies of anything important.

With less than a week to Accession Day, the tourist season was reaching its peak. This year there were more foreigners in London than ever; the Government was loudly proclaiming this as evidence that Britain was once more a civilized and prosperous land. 'You've never had it so good,' some politician had said. Having it this good meant the police had to work twelve-hour shifts six or seven days a week, with no possibility of any leave until October.

The electricity workers, dissatisfied with their pay, had declared for strike action; if the lights went off tonight, every footpad and twister in the West End would have a rich harvest.

Scipio was personally responsible for 4,222 unsolved cases, twenty-three of them murders. He sipped at his coffee, knowing it would burn his tongue. It did. And it tasted of brick-dust.

A tourist – Dutch? German? Danish? – had come in. Big nose, big moustache, hair white, age about fifty. He wore a white cambric shirt and those fashionable particoloured stretch-tights that showed off his legs to good effect. Muscular thighs and calves. A keen horse-rider, perhaps. More likely a cyclist. Still looked ruddy stupid, though. Anyone dressing like that over the age of thirty-five looked stupid. And he carried his belongings in one of those leather shoulder-bags which were all the rage with the youngsters.

The silly man was complaining to Sergeant Hopton that he had visited a whorehouse and the woman had tried to flay his arse with birch twigs. It was clearly an innocent misunderstanding caused by language barriers, but he wanted to file for assault.

Constable Glyndwr had had a frightful row with his boyfriend. Scipio knew this because the topmost piece of paper on his desk referred to a severe domestic disturbance at Glyndwr's lodgings. He picked up this sheet and consigned it, too, to the bin.

Glyndwr had an I'm-going-to-hit-someone-tonight-you-see-if-I-don't look under his abundant, carefully-plaited moustaches. He sat at his desk filing 9-mm rounds into dum-dums and glared murderously at the squawking Dane.

King Edward II mumbled to himself. Although it was patent that His Majesty was a mere vagrant who was no more of royal blood than a stray dog, every pretender to the throne had to be flattered. The last shift had acted by the book and summoned a Senior Outreach Worker from Debrett's Peerage. The Honourable Mrs Caroline Newnham-Fame, a woman of considerable energy and surprisingly coarse manner, had tested His Majesty and failed him comprehensively. She had been leaving as Scipio arrived ten minutes ago. 'Complete bloody lunatic,' she had barked as she packed away her reference books and portable polygraph. 'You know, Inspector, on most of the occasions I get called out to establish anyone's pedigree, I find they're lying. I sometimes despair of ever meeting anyone of any real breeding . . . I say, I bet you're of noble blood, though. To be a black fellow in this country usually means you're of slave stock, which means you're probably from West Africa. You might be descended from one of those Ashanti kings, some frightfully bloodthirsty fellow with three hundred wives. Want me to try and track your family down?'

Scipio had declined politely. He was not descended from any African nobility. If he had been, he would never have been enslaved. QED. But at least the Hon. Mrs Newnham-Fane had some idea of his origins. A lot of people assumed he really was the ancient Roman general, or at least some vague figment of long-forgotten Latin lessons suddenly made flesh.

Edward II had been brought up from the cells and awaited the evening shuttle-bus to the loony bin and told anyone who wished to listen that he was a martyr to haemorrhoids.

Scipio looked at the piles (piles?!) of paper once more.

He could not work in these circumstances. He would go and look at this spade-murder himself. O'Rourke was perfectly capable of dealing with it, but he just had to get out of this bedlam.

As he stood up and took his jacket from the back of his chair, a slim young man in a suit that had almost certainly been issued by a reception centre, all baggy trousers and boxy, padded shoulders, appeared beside him.

'Detective Inspector Africanus, sir?'

'What?' he snapped.

'Er, I'm to be your 'prentice, sir.'

'Oh Lord, no, please! Why me?!' he wailed.

Scipio most assuredly did not want a 'prentice. In his time, he had been obliged by law to play wet-nurse, protector and father-confessor to eight new retreads – six men and two women. Four of them, to be sure, had become successful rozzers (three now outranked him), but there had been failures, too. One had chucked in the force to become a nun, one had decided to open a cheese-shop in Covent Garden, another had run off to become a circus-acrobat. One was in The Scrubs for fraud. For all that, the Central Resettlement Office's files obviously still had a high regard for Scipio's abilities as mentor.

Either that or someone there hated him.

'Please stop looking at me like that,' he said to the newcomer. 'Have you never seen an overheated and irritable black man before? Who the blazes sent you here and why was I not warned?'

'Sorry, sir. For staring, I mean. I came up a week ago. I've come from the West Malling reception centre. In Kent. When they suggested police work, it sounded jolly interesting . . . They did say you'd be expecting me.' He proffered a piece of official paper. Scipio did not bother to read it. If the lad had only been here a week, he would have some education. And he spoke near-enough Standard English. The centre would be trying to save on bed space by leaving Scipio to do the inducting.

'Name?'

'Boswell, sir. Guy Boswell.'

'Origins?'

'Born in Brighton, 1915. Worked as a journalist for a while, then joined the Royal Air Force in 1939. Killed in action a year later to the day. I was a fighter pilot. Took a load of Jerry bullets up the jacksie, that is, I was, er, shot down by a German aeroplane.'

Twenty-five years old. Probably went to one of those

public schools. Tall, healthy-looking. Keen, open face. Eager to please. Ashamed that he'd been killed. He had let the others down. Handsome in a Mummy's boy sort of way. Positive. Everything is jolly fun. But sensitive, too.

Nice fellow.

Nice fellows do not always make good coppers.

'You paint, or write stories, or poetry, perhaps?'

Boswell's jaw dropped, then he broke into a smile. 'I say, sir! Could you really tell that about me just by looking at me? Yes, I do sort of dabble in painting, nothing especially good I'm afraid. And I'm very keen on poetry, though I don't, can't, write it myself. How on earth did you know?'

How on earth had CRO decided to recommend this man for the police?

'Observation equals good copper, Boswell. Lesson one.' After eight 'prentices, he had started to acquire an alarming number of trite maxims.

'Should I write that down, sir?'

'I would greatly prefer you to commit it to memory.'

'Right-oh, sir. Observation equals good copper.'

'Boswell,' said Scipio, returning his jacket to the back of the chair. 'You have precisely five minutes to demonstrate to me that you are not a complete clown. Have you any idea how you can do this?'

'No, sir, none whatever.'

'Then you will pull that chair over there to my desk, you will sit down and you will tell me about your career as an aviator.'

Scipio realized that the Danish tourist at the front desk was drunk. He had pulled down his trousers and was showing Sergeant Hopton the weals on his arse.

Glyndwr was getting up to hit him.

'Constable Glyndwr,' Scipio shouted, 'return to your desk at once and find some useful work to do. I remind you that regulations clearly state that tourists are valued guests in Great Britain, and should therefore only be clouted in order to protect oneself or members of the public.'

Glyndwr shrugged and sat down.

'What time is it, Boswell?'

'Sorry sir, I don't have a watch yet.'

'Well get one. Do you have any money?'

'Yes, sir,' said Boswell, pulling a chair over and sitting down. 'The reception centre gave me twelve pounds and fifteen shillings to tide me over until my first pay-packet. I understand it's the standard amount.'

Scipio reached behind him and fumbled in his jacket pocket and found his own battered wristwatch. Just coming up to six.

'We'll leave your story for a moment, Boswell. I want to listen to the news headlines. Then you can tell me your thrilling tale of derring-do.' He opened the top drawer of his desk and took out his transistor-radio and turned it on.

The Danish tourist was demanding that Hopton take a photograph of the injuries to his bottom as Big Ben chimed on the radio.

Good Evening. This is the BBC Home Service broadcasting from London, and here are the news headlines at six o'clock on Monday, the eighteenth of August 2008.

Things Unborn

His Majesty the King today began a busy week of engagements which will culminate on Saturday with the Accession Day celebrations. This afternoon, he officiated at the opening ceremony of the new wing of the Public Record Office at Chancery Park in London. The new facilities will allow any member of the public, free of charge, to search official records in order to trace their forebears, their descendants and other relations more rapidly than ever before. His Majesty became the first person to use the new filing system, which boasts more than five million family files and an estimated eighty million index cards on individuals. His Majesty shared a joke with staff, saying he wondered if he had any wealthy relative in whose household he might find employment as a gardener or turnspit. In a short speech afterwards, he told Public Record Office workers that they were engaged in vital and worthwhile work. He said that for many people, being reborn into this world was a shocking experience, but that being able to trace even distant kinfolk quickly would alleviate much of the alienation and distress experienced by all retreads.

A man has been found guilty of the murder of two young children in the Collyhurst area of Manchester in February. The jury at Manchester Crown Court decided within half an hour that Arise Hampson, aged twenty-three, had cut the throats of the twin boys Albert and George Higgins and then left various items associated with the Jewish religion at the site of the crime. Hampson, a retread from the seventeenth century, is a member of an extremist Protestant group and is thought to have been trying to stir up anti-Jewish feeling. He has not spoken throughout the trial except to say that he did not recognize the authority of the court. Chief Inspector Lancelot Bickley of the Lancashire Constabulary, who led the investigation, said that Hampson had committed a vile crime and compounded it by trying to blame an industrious and wholly inoffensive group of people. He paid tribute to the hard work of his officers and said that troublemakers would always be defeated by careful policing and modern forensic science. Hampson will be sentenced next month and, given the premeditated nature of his crime, is expected to face the death penalty.

The London County Council Board of Works has published the report of the Jennings Commission which was established two years ago to consider the feasibility of reopening some or all of the old London Underground Railway. Engineers say that repair works to the infrastructure and the building of new rolling stock on a number of the lines could be completed within three years at a cost of not less than twenty million pounds. A spokesman for the Council said that budgetary considerations would not permit work to begin this year, but that a bond issue will be considered next year to finance the project.

The Minister of Health, the Right Honourable Miss Daphne Bradshaw has announced that there is increasing concern among doctors that over one-third of the adult population of England, Wales and Scotland is overweight. Miss Bradshaw said that too many people were consuming cheap, fattening foods to the detriment of their own health and to the resources of the public medical services. The Whig Party spokesman on moral issues, Sir Wisdom Greene, said that while in govern-

ment, the Labour Party had promoted the sin of gluttony when the Prime Minister, the Right Honourable Mr Gordon Brown, had intervened to reduce the import duties on the sugar and cocoa beans used for the manufacture of chocolate bars. Sir Wisdom said that gluttony was an evil akin to drunkenness and that all true Englishmen preferred plain, honest food. Miss Bradshaw later countered that it is no business of government to regulate people's dietary habits but simply to advise those who may be innocently harming themselves because of ignorance, or because they were born in an age which equated corpulence with prosperity. She said that the Government would be launching an education campaign in the autumn through schools, adult education centres and the radio and television.

The Continental Department of the Reception and Resettlement Service has announced that Mr Keith Douglas, a poet who was killed in France in the latter part of the Hitler War, has been reborn. Mr Douglas, who was found close to the place where he had been killed in Normandy in 1944, has been in the care of the Dover reception centre for the past two weeks. Listeners may be interested to know that Mr Douglas has consented to be interviewed on the Home Service's poetry programme next Thursday.

Overseas news, and in the American presidential campaign, the Democratic Party challenger, Senator Gary Hart, has said that if elected he will use the presidential powers of pardon to release Mr Robert Kennedy from prison. Mr Kennedy and his brother President John F. Kennedy were impeached and

27

sentenced to several life sentences during the 1960s for their part in starting the Atom War. While the former president died in a federal prison in 1978, his brother, who was Attorney-General in his government, has survived. Senator Hart says that he should now be released on humanitarian grounds given his old age, and that the American nation should put the traumas of the twentieth century behind it. His opponent in the forthcoming election, the Republican President James Garfield, has so far refused to comment.

It is now three minutes past six. At half-past six, in the Literacy Hour, Will Beddoes will be looking at application forms for employment, and recommending some of the best books and comics for adults who are just starting to read. But first, today's episode of The Archers, *in which Cecelia is becoming increasingly nervous about the impending visit of one of her Tudor ancestors, while in* The Bull, *Old Percival sees the opportunity of an evening's free ale when a collector of folk-songs pays a call . . .*

Detective Constable Jenny Pearson leaned against a lamp-post and feigned interest in the sermon. Her skirt ran to well below the knee and she wore sensible shoes and a big, shapeless grey jacket full of pockets. She hadn't gone the whole hog and put on a poke bonnet, but her appearance was sober enough to intimate that she would seriously consider renouncing sin and prepare for the return of the Lord.

This small patch of empty ground had been a bomb-site for years. Recently, the Bulls had taken it over, cleared the weeds and rubble and erected a small wooden platform where one or another Upright Man prated as long as the weather was good.

She liked standing pad. You never get tired of people-watching. It was out of her normal line of detective work, but with the tourist season at its height, it was important to ensure that as few as possible fell victims to crime. She and Trevor had been pulled from their usual caseload and told to hang about in likely spots. Sooner or later, business would come their way. It always did.

Trevor Mills, her oppo, stood a few yards away, pretending to study the prize-fighting form in the *Evening Standard*. Trevor was a decent enough cove, though he spoke little and was tautened up by the demon in his soul, probably because he was a native, of which there were comparatively few left in London. Born in 1960, he had lived through the aftermath of the Atom War, then the Feudal Wars, the food shortages and plagues. Both his parents were long dead – natives didn't have the retreads' immunity to the radiation plague – and he acted as though his time would be done imminently, even though he was almost fifty and still in rude health. So sometimes he went cammy-karzi, acting like he didn't care whether he died or not, getting them both into dangerous corners. He probably hoped that if he died prematurely he would awake in another world, like the retreads had done here.

Trevor usually dyed his hair, too. It would be darker on Monday than on Friday, but not for now. Trevor was an excellent pad (he had taught her much of her streetcraft), and he knew that making himself look his age meant that fewer people would take any notice of him. Now he stood there in bottle-green corduroy trousers, a bulky tweed jacket and flat cap like any other working man making his way home for the night.

The preacher had gathered a small crowd, part local, part tourist, and was babbling about the coming of the millennium, the thousand-year dominion of the righteous, the imminent return of the Lord in glory, the necessity of destroying the Liberal Settlement, of overthrowing the Catholic monarchy and destroying King Richard, who was in reality the Antichrist, and of instituting a government of the saints to prepare the way.

Rozzers had little time for God-botherers. All the while the Upright Men prated about righteousness, their secret society, the Antient and Honourable Order of the Sons of John Bull, was a criminal organization, plugged into every lay and racket there was, a haven to every low spicer in England.

She noticed a boy, ten or eleven, at the edge of the crowd, no more interested in the sermon than she. Black trousers and navy jacket, sealskin hat and a black band around his right arm, as though in mourning. He had beautifully clear skin, big shiny blue eyes. Oh! He was adorable enough to be one of the sprogs on the television ads exhorting people to eat frozen peas, or adopt retread kids . . .

Too plausible by half.

Ah! This was the life! Jenny's mother was a retread, and in her last life she had been condemned to drudgery and ignorance as a farm servant, then, had she lived, to drudgery and ignorance as some smallholder's wife. Here, she had chosen her own man and her own future. Jenny would do the same, she had her own job, her own money, an education, she could choose her own husband (but not yet!) . . .

Trevor folded his newspaper under his arm, looked at his wristwatch and glanced towards her. She made a tiny nod of her head in the kid's direction. Trevor yawned and took the strap of his canvas bag containing his radio and gun and set it over his right shoulder.

The kid was on the lay, right enough. But did he have any stalls? With his Little Lord Fauntleroy looks and his nimble fingers, he'd be a valuable property. He'd have accomplices, a putter-up . . . Jenny moved the strap of her own handbag into place.

Her eyes worked the crowd furiously, looking for the boy's partner while he stood, hands in pockets, as though in a sweet-shop with a pound to spend.

'And I say unto you,' preached the Bull, 'the presence of a CATHOLIC on the throne of England is an ABOMINATION in the sight of the LORD, as were the DISGUSTING vices practised by the DAMNED peoples of SODOM and GOMORRAH.'

The Upright Men spoke as their pamphlets read, with the occasional word picked out in capitals to keep you awake.

Quick as a Saxon running from soap, the kid dipped a side-pocket of the sports jacket of a man in front of him.

And came out with his reader. You had to admire it.

The flat was a chubby little cove in glasses and straw boater, who remained unaware his pocket had been picked, and stood shaking his head and grinning smugly at the Upright Man's nonsense. A tourist.

'It is written in the SCRIPTURES. His RETURN IN

31

GLORY is imminent. And that those RIGHTEOUS who would be SAVED must RISE UP as a great and mighty ARMY . . .'

The kid had the wallet inside his own jacket and sauntered off at a smart pace. Trevor was already away, walking fast as though heading up the Avenue, working his way around in a narrow arc to block the kid's escape. Jenny strode straight after the boy.

The kid walked into Trevor as he reached Shaftesbury Avenue and saw he was trapped as Jenny closed in behind him.

'You're under arrest,' she said while Trevor got the bracelets out. 'On suspicion of theft. By law I must warn you that you are not obliged to say anything, but anything you do say will be noted and may be used in evidence against you. Do you understand what I am saying?'

Great glycerine tears gushed out of his lovely dark eyes. 'Oh please don't take me away!' he wailed. 'Please!' Sob. 'You can't be so cruel as to do a thing like this!' Moan. 'I beg you to have a little decency of sentiment.' Whinge.

Instantly, a crowd gathered around them. This was better sport than the Upright Man's huckstering.

'Can you not see I am in mourning for my poor, poor mother?' Blubber. 'Please don't take me away!' Snivel. 'You ma'am, I beg you to have a woman's sensibility and not make me go back to that life.' Howl. 'That piteous existence of utter degradation!'

The boy collapsed, grovelling in the gutter. Trevor repeated the caution, once again asking the brat if he understood his rights. The kid carried on howling, implying she and Trevor were procuress and pimp.

Little swine.

Trevor grabbed the kid by the arm and yanked him upright, fumbling with the cuffs in his other hand.

'What's goin' on here, bub?' said an American tourist at her side.

'We're taking him in for theft. We're police officers,' said Jenny.

'Oh nooooo! My poor mother!' screamed the kid. 'I'm so sorry Mama! I promised you I would never again submit to doing those terrible things with men!' He continued, now thickening the plot by introducing a crippled sister he had to support.

'Oh yeah?' said the Yank, two of whose friends had appeared at his side. 'You sure look,' he said to Trevor, 'like a goddam fruit to me. Let the boy go!'

Trevor had the cuffs on one of the kid's wrists.

'Me and my buddies here are war-veterans, you know. We can handle ourselves. Now either you show us some ID or you let the kid go.'

Jenny sighed and opened her bag and rooted around for her warrant-card. 'I appreciate your public-spirit, but I assure you we are plain-clothes police officers, and this boy has just stolen . . .'

'Hey! That's my billfold!' exclaimed one of the Americans, pointing to the gutter where the kid had dropped the wallet to distance himself from the evidence.

As Trevor looked down, the kid pulled free and ran. The crowd, half-convinced the brat was trying to escape a life on the twang as a gentlemen's plaything, broke to let him through.

'Awwwww DAMN!' yelled Jenny. Trevor was already running after the kid. She took off after him, uselessly waving her silver slice in the Yank's stupid, bloated, pop-eyed face.

It was almost seven-thirty. The Avenue was crowded with people off to the theatres, music-halls or cinemas, or looking for somewhere to eat.

She pushed her way through herds of Americans, Anzacs and Indians, through gawking crunchers up from the country, past Londoners going about their business, past gangs of swells and swivellers, past dollymops and biddies trawling for Johns.

Trevor was about a hundred yards up ahead, galloping past the big Wimpy restaurant.

On she ran, past scaldrums begging for passing change, showing off their faked diseases and injuries.

Trevor was getting further and further away. He disappeared behind a one-man band playing for the queue outside the Locarno Music-Hall. Her chest ached. She dodged out into the road to avoid the queue. Behind her a car honked, she glanced back and nearly ran into a hansom.

Trevor was waiting at the corner of St Giles High Street.

'Holy Land?' gasped Jenny, fighting for breath.

Trevor nodded grimly, taking the radio from his bag.

'That's that, then.'

'No it isn't,' said Trevor. 'I could have caught him if I'd wanted.'

'Eh?'

'While our tourist friends were kicking up a fuss I slipped my peach into one of his pockets,' he said, tuning the radio to the frequency of the miniature radio-beacon he had slapped on the brat. 'I don't think he noticed.'

Last year, some bright spark at Scotland Yard had bought a gross of these newfangled miniature radio transmitters from India saying they would be of great assistance in the fight against crime. Some popular newspaper had nicknamed them 'peaches' because they would peach – inform – on a suspect's where-abouts. At Bow Street, everyone thought they were a silly and pointless gimmick, and only Trevor had bothered to draw one from the stores.

'Trevor, why in Heaven's name do we want to play kiss-chase through the Holy Land?'

'Because he might lead us to something interesting. We might get a whole thieves' kitchen, Fagin and all. Instead of getting one snot-nosed chavie, we might net a whole firm.'

'We might also get killed.'

Trevor shrugged. His radio started squeaking. 'This way,' he said, crossing the road.

She followed.

'It was a nice story,' said Scipio to his new 'prentice as they walked out of the back of the station and over to the car-pool.

'Thank you, sir,' said Boswell, who had related how he had been shot down by a German fighter aircraft in 1940. 'We got plenty of practice in the mess, yarning to one another about the scrapes we'd got into during the day's work. I wonder how the rest of the squadron did that day.'

'You should be able to look it up,' said Scipio, fumbling in his pocket for car-keys.

'Sorry?'

'The next occasion on which you have a few hours to spare – and I can promise you that will not occur for some weeks yet – you can go to the Public Record Office, and see what happened to the rest of your comrades that day and later.'

'Really? Will they have all that?'

'One cannot guarantee it, but history and historical records are terribly important here. Infinitely more so than in your last life, for reasons which may be starting to dawn on you.'

Boswell stopped walking, looked agitated. 'I say, Inspector . . .'

'Yes?'

He shook his head and sighed.

'Oh, nothing.'

They reached one of the big old Humber Odyssey squad-cars. Scipio patted it on the bonnet. 'Our chariot, Boswell. We have six of these. They are twenty years old but they have never let us down yet. Which is as well, because the Met will not give us the money to buy any new ones.' He climbed into the driver's seat.

'It's funny, sir,' said Boswell, getting in beside him. 'This car doesn't look too different from the police cars of my previous life. A little bigger, perhaps. At the reception centre when they told me I had died and woken up nearly seventy years later I thought this world would look very different, but it doesn't in all its essentials.'

'It may look similar,' said Scipio as he started the

engine, 'but I can promise you that it thinks a whole lot differently. You are right, though. For someone from your time, there are only a few signs of technical progress here. Televisions and transistor radios are about it. It's the consequence of the Atom War and the anarchy and Feudal Wars that followed it. We have all been too busy trying to survive to have the time to invent anything. That is now starting to change, of course.'

To get the vehicle out of the cramped car-park took a considerable amount of application. Scipio fumbled with the gears and cursed quietly as he manoeuvred the thing backwards and forwards until, at last, he had a clear run at the open gates. He pushed her out into the street, narrowly missing an omnibus.

'It is your girl you are wondering about, no?' he said, once they were under way.

'Sorry, sir?'

'You were about to ask me a question a moment ago. You want to know that happened to your girlfriend or fiancée.'

'How did you know?'

'At the reception centre they will have told you of your parents' fate, and that of any brothers or sisters you had, although your demeanour is that of an only son. Back in the station you took no particular notice of any of the male officers, but you gazed distractedly upon the very shapely form of WPC Hobbs as she helped to wrestle that drunken prostitute down to the cells. Therefore I deduce it is your girl you are wondering about.'

One of the few consolations in serving the night shift

in summer was that you did not have to endure the London heat by day. The sun was low in the sky, now dipping behind tall buildings, now flashing out again to ambush them. He rolled the window down and drank in the air.

Ah yes! Being abroad on an evening like this knocked being in the station into a cocked hat.

'Pamela,' said Boswell at length. 'We weren't going to be married or anything, but we were getting pretty serious. I miss her terribly.'

Scipio glanced across at him. Not blubbing, but lips pursed, chin jutting out. Taking it hard.

'I am sorry, Boswell. Truly. Do not be ashamed of your sorrow.'

'Thank you, sir.'

'The pain is very common. Initially when people wake up here and find they have been given a second chance, they are usually delighted. Then, after a few days, the anguish and loneliness of knowing that you have left loved ones behind starts to set in. We call it the mourning sickness.'

Scipio could barely remember what it was like to be reborn, but in his case, he hadn't left anyone he truly cared about behind. But he had been in Arcadia long enough to have developed his own drill for dealing with depressed youngsters.

First kindness, then change the subject . . . He fished his cigarette-case out of his breast pocket and passed it to Boswell, saying, 'Have one and light one for me as well.'

From the corner of his eye, he noticed Boswell admiring the solid silver case and the inscription on it.

He read it out loud. 'To Major Scipio Africanus, from the private soldiers and non-commissioned officers of the Fifth Mechanized Infantry Regiment, in admiration and gratitude for your courageous leadership and tireless concern for the welfare of your comrades. August 1979.'

The young man struck a match and passed him a lighted Great Zimbabwe. African tobacco was more expensive than American Virginia these days, but he had made it a matter of principle to buy African after the old colonial regimes in Kenya and the Rhodesias were overthrown.

'You fought in the Feudal Wars, sir?'

'As a question, Boswell, that will not do. It is a waste of time and of breath, and were you engaged upon a police investigation when asking it, you would be squandering the taxpayers' money. Of course I fought in the ruddy Feudal Wars. That is what the cigarette-case tells you.'

'Sorry sir.'

'Stop it. You are here to learn, not apologize all the time.'

He turned into High Holborn and straight into a traffic-jam. They were stuck behind a bus, breathing in its diesel fumes. Still better than being in the office, though.

'How did . . . ?' Boswell fumbled with the question all his 'prentices wanted to ask.

'Let me assist you. What you are trying to ask is how on earth did a blackbird, a coon with no formal education, rise to high command in the Coalition army?'

Boswell turned red. How affecting!

'There are two answers,' he continued. 'Either I was a supremely gifted tactician and leader of men, or they were absolutely gopping desperate. The truth, of course, lies somewhere between the two.'

The traffic was not moving at all. He killed the engine, leaned back and took a deep drag on his cigarette. The streets were getting too busy these days. Even ten years back most of the traffic had been buses, taxis, vans, lorries and a bewildering variety of horse-drawn vehicles. Now more and more people could afford cars and the petrol to run them with. One saw fewer and fewer horses on the streets these days; keeping prads was too much like hard work anyway.

Kitty was always on at him to buy a car, saying how good it would be to take the kids on picnics in the country at weekends. He could probably afford it, too.

'Your story, Boswell, the business of your fighter aircraft and the Messy-whatchamacallems—'

'Messerschmitts, sir.'

'Yes, those . . . Anyway, you are a well-educated young man from a recent time in our history. You are also a dashing military hero. These things qualify you to move in the highest circles . . .'

'Oh, I don't know about any of that, sir. I can't dance a step, and I hardly know how to hold a soup-spoon properly.'

'Then you had better start learning unless you wish to be a flatfoot for the rest of your life,' said Scipio. 'What I meant to tell you was that while I was intrigued to hear of how you died, it is considered vulgar in polite society to describe your demise in excessive detail.'

'Thank you, sir. I'll remember.'

'Apart from the high Victorians,' said Scipio, distractedly. 'They are besotted with death, particularly the women. Do not ever get involved with a Victorian woman, Boswell – or with a hereborn who has been brought up as such. You will be there on the sofa wanting to get spooney, and she will be next to you trying to decide what sort of mausoleum the pair of you should have when you have expired prematurely of the consumption in one another's arms. 'Tain't decent, I tell you.'

He flicked his cigarette end out of the window and noticed they were stopped by one of those fashionable new curry-restaurants that were opening all over town.

'You'll be going to places like that, soon,' said Scipio.

'The Taj Mahal Curry Palace,' Boswell read the sign. 'Isn't curry hot stuff they eat in India? I had a retired uncle who'd been an officer in some Indian regiment. He once made me some mulligatawny soup when I was a boy. He thought it was a great treat. I thought it was horrible.'

'I would agree with you there. Ghastly foreign muck. Give me a plate of roast beef any day. Ever been to India, Boswell?'

'No sir.'

'I once spent four weeks there some years ago. I was working on a case which necessitated my taking the flying boat from Southampton to Calcutta. We took off from Solent Water on Wednesday morning, and landed in the Hoogly on Saturday evening with innumerable stops in between. I promise you, Boswell, the entire experience was more educational than two years at any

Oxford college. India ain't like here. The whole country was left unharmed by the Atom War so you'd think the place would be very prosperous, and so it is, for many. Look behind us.'

Boswell turned in his seat to look at the white van which was just as grounded as they were in the jam.

'Edward Briggs, plasterer and general decorator, telephone Cheapside 77493,' he read the words painted on the bonnet. Scipio looked in the rear-view mirror. Mr Briggs, if that was he, sat impassively at the wheel of his vehicle, pointedly taking no notice of the police car in front of him.

'And the radiator-badge?'

'Tata,' said Boswell, reading the chrome-plated badge.

'One of India's great industrial dynasties. It is the ambition of every stout-hearted English tradesman to own a Tata van, despite the availability of cheaper, though poorly designed and mechanically unreliable British alternatives. Well over half the households in the land have a Bombay Electrical Company television, while every last living one of us drinks tea harvested and exported by the Prabakaran Brothers.'

'The people of India are doing well for themselves then,' said Boswell. 'I always thought they would fare better once they were independent.'

'Some of the people of India are doing well,' said Scipio. 'But you never saw such a contrast between wealth and poverty. There are millions living there in conditions which not even the meanest, most ignorant retread from the Dark Ages has to tolerate here. Accordingly, many Indians with the skills and courage to do so, come to this country. Not just from India; we also have Indians from East Africa as well as Mohammedans from Pakistan. They are a great asset to us as they are hard-working and ambitious and take nothing from the social welfare funds. My only fear is that if many more of them come, then they will start to fall victim to the bigotry of the masses. The English do so hate people different from themselves.'

'Have you ever encountered bigotry? As a black man, I mean . . .'

'Yes, of course. Every day. Most recently from you.'

'Oh I say, sir! That's a bit unfair . . .'

'Lie to me as much as you wish, Boswell. I have been a copper for a very long time and can usually tell when I am being lied to. But only a complete fool lies to himself. I saw your face when you showed up at the station asking for me. It's a look I've seen from natives and retreads alike millions of times. The look that says, do I really have to do business with this darkie, this benighted savage who's only fit to slave on a West Indies sugar plantation?'

Boswell was silent for a while. Eventually, he said, 'And how do you deal with it, sir?'

'I try to deal with everything as it comes, Boswell. Without prejudice or preconception. It ain't always easy, of course. Let us make that rule number two of being a good rozzer.'

Somewhere in the traffic queue up ahead of them, horns were being sounded in frustration. As a responsible adult, Scipio wondered if he should get out and attempt to resolve the problem, even though traffic was not his domain.

43

Half a dozen young lads hopped off the bus in front of them, tired of waiting. Straw boaters, striped blue blazers, silk neckerchiefs, sensible haircuts. Late teens, a bit of swagger, but not too much. Not your regular centre-of-town mashers. None of them looked like retreads; they'd all been born here. Respectable families – at least three of them had the same blond hair and oval faces. Probably on their way to a hop organized by one of their fathers' guilds or unions. Not a church function. The boys looked a touch too worldly to tolerate organized dancing to waltzes with strict rules on how much you could touch the girls. No, they would be dancing to beat and badmash and jazz music from the hit parade and hoping to get in a grope or two before the evening's end.

'Listen, Boswell, I am not bothered or offended that you, a privately educated young gentleman, should be momentarily shocked to be taking orders from an African. All I ask is that you start to realize that a lot of things in this world are not as they seem.'

'Yes, sir, thank you, sir.'

A pause, then, 'Are there a lot of, um, black people here, sir?'

'There are a few Africans like myself here, a handful of men and women who were once servants, slaves or sailors. In the eighteenth century the African population of London was probably around 10,000. Naturally, a lot of them died prematurely and have come back since. So we are a common enough sight. There are also a few Caribbeans who came over in the years immediately before the Atom War and managed to survive it. In fact, I should not be at all surprised if those young swells over there' – he pointed to the lads who had jumped off the bus – 'were going to a dance at which they will be entertained by black musicians from Bristol, Liverpool or Leeds. Those cities were unharmed by the Atom War and have large Caribbean communities. Because of the prejudice they suffer when seeking work, many make a living as musicians.'

'Really?'

Scipio's own eldest son was a musician. An increasingly successful one.

'Oh yes. You would not wish your daughter to marry one of us, but we do make such superb entertainers, you know . . . I am being sarcastic, by the way.'

The traffic started to move once more. Scipio started the engine and edged the car into Oxford Street, which was teeming with people now that the shops were permitted to stay open late during the summer months. All of this area had been destroyed by the Atom War and the buildings, most of which had been hurriedly thrown up in the 1980s of concrete, steel and glass, were starting to look very shabby.

They found themselves in another traffic-jam, this time stuck behind a horse-drawn cart of manure.

'I say!' said Boswell. 'Here I am clinging on to your cigarette-case. You'd better have it back.' Scipio took the case and returned it to the inside pocket of his jacket. 'I read all about the Feudal Wars at the reception centre,' said Boswell. 'You'll have to tell me all about your adventures one day, sir.'

'Oh I shall, Boswell, I shall,' said Scipio drily. He would, too. Historical education was a far too important business to leave to government pamphlets and library books. 'I will relate tales of bravery and heroism the like whereof you do not hear outside the operas and television dramas. Then I shall top it with the story of how my regiment and I captured the entire City of Bristol for the Coalition bloodlessly. Well, almost bloodlessly. There was only one casualty, and he was a Fascist.'

The traffic started to move again, but Scipio was barely into second gear before he had to stop at a Belisha beacon to allow a nursemaid pushing a pram to cross.

'And then,' he said, 'if the BBC ever re-shows it, I shall sit with you while you watch *The Dashing Mechano*, the BBC's comic play about my exploits.'

'Gosh!' said Boswell. 'What's a Mechano, by the way?'

'Slang usage for mechanized infantry during the Feudal Wars. One of the advantages we enjoyed over the enemy was that we were plentifully supplied with motor transport by the Americans. Even though the United States was sorely hurt by the Atom Wars, President Carter managed to spare us arms and equipment to re-establish democratic rule. The trucks allowed us greater mobility. I was for a time acting commanding officer of the Fifth Regiment of Mechanized Infantry.

'Gosh!' said Boswell again.

'Do you know what a rake is?' said Scipio.

'A thing for making straight lines in flower-beds?'

'Try again.'

'Oh, I see, a chap in a big wig who likes to tumble comely trollops in coaching inns, loses the family fortune to unscrupulous bawds, and then dies of the pox – or a rotten liver – at the age of thirty-five.'

'Correct,' said Scipio, 'and the author of *The Dashing Mechano* is the original rake, my Lord Rochester. I do not know what killed him, but it was probably syphilis. He also wrote poetry, most of it plainest filth, but some of it quite exquisite.'

'I know Rochester. I went to an undistinguished public school in Surrey where the head's principal passions were cricket and divinity. Seneca was not really approved reading, but when I was there I went through a stoic phase. I memorized some lines of Seneca's *Trojan Women* which Rochester had translated very freely.' He recited:

'After death nothing is, and nothing, death:
The utmost limit of a gasp of breath.
Let the ambitious zealot lay aside
His hopes of Heaven, whose faith is but his pride;
Let slavish souls lay by their fear,
Nor be concerned which way nor where
After this life they shall be hurled.
Dead, we become the lumber of the world,
And to that mass of matter shall be swept
Where things destroyed with things unborn are kept.
Devouring time swallows us whole;
Impartial death confounds body and soul.
For Hell and the foul fiend that rules
God's everlasting fiery jails
(Devised by rogues, dreaded by fools),
With his grim, grisly dog that keeps the door,
Are senseless stories, idle tales,
Dreams, whimsys and no more . . .'

'Well that is hogwash, ain't it?' said Scipio. He, too, fancied himself as something of a stoic, but the sentiments were Rochester at his most atheistical.

'Oh I don't know,' said Boswell, slightly hurt. 'It's easy to be wise after the event, isn't it, sir? What's Rochester like?'

'The very devil. The mint of all mischief.'

'I say, sir, didn't you say that we were going to Bloomsbury? Isn't this the wrong way?'

'Correct,' said Scipio. 'We are taking a small detour to the end of Oxford Street. I wish to show you something.'

'What area are we responsible for anyway?' asked Boswell.

'Our patch covers most of the West End, Regent's Park, Soho, Mayfair, Bloomsbury, Covent Garden,' said Scipio. 'We are the swells of the Met, blessed with the most spectacular villainy.'

The traffic was moving properly now. Scipio decided to risk overtaking a pantechnicon which seemed to be unsure of its bearings.

'We have relatively few pre-Tudors on our manor,' he said. 'Medievals, ancients and Anglos find it wearing to cope with noise and machinery.'

'And the language, too, I shouldn't wonder,' said Boswell.

'True. You cannot prattle any old cant at foreign tourists. The Yanks took a pasting on their eastern side during the Atom War, but all other industrial countries suffered worse. There is no order in most of Eastern Europe and much of the mainland of Asia. It is all petty fiefs and competing warlords, much as things were here until after the Feudal Wars. In the civilized world – and that is a relative term – Yank money matters a lot. But we get a lot of tourists from other industrialized countries which were not affected by the Atom War. Indian, Canadian, Australian, South African, Kenyan, Nigerian and New Zealand money matters to us as well. All places where the flavour of spoken English is decidedly twentieth-century.'

'I must read up on the history of the world since my time. One feels so stupid knowing so little of what's happening in the rest of the world.'

'Luckily for you there is not a great deal to learn. The Eurasian landmass went back to the Stone Age, or the Dark Ages, is all you need to know. When the Atom War broke out there was fighting in northern Europe already, then the Americans and British and Russians began using atom weapons. Even in areas unaffected by the bombs, there was fighting, disease and famine. Because of all the dust in the atmosphere the sun did not shine properly for years. Harvests failed and millions starved. Now the west of Europe is comparatively civilized, though their conditions are scarcely as prosperous as ours. Russia and China are divided into petty kingdoms run by warlords. Many countries which escaped the worst of the Atom War are prospering. The United States is the greatest power in the world, and here in Britain we are struggling towards the sort of life people would have had in the 1970s had the Atom War never occurred. We are now sufficiently well organized to permanently station reception centres on the Continent, with armed guards if necessary.'

'On the Continent? But why?'

'To rescue the men who died in various of Britain's wars down the centuries, of course . . . Here we are.'

Oxford Street ended, the crowds had disappeared and in front of them stretched what seemed to be several acres of wasteland.

'Do you know where we are, Boswell?'

'Didn't this used to be Marble Arch?'

'Correct. A bomb fell close to here during the Atom War. The area immediately in front of us has never been rebuilt.'

The ground had been flattened. It wasn't up to the standard of the pitch at Lord's, and grass only grew on it in untidy clumps. But it looked as though someone was trying fairly hard to stop it from becoming overgrown. They were separated from the area by a well-maintained fence of shining barbed wire. Scipio nodded towards his right. Boswell followed his gaze and saw a wooden scaffold, topped by a little roofed building, open on all sides. A policeman stood in it, next to a searchlight.

'So what is this?' said Boswell, 'the border with Hell?'

'I bring all my 'prentices here,' said Scipio. 'We are at the edge of the Bow Street patch. The other side of this area is the responsibility of the Paddington Green station. Bow Street and Paddington are jointly responsible for this area in front of us. About two hundred yards ahead is what used to be the place where the Edgware Road and Oxford Street met one another. Before that, it was the site of the Tyburn Tree. Between the hanging of William FitzOsbert for sedition in 1196, and that of John Austin for robbery in 1783 – memorize the dates, Boswell – it has been estimated that anything between fifty and eighty thousand felons met their deaths in the small area immediately before us.'

Boswell understood. The area was fenced off and observed by policemen day and night because retreads usually – though not always – reappeared at or near the place where they had died. Anyone who appeared in the vicinity of Marble Arch was very likely to have been convicted of a capital crime.

'Wait a minute, though,' said Boswell. 'Weren't a lot of the people hanged here for trivial offences, like spitting on Westminster Bridge, or stealing hankies, or pinching food to feed starving families?'

'True enough,' said Scipio. 'Many victims of the Fatal Tree were wholly innocent of any crime. Others were children, or insane, or poor mothers driven to distraction by howling babes. A great number were nubbed for crimes of no consequence. But a few of them, a very few of them, Boswell, were possessed by evil. That is why the Metropolitan Police like to be the first to greet every retread who comes up at Marble Arch. We like to know precisely who is being set loose on the streets.'

Jacob Malahide sat at the bar, steadily drinking his way through a bottle of Lickpenny Nan's best satin. Two bottles of gin had been his only companions the night before he was hanged and he drank the stuff because it reminded him of how miserable things could get. And of how he had been chosen by God to live a better life.

He was half-watching the news on the television set on a shelf above the bar. Poor young Arise Hampson had been framed for a crime committed by the Israelites up north, while Dick the Shit and his cronies were living higher on it than usual now that it would soon be Accession Day.

Well, thought Jacob Malahide. So be it. But not for much longer. England would soon be entering a much happier state.

The weather would be hot and sticky for several more days, the man on the television said.

There was a banging and commotion at the door. Malahide turned, stroking the ivory handle of the chiv under his shirt, tucked into the waistband of his britches.

It was only the fop Rochester and three of his pals. They visited often, usually in full Restoration fig, all puffed-up in their big wigs and heavy clothes held together with brightly coloured ribbons. The hot weather had the better of them now and all wore loose breeches and expensive embroidered white shirts. They had all abandoned their wigs, too, and went bare-headed. Most of them, including Rochester, had shaved their heads.

Well bad cess to them. Malahide returned to his glass.

'I have not passed a day in sobriety since leaving my mother's tit,' yelped Rochester, banging his long cane on the floor. 'Bring us drink, and bring us the most handsome puncks in the house! This hot weather is eating me up with lust and I will beslubber myself with the most ruttish young cock-chafer you have. And no more than fifteen years of age, if you please!'

The fop and his cullies called themselves Mohocks. Rake-hells, said other people, always drinking and wenching, or smoking bhang or taking morphine, always up to no good.

They were filth. Soon they would pay for their Godless ways.

The wantons behind the bar kept well away from Malahide, and toadied to the Mohocks, pouring out big drains of port, sack and satin.

Jacob Malahide was the Order's pastor in Covent Garden, collecting tithes and seeing that his flock of publicans, whores and shopkeepers did not stray. It amounted to picking up the money, hanging around in ale-houses or here at Lickpenny Nan's and occasionally giving people a taste of the wrath of the righteous.

It was no sin to take poppy from people who had earned it sinfully. It was going to a righteous cause.

Nan Heycock – she was called Lickpenny Nan as she wasn't always inclined to trust the quality of a customer's tin – waddled in. She was a chubby little bitch who could jolly the customers, especially the wealthy ones, but who hated him for taking her tithe. She glanced at the bottle of jacky in front of him and gave him an ugly look.

A cuckoo, she had called him, aye, and a lot else until he took his chiv to the face of her most expensive tart. That slut wouldn't lead men into sin again.

Heycock did the amiable with Rochester and his cullies, reckoning up how much she would make them pay for the evening's twisted pleasures. Rochester was one of the few titled retreads with the money to go with it, writing his bawdy plays for the BBC and the theatres and acting the fool in his frills and breeches and peruke as though he were still rogering his way through the court of Charles II.

Malahide was a political Bull as much as a religious

one. He cursed the Liberal Settlement, cursed the memory of T.E. Lawrence and venerated that of the Duke of Monmouth. Back in the seventies, he'd fought under Monmouth's banner in the last days of the Feudal Wars. But the day he actually swore the Order's oath was the day they passed the Act of Accession. The day Richard III became king again.

Dick the Shit was a paper king, a decoration of the Liberal state and a pretty come-on for the tourists who flew into Croydon airport to gawp at free-born Englishmen like they were menagerie animals at Vauxhall Gardens. But putting a Popish child-murderer on the throne was still an insult to every decent Protestant.

Jacob Malahide wanted to make England great again. So did everyone in the Antient and Honourable Order of the Sons of John Bull. Folk who had died in a previous age were coming back to life; what else could that mean except that the Lord had decreed that His return in majesty was imminent?

Only people who had died prematurely – of disease, in war, in childbirth, accidents, murders – were coming back . . . These people were all being given a chance to redeem themselves in the eyes of their Creator. The nation had to cleanse itself and make itself worthy of that gift.

'Mother Heycock, may I present to you Saint Ethelbright,' Rochester yelped to Lickpenny Nan. 'We have brought him here as he is sore needful of kind and tender usage.'

Malahide looked, curious. The Popish saint was a skinny pock-faced youth. What did a boy know of leading a righteous life? And if he was so whoreson saintly, what was he doing in a trugging-house? This proved the vanity of the Romish church.

The rest of the trollops were wandering in, all eager to oblige, particularly to be of service to my Lord Rochester. It being the tourist season, most were dressed in the modern fashions, in short skirts and painted faces. The fatter ones, who did good business with Englishmen but were less popular with tourists, stood around in the background.

Damn them! They were deliberately leading men into temptation. He would have to fuck one of them himself later.

'I fancy that the saintly Ethelbright will require mortification of the flesh,' said Rochester.

'Ooooh, I see,' said Lickpenny Nan, all businesslike and looking the boy, who was marinated as a navvy on Friday night, up and down. 'Well, your Lordship knows we're very good at seeing to a man's spiritual needs.'

The Order deplored drinking, smoking, gambling, the wearing of elaborate clothes, whoring and sodomy; the theatres and cinemas were corrupting, radio and television were despicable and all music save simple hymns was the work of the Devil. Jacob Malahide indulged all these vices; it was necessary. He had to consort with sin to carry out his duties to the Order. The Order needed money, and who better to get it from than sinners?

Rochester, seeing Malahide, walked over to him as the rest of his Mohocks fondled the squealing trollops.

'Good evening to you, Jacob Malahide,' said Rochester brightly. 'Is the Kingdom of God yet to hand?'

Malahide straightened on his stool and looked the fop

in the eye. 'Your Lordship should not make light of the Order.'

'Oh but I do not,' said Rochester, mock-serious. 'This very day I have contrived the most sacred sport, an almighty fart in the faces of the Pope, of Cardinal Campion and all the Romish fools.'

Rochester was an atheist. He had proclaimed it loud enough often enough. He lowered his voice. 'Young Saint Ethelbright here has been lodged at the Cardinal's residence since his rebirth some weeks ago. Whilst he was cloistered this afternoon, we paid a visit and spirited him away, making pretence that we were about Rome's business. We have plied him with drink, and this night I shall closet him with one of Mother Heycock's choicest trollops. She shall mortify his back and then baptise his prick. By tomorrow morning, he shall be a saint no more.' Rochester giggled like an excited child. 'What think you, Jacob Malahide? Is it not an exquisite thing to take a man who died a saint and to de-sanctify him thus?'

Malahide shrugged. It was idiocy. So it was with everything that Rochester did.

Jenny Pearson stood in a doorway in a long, very narrow alley. Its only illumination was the thin crack of evening sky running its length. It resembled a crone's smile; the clean blue of fresh air contrasted with the diseased dereliction of the ragged, irregular line of buildings. Apart from an alehouse further down, not one could boast a full face of intact plaster.

Trevor waved his radio around, seeking the best direction.

The Holy Land had a distinctive smell; bad sanitation, damp cotton, toasted herrings and boiled cabbage under a miasma of chip-fat. The area had not been built, it had just happened, a rag-tag collection of half-destroyed buildings which had survived the Atom War and which had been added to, pulled down, improved and worsened ever since. Originally, the area had provided cheap housing in the middle of town for the immense army of labourers who had been rebuilding London and Westminster after the Atom War and Feudal Wars. Most had since moved on to decent housing in the suburbs or the council estates to the south of the Thames. There were still a few respectable people living in the Holy Land because of the dirt-cheap rents, but their numbers were diminishing with every time their home was burgled or one of their neighbours was robbed. Now the Holy Land was the Underworld, a home of thieves, prostitutes, druggies, gangsters and assorted other feral natives and retreads who wanted nothing to do with the Government or police.

And Trevor had made them come in here. The sooner London County Council made good its promise to demolish the whole area and disperse its inhabitants to other homes, the better.

After ages on the tramp following radio signals from the gonoph brat, Jenny was getting sick of it.

It would soon be dark and even more dangerous. They stood in one of the most thickly populated regions in the world, but not a soul was visible.

The Holy Land ran from St Giles High Street via several warrens into part of what had once been Soho.

On the map, the area looked insignificant; but it also went high into the air and deep into the ground, a muddled labyrinth of stairs, lanes, alleys, footbridges, tenements and yards. Most people here were retreads from the eighteenth and nineteenth centuries and their children, the lowest oiks in central London among them, those who had always been city folk. They happily lived atop each other, whole families sharing tiny, damp, lightless rooms and netherskens, because this was the way things were ordered, and now most could afford televisions, transistor radios and cheese-burgers as well. Perhaps a quarter of the menfolk had straight employment. The rest skived on social welfare payments, or they were on the lay. Usually both.

The police were not welcome here. The locals could easily smell a rozzer, even one in mufti.

The signal was strongest as Trevor pointed the radio further on down the alley.

'I'm only flymy for another half-hour,' she said. 'We don't know if the kid's still got the peach on him. He might have found it and stuck it on a cat or something. We can't stay here after dark.'

They walked on, past tiny windows and doors. Somewhere, a transistor radio tuned to the BBC Light Programme blared out 'Johnny Todd', a traditional song about a man who lost his sweetheart because he went to sea. She had sung the same song in the choir at school, but this version had been turned into something moronic, with a full orchestra and irritatingly repetitive melody. These modernized folk tunes had been around for decades, and were still loved by older people from every era, and they'd probably still be around when

Jenny was in her dotage, no matter what the younger jazz or beat musicians said.

Women screamed, men shouted, children cried, dogs barked, but they didn't see anyone.

She knew damn well that plenty of people saw them.

Her own radio crackled. Sergeant Hopton was calling every five minutes to see they were all right. She pumped the transmit button twice in acknowledgement.

Something splashed to the ground just in front of her. The contents of a chamber-pot. She looked up and saw nobody.

A set of stone steps ran off to the right. Trevor motioned her to follow. His radio was turned very low, but she could hear the pulses getting stronger.

They came up into a wide yard, surrounded on three sides by high tenement buildings. These had windows, about half of them broken and covered with boards or stuffed with rags. Everywhere washing hung on lines, some strung across the full width of the yard.

'It's the filth!' came a woman's voice close by. 'If you've got it, hide it!'

'It's stopped moving,' said Trevor. 'If he's still got the peach, he must think he's lost us.'

He pointed right. There was a large arched entrance to the building. Trevor led on. It felt like entering the maw of Jonah's whale.

'Up,' he said, pointing to a ramshackle wooden staircase smelling strongly of urine, of vomit and stale cider. They stepped over a stinking heap of rags which, she realized, was a man.

Something came thumping down the steps towards them. Both pressed themselves against the wall. A small lacquered wooden cabinet, a choice piece from a prosperous town house, crashed on down past them, falling to splintered sticks as it went. Trevor reached into his bag and took out his Browning automatic. Jenny took out her own gun, a snub-nosed .38 revolver she'd paid for herself. The Women's Branch of the Police Union were still lobbying for standard-issue pistols that didn't break your delicate little ladylike wrists when you fired them.

Trevor led on, gun in right hand, radio in his left.

Why was she risking painful or disfiguring injury, or even death, just to catch a dipper?

They reached the top of a flight. A dim, deserted corridor of bare floorboards strewn with cheap kids' toys and old newspaper ran off to their left for about 300 feet. Semi-literate graffiti adorned the walls – names, declarations of affection, obscenities.

They moved quietly down the corridor, trying not to make the boards creak. The almost continuous tone from Trevor's radio seemed hellish loud.

He pointed to the next door along, switched off the radio and put it into his bag. Jenny pumped the transmit button on hers.

'Sarge,' she whispered to Hopton at the other end. 'We're entering a room on the third floor of Disraeli Mansions, just off Catgut Alley. Have the Horse Artillery saddled up and ready if we need it.'

'It's on its way already, Pearson,' said Hopton. 'Good hunting, girl.'

Clutching her gun right-handed and supporting her wrist with the left, she pressed herself against the wall beside the door.

Trevor stood in front of the door, holding his massive gun pointed upwards. Like a cat preparing to spring, he drew himself to his full height, every perfectly-honed muscle bulging and undulating.

He sprang forward, crashing his shoulder and upper arm against the door. It gave way at once, just like in the American cop films that every male rozzer adored. Trevor burst through and fell to one knee in a perfect, practised movement, holding the gun out in front of him two-handed.

Jenny swung through 180 degrees to stand behind him, arms outstretched, gun cocked, squinting along the notch and blade at the top of the barrel.

Scipio jerked the car to a halt outside the substantial town-house in Russell Square and looked at his watch. They'd have been here in half the time if they'd walked.

'Come on then, Boswell. Let us go and see what manner of villainy we are dealing with this evening. I hope you are not scared of the sight of blood.'

Boswell had been in a war. He had probably witnessed a few ghastly things.

Aye, but he'd never had to stand there rooting around for clues in them, had he? He would learn what sort of stomach the youngster had soon enough.

A police van and another blue Humber squad-car were already parked outside the house. There was a small knot of curious bystanders, the usual combination of concerned neighbours, ghouls and sensation-seekers.

The whole square had been rebuilt after the Atom War. Scipio had no idea what it had looked like before, but it was now one of the choicest addresses on the manor. The builders had done a pukka job here; the houses were gracious brick-built five-storey jobs, all fronted with smart iron railings and plenty in the way of windows. The speculator who'd put them up had also bought himself a load of stone-carvers (medievals, probably) to add some flummery over the doors and windows.

The front door was open. Boswell followed Scipio as he elbowed his way through the onlookers. 'Inspector Scipio,' hissed one of them to his neighbour in a tone that sounded gratifyingly awestruck. Well, he had been in the newspapers plenty of times in the past, talking about a case or giving evidence in court, and he had had a TV play made about his Feudal Wars exploits.

'Remember thou art mortal,' he muttered to himself.

'Sorry, sir?' said Boswell.

'Latin for "pride comes before a fall".'

The uniformed constable standing at the front door saluted them and directed them towards the basement.

The room, well below ground level, was among the servants' quarters, though it was empty. Might never have been used at all. Completely bare, whitewashed walls adorned with a few cobwebs. Single light-bulb hanging from the ceiling. No shade. A small, barred window looked out on to street level.

'Oh Lord!' said Boswell behind him.

The floor, though, looked fairly new. Varnished Scots pine, along which ran several rivulets of blood radiating from the mess of mincemeat, bone and offal where a man's head had once been.

Boswell was trying not to look.

Scipio had seen worse. The MO had passed through and covered the head and hands of the victim with plastic bags, the better to preserve any evidence which might adhere to them. It was marvellous what they could find under a dead man's fingernails these days.

The deceased lay belly-down on the floor close to a big, rough hole in the floorboards. He wore black knee-britches, black stockings, black shoes and a plain black jacket. Next to the corpse was a bag of tools, a pickaxe and a blood-stained shovel.

Sergeant O'Rourke came in, wearing, in spite of the hot weather, his usual heavy tweed suit, wing-collar and bow-tie.

'Detective Sergeant O'Rourke,' said Scipio, 'I thought I would escape the dusty confines of the station to take a look at this. It is, I own, most intriguing. What light can you shed upon it?'

'Hard to say, boss,' replied O'Rourke – Uncle Seamus to his colleagues – in his gruff Irish tone. 'His reader was over there on the floor.' He reached into his pocket and pulled out a plastic bag with a cheap leather wallet in it.

'No lettuce, just some calling-cards.' He handed one to Scipio. 'The scene-of-crime boys have just finished, as has the Medical Officer, who'll be back to collect your man in a minute. Says he's been dead six to eight hours.'

Scipio looked at the calling-card and handed it to Boswell. No address or telephone number, just a name. Richard Haseldich.

'Who owns the house?'

'Cove by the name of Lilley,' said O'Rourke.

'Something in the City, not short of a shilling. Rumoured to be a bigwig in the Bulls. He's taken his family to Bath for the season.'

'I know him,' said Scipio, turning to Boswell. 'A businessman, deals in grain. From about my own time. I have a feeling that he was a merchant in his previous life too. A trader in slaves. The more successful eighteenth century retreads still go to Bath during the summer. Bath has become their favoured holiday resort, just as it was in the old days. It is a marriage market for their offspring, whether natural or adopted retreads. They have made Bath their own, a place where they do not have to mix with your kind.'

'My kind?' asked Boswell.

'People telling them what to think about democracy, hanging pickpockets, religious toleration, high-cholesterol diets and arranged marriages.' He turned to O'Rourke again. 'Who found him?'

O'Rourke recited the known facts with his customary brevity and precision. 'One of the servants next door saw a large man making off through the back garden around half-past two. He was carrying a box. She dithered. She knew the Lilleys were away and thought the man might be a labourer come to weed the garden or something. But she worried all afternoon that he might be a thief and rang the police three hours back. The patrol constable gained entry through a back door and found the body. The neighbour gave a vague description of the man she saw as being fat, clumsy, brown hair, bumfluff moustache and pock-marked face. Aged mid-twenties.'

'And the deceased?'

'Not sure yet, sir. I radioed the station and got the work done on Richard Haseldich, if this is he. The closest match is a wealthy barrister killed fighting for Parliament during the Civil War. He came up three months ago. Spent two weeks at the Chiswick Turnpike reception centre where he was signed up for a law course so's he could start practising again. The Bar hasn't heard from anyone of that name.'

Scipio stepped forward to look down the hole which had been torn in the floorboards, and motioned Boswell to look, too. A foot beneath the floorboards was thick, moist brown clay. This, too, had been gouged into.

'Any kinfolk or affinity?' he asked O'Rourke.

'The usual ancestors and descendants and a few cousins. Nothing close, though. No wife, parents or children that we know of. I'll have it followed up.'

To one side of the hole there was a square indentation at the bottom, as though a box had been lifted out of it.

'Sergeant,' said Scipio, 'what do you think?'

'My first thought was that this might be our own little Hereford Hoard, sir, but that doesn't really fit at all, now does it?'

'Apprentice Detective Constable Boswell,' said Scipio, 'meet Detective Sergeant O'Rourke, one of the canniest rozzers on this manor. Once you get to know him better, you will be permitted to call him Uncle Seamus. Uncle Seamus, meet my new 'prentice.'

'Another one!' laughed Uncle Seamus. 'Faith, I hope he doesn't go the same way as the last.'

'Trust you to puncture any pride my adoring public outside might have puffed up in me.' He turned to Boswell. 'Detective Sergeant O'Rourke is referring to my previous charge, who decided that police work was not to his taste and ran off with the circus.'

'I think I'll join him,' said Boswell.

'Why Boswell, I do believe you are turning green.'

'Ah leave the lad be, sir,' said Uncle Seamus, slapping Boswell on the back. 'Sure the sight of your first corpse is enough to turn any ass from his oats.'

Scipio shrugged. He could not remember his first corpse. He might have been four or five years old, in the stinking hold of a wooden ship bound for the West Indies. Not something you would dwell on if you wanted to remain sane.

'So Boswell,' he said crisply. 'Go outside, puke up, then go and find another job, or stay here and start thinking like a peeler.'

Boswell decided to avoid the issue by changing the subject. 'What's the Hereford Hoard?' he said, looking away from the corpse.

'Imagine,' smiled O'Rourke, 'that you're a big-shot during the Dark Ages, with a gang of armed men terrorizing the locals, molesting the womenfolk and confiscating all their valuables. Then one day you're out fighting and your pagan gods desert you and you receive a mortal wound. Before you pass away, you instruct your kerns on the funeral arrangements. In them days they thought the afterworld was a lot like the one they'd come from, so they'd need some earthly possessions to see them through . . .'

'This particular potentate,' said Scipio, continuing the story, 'was buried with a modest fortune in gold, silver and jewels. Then he woke up here, eleven hundred years later.'

'As you well know,' said O'Rourke, 'we are all reborn naked. When we arrive here we show up without a stitch of clothing. No jewellery, wigs, false limbs, gold teeth, nothing. We awake naked as God or nature made us.'

'On the credit side,' said Scipio, 'we are cured of our ailments and mutilations. Your average retread is filled with wonder to be reborn with a full set of healthy white teeth.'

'Now the question is,' said O'Rourke, 'is our king entitled to dig up his treasures – assuming they're still there – and do what he likes with them?'

'Because,' said Scipio, 'providing for him in the afterlife was precisely the purpose for which they were buried with him.'

'There is no doubt in your man's mind,' said Uncle Seamus. 'Himself and some trusted butties traipse off to some field near Hereford to dig him up. They find his old bones . . .'

'Which is spooky, no?' said Scipio.

'These he throws away,' said O'Rourke. 'But the heap of geegaws he takes to the nearest jeweller looking to sell so's he can live this life in due and fitting dignity.'

'At which point the Government steps in,' said Scipio, 'and declares the lot treasure trove.'

'Naturally,' said Uncle Seamus, 'our warlord is not about to take this as it comes, but not having enough men-at-arms to overthrow the Government, he goes to law.'

'He lost,' said Scipio. 'This was one of a number of cases which established an absolute point of law—'

'That just as man is born naked,' said O'Rourke, 'so is he re-born naked.'

'Meaning,' said Scipio, 'that not even a king has any right in law to property he owned in his previous life.'

'Whether it's land, gold plate, or a clod of earth,' said O'Rourke.

'You can keep titles, of course,' said Scipio. 'The law is not concerned if you want to call yourself General This, Lord That or Bishop The Other.'

'Though that doesn't mean you'll get your old job back,' chimed in O'Rourke.

'And you cannot keep a spouse, either.'

'Why on earth not?' asked Boswell.

'Well, imagine that the previous Mrs Boswell – if there was one – died before her time and then fetched up here,' said O'Rourke. 'Sooner or later she might take it into her head to remarry. What happens then, if, say, ten years later, Mr Boswell arrives here. He can't lay any claim to Mrs Boswell as she is now Mrs Someone Else.'

'Quite apart from which,' said Scipio, 'the former Mrs Boswell is now ten years older than she was when Mr Boswell last knew her.'

You could tell that Boswell was thinking of his fiancée from his last life. 'There's no way of knowing when someone is likely to turn up, is there?'

'None whatever,' said Scipio. 'Retreads have been arriving here since the Atom War and as far as we can tell they have appeared at a more or less constant rate ever since.'

'It's got to stop sooner or later,' said O'Rourke. 'After all, there are only so many dead people in the world. And babbies and them as died of old age aren't showing. That narrows it down a little.'

Boswell had not thrown up yet and, in truth, the room didn't smell too pleasant, even though it was cool down here below ground. Scipio motioned Boswell and Uncle Seamus upstairs.

'You are not even permitted to own any mortal remains that might be left of you from your previous life,' O'Rourke explained to Boswell on the stairs. 'This might seem unfair, but there's sense in it. There was a case many years ago when a minor saint came up and took exception to the fact that a cathedral possessed some of his bones for the purposes of veneration by the pious. He took legal action, but lost.'

'Whether or not the dead bones of this man who lived once more retained their healing powers—' said Scipio.

'If they had any in the first place . . .' interjected Uncle Seamus, laughing.

They entered a spacious withdrawing-room on the ground floor, furnished in a plain, puritanical style, an owner's conceit, an escape to the confident certainties of his old world. No television or telephone. The only mod. con. was the electric light. The walls were whitewashed and the furniture was all of hard, plain oak.

'Any servants around?' he asked O'Rourke, who shook his head.

Boswell opened a sash window looking out on to the street and leaned out, pulling greedily on fresh air. O'Rourke sat himself upright in a chair, hands in his lap, as though waiting at court to give evidence.

Scipio could not remember when he had last seen such an uninviting room in such an expensive house. Perhaps it was just for formal occasions, but there was something cold, antiseptic about it. It had no personality. Not even any pictures on the walls. No books either. A queer place.

Boswell came back into the room and closed the window,

'So, Boswell, walk us through it.'

'Well,' said Boswell, 'from what I can see, this chap didn't commit suicide. In view of what you've told me about buried treasure, I deduce the deceased and an accomplice broke into the house while the owners were away. They were looking for goodies that were buried by someone – possibly the deceased – in a previous life with a view to surreptitious recovery and cheating the State of its pound of flesh.'

They read a few racy novels and they all think they're Sherlock ruddy Holmes. 'Nonsense, Boswell. There is but a small hole in the cellar floor and the floorboards are of recent installation. If a man buries a chest in the ground hundreds of years previously, does it not seem odd that he can once again find the exact spot where he left it? This house had not been thought of during the seventeenth century – though there might have been one on this site previously – but is it not the most magical coincidence that a man discovers his treasure with virtually the first blows of his pick? Whatever was buried under the floorboards was buried well within living memory.'

'So what next, boss?' asked O'Rourke.

'Discover all you can about the late Mr Haseldich. And about the owner of this house, this Lilley fellow.'

'Shall I ask our colleagues in Bath to pick him up?'

'No. We cannot profit from generating more paperwork at this stage. Boswell, for what it is worth, you should know that we have a most curious and unusual case here.'

Jenny let her gun down. 'Police,' she said, addressing the man who sat on the floor examining a handful of coins. 'Are you related to this boy?'

The man shook his head. Six feet-something tall, fat, and probably quite strong. His grimy grey trousers were held up with a heavy belt beneath a white shirt and a flash brocade weskit covered in embroidery, egg and ketchup stains.

The room had a single sash window, a threadbare carpet, a bed, a table and a couple of rickety chairs. In the middle, sitting cross-legged beside the man, was their quarry, admiring the contents of a soil-caked wooden chest the size of a television.

'Arrr, Jim Lad!' said Trevor. 'I suppose,' he said to the kid, 'your poor sainted mother left you this lot in her will.'

The kid said nothing. Trevor entered the room. She followed, closing the door. It creaked open again. Trevor had burst the lock off.

'Where did you get this?' Jenny asked the kid, pointing to the box. It was filled with what appeared to be gold and silver coin, some of which was scattered on the floor next to it.

'It's not mine,' he said crossly. 'Numps here found it on some waste-ground.'

'S'right,' said the fat man. 'I digged it up from one of the bomb-sites. In the East End, it was. I had a special treasure-map.'

'Shut up, Numps,' said the kid. 'Don't tell them nothing.'

Jenny took out her radio. 'Sarge, we have the kid. He rooms with a big cove name of Numps. They've got a wooden chest full of coin. Sovs and testons. Mean anything to you?'

Trevor told the man and boy to spreadeagle on the floor, on their bellies.

'I don't know,' Hopton's voice came back. 'Let me have a look in the files.'

'You're both under arrest,' Trevor said to the boy. 'You are not obliged to say anything, but anything you do say will be noted and may be used in evidence against you. Do you understand?' The kid said nothing. Trevor turned to the fat man. 'Did he understand?'

The man turned his face sideways. He was in tears. 'He's only a kid. Please don't take him. Arrest me instead. I committed a crime. I committed a capital felony, I did.'

'Shut up, Numps!' said the kid coldly.

'Ain't it a bleedin' shame,' said a woman's voice behind them. 'The filth thinks they owns the place, don't they?'

A knot of residents had gathered by the smashed-in door.

'Yeah, awful is what it is,' agreed another woman. 'Running around with them bloody great guns fit to frighten the life out of decent folk.'

'It's bullyin', I tell yer,' said an elderly man. 'See, they can't even arrest a boy an' a bloke who's simple in the head without smashin' the door in.'

Trevor knelt by the boy, reaching for his handcuffs.

'Stap me!' said one of the bystanders, pointing to the chest, 'look at all the swag in there!'

There was a murmur of conversation among them about the likely value of Numps's treasure chest. Jenny spoke quietly but urgently into her radio. 'Sarge, we might have a problem. The natives are deploring the constabulary, and coveting the treasure chest. Let's have some back-up at once.'

'We're on the case,' said Hopton, 'keep your channel open. The relief column is already on its way.'

''Ere, Tom, come 'ave a look-see,' said one of the locals at the door.

The crowd parted for Tom.

Tom was My Brother Sylvest made flesh. An unyielding mountain of a man with a chest the size of a soccer pitch that was bare beneath a leather jerkin. He wore trousers that barely reached below his knees. There was no sign of life in his cold shark's eyes.

As Trevor looked up to see Tom, the kid brought his fist up. She tried to yell a warning, but it was too late to stop Trevor being thumped in the crotch. For a moment, everything froze, then Trevor collapsed in agony.

Jenny brought her gun up to stop the kid.

No! She couldn't point it at a child!

Something numbed her arm. The gun fell to the floor. The kid rushed past her in a black blur. She looked to her side, wondering what had happened.

Tom grasped her forearm in his cannonball fist. She hit at him with her left hand, banging his stomach pointlessly. Now he grabbed her left arm with his other hand and pulled it slowly, inexorably towards his mouth.

73

'Trevor,' she yelled over her shoulder. 'Shoot the bastard!' Trevor was still on the floor. She felt her hand being brought into contact with the big man's stubbled chin, his lips. She spread her fingers, scratching, and worked her legs uselessly, trying to kick something vulnerable, but only contacting thin air or solid muscle.

She looked around. Trevor was still on the floor. Numps, the fat man, had stood up. He yanked Trevor's gun from his hand.

Tom pulled her thumb into his mouth. She knew what was coming. She'd heard about it often enough. She'd even seen one of the victims. Mind over matter, she said to herself. Two months' sick leave, at least. Almost as good as a paid holiday . . .

If this big swine didn't go on to kill them.

Two months. Time enough to decorate the flat, tidy the garden, make some new clothes, perhaps a holiday in Cornwall . . .

Still he held on to both her forearms.

Numps passed her, as quick as 18 stones of fried egg and stupidity could go.

Her fingers clawed impotently at leather skin. Tom had her thumb in his mouth. She tried to wriggle it free of his back teeth. She failed. She felt his teeth closing, told herself it was only her left hand, prayed for their back-up to arrive this instant, prayed to see Constable Glyndwr come thundering in like the Angel of Death with a sawn-off shotgun in each hand and the scales of justice dangling from one of his plaited moustaches.

Tom and her thumb. Tom Thumb – ha-ha!

She was getting hysterical, fighting an urge to laugh and scream all at once.

Big Tom's teeth tightened. Pressure turned to pain.
Pain turned to agony.

Tom was doing it slowly, like he was relishing a
delicately flavoured cut at a nobby chop-house.

'Look out, Tom!' someone said. Behind her, someone
scrambled across the floor, trying to get her gun.

Tom carried her along for a couple of steps. He
kicked. She heard Trevor's voice letting out a distended
oath.

She heard the dull popping of the gristle in her hand.
Pain shot all the way up her arm.

She wouldn't give him the satisfaction of screeching.

She spat in his face, hoping to startle him long
enough to get herself – or at least her thumb – free.

Her feet touched the floor again. Her legs gave way
beneath her. She collapsed, sitting. She tried to support
herself with her left hand. The pain returned. She
looked at her thumb. There were two huge black
blotches on it, but it wasn't cocked at any strange
angles, and she could still move it, and there was no
blood, and . . .

The crowd at the door were laughing, cheering on
their champion. Trevor was standing, as though to
defend the treasure chest and square off against big
Tom.

She scrambled over to her gun, breathing hard, trying
to ignore the pain in her thumb. She picked it up,
reminding herself not to try and steady her wrist with
her left hand. She turned to point it at Tom.

But Tom and all his friends had gone.

She blinked, shook her head. The doorway was clear
of people.

'Are you all right?' said Trevor.

'Nothing a bottle of gin, a handful of aspirins and two months' sick leave won't fix. And you?'

'He broke one of my teeth when he kicked me. Ssshit, I hate going to the dentissst.'

The sound of footsteps rumbled up the corridor outside, then stopped. A shape in blue shot past the door and thumped against the wall next to it.

'It'ss all right. There ain't nobody here but uss chickenss,' said Trevor.

The door was blocked by the massive form of Constable Glyndwr clutching a pump-action shotgun.

'Bloody 'ell,' he growled. 'What you two doin' runnin' around Holy Land all on your own anyway?'

'That's a question I've been asking myself, Glyn,' she said.

'Come on then, love. Let's get you 'ome, and him to hospital.'

Dorcas Chubb led Saint Ethelbright into one of the luxury rooms and closed the door.

Ethelbright stood, swaying a little, screwing up his eyes. He reeked of drink. Brandy, perhaps.

This, she supposed would be difficult. Drunks usually had problems doing their business. Some of them would then get nasty.

When Lickpenny Nan had told her she was going to see a saint, she had imagined an old man with a beard and upturned eyes and one of them rings of light around his head. Just like you saw in the print-shop pictures that the medievals and northerners (they couldn't help being Papists) liked to put on their walls.

Saint Ethelbright was a skinny, consumptive runt about her age, maybe a little older, dressed in baggy trousers and a shapeless, collarless shirt that was too big for him.

He fell on to the bed, spifflicated as a two-year sailor on his first night back in Tiger Bay.

She hated doing for God-botherers. They either wanted to be thrashed, which made her arms ache, or they wanted to thrash her, which was worse. Nan was very strict about this; her girls were to be treated with respect, she always said. But that didn't stop them wanting to do it. Let a man thrash you, Nan said, and you wouldn't be long for this world. Nobody could tell what sort of devils men had in them, she would say.

Elder Saltonstall would like to thrash her, and worse, she knew. He was a very esteemed Upright Man, who came to see her twice or thrice a week. He might be a man of God, but he fornicated like a demon. He called her such terrible names when he was doing his business. It was all she could do to stop him from thumping her while he was at it. He'd call her a bitch and a whore, but if she was really so bad then why did he keep coming to visit her? Why did he like her to pretend she was a 10-year-old girl when she was actually seventeen? And why did he never bring her any presents like some of her other gentlemen did?

She sighed. It was all too confusing. Well, in another few years, she'd have enough in her Post Office account to quit this lousy business and perhaps open a shop or something.

Perhaps she might meet a nice gentleman who would take care of her, though it didn't seem likely. Nearly all men were selfish swine, from what she could see. It might happen, though. It had happened to Cigarette, one of the other girls. She'd ended up marrying a very respectable banker from over Chelsea way. Now she was so grand she wouldn't even give her old friends a second look in the street.

The saint lay still, face-down on the bed. Ethelbright. Funny name. Ethel Bright sounded like the name of a strumpet or a cheeky shopgirl in a television comedy, or one of the music hall funnies.

When she started this lark two years ago, she'd imagined that going with bobtails would be sinful for a man of God. Perhaps it was, but she couldn't know for sure. She had Salty, now Ethelbright as well.

She took off her blouse, folded it neatly and lay it over the back of a chair next to the bed.

Nan always said that men had such responsibilities and worriment that women could never understand what drove them. Especially religious men.

Elder Saltonstall, Mary said, had suffered for his religion, had been a martyr. In his last life he had been branded by the public hangman after attacking the bishops. She knew as much. When he was doing his business, the letters would stand out in red on his cheeks.

She unzipped her short skirt and put it on the chair. She looked at herself in the mirror that covered one of the walls. In her black stockings and silly black corset she looked ridiculous. But it was a good face, a nice complexion, and natural blonde hair. She was, after all, only seventeen. There was still plenty of time to get out. It wasn't so good here any more, now that bastard

Malahide and his bullies were frightening the girls and taking a poke at the kitty. Fair do's, Lickpenny Nan took half their earnings, but she looked after them. Malahide was different. He was very nasty. Malahide would love to thrash her. He'd thrashed some of the other girls. Aye, and he'd taken that wicked knife of his to poor Mary Cooper's face. Ruined her looks completely, he did, the bastard.

As long as she was going with Salty, who was Malahide's boss, he wouldn't touch her. That was some comfort.

Ethelbright breathed heavily. He looked happy to stay the way he was, but Lord Rochester was paying a pretty sum to see the boy got all the kind and tender usage the house could offer.

She walked over and stood by Ethelbright's head. She coughed. One of his eyes opened, then the other. He sprang upright, then backwards and climbed clumsily to his feet. He looked towards the door.

She stuck her hand down the front of the corset and pulled out the key, waved it a few inches from his eyes, then dropped it back between her dugs.

Ethelbright fell to his knees in the middle of the floor, clapped his hands together hard enough to crack a walnut, and babbled prayers in his ancient language.

She knelt on the floor in front of him, fondling her boobs.

He closed his eyes and prayed harder.

Lawks, this was going to be difficult!

At length, he opened his eyes again. He saw something over her shoulder and pointed.

On the window-sill was a bundle of fresh-cut birch

twigs, set in a vase of water to keep them whippy.

She sighed. Ethelbright was going to be just like Salty.

She stood and walked to the window-sill, took the birches from the vase, shook the water from them and went to stand in front of the boy.

She slapped the palm of her left hand with the twigs. The boy nodded hard and pulled off his shirt. Beneath it he wore an undershirt made of what looked like horsehair.

She heard a faint creak and looked to see the door opening. Nan would be looking in to see how she was faring. But instead of Nan, Lord Rochester himself appeared.

'And a good evening to you, Dorcas,' he said pleasantly, sitting himself down on the bed.

He knew her name!

Saint Ethelbright crossed himself and stood up, stone cold sober. He looked at Rochester, who nodded at him. He sat himself down quietly on the chair by her bed, taking care not to rumple her clothes.

'I do hope that you will pardon this intrusion. I have just left one of your colleagues in a neighbouring room in order to pay this brief visit. I've been watching you, Dorcas,' said Rochester, patting the bed next to him.

What on earth was going on?

No good was what. Rochester might pay well, but he was a madman. Reluctantly, she sat down.

'You have a good figure, young lady,' he said. Like Ethelbright, he stank of booze, but he didn't appear even a little bit drunk.

It was like the pair of them had been pouring drink over their clothes, but not down their throats.

'Yes,' he said, leaning over her cleavage. He breathed in like her tits were a vintage wine.

'And so fresh,' he said. 'You smell of nothing more unwholesome than talcum powder.'

That was true enough. She liked to have two baths a day. Three on the days when Salty came to see her.

'Fashions change all the time,' he said. 'Sometimes the most desirable women are supposed to be skinny and consumptive, at other times, we like 'em buxom. Your figure, my dear, is perfect for the moment. You have lovely clean white skin, large, shapely breasts and a plump but shapely bum. I'll wager few of your cullies can resist the temptation to slap it, or grab big pawfuls of it and maul it about like a baker kneading forty pounds of dough.'

She couldn't help laughing at this. 'You're right there, your Lordship.'

Gently, he took her chin in his hand and turned her face towards him. This was the first time she had looked him in the eye. His eyes were an odd grey colour. There were little wrinkles around them. On his shaved head, over which he usually wore a peruke, she could make out the tint of his hair. Getting a little grey, by the look of it. The man must be getting on for fifty.

'Dorcas, I am, to put it charitably, a man of the world. I have spent a great deal of my life – this one and the last – in the company of trollops and I know whereof I speak. If you stay in this business for another three years, your looks will be gone, ravaged by drink or drugs or disease or overeating. Or perhaps even by the fists or knife of a punter. Do you want that to happen?'

Now he was frightening her again. She shook her

head. She wished she had more clothes on.

As though he could read her mind, Saint Ethelbright stood up and brought her skirt and blouse over to her.

'Please, Dorcas,' said Rochester, 'have no fear of me. I want to help you. I do a lot of work for the BBC and in films. With your looks, you could do well for yourself. If you can act, so much the better, if not, I might be able to get you on to one of the game shows, like *Double Your Money* or *Ask the Ancestors*. All you have to do is wear nice clothes and smile a lot while the rabble in the audience applauds the prizes. It is, I promise, very easy work.'

Why was he giving her this guff? If he needed to get round her all he had to do was pay, and he had plenty of tin.

Saint Ethelbright sat down again and reached into his ragged clothes to produce a cigarette and a box of matches.

'Your Lordship has me all confused,' she said. 'He' – she indicated Ethelbright – 'is not a saint, and you would not burst into the room as I'm trying to do the business with these' – she realized she still had the birches in her hand – 'in order to tell me I've got the star quality. Please don't play any more games with me, sir.'

Rochester took one of the birches from her hand and stood up. 'Would you like to be on television and in films, Dorcas? Would you like to escape the clutches of Lickpenny Nan and Jacob Malahide? Hmm?' He was running the end of the birch along his fingernails, as if to clean them.

Was it clever to answer a question like that? She said nothing.

'I'll take that as a "yes",' he said. 'Do you think you can act?'

'I've never tried, my Lord,' she said evenly.

'On the contrary,' said Rochester. 'You do it every day. You come into this room with some swag-bellied hussington who hates himself for being unfaithful to his wife, or just for having to use dollymops, and you pretend that he is the greatest love of your life. Nan tells me that you are also especially talented with the birches, at playing the stern schoolmarm chastising her unruly boys. She further informs me that you are also adept in taking the part of a nurse.'

She shrugged. Playing pretend was part of the job at what Nan liked to say was 'an 'igh-class establishment'.

He sat down next to her again. 'This is for you,' he said, producing a small suede leather purse. She took it. It was heavy. She pulled open the drawstring at the top. Inside was about £100 in gold sovereigns. Enough to live on the fat for three months.

'There will be more,' he said. 'And I give you my word that I will do everything in my power to find you glamorous and fulfilling employment at the BBC or in motion pictures.'

'And in return?' she said, rolling one of the coins around in her hand.

'All you have to do, Miss Chubb, is act, is to continue as normal,' he said. 'And keep your eyes and ears open and answer some questions for me. Nothing more. But I have to warn you that if you do not keep our little secret, then your life will be in mortal danger. Not from me, I hasten to add, but from others.'

She could imagine. Whatever Rochester was proposing

would probably not be much to Jacob Malahide's liking.

'And so to work, what?' he said. 'I want you to tell me all about a gentleman who has been visiting you of late. But first, since Ethelbright here is a saint and he don't fornicate, I would deem it shameful to waste your talents in mere talk. Why don't you get undressed again, my dear?'

Jenny Pearson yelped as the duty quack, a small balding man with bottle glasses, wrapped a bandage around her throbbing thumb.

The evening held all manner of new displeasures. She had never seen the inside of the first-aid room before, a windowless cell with peeling vomit-coloured paint on the walls, a bare light-bulb and a creaking bed with an ass's breakfast mattress on which she now sat. The whole of one wall had half a ton of paper and files stacked against it while the builders were in.

Damn the gonoph pickpocket, damn his big foolish cully with the box of treasure, damn big Tom the thumb-biter, damn—

The light went out. The sawbones tweaked her thumb again.

'Power workers' strike,' he muttered as she bit her lip. 'There should be a law against it.'

Trevor had been dragged off to Charing Cross Hospital for X-rays. After Glyndwr had driven them (and the treasure chest) back to Bow Street, the doc declared that Trevor had a broken nose, and possibly a broken jaw. Trevor, the Atom War survivor, was unenthusiastic about X-rays. They had been the death of his entire family.

The light came on again, buzzed faintly. The door burst open and Inspector Africanus came in.

'Nothing broken,' the quack said to the Inspector. 'Send her home for the rest of the shift.'

The Inspector nodded. 'Glyndwr has called from Charing Cross,' he said to her. 'If I understand his gruntings and hawkings correctly, Constable Mills will be off the strength for a while. Now, this business of yours in the Holy Land; you say that Numps was the big man's name?'

'Yes, sir. Do we know him?'

'We are checking the Public Record Office index. I do not anticipate any success. Numps is just a nickname from the 1700s. It means "simpleton".'

Really? What a surprise.

'I am intrigued by this box of baubles. You had the impression it was a recent acquisition?'

'Yes, sir,' she said. The doctor was packing his bag and preparing to leave.

'It was a good idea to slap the peach on the kid to get him to lead you to his lair. If the thing is still on the boy, we shall have them.'

'It was Constable Mills' idea, sir. I wanted none of it.'

'No matter. It took a lot of bottom to do what you did, and you might have incidentally solved a tricky-looking murder case. I will see that it is entered into your staff records.'

The quack nodded to the Inspector and left, letting a prescription for some ointment and pain-killing pills flutter into her hands.

'Couldn't I have a week off instead, sir?' After all she'd suffered she had the right to talk flash to the boss.

He shrugged. 'With Accession Day almost on us? Constable Pearson, please do not think me mean-spirited, but there is a political imperative here. Last year, in the week before Accession Day, you caught twelve pickpockets, all of them preying upon foreign visitors. I have looked at your records. I have no doubt that you will be similarly successful this year. If we assume that each of those twelve dippers took five victims per day, we finish with a total of sixty persons daily who have had their holidays ruined. They do not visit the country again, and they advise their friends and kinfolk against it. The result is ultimately the demise of a valued industry which provides thousands of Londoners with honest industry and money. Now what, I ask you, is a little pain in your thumb when set against this great mass of prosperity and happiness you are guarding? Do you now understand why I should rather immerse my feet in boiling water than lose the use of your good self, the best pad in London . . . Go home, embrace Morpheus for a good ten or twelve hours and I shall see you tomorrow.'

Jenny thought of a word that she would never have said out loud.

Still, it was nice to be appreciated.

After sitting at his desk for ten minutes, Scipio realized his powers of concentration were gone. It was getting late and the uniformed officers were dealing with their usual caseload of drunks, beggars and petty, noisy nuisances. Besides, he himself had an interesting case rattling around his brain, something he turned over and about, chewed and prodded from every approach. A bizarre murder, and now Constables Pearson and Mills had recovered a box of treasure which might or might not have been the object concealed in the hole in the ground at the site of the murder.

Boswell sat at Glyndwr's desk while the latter was out striking terror into the city's criminal classes, leafing through a manual on police procedure.

'Boswell,' said Scipio. 'I am being remiss in my duties towards my new 'prentice. I forgot to enquire as to whether you have a place to stay.'

'Yes, sir,' said Boswell looking up from his book. 'I'm in Highgate with an ancestor of mine, Sir Digby Lovejoy. I believe the expression is that I am of his affinity.'

Whenever a new retread came up, the reception centre would try and put him or her in touch with some relatives, however distant. It eased people's passage into this world, it connected them with a family network who might be able to help them find work and accommodation. And it did something to prevent people from the same eras all crowding together in separate little parishes – ghettos – of their own.

Down the years, family clans had formed, usually headed by a nobleman. Some people would say they were of the affinity of Lord So-And-So or the Earl of Whatsit, even though most of these noblemen had their titles and little else. Many retread nobles prospered by persuading their kinfolk to work for them because that was the way the world should be ordered. Most of these affinities were loose and informal. But some were becoming close-knit and powerful. Some had made criminal clans of themselves.

'Affinity ain't a word I like, Boswell. It smells of feudalism. I prefer "family".'

'I see, sir. Are you a member of a family?'

'I suppose I am head of one. I married an African-Caribbean woman many years ago, and we have three children of our own. We have also adopted or fostered a further twenty retread children. The reception centres have Mrs Africanus and me marked down as conscientious parents of other people's children. Most of 'em are black, and many now have children of their own. Indeed, you might say that I am head of the Africanus affinity. That dignity will doubtless pass in due course to my son, John, who is a well-known jazz musician. Well, I say "jazz" although the term the youngsters use for his particular musical form is "badmash". The word is Indian for rascal or hooligan, but somehow it got over here, perhaps because it mixes nicely with "masher".'

'What's a masher, sir? Nothing to do with golf, or potatoes then?'

'A masher is a young dandy, often one who is partial to badmash music, but only as long as it don't mess up his hair or expensive striped jacket or embroidered waistcoat. The music is noisy, exuberant stuff for clever kids partial to its swagger and rebelliousness. Though no one would admit to it, badmash is for students and middle-class kids – the nobs. Beat music, on the other hand, which can also be noisy and exuberant, but which is more repetitive and where the words have little or no meaning, is for oik kids, the lower classes who may *also* be mashers – understand that masher is purely a fashion term and does not necessarily denote any particular musical taste . . .'

'Right-oh, sir.'

'And the oiks' parents listen to music hall comedy songs, sentimental ballads or syrupy orchestrations of folk songs.' Scipio stopped talking. How on *Earth* did he get to be such an expert on popular music? Oh yes. 'This at least is what my son tells me. I know little about the musical and sartorial tastes of the masses and the young and care even less.'

Boswell's eyes widened.

'I keep thinking that this is all a delirium,' he said at length. 'I half-expect to wake up in the hospital in 1940, covered in burns and with some angelic nurse shoving a bed-pan under me.'

'You will get over it,' said Scipio. 'I have been here thirty-four years and sometimes I still awake thinking I must rush to put on my jester-suit and attend the Master's levee.'

'Sorry?'

'Levee. Big-wig's getting-out-of-bed ceremony. I was a slave. Or servant. The difference is a legal technicality, no more. As a child I was abducted by slavers from a home somewhere in West Africa, then taken to England and given or sold to a nobleman who lived near Bristol. I was dressed like an organ-grinder's monkey and renamed for some hero of European antiquity. I was treated with affection but offered no hope of dignity and died just as I reached manhood.'

He returned to his desk and the mountain of bumf on it. Division had sent down a request marked 'most urgent' that he ask his officers their attitude to proposed changes in the design of charge-sheets. He shook his head irritably and threw the request in the bin. Sorry, never received it. Oh I did, did I? Ah, well, we had the builders in, you see. We must have lost it in the confusion. Too bad. Never mind.

'Rule three, Boswell. Seek opportunity in every adversity.'

Boswell looked up from his manual. 'Sorry, sir?'

'Nothing. By the way, do you have a grave?'

'Um, I don't know, sir, the idea never occurred to me. I crashed on to dry land, so I suppose I must have.'

Confound it, I need spectacles, thought Scipio as he consigned more paper to the bin. All this paper is ruining my eyesight.

'The doctors say that visiting one's grave is a tonic. I saw mine a few years ago.'

'How did you feel when you saw it?'

'Nothing much. It was in some ways useful. I had my wife and children with me at the time. My son and I spoke to one another at length for the first time in years.'

O'Rourke and another constable came in carrying string bags full of newspaper packages. They moved around the room, doling them out.

'Ah!' said Scipio, putting his fountain-pen down, 'eight-thirty! Supper time! This is a quiet part of the shift, so we eat.'

The station canteen had fallen temporary victim to the builders, and their regular slop-jockey pensioned off for the duration. A mercy, since the man was incapable of preparing anything other than stews accompanied by thick slices of tasteless white bread generously coated in margarine.

O'Rourke placed parcels in front of Scipio and Boswell. Boswell unwrapped his fish supper. The fare of what to Boswell would have been the labouring classes, caked in salt and drenched in vinegar. Despite viewing a corpse, he found he had an appetite, unwrapped it and began eating quickly.

Scipio watched him. 'Boswell,' he said, 'look around you, in this room, the streets. What do you see?'

Boswell shrugged. 'I'm sorry, I don't follow . . .'

'What do most of the men in this room have in common? Aside from you and me?'

Boswell looked around. A dozen policemen ate their fish suppers with evident relish. Some were in uniform, some in civvies, few were as tall as him, but . . .

'They're all overweight,' said Boswell. 'I noticed it in the streets first. A lot of younger men wear tight-fitting breeches and tights as if to show off their slimness . . .'

'Precisely. You came from a well-to-do family at a prosperous time in history. As you look around here, you probably consider it a mess – huge areas laid waste, millions killed by war, others dying of the radiation plague, political unrest . . . And daily more folks arrive here. To most of them, this is Arcadia. Not Heaven, but demonstrably not Hell either. They arrive healthy, at the same age at which they died, their memories intact. In their last lives, few could ever be certain if there would be food from one day to the next. Now they are in a gastronomic paradise, and they eat. They eat because food is abundant, because there is an undreamed-of variety of tastes and textures, they eat because being fat was the mark of wealth in their last lives, and they eat to comfort themselves, to forget their terrible uncertainties. Four per cent of all the money earned in Britain is spent on chocolate bars alone. Of these, the biggest selling chocolate bar is a thing filled with sticky stuff called a Chocolate Heaven. You see, Boswell? We have died and gone to Chocolate Heaven.'

Scipio unwrapped his fish and chips and began to eat.

'This murder we saw today,' said Boswell, in between ravenous mouthfuls. 'Do you ever wonder where the dead go from here? Is there another world somewhere else where they wake up?'

'Is there any sense in wondering?' Scipio carried on eating.

Boswell turned back to his police manual. He had reached the section outlining procedures for dealing with retreads. Around a hundred and fifty a day arrived in London alone. If a police officer was called to a resurrection, he was to ensure the subject was kept warm, his or her nakedness covered, given reassuring noises, and despatched to the nearest reception centre for registration and induction.

Scipio left half his food. He never had much of an appetite in hot weather. Like every retread, he had once regarded wasting food as something close to murder, but these days he believed that giving second helpings to his overweight officers was even worse. Rather than share it, he bundled the remains into a newspaper ball and threw it towards a wastepaper basket two desks away, then belched.

'What about the murderer?' Boswell asked. 'Will he be hanged when we catch him?'

'He will stand trial, after which he may well hang.'

'I'm an abolitionist myself. At least I was last week.'

'In my day, an abolitionist was something altogether

different,' said Scipio darkly. 'For what it is worth, I know of few cases where hanging did any good, and one or two in which it did incalculable harm because the victim was palpably innocent . . . Boswell, are you a Marxist?'

'I call myself a Socialist. My eldest brother fought in the Spanish Civil War.'

'Never heard of it. Boswell, there are Marxists here, but their brains are somewhere else. Life here is not about how much you own, because most here own far more than they did in the past. What matters is why we are here. The men of science have unproven theories about resonances and auras of the dead lodging in the earth and brickwork and elsewhat. But empirical science is nobs' business. For the majority, for us oiks, what matters is God; they say the Almighty is giving them a second chance. Some say that the Almighty is giving them the opportunity to live more righteously, while others say that they have been delivered from their medieval hovels or hellish Victorian slums as a reward from on high. Who is right? What also signifies is when you came from. Those who are best equipped to cope with the twenty-first century are those who died most recently. The forces that drive this country are religion and knowledge, not money.'

'Did you kill during the Feudal Wars?'

'Yes,' said Scipio, lighting a cigarette. 'And at the end of it, on the day they stretched the neck of Monmouth, I cheered myself hoarse. And I am not a man ever given to public displays of emotion. Call me vindictive if you will, but it meant that Monmouth and his band of cut-throats, liars, aristocrats and God-bothering lunatics would not enslave me or anyone else, and there was finally an end to the killing.'

'I see that,' said Boswell, 'but there's something I don't get. Is killing – here I mean – such a terrible thing? Perhaps those who die prematurely here get another chance in another world somewhere else.'

Scipio shrugged and puffed smoke-rings towards the ceiling. 'Only a few are foolish or courageous enough to want to find out. That is something you learn very quickly. Nobody wants to die again, and nobody wants to be deprived of the love of their families or the good-fellowship of their friends and comrades. So many of us have come here as orphans, agonizingly sensible of our loneliness in the universe, so we work very very hard to cultivate the love and comradeship of others. You lived during a war yourself. You must know that murder is still the greatest crime of all.'

Boswell nodded, and carried on eating, though he did not look as though he completely understood.

'Any chance of any scran over here?' screamed Edward II from his position in the public area. He rattled his handcuffs against the radiator to which he was affixed to emphasize the point.

'You'll be fed later,' growled Sergeant Hopton from the desk.

'This is no way to treat a king,' yelped the Pretender. 'Reminds me of the time I was in that Berkeley Castle.'

Hopton shrugged. 'Then perhaps you shouldn't go round causing trouble. You're no more King Edward II than I am. Now calm down. Some people will be coming along to collect you later. You'll be treated kindly, I promise.'

The man seemed happy at the thought of the kindness he would receive. He smiled, then nodded. Then, quite promptly, fell asleep.

'Well now,' said Uncle Seamus, pulling a kingsman handkerchief from his breast pocket and wiping off his fingers. 'Shall we have a look at the prize our colleagues brought back from the Holy Land?'

'A good idea,' said Scipio. 'Glyndwr left it in the evidence room. Better use some gloves.'

The sergeant nodded, took a fresh pair of plastic gloves from the top drawer of his desk and set off. Now there was another man who was too fond of his grub. All Irishmen, in Scipio's experience, were the same.

'The Irish,' he said to Boswell, 'are if anything even more committed to their affinities and clans than the English, you know. Uncle Seamus over there takes a fortnight's holiday without fail every March and repairs to Kilburn, where he meets up with assorted O'Rourkes and their affiliated in-laws for ten days of drinking, dancing and, above all, eating. There are no nobles among them, but some are exceedingly wealthy men who have prospered from the rebuilding of London.'

The young man looked thoughtful. Wanted to say something, then thought better of it.

'What, Boswell?'

'I was wondering if police officers could ever be, er, morally compromised by their family ties.'

'Certainly. It has happened even among officers at this station. But not Sergeant O'Rourke.'

'No, no, of course not,' said Boswell, reddening in the face. 'I never meant to suggest . . .'

'It was a good question, Boswell. The worst thing

about this job is that it makes you suspicious of everyone.'

O'Rourke had had to get help. He and a uniformed constable came in, straining to carry the heavy wooden chest. They set it down carefully on his desk. Scipio, Boswell and some of the other officers gathered round. Several of them gasped as he opened the box with a gloved hand.

Most of the coin in it was – or appeared to be – silver. About a third of it was gold.

'Our man buried these in his house in recent years,' he said. 'This little lot definitely isn't something that someone cached away in a previous life.'

'Who?' asked Boswell.

'Mr Lilley,' said O'Rourke. 'Who else? Haseldich, the man who got killed, wouldn't want to hide his own readies – assuming he had any – in someone else's house.'

'How can you be certain they weren't hidden in another century?' asked Boswell.

O'Rourke flipped a coin to Boswell, who only just managed to catch it. 'Look whose head's on the back.'

It was a sovereign. Saint George was slaying the dragon on one side, while on the other was a man's head in profile, and the legend '*Ricardus III D.G. R. Brit*'.

'I don't suppose he's *Ind. Imp.* any more,' said Boswell.

'No, King George from your own time was the last Emperor of India. And until none too long ago, the Indians could have come over here and made Britain a colony of their own – if they'd been bothered.'

King Richard had a noble, dignified profile, that of a young and able man. 'And what about *Fid. Def.* – Defender of the Faith?'

'Ah,' smiled O'Rourke. 'The Liberal Settlement keeps a brick wall between Church and State. People would ask whose *Fid* he'd be *Deffing*.'

'So who is head of the Church of England if not the King?'

'The King is a theoretical Catholic, and a practising agnostic,' said Scipio. 'The Church is governed by its synod. Not a happy state of affairs for a lot of faithful men. They preferred it when they had a Protestant king. Kings are sort of not quite human, a bit closer to God in the great scheme of things. A king can head a church . . . but a committee of bishops? To many, that does not seem right.'

'Some people disapprove?'

'Quite a few,' said Scipio. 'Catholics and Protestants.'

'That reminds me,' said Boswell. 'I keep meaning to ask if any other kings and queens have been reborn. Not all of them died of old age.'

'Ah well now, you'd be thinking of King Charles I to start with,' said O'Rourke.

'He was reborn ten years ago,' said Scipio, 'saw that his throne was already occupied and decided – or was quietly persuaded – to retire to a monastery on one of the Scottish islands. Quite an austere place, I believe.'

'Wouldn't he want his throne back? Divine right of kings and all that?' asked Boswell.

Uncle Seamus shrugged. 'Sure he'd be the start of another civil war if he began making trouble. No, we're all better off with him up there freezing and saying his prayers.'

'There are,' said Scipio, 'people keeping an eye on him. Not government people, but those committed to the preservation of the Liberal Settlement. If King Charles I grew troublesome, he would not be long for this world.'

'Gosh!' said Boswell. 'Any more monarchs?'

'Plenty of obscure Celtic and Anglo-Saxon potentates you've never heard of,' said O'Rourke, 'including ten Boadiceas and several dozen claiming to be King Arthur. There's also quite a few princes and princesses who might have ruled had they not perished first. But the only other famous king is William Rufus.'

'A Norman thug with a bad personality who was shot with an arrow while out hunting,' recalled Boswell. 'Accident or assassination no one knows.'

'Oh, but we do!' said Scipio. 'William Rufus is by all accounts a difficult character, consequently he is *most* unlikely to gather any supporters were he to make a bid for the throne.'

'He now breeds racehorses somewhere in Berkshire,' said Uncle Seamus. 'I put a few shillings on one of his nags at the Cheltenham Gold Cup last year. Lost the bloody lot.'

'What about Anne Boleyn?' said Boswell. 'She's the start of all this Catholic–Protestant nonsense. If it hadn't been for Henry VIII wanting to have his wicked way with her we'd probably all be Catholics.'

'No sign of her,' said Scipio.

'There are plenty of Papists around,' said O'Rourke. 'I'm a Papist, like most other Irishmen, quite a few

Scots, several northern English and anyone originally born between the tenth and fifteenth centuries as well as quite a few from before that. We take our orders on matters of faith from San Francisco. That's where the Papacy moved after the Atom War. Now, look at these.'

Uncle Seamus stretched out his massive paws to display a handful of shillings and florins. They were much smaller than coins of the same denomination in Boswell's last life.

'Look at the dates on them,' said O'Rourke. 'Nothing before 1990. People from olden times don't put too much faith in paper money. These are silver. Before 1990 there was less silver in 'em. They had a core of copper or some sort of alloy, and people didn't trust them. A lot of trade, especially among retreads from the distant past, was carried out by bargain and barter. The Government didn't think this was a very efficient way for a modern economy to conduct itself, so in 1990 all silver coin became fully silver again. All the old stuff with the base metal in the middle was recalled or was driven out of circulation and everyone trusts the coinage these days. More or less.'

'So why would anyone want to bury their money. Aren't the banks safe?' asked Boswell.

'The banks are perfectly safe. You're the 'prentice — you work it out.'

'Got it!' said Boswell. 'The tax-man!'

'Aye,' said O'Rourke, reaching into the box again. 'Your man Lilley is wealthy. He'll be there on his holidays in Bath, drinking brandy and roaring curses on the Liberal Settlement and King Dick. Not only does he want to keep his wealth, but he'll be most particular about not wanting to give any to a state he wants no truck with. Something you'll learn at the end of the month, me boyo, is that the taxes here are something wicked. Nine shillings and threepence in the pound if you're on more than five hundred a year . . . But how else do we pay for the reception centres and the schools and hospitals and the BBC and the roads and railways . . .?'

'And the police!'

'Oh aye, the police, too,' beamed Uncle Seamus.

From the bottom of the box he pulled a roll of brown leather, like a tobacco pouch. He unwrapped it and spilled its contents on to the table.

'Uncut diamonds!' gasped Boswell. 'Any idea what they're worth?'

Scipio clasped the young man on the shoulder. 'Probably more than you're going to earn in this lifetime. Or the last one.'

'Chief,' said O'Rourke, 'what say you we all just stuff our pockets and go? I always fancied taking the Flying Boat to Mombasa . . .'

He was putting the diamonds back into their bag, and dropping coins back into the box.

'Okay,' said Scipio.

'I don't know, though,' said O'Rourke, hesitating. 'Africa sounds awful hot.'

'You are right,' said Scipio. 'Let us forget it until the winter. After all, we get boxes of treasure passing through here all the time. What is our hurry?'

Suddenly, all the lights went out.

'Bleddy power workers!' yelled King Edward II through the darkness. 'They should count themselves lucky they've got jobs at all. I'll give the Electrical Supply

Guild what-for when I reclaim my rightful throne. Have the blimmin' lot of 'em in the Tower, so I will.'

'Someone find us some candles,' yelled Scipio. It would still be daylight outside, but there were no windows on this part of the building.

'It's more than a Christian skin can stand,' said Uncle Seamus. 'Stuck in here in the dark with a lifetime's opportunity to run off with a fortune in coin and diamonds.'

'Look on it as a test, Sarge,' said Boswell's voice from somewhere.

Uncle Seamus sighed, then laughed.

The lights kept going off, then on again. Scipio now had a candle planted on his desk, half-hoping that some clumsy flatfoot might knock it over and accidentally set fire to all his paper. Glyndwr had almost done it, too, on returning to the station, but had turned to catch it at the last moment. The only damage was a solidified pool of wax on top of a very important memo about the correct way of filling in expense-claim forms.

Boswell was trying hard to stay awake as he read his manual, probably exhausted by all the brain-work he'd had already that evening.

'Inspector!' shouted Hopton from the desk. 'We have a fix from DC Mills' peach!'

'Excellent,' said Scipio, getting up from his desk. 'Who, where and is it moving?'

'PC Smith, in Covent Garden. I've had all the patrol officers switching to its frequency every five minutes. He's just found it. It's stationary. And boss, you're going to love this . . .'

'I very much doubt it.'

'It's at a stew, just round the corner from here.'

'Right!' shouted Scipio. 'Tell Smith to stand pad and keep low until we arrive. Boswell! Stick with me. Glyndwr, you are with me, too. O'Rourke, take two men and cover the back of the house. Do not enter until I say so. Remember they took DC Mills' gun, and may have other weapons. The man may be extremely dangerous. The kid is a poisonous little brat, but please, everyone try your best not to kill him. It would look terrible in the newspapers and means a week's worth of paperwork for me. We shall take the cars. Get Boswell a bundhook, O'Rourke – and I want everyone in armour!'

O'Rourke got up, took a massive bunch of keys from his jacket pocket and went off to the arms cupboard.

'Do you know how to use a revolver, Boswell?'

'Um, sort of. We were trained, sir, though I'm a lousy shot.'

'It ain't about being a good shot unless you are cornered. A gun is a tool for getting the other fellow to do your bidding. Its lethal function is secondary.'

O'Rourke emerged with an armful of blue bulletproof waistcoats. Some peelers said they should be wearing them all the time. Others said it would make them look frightening, and not like the old-fashioned, trustworthy British bobby who had done so much to make the country a civilized place when a lot of others were going to the dogs.

It was academic either way. There weren't enough to go round so they only got issued on gala occasions.

Scipio took one from Uncle Seamus's arms and helped him into it. 'Proof against low-velocity bullets and knives,' he said. 'Fasten all the buttons at the sides.'

O'Rourke passed him one of the station's stock of elderly Webley revolvers. He broke it open. It was fully loaded. He gave it to Boswell.

'Safety catch here. Keep it on unless you need to use it. Put it in your pocket for now, but do not expect to be able to draw it quickly. The hammer will almost certainly get caught on your clothes.'

'Yes, sir.'

'I shall find you an automatic and show you how to use that when I get a chance.'

'Oh, I always love this bit,' said O'Rourke, who was struggling to get his own weskit on over his ample stomach. 'Did you know, Mr Boswell, that the body produces its own drug when it's agitated? Nothing licks the excitement of getting ready to go and get killed.'

'Oh stop it, O'Rourke. None of my 'prentices have perished in the line of duty yet,' said Scipio. 'Come on then,' he added, leading them off down the corridor to the car-park at the back. Glyndwr followed, cradling his pump-action shotgun.

Two Humbers stood waiting. O'Rourke climbed into the back of one, with the two other officers he was going with. The car's engine coughed into life and it pulled off quietly.

Scipio climbed into the driver's seat of the other, motioning Boswell to get in beside him. Glyndwr got in the back, still feeding his voracious cannon. 'I suppose you imagined that this would be a more cerebral profession,' said Scipio starting the engine. 'It is not like your Sherlock Holmes or Mrs Christie stories. It is truly fortunate that most criminals are far stupider than even the average rozzer. The secrets of our success are common sense and being organized.'

'An' 'avin' more fire-power,' growled Glyndwr from the back seat.

'Glyndwr, your faith in the tools of your trade is touching,' said Scipio. 'Have you been introduced to my new 'prentice yet?'

Boswell turned in his seat to shake Glyndwr's hand. 'Pleased to meet you,' said Boswell. Glyndwr grunted, assessing the new boy. Evidently he met the Welshman's approval. 'You was a fighter pilot I hear?'

'Yes that's right?'

'Spitfire or 'urricane?'

'Hurricane.'

'Pity. Spitfires is more romantic, I always thought. What squadron?'

This was probably the longest conversation Glyndwr had had all week. The man was an artist in metal. Scipio had seen the models and sculptures he made with his big, clumsy-looking fingers. Evidently his interest in the 'prentice was cerebral rather than carnal.

Probably just as well, really.

Jacob Malahide had stopped drinking. There was something really bad going down. Earlier on, one of the Brethren had dropped by to say the rozzers had been over at Elder Lilley's house. He couldn't take a looksee himself as he was too well known in the parish. He would have to let Elder Saltonstall know later.

Aside from Rochester, his Mohocks and the Papist saint, it was a quiet evening. Three Yank tourists were getting their ends away upstairs, as were a few of the regular toffs – middle-aged pen-pushers from Whitehall who had doubtless told their wives they were working late.

He sat at the bar, nursing a cup of coffee and smoking a Wild Woodbine. Lickpenny Nan came rolling up. 'Something strange, Brother Jacob.' She used the word 'Brother' sarcastically.

'What?'

'There's a young kid and a fat cove in my apartments, come over the back wall, they did. Said they needed to see an Upright Man and quick.'

Malahide slid from the stool and went to a heavy oak door marked 'Private'. Nan followed. At the end of a narrow passage was another door. Through here was her own parlour, a room with huge French windows, whose walls were hung with stupid pictures in pear-wood and burl-elm frames of kids wearing rags and looking all sad with over-sized eyes, or white horses galloping along a seashore. The furniture, all fussy Louis Quinze stuff made of plastic and chipboard, was covered in china trinkets or pots growing nettles. The stingers were in season and some coves liked being thrashed lightly with them. Nan referred to them in her cod-French as a 'speciality de le maison', like the place was some fancy eating-house.

The kid and a big fat spack stood in the middle of the room. He had a nodding acquaintance with the pair of them. The kid was a dipper who'd always come on respectful, the spack was his mate. Maybe he was a margery, and the kid his girlfriend.

'Jacob Malahide,' said the kid, 'I'll tell you no lies . . .'

Malahide said nothing, just nailed the kid with a

stare. Heycock was stood behind him. He waved her away. She frumped out, muttering something in the cant she used with her sluts, thinking he didn't understand her.

'The rozzers are on to us, Mr Malahide,' said the kid.

The spack was staring at the floor all contrition-like. Malahide didn't like the smell of this one jot. They could be leading a Lord Mayor's Parade of trouble this way.

'I've resisted arrest twice,' said the kid. 'For dipping. Numps here killed a man. They're after him, too.'

'Why did you kill?' Malahide asked Numps.

'He was defending himself. The man came at him with a shovel—'

'I didn't ask you,' said Malahide. 'Why?' he addressed the spack.

The big fool started crying. 'I didn't mean to, honest I didn't. He just asked me to stand crow while he cracked a house . . .'

'And the cove wanted to keep all the tool for himself,' said the kid. 'He wouldn't let Numps have his fair shar—'

Malahide pulled out his chiv, grabbed the kid by the hair and held it in front of his eyes. 'Look close, chavie . . . Two blades, just a tiny bit apart. You know what happens if I cut you? It's really hard for the quacks to fix, they can't sew it up. It'll hurt like mad and you'll lose your pretty looks. Now shut your trap, and let Numps talk.'

'Don't hurt Uriah, Mister Malahide, please,' wailed Numps. 'It's the truth! I met this cull in the streets. He took me to an alehouse, bought me a drink and said how

I was a big strong fellow and could I help him with a job? He said there'd be good money. I didn't tell Uriah here about it. I thought it'd be a surprise. He's always telling me how I'm no use for making us a living and how it's his brains keeps us in style. I was going to show him.

'So I met this bloke this morning where he said. He's got a shovel, a pick, and an axe and an electric saw and such, and we cracked the house. He must have known all about it. He took us down to the cellar and we tore up the floorboards and started digging. Just where he says it'll be there's this big box with loads of stuff, gold and such. I thought with all that Uriah and me could buy a little house and live there and stop grafting, but I had to get rid of the cove. So I hit him some. I suppose I must have killed him.'

Malahide let go of the kid. 'Where's the swag now?'

'The rozzers have it. They came to our room a while ago. We ran away. We had to leave it there,' said Numps.

'Apart from this,' said the kid. He reached into his pocket and held out a dozen gold sovereigns. Malahide took them. Their solid, reassuring weight in his fist felt real enough.

'And now you want the Order to help you?'

They both nodded. He pocketed the coins. The big man would have a strong back, and the kid was smart. Both were useful. The Order would have to hide them. That was easy enough. But the law was on to them. Were they worth the trouble?

He made his decision.

'You are both sinners,' he said. 'There is yet a chance of redemption. You will work unceasingly for the Order to prepare the way of the Lord. Fail us, and we shall throw you to the rozzers. Or worse.'

He put the chiv away and felt the coins in his pocket. Suddenly, he felt a heaviness in his stomach, his face started sweating.

'Where was this house you cracked?' he asked coldly.

The spack started shaking.

'Answer!' he yelled.

'Russell Square,' said Numps, timidly.

'Name the cove you killed?'

'Hasel-something,' said Numps.

'Haseldich?'

'Might be . . . I, I can't remember rightly. I used to know him a bit in my last life. We met in the streets. He asked me to help him.'

Haseldich had come up recently and joined the Order. Elder Lilley had a house in Russell Square where one of the Brethren had seen the rozzers this evening. Elder Lilley was the Order's treasurer. The money was needed soon. Everyone in the Order knew that great events would soon take place.

'Mister Malahide?' said the kid.

'Shut up, I'm thinking.'

But now it looked like Haseldich had betrayed the Order. If he had been taking the money for the Order's purpose he would have got some of the Brethren to assist him. Instead, he had enlisted a big strong idiot without the wit to ask awkward questions who he thought would help him do the job in return for a pat on the back and half a crown.

No doubt about it. Haseldich had been trying to take it all for himself!

Well, Haseldich had paid for his treachery, but he had bequeathed a cartload of worry. Jacob Malahide did not know what to do. The kid and the spack would probably have to pay, too, but the Elders would want to question them first.

Jacob Malahide considered, as the pair of sinners trembled before him. Again, he fondled the coins in his pocket.

Something wasn't regular about them.

One was not a coin, but a small, round thing, one side of which was sticking to his finger. He took it out.

'What's this?' he asked the kid, holding out the tiny piece of nob machinery. 'Did you dip it?'

The kid came forward. 'I don't know,' he said.

There was a muffled commotion from the direction of the bar. One of the trollops out front shouted something about Police.

'Agreement's cancelled,' he said to Numps and the kid. 'Get out of here. You will pay dear for this.'

It was too late. Through the French window, the beams from three powerful electric torches played along the top of the garden-wall.

'Come on Numps!' said the kid. 'We'll try and get out the front!'

The kid pulled out a massive automatic popp. This would look very bad for the Order. He tried to block the kid's way. He saw Numps' huge fist coming straight at his face.

He fell, vaguely heard the big spack saying, 'Sorry, Mister Malahide.'

He looked up. Three big, ugly rozzers were at the window. In a moment, one of the panes fell inwards. An arm in blue shirtsleeves was reaching in to unlock the door.

'Thank heavens you're here, officer,' he said, 'they threatened me with a gun. They went that way.'

The rozzers ran off through the door. Jacob Malahide decided it was prudent to make himself scarce, too. Besides, he needed to speak with Elder Saltonstall urgently. He would leave by the French window and over the wall.

They parked a few yards down the road. When O'Rourke radioed that he and his men were in position at the back of the building, Scipio led Boswell and Glyndwr out of the car and straight up to the front door of the brothel, where, on the lintel was inscribed the words 'KIND AND TENDER USAGE'.

Boswell's eyes widened. Poor simple boy. 'I say, sir, is this a . . . ?'

'Yes Boswell, it is.'

'Isn't it against the law?'

'Rule number four, Boswell. And you will not find it in any police manual, or the statute books . . . Our calling is to protect people and property from criminal acts. It is not to regulate public morality. A good peeler fights crime. He endeavours not to waste his time in fighting sin.'

Scipio knew the place. High-class stew. Run by a middle-aged woman named Heycock, alias Lickpenny Nan. Late eighteenth-century retread. Bit of form for procuring and immoral earnings, but nothing egregious. Worked under her own sail. No known mob affinity. They could close the place any time, but the paperwork and the court time would be frightful. Besides, she'd only set up shop elsewhere. Or all her girls would go on the streets, making a nuisance of themselves, or being preyed on by mobs and ponces. As long as women were going to sell themselves, it was best they do it from places like this, which were orderly and where an eye could be kept on them.

Glyndwr banged on the door, shouting something that might have been, 'Police! Open up!'

A fat, jolly little woman who looked more like a farmer's wife than a madam – Lickpenny Nan Heycock herself – appeared and held it half open.

'Why, good evening, gents,' she giggled. 'And what lovely weather we've been having of late. Yes, really lovely . . .'

She looked nervous. And pale. Worn out by something. Probably not the cares of running a business.

Scipio edged her aside with the flat of his arm and walked in. 'This is a disorderly house,' he said. 'It will go badly for you if you do not co-operate.'

She let them through and bowed a little.

Lickpenny Nan was glad to see them.

They walked into a spacious, deserted room. Along the length of the left wall was a very well-appointed bar. At the far end of the bar a wide staircase led upwards, doubtless to the kind and tender usage. To the other side of the stairs was a small doorway marked 'Private'.

The place reeked of genteel depravity; red carpets, red flock wallpaper, red plush seating, polished mahogany tables. Gilt cherubs adorned the wall-mounted light fittings. When Boswell saw the ceiling, he let out an audible 'Good grief!' Supported by four thick columns through the middle of the room, it was painted in vivid colours and depicted a right old bacchanal. Plump women yielded to the advances of mightily muscled swains while satyrs played lutes and filled their wine-goblets.

'Mother Heycock,' said Scipio, 'we are seeking a fat man and a boy aged about ten or twelve on suspicion of murder.'

The woman said nothing. Just angled her eyebrows towards her shoulder.

'Glyndwr, you stay here. Do not let anyone out. Boswell, come with me.'

The lights went out.

'Come on, Numps!' came a boy's voice from the direction of the door at the foot of the stairs.

The bang of a gun filled the room, crashing over into all his other senses, filling even the darkness.

Scipio drew his Browning automatic from his shoulder-holster and pointed it in the general direction of the gunshot, though with the noise bouncing off all the walls it was hard to tell exactly where it had originated.

There were screams and shouts upstairs. 'Who put the lights out?' asked a voice. American.

Ruddy power workers' strike.

The lights came on again. Boswell reappeared from behind a pillar, holding his pistol at his side, his knuckles white and tense.

Scipio made for the cover of another pillar and quietly motioned to Boswell to get back behind his. The shot may have come from behind the bar.

Three middle-aged men in spectacles and shorts came down the stairs at the side of the bar and into the room.

There was no sign of Numps or the kid.

'Was that gunplay we heard?' said one of the men. American accent. 'Sure sounded like gunplay to me.'

'Figures,' said another. 'Everyone in here's hiding behind chairs an' stuff.'

'Do you guys think,' said the third, 'we should do the same?'

The lights went off again. One of the Americans swore and said something about going upstairs to get dressed. The others agreed. One of the stairs creaked as they left.

A torch-beam lanced into the room from a door at the far end.

'What's happening?' shouted O'Rourke from somewhere beyond the light.

'We think they are both in here somewhere,' yelled Scipio. 'They fired a shot a moment ago.'

Three shots crashed out. This time, he saw the muzzle-flashes. From about where the top of the bar would be.

The lights came on again. The television above the bar flickered into life. The sound was turned down. A solemn man at a desk was speaking to camera with a picture of Prime Minister Mr Gordon Brown behind him. The evening news.

Glyndwr appeared behind the pillar beside him, next to Boswell. The burly Welshman sprung out, cocked his shotgun and fired four times along the top of the bar.

Mirrors, bottles, glasses disintegrated as he shot.

113

Amber, red and green and clear liquids fell, thick shards of glass dropped, splinters flew up and out into the air and dropped like fine powdery snow.

Glyndwr's intention had been to frighten rather than kill. He retreated behind his column to reload.

Scipio's ears ached. He was getting too old for this nonsense.

The lights died once more. They heard feet or knees crunching along broken glass.

'Give yourselves up now,' shouted Scipio.

'God's sacred breeches!' said a male voice from the foot of the stairs. 'Rochester, methinks that something disagreeable is afoot.'

'Granville, you clouterly old gibb-cat,' came another voice from the same direction, 'the poor harlot who deigned to swive you this evening was the only one to suffer anything disagreeable.'

Another male voice laughed behind them.

'Police! Go back!' shouted Scipio. 'There's a madman with a gun down here!'

'More than one madman, I fancy,' said the voice called Rochester. *The* Rochester? What was he doing here?

Milord Rochester in a whore-house? What was a goldfish doing in water?

'I'll surrender myself,' came the boy's voice from behind the bar. 'I'm jumping over now! Please don't shoot me. I never committed any murder. It was Numps. It was nothing to do with me.'

The lights came on again, as did the television, this time for some reason with the sound turned up. The weather tomorrow would be hot again.

The kid jumped over the bar and on to the floor in front of Boswell, who leapt out and swiped the brat by the scruff of the neck, pulling him to the floor and dragging him behind his pillar. Someone tossed a pair of handcuffs, which landed by his side.

He took both of the kid's wrists and clapped the bracelets on, ratcheting them as tight as he could. Good man.

'Bless me!' said a shaven-headed man in a white shirt embroidered in bright flowery patterns and baggy trews standing at the bottom of the stairs. 'What trumpery is this? All the King's horses and all the King's men to capture a boy?'

Yes, Rochester all right. Was this something to do with him?

Rochester noticed Scipio. 'Well, I'll be buggered! Gentlemen,' he said to his companions on the stairs behind him, 'I do believe we are being shot at by Major Scipio Africanus, conqueror of Bristol, hero of my own masterpiece, *The Dashing Mechano!* Good evening to you, sir! Let us do as he commands!'

Before Rochester could move out of the way, a fat, clumsy, desperately unhappy-looking young man – Numps – emerged from under the bar. He grabbed Rochester around the neck and pulled him backwards. He pressed his own back against the wall and pushed a gun into Rochester's temple.

'Don't come any nearer,' said Numps. 'Or I'll shoot this gentleman, so I will.'

Rochester looked more amused than frightened. 'You only speed me on my way, changeling,' he said.

'Uriah, help me,' said Numps piteously. 'Why did

you give yourself up? You told me we was partners grafting together.'

Boswell pulled the brat's head up. 'Tell him to give himself up,' he hissed.

The lights fizzled, then went off again. There was a small commotion, then a rushing noise as though a powerful gust of wind had come through an opened window. Scipio's ears popped.

Small pinpoints of light, every colour of the rainbow, danced around like fireflies in the middle of the room.

The wind was not blowing, but sucking. His hair flopped forward, drawn towards the lights, which moved more and more quickly. Next to him, a chair bumped to the floor.

The coloured lights began to resolve themselves into human shape.

The electricity came back on. A thin, naked man in his twenties lay in the middle of the room. He stared at the ceiling, running his hands over his body. His mouth gaped open further and further as he contemplated the painting of the orgy on the ceiling above. 'Be this Heaven?' he whispered to himself.

'Aw lawks!' said Lickpenny Nan Heycock from the other end of the room. 'That's always happenin' in 'ere, people comin' up at awkward moments.' It was as though she were apologizing for a stain on the carpet. 'They must've built this place on a plague hospital or lazar 'ouse, or something. Me walls is full of resonances, is what it is. Look at 'im, poor bewildered soul . . . Numps, can I go and get a blanket for 'im?'

'Don't move! This is one of your clever rozzer tricks!' said Numps, his finger visibly flexing on the trigger of the gun. 'I'll not hang, d'you hear me!'

'Numps!' shouted Scipio. 'It is not a trick. The man is a retread. He has just come up in the middle of all this. Put your gun down. I give you my word that you will be treated fairly.'

There was some movement among Rochester's cronies at the foot of the stairs. A barefoot, pock-faced teenage boy, in clean but well-worn clothes – just breeches and a ragged woollen shirt – pushed his way through. In his right hand, he held a clump of birch twigs.

What on earth was going on?

'That's Saint Ethelbright,' said Rochester, sounding mighty amused, even though Numps still held a gun to his head. 'Numps! This young man is an Anglo-Saxon saint. Let him look after the retread.'

Saint Ethelbright? Scipio had never heard of him. It was in the nature of a lot of saints – and Protestant martyrs – that they had died early and violent deaths, and some had certainly came back as retreads. There were special procedures for looking after these individuals, and as a peeler, Scipio fancied he knew the names of most of them. But Ethelbright? You would remember a name like that.

Saint Ethelbright walked into the middle of the room and looked at the newly arrived retread. He turned to look at Numps and Rochester. He was just a boy, probably not eighteen. Desperately thin (from too much fasting? The Catholics were great ones for the fasting), close-cropped mousy hair, stooped shoulders.

Ethelbright returned his gaze to the retread, who now sat upright on the floor, rubbing his eyes. Ethelbright turned and walked to the bar, brushing past the trembling Numps and his captive Rochester as though they did not exist. Scipio winced as the boy walked, broken glass cracking like gravel under his bare feet. At the sink, he turned on a tap, turned and found an intact pint mug on a shelf and filled it.

He walked past Numps and Rochester again, bearing the water in one hand, his twigs in another, his bloodied feet leaving dark stains in the red carpet as though he had just emerged from the bath.

He kneeled next to the retread and put his birches on the floor. He took the man's free hand and pressed the glass of water into it, then guided it to his mouth. The man sipped slowly. Now, the boy pulled his shirt off and gently placed the garment on the man's back.

'*Thu neart on Heofonum, thu neart on Helle, thu eart othrum sithe on life*,' he said. The retread shook his head, not understanding. Ethelbright frowned slightly. '*Non Excelsis est*,' he said, '*sed non aut Inferi. Deo gratia, iterum vives*.' Not Heaven, but not Hell either. By the grace of God, you live again. Or words to that effect. One tended to pick up a bit of Latin, the language of the medieval church, here and there on the job.

Ethelbright picked up his birches and stood to face Rochester and Numps. He began to hit his back with the sticks, first over one shoulder, then the other. Again and again he beat out his remorseless rhythm, the only sound in the room, opening superficial wounds in his flesh, lightly mutilating himself as though to take away a few of the lesser sins of the world.

After two or three minutes, he stopped and dropped the twigs to the floor. Holding out both arms either in embrace or challenge, he looked Numps in the eye.

Numps shook and sweated, his lower lip trembled. Did he realize he had nothing to lose? It was no certainty he would hang if he gave himself up. If he did not, he would surely be shot. Perhaps the humility of Saint Ethelbright was what impressed him most, but suddenly, his gun-arm collapsed, his grip on Rochester's neck loosened. The heavy gun fell to the floor, cracking a thick shard of mirror-glass.

'I never meant to kill no one,' he said. 'I just thought I could get the money so's me an' Uriah could have somewhere nice to live. That's all.'

He collapsed to the floor and sobbed uncontrollably.

The room came to life. O'Rourke rushed in from the side-door to put the cuffs on Numps, then Scipio and Glyndwr emerged from behind their pillars. Rochester's cronies came out into the room, chattering excitedly. Lickpenny Nan Heycock shouted to one of her girls to fetch a blanket for the confused retread, who still sat on the floor clutching his mug of water.

Boswell stood and unbuttoned his bulletproof jacket. The kid was still lying on the ground beside him. He dragged him upright, keeping a tight grasp on his shoulder.

Scipio walked over to Boswell and looked at the kid. The kid stared at the floor, more in dumb insolence than shame.

Glyndwr and O'Rourke took Numps and the boy away. Scipio clapped Boswell on the shoulder. 'I didn't disgrace myself, did I, sir?' he said. Eager to please as ever. More worried that he would let the side down than about being shot.

'You performed your allotted tasks quite adequately, Boswell. We shall make a rozzer of you yet.'

'Thank you, sir.'

'Now Boswell, the night shift is long from over. From tomorrow we will be working days for a week or two. It is one of the vagaries of the duty-roster. I fancy that you have had too much to take in for one evening, so leave your weskit and gun with Uncle Seamus outside and go home for some sleep. Be back at eight in the morning.'

Boswell nodded. Suddenly, he did look tired. 'Thank you, sir. If I rush, I should be able to get a bus now. Good night, sir.'

Nan Heycock was fussing over the mess that had been made of her bar, while one of her girls had produced a telephone from behind it and was dialling 222 to get someone from the Westminster reception centre to come and collect the new arrival.

Scipio nodded. Rochester and his cullies were at the door, too, making to leave quietly.

'My Lord Rochester,' said Scipio, 'a word with you and your pet saint, if you please.'

'My apologies, Mechano, but we must leave at once. Saint Ethelbright here is due back at Cardinal Campion's palace.'

Ethelbright had left his shirt with the retread. Someone had found him a blanket, which he now held wrapped tightly around his chest.

'No, Rochester. Here please.'

Rochester shrugged, left the saint and his friends at the door and came over, smiling pleasantly. 'How have you been keeping, Mechano?'

'I am well, thank you. What do you know of this evening's proceedings?'

The man didn't really look the part without his big wig, though only a *complete* lunatic would wear one in this hot weather. With his shaven head and expensive clothes, he looked more depraved than ever.

'Nothing, I assure you. My friends and I had thought to make sport of borrowing Saint Ethelbright from the Cardinal for the evening and taking him here to render him a little less saintly. I'm afraid our plan came to naught. He was well able to resist the wiles of Nan's most personable trollop. As for this business with the young man, the boy and the gun, I fear I can tell you nothing.'

'They were on the run. Suspected of murder. Why would they come here?'

Rochester shrugged, but still met his eye. His look was a mite too challenging. He knew something, but wit alone would not get it out of him. Well, Lickpenny Nan would be more forthcoming, or she would be out of business.

'I have a good memory, my Lord. When I studied for the examinations for the post of Inspector of Detective Police, I had to do a great deal of reading, including Butler's *Lives of the Fathers, Martyrs and Other Saints*. Or at any rate those passages pertaining to *English* saints. I was assured that it might one day become useful in my line of work. So, despite all my scepticism, it has proved. There is no Saint Ethelbright. Who is this boy?'

'I tell you, Mechano, he is an Anglo-Saxon martyr from Northumbria. He don't speak a lot of modern, I'm

121

afraid, as he's just come up recently. Your Butler must have missed him.'

Scipio beckoned the boy over. He came quickly enough. His feet were caked in drying blood.

'I am going to have to arrest him,' said Scipio, watching the boy's face carefully. He blinked and recoiled ever so slightly. He understood modern English right enough.

'No,' said Scipio. 'It ain't worth the trouble. I will leave him free if you promise to take him to a hospital to get all that broken glass out of his feet. Take the blanket off, boy.'

Ethelbright looked at him blankly. Rochester nodded at him.

The teenage saint dropped the blanket, but kept his arms crossed over his chest as if he was cold, or trying to hide his nakedness.

'Rochester, he may be saintly. All that business of walking on glass or giving himself the once-over with the birches requires a certain amount of bottom, but he is no more a saint than you are.'

Rochester raised an eyebrow. Scipio grabbed the boy's wrists and with some trouble – he was remarkably strong for such a scrawny specimen – wrenched his arms away from his chest.

His ribcage stood out under skin as white as dough. You could actually make out his heart beating beneath the tattoo. A picture of an intricate knot of brown rope beneath a vivid red seal with the impression of a crown in the middle.

An expensive, expert piece of work for a young man who had rejected the vanities of the world.

Ethelbright was a member of the Sealed Knot.

And definitely no saint. Not in Scipio's book, at any rate.

Rochester threw up his arms and smiled in mock-surprise. 'Well there's a thing!' he laughed. 'Listen, Mechano, I know my word is almost worthless, but I promise you that Ethelbright has nothing to do with what passed this evening.'

Scipio wanted to believe him. He dreaded political cases.

A man and a woman in the light blue uniforms of the reception service came in, nodded greetings and took charge of the retread on the floor. The man glanced up at the obscenities on the ceiling, smiled and shook his head. 'You probably thought you woke up in heaven, mate,' he said to the retread while his colleague opened a small bag and took out a stethoscope and pressed it to his chest.

'Get your saint here to hospital, Rochester,' said Scipio. 'And do not leave London. If I cannot find you easily, I shall issue a warrant for your arrest.'

Rochester grinned. 'Ever the Dashing Mechano,' he said. 'Don't worry. I'm not going anywhere.'

Lickpenny Nan was at the bottom of the stairs apologizing to her American customers for all the fuss and hoping they were not too put out. They were being frightfully sporting. Well, it had made the evening a little more exciting, had it not?

'Mother Heycock,' said Scipio to Lickpenny Nan as Rochester, his saint and their cronies went off into the night. 'A word, if you please . . .'

THINGS REMEMBERED (1)

JACOB MALAHIDE, ALIAS JACK RACKSTRAW

THE STONE ROOM, NEWGATE PRISON, THURSDAY, 6 JUNE 1753.

'You, prisoner that lies within, who for wickedness and sin, after many mercies shown you, are now appointed to die tomorrow in the forenoon, give ear and understand that tomorrow morning the greatest bell of Saint Sepulchre's shall toll for you in form and measure of a passing bell, as used to be tolled for those at the point of death, to the end that all godly people, hearing that bell and knowing that it is for your going and your death, may be stirred up heartily to pray to God . . .'

The sexton droned on . . . At first, Jack Rackstraw had been glad to hear the man's voice, just for the companionship. Now he tired of it. He had never been so weary in all his twenty-two years.

After the warrant for his death had been signed three days ago, he had been moved from the stinking, filthy room he shared with thirty other men and women. He was glad to be away from them. They were the meanest folk for the most part, and their chatter gave him the head-ache.

Now he was alone in the Stone Room, the hold for condemned prisoners. He had only seen the jailers and the reverend. He could not tell if his isolation was a luxury or a curse. Despite the quiet, he still could not sleep.

No one had come to pay a visit. Not even his own brother.

The room was dark, windowless except for the grating that looked out on to the corridor whence jailers and visitors approached. The bars on it were thick as a man's wrist.

He had a table and chair and a straw mattress.

The sexton, his prayer finished, looked through the grating, shook his head and walked away. Even at this distance, Jack Rackstraw could smell the drink on the man's breath.

All day, Jack Rackstraw had stood at the grating, polishing the King's iron with his eyebrows, hoping for news of a reprieve, or mercy, or just a visit from someone. None had come.

On the table, the second-to-last of his candles guttered and spat its last. Quickly, he lit the other from it.

The candles, the table, the chair and the mattress had had to be paid for. He could not afford it. Here in Newgate, 'the Whit' the flash lads called it – 'the Whit be burned' was their toast – here a man had to pay for every small comfort. The jailers said that a dowager who dispensed charity to poor prisoners had been his benefactress. She had also paid for his food, and the two bottles of gin which now stood on the table.

There would be no reprieve. He knew that the King's mercy would not be extended to him.

He lay on his mattress, closed his eyes and stretched his aching legs, craving sleep.

Tomorrow, Friday the seventh of June in the Year of

Our Lord seventeen hundred and fifty-three, would be his last on this earth.

In the morning there would be more prayers, and the promised bells of the Newgate parish church. In the morning he would go west, riding to Tyburn at the cart's arse, sitting behind his own coffin, sitting facing the rising sun, sitting with a noose bound to his chest. Beside him, the parson would read his devotions.

He could stand in the cart if he wished. He did not know if this would be wise. It depended on how the crowd took to him. They might be moved to admiration by his stoic fortitude. More likely they would jeer and pelt him with shit and cabbages and dead rats.

Out in the crowd, the dippers would have good work. Men animated by detestation were less mindful of their pockets and purses than those nodding in thoughtful and sober approbation. Perhaps the chaunter-culls would hawk his printed lamentations, 'The Last Dying Speech and Confessions of Jack Rackstraw', fakements they had spun of their own invention without ever meeting him.

And beside him in the cart, the parson would still be reading from the scriptures. Provided he was not pre-occupied in protecting himself and his garments and his fancy wig from missiles intended for Jack Rackstraw.

He knew how hangings were conducted. He went to every Tyburn Fair he could. He knew what would happen in the morning.

Perhaps Mammy Douglas would do a good trade. Perhaps gentlemen and ladies would pay her a few guineas each to accommodate their bums of quality on her bench near the Tree. Would there be ten or twenty thousand out to see him turned off, like Jack Sheppard or Jonathan Wild back in the old days?

The cart would press on towards the Tree, through crowds becoming denser. Men would clap the shoulders of those in front of them and shout, 'Hats off!', not as any sign of respect, but the better to see him. If there was a sizeable crowd, the magistrates would call out the dragoons to keep order.

And still the parson would blabber. Where was the use in it? Jack Rackstraw was either damned for all eternity, or the Almighty would know that he was not responsible for the crimes he committed. He had been led into temptation.

The cart would be stopped under the nubbing chit, the three uprights supporting crossbeams from which dozens of men and women were frummagemed each year. The Tyburn Tree. The deadly nevergreen that bears its fruit all the year round.

Now he would stand. There would be hymns. To die a decent Christian, he would accompany the parson in reciting the Hanging Psalm: 'Have mercy on me, O God, according to Thy loving kindness: according unto the multitude of Thy tender mercies blot out my transgressions. Wash me thoroughly from mine iniquity and cleanse me from my sin. For I acknowledge my transgressions: and my sin is ever before me. Against Thee, Thee only have I sinned, and done this evil in Thy sight: that Thou mightest be justified when Thou speakest, and be clean when Thou judgest. Behold I was shapen in iniquity, and in sin did my mother conceive me . . .'

Now the prisoner makes his speech. What should he say? The sheriffs and magistrates liked the condemned man to say he had led a life of wickedness and that his suffering the ultimate exaction of the law should serve as an example to divert any young man contemplating idleness and vice into a more righteous life.

But what reason did he have to repent? Why should he recite any dismal ditty? He had been overtaken by evil. His thoughts and actions were not his own when he killed the woman. And the brats. He had only tried to shut up their whining and blubbering.

This was not how it should be. He should be wearing a fine white suit, paid for by his friends and admirers, decked out with ribbons and posies and white gloves. Being showered with flowers by the crowd, bowing all gallant-like to the ladyships in the high windows. Riding like some ancient pagan king entering his city in triumph – that was the way to hang. That was the way the best lads went at it.

But the mob would not understand why he had done wrong. The mob would simply hate him.

After he exhorted the crowd to shun viciousness, he would put on the shroud, a coarse white nightgown of a thing. Then the hangman would put the rope around his neck, while the hangman's mate scrambled up the chit to secure it to the cross-beam. He might give him time to prepare, to offer up a few prayers. But not long if the mob grew impatient. If they were eager to see him dempstered, they would hiss and throw stones.

When he was ready, he would bow to the sheriffs and nod to the hangman.

The hangman would slap the nag to whip the cart

away, and Jack Rackstraw would cry cockles.

The rope would slowly tighten around his neck. His face would twist to a scowl, his eyes would swell like two scalded gooseberries in a tart. As the rope squeezed the life out of him, his legs would dance a jig on thin air.

The hangman might let his friends speed his death by pulling on his legs. If he had any friends remaining. But if the crowd loathed him as much as he feared, they would not permit anyone to come close to ease the torment of the man who had violated and killed a young woman and her two children.

Would the Shadwell boys turn out to see him away? The coal-heavers always looked after their own when they hanged. Many coal-heavers did hang, after short, glorious lives. Years ago, James Mahoney had tried to talk him around to joining him one night in the Ship and Shears. 'Come with me, Jack, do as I do and money shall never be wanting. I live well upon the lay and have everything at command. We cannot be hanged more than once . . .'

Mahoney was Irish. He had lived well, and died well. All the Irish Shadwell boys had had a wake for Mahoney after he was turned off. They had drinking and games for days. And songs, too:

> Though sure it's the best way to die,
> The Devil a-better than living,
> For sure when the gallows is high,
> Your journey is shorter to heaven.

But James Mahoney had robbed the rich. He was never a murderer.

Jack Rackstraw had been condemned for the murder of a woman and two babes. If the Shadwell boys came to Tyburn, it would not be to wish him well. Nor to rescue his mortal remains from the College of Surgeons and see that he got a decent Christian burial.

He would take ten or twenty minutes to die. At the finish of it, his corpse would be taken to Surgeons' Hall. That was the law with murderers. By the evening, he would be dissected, hacked up by the anatomists. Like the picture he had seen in the window of a print shop, there would be holes in his skull where his eyes had been, a man with rolled-up sleeves would pull out his bowels for the edification of the surgeons and students. The man with rolled-up sleeves would grasp Jack Rackstraw's heart, wrench it out and throw it to his dog.

Could he get to Heaven without a body? Would he be able to take part in the Resurrection if he had been dismembered so? Wheresoever he arrived in the next life, if there was one, he would change his name. He would call himself something else. Jacob. He would call himself Jacob because he was a good, God-fearing man. And Malahide. That was his mother's name. He would be Jacob Malahide.

The shame was too much for a man to bear.

He was going to roast in Hell. He would be damned for all eternity. It was not his fault. If only the woman had not tempted him.

If only he had another chance to live a righteous, Christian life.

The chapel clock struck midnight. Jack Rackstraw, unable to sleep, opened his eyes and got up from the mattress.

Things Unborn

At the table, he tried to uncork one of his bottles of gin. But it fell to the flagstones and smashed because his hands were trembling.

II

TUESDAY, 19 AUGUST 2008

Vast numbers of our people are compelled to seek their livelihood by begging, robbing, stealing, cheating, pimping, forswearing, flattering, suborning, forging, gaming, lying, fawning, hectoring, voting, scribbling, stargazing, poisoning, whoring, canting, libelling, free-thinking and the like occupations.
– Jonathan Swift, *Gulliver's Travels*

'Let us pray . . .'

Jacob Malahide and Elder Lilley bowed their heads as Elder Saltonstall spoke.

'Oh Lord, thou has sent us this tribulation, but in your goodness you have justly smitten Richard Haseldich down. Please give us the strength and wisdom to carry out your plan, and guide our counsel this day. Amen.'

'Amen,' repeated Lilley and Malahide.

They sat down around a small trestle-table in the alehouse's upstairs function-room. The kind of place where poor folk would have their wedding-breakfasts, or fraternal societies or guild branches would hold their monthly meetings.

Saltonstall sat silently for a moment, as though thinking hard or deep in personal prayer. Dressed in a plain black frock-coat, black breeches and stockings, and over 6 feet tall, he was a very imposing presence. Even more so when he was standing up addressing a service or prayer-rally.

'Well?' he said to Lilley at last.

Lilley looked nervous, and so he should be. A man had been found dead in the basement of his house, and whoever had killed him had taken most of the Order's cash reserves. Lilley had been in Bath last night but had caught the train back to Paddington when he had heard about it.

Lilley sighed. 'I believed that I could trust Haseldich. He was my deputy, as you know, and I told him where the funds were concealed, thinking it as well that someone know in the event of my not surviving the coming days. I own I misjudged him. He became greedy.'

'He has paid for his greed,' said Saltonstall. 'He roasts in Hell as we speak.'

That was a satisfying thought.

'This is a set-back,' said Saltonstall. 'We had need of that money to help prepare the way for the rule of the saints.'

Saltonstall clenched his fists on the table, trying to control his anger. Malahide had seen it a few times before. The blood rushed to the Elder's head and strained against his skin. As it did so, you could see the scars in livid red on either cheek. A big 'S' on the left, and an 'L' on the right.

In his first life, in the reign of Charles I, Elder Saltonstall had written a broadside attacking Archbishop Laud for the treasonable Papist he was. He had been fined £3,000. But the evil had not stopped there. Saltonstall had been pilloried, his ears nailed to the wood, then cut off. Then the hangman had pushed red-hot brands in the shape of letters into his cheeks. One letter denoted 'schismatic', the other 'libeller'.

Elder Saltonstall had been killed in the Civil War, fighting for the Good Old Cause. When he returned, the Lord had given him back his ears, but the faint outline of the letters burned into his face was sometimes still visible. Usually, any injuries you had from your last life were cured in this one. The scars of the branding were not as livid in this life as they would have been in the Elder's last one, but you could still make them out. The Elder regarded this as a sign of faith, a mark of God's covenant with the Upright Men.

Elder Saltonstall brought his fists crashing down on the table. 'Damn you, Lilley, damn you for a muddle-headed fool! If we fail now it will be your doing! Your fault!'

Lilley, normally a very grand-mannered fellow, looked very contrite. Rather than take it in the face, he was staring down at his expensive tailored pinstripe suit (he only wore his full Georgian fig in Bath). 'I am sorry, Brother, I . . .'

'Brother!' screamed Saltonstall. 'You dare call me "Brother" after what you have done? It will be a long time before you have the right to call any of us "Brother" again!'

Saltonstall closed his eyes and breathed deeply and took a small silver box from one of his pockets. From it he took a small pink tablet and put it into his mouth. Something for his nerves, perhaps, or his heart, though to Malahide it looked mighty like those amphetamine pills you could buy on the streets in some parts of town. That wouldn't calm him down at all.

'Never mind,' he said at length. 'This will not prevent

us from carrying out the Almighty's plan. We will proceed as before with our agitation, and by this time next week, the stinking Papist Liberal Settlement, this vile democracy will be at an end. The country will be in the hands of honest, plain Protestant men. The Catholics and the Jews will no longer have any influence upon our destinies and we can begin the work of creating a land fit for His return in glory.'

'Amen!' said Malahide.

'Amen!' said Lilley.

'Is this . . . business,' said Saltonstall, glaring at Lilley, 'likely to cause us any more worriment?'

'It might,' said Malahide. 'The cove who killed Haseldich, and the kid who was with him, came looking for me last night, hoping the Order would find them some manner of sanctuary. And the police came looking for them. I don't think that Lickpenny Nan or any of her harlots would peach me up, though. Not if they know what's good for them.'

Saltonstall nodded. 'As you know, I visit that house of ill-fame frequently. I am giving spiritual counsel to one particular young lady there. I shall have to avoid the place for the moment.'

The idea of avoiding Lickpenny Nan's because the police were likely keeping an eye on it made the Elder all the more angry. It was like the man was some kind of volcano, always about to explode if anything disturbed him too much. Well, he carried a lot of responsibility, didn't he?

'I heard afterwards that Africanus, you know, the famous blackbird peeler, was at Elder Lilley's house getting himself an eyeful of corpse. And he turned up at

Heycock's later. He was there when Numps and the kid were arrested.'

'It is not a man whereof you speak, Brother Malahide,' said Saltonstall. 'He's a baboon, a mere African savage, a jungle creature. He will cause us no problems. Why don't we catch him? Lilley here could sell him to the plantations.'

Lilley in his last life had made a lot of money in Liverpool, dealing in sugar and slaves.

'I jest, of course,' said the Elder. 'The police will cause us fewer problems than you think. We have an agent among them.'

'We do?' said Malahide. This was the first he had heard of it.

'A man who has been a loyal and diligent copper for many years,' said the Elder. 'It may prove politic for him to show his hand soon, should the need arise. I also have a man coming to assist us. A specialist in weapons and certain other infernal devices. If this savage causes us any more distraction, he will doubtless be able to kill him.'

It would be as well, thought Malahide. The Elder said that the blackbird was a mere savage, but he wasn't so sure. The policeman had a fearsome reputation. Perhaps he used sorcery.

'Now Brother Jacob,' said Saltonstall, 'are the rest of our plans in place?'

'Yes Brother,' said Malahide. 'Myself and two of the lads took the Reverend Harry Seymour, as he likes to style himself, from his lodgings four days ago. We thought it best to take him early, just to be sure we had him.'

'And where is he now?'

'Safely in our most secret hiding-place, Elder.'

'Good. Now let us move to discuss the rest of our design. But first, Brother Jacob,' said Saltonstall. 'Some refreshment, if you please.'

'At once, Brother,' said Malahide, getting up to go downstairs for a jug of porter.

The Standard of England alehouse in Bermondsey was about as ordinary-looking a place as you could find, set in the middle of an estate of council housing. Courts, for the most part; square brick tenements built around a yard where the kids could play soccer and cricket or the more prosperous could park their cars and vans. Most people here were eighteenth-, nineteenth- or twentieth-century retreads, and their hereborn families. A lot of them worked in the docks, warehouses and railyards. Almost all were Protestants. There were few Catholics here.

'Good morning to you, Brother Jacob,' said Ned Hampson, the landlord, as Malahide reached the bottom of the stairs. Hampson was a stout man, well able for trouble (you had to be if you were an alehouse keeper hereabouts) and a loyal member of the Order.

'We'll be needing some refreshment if you please, Brother Ned.'

'Right you are,' said Hampson, who dipped behind the bar and started pumping porter into a big blue jug.

The pub only had one bar; rough wooden tables and chairs, whitewashed walls decorated with prints of famous battles. The floor was bare boards. There was a billiard table and, in the far corner, a juke-box which for the most part played ballads and popular music hall numbers by people like Al Bowlly and Billie Piper. Ned wouldn't have any of that modern beat or jazz rubbish here.

There was no one else in this early in the morning, and from the streets outside came the sounds of traffic and of folks going about their business. From somewhere up the street, a hurdy-gurdy wheezed out a tune.

The door opened and a tall young man in very strange clothes entered. Bell-bottom denim trousers and a loose-cut leather jacket with a lot of pockets on it. His hair was blond and cut short-back-and-sides. He had a big blond moustache over thick lips, and over his eyes he wore an outlandish pair of dark glasses, which he did not take off, even though the inside of the pub was gloomy.

Yank tourist, probably.

He walked up to the bar and leaned on it, looking at Ned.

'Sorry mate, we're not open until noon,' said Ned.

'Yeah?'

'Yes, sir,' said Ned brightly. 'Two hours' time.' He placed the jug of porter on the bar and turned to get some pewter mugs.

'I see you're serving some people here,' said the stranger. American accent all right.

Enough of this nonsense, thought Malahide, and walked over to the man, who was a good foot taller than him. 'He said he's closed. Now go.'

It was impossible to tell what was going through his mind because of the sunglasses over his eyes.

He shook his head slowly.

Malahide reached into the waistband to pull out his

chiv. Nothing serious, just give him a bit of a fright.

Something happened and he found himself on the floor.

The chiv was a good couple of feet away. He fancied the knife had been knocked from his hand and the bloke had kicked his feet from under him when he lost his balance. He reached for the knife, only to see a soft brown leather boot kick it away.

'Do you keep ice?' said the man's voice above him. He was talking to Ned.

'No,' said Ned. 'Now please leave or I'll call the police.'

It was an empty threat. A man like Ned Hampson never got the law involved.

'No, I don't think you'll do that,' said the Yank. 'I'll just have a glass of lemonade, please. It's mighty hot out there.'

Malahide got up. There didn't seem to be any broken bones. He walked over to get his knife. The stranger did nothing to stop him.

Ned was still looking daggers at the stranger. 'Lemonade,' said Ned quietly and reached down under the bar and produced a sawn-off shotgun which he pointed evenly at the man's chest.

'I said we are closed until noon, which is academical in your case, cully, 'cos you're barred. For life.'

Malahide put the knife back into his waistband. Ned could deal with this joker on his lonesome.

The Yank shook his head, smiled and took off his specs. 'We have gotten off to an unfortunate start. Do I have the honour of addressing the landlord of the Standard of England alehouse in Bermondsey?'

'You do,' said Ned, not lowering his gun.

'Then ask me how many beans make five.'

'You what?' said Ned.

Malahide approached the man again. 'How many beans make five?' he asked.

The man turned to him, saying rapidly, 'A bean, a bean, a bean and a half, a bean and half a bean.'

'It's all right, Ned,' said Malahide, glaring at the man. 'It's one of the Elder's riddles that he gets people to use to identify them as friendly. He's with us. Cocky fucker, though, ain't you?'

The man shrugged. 'The name's Miller, Ethan Miller. Elder Saltonstall is expecting me.' He held out his hand for Malahide to shake. Malahide did not take it.

They went upstairs. Ned followed on with the porter and mugs on a tray. And a glass of lemonade for Ethan Miller.

It wasn't yet eleven, but the heat was already bothering Jenny Pearson. The sun hurt her eyes and her heavy, nondescript clothes were making her perspire. If she wasn't careful, the sweat would break through into the armpits of the grey woollen jacket she wore over her long white dress. In this job, something like that would be a disaster, because it would make her feel self-conscious, and if you feel uncomfortable, you can't be inconspicuous.

Apprentice DC Boswell stood across Oxford Street from her. He was taking a great deal of interest in a news-stand, looking at the comics, the *Magnet*, the *Hotspur*, the *Dandy*. Those things were aimed at children, but were actually bought by a lot of adults as well because they were easy to read and, to the uneducated, the brightly coloured funny stories or adventure tales were fascinating.

The traffic was ill-tempered in the way that only a combination of motor-vehicles and horse-drawn carts, and the occasional hansom cab (tourists liked them, locals never bothered with them) could be. Motorists bashed their steering-wheels or honked their horns at the least affront. Some cab-drivers swore abundantly, others adopted a mulish peasant impassiveness and refused to make way for cars.

She moved on steadily up the street. A woman on her own would draw attention to herself if she stood still for too long without a good reason. Sergeant O'Rourke, Uncle Seamus, had originally shown her how to do street-work a few years back, when no women officers were assigned to it. There was a good reason for this, he had said; every man under the age of seventy-five who wasn't a molly looked at every woman under the age of forty that he passed by. In truth, most men looked at a certain part of you, which was why big shapeless jackets or coats were so important. If you were a young woman, even an ugly one, it was much harder to pass unnoticed.

Jenny Pearson was not, she fancied, ugly. She had a pleasant enough face with a good complexion, though her nose was a little on the big side. She was of average height and entirely average build and bust. Her bottom was fairly big compared to the rest of her. She hated it.

She looked ordinary, she told herself whenever the men in the station made remarks which were meant as compliments to her streetcraft, but which could come out sounding like insults to her looks. Every weekend, or if she was going out shopping or dancing with her friends, or on dates with men, she felt the need to wear the loudest clothes she could, as if over-compensating for keeping her personality in check for the rest of the week.

There was a commotion further back down the street, more shouting and honking of car-horns.

A parade. She looked at Boswell, who caught her eye. With a tiny movement of her head she motioned him to cross over to her. He understood and threaded his way through the slow-moving traffic. Good man. Perhaps this wouldn't be so hard after all.

Trevor was off with a broken nose and, the hospital had confirmed, a broken jaw. Inspector Africanus had assigned Boswell as her oppo this morning, saying he needed a few weeks on the streets before they'd move him on to detective work proper. The boss had added that once the tourist season was over and she was back in her usual line, she would show Boswell the elements of detection. All the Inspector's soothing noises about how she was the ideal person to teach the new retread the ropes, and all his instruction to Boswell as to how he was to do exactly as she told him, hadn't made her any happier. Few men, particularly retreads, liked being given orders by a woman.

Boswell arrived at her side, jacket draped over one shoulder. Dressed in his reception-centre-issue suit and tie, he looked just as uncomfortable in the heat as she was, but at least he could take his jacket off.

'What's happening?' he said quietly, without looking

at her directly, still pretending they were nothing to do with one another.

'It's all right,' she said. 'Walk with me a while as though we're brother and sister or husband and wife.' Another reason for being partnered with a man for padwork. Other men didn't look at you so much if you had a man with you. You were spoken for, some other cove's property.

At work, she always wore a plain band of gold on her ring-finger.

The parade came on. Cars, lorries, carts and vans pulled aside for it with the worst possible grace. It was led by an amateurish brass band which sounded like a herd of elephants being tortured. Through the cacophony she picked out some hymn she half-remembered from assembly at Ealing Grammar School for Girls.

Behind the band came around 150 people, mostly men (didn't they have jobs to go to?), marching along the middle of the street in a manner calculated to cause maximum irritation. Hatchet-faced Puritans, plainly dressed, pursed hen's bums of lips, disapproving of the rest of us but content in themselves that they were God's especial preoccupation. Some carried banners warning that HIS RETURN IS IMMINENT or that THE LIBERAL SETTLEMENT IS AN ABOMINATION.

For some reason, her bandaged thumb, which had been giving her less gyp than she had expected, started to hurt again.

She felt a bead of sweat trickle from her left armpit and into her blouse. She took Boswell by the arm and guided him beneath the awning of a toy-shop.

'My mother always said it was rude to discuss religion and politics,' said Boswell, momentarily distracted by an enormous Tri-ang train-set in the window.

'The Antient and Honourable Order of the Sons of John Bull,' she explained. 'Puritans. Protestant hardliners. They don't like the Liberal Settlement because it gives equal favour to Catholics. With a lot of retreads from before the Reformation, though, you have to treat all religions alike or we're back to the Feudal Wars.'

'Are they' – he pointed to the parade – 'all retreads themselves?'

'Most of them are, I imagine. Some will be hereborns, but very few natives.'

'Sorry?'

'Natives, people like my own father or DC Mills, whose job you are doing. People who were born before the Atom War and who survived it. Because of the horrors they have seen, they tend to be more sceptical than retreads in matters of religion.'

'I see. And I suppose that a lot of them are retreads who think that the Almighty has brought them back to life once more in order to live a better life.'

An elderly couple walked past. She heard the man mutter to his wife, 'Bleedin' God-botherers.' A few of the frustrated drivers sounded their horns or made obscene gestures.

'They're not universally popular then, I see,' said Boswell.

'Where people have religious doubts, they will always have some support,' she said. 'Have you yet satisfied yourself as to why you have been reborn?'

144

Boswell shrugged. 'I was never very religious.'

'No, nor me, but I'm a hereborn. I've never been through the trauma of dying and coming back to a strange world. Most retreads think it's God's work. They think that the Almighty has offered them a bargain and that they must live more righteously. The Catholics are the same, but they're not as well-organized or noisy. Nowadays, of course, we have law and order and plenty of food and work, and houses with running water and electricity and televisions and radios, so you hear a lot of retreads saying they've been sent here as a reward for being righteous in their last life.'

The parade crashed, tramped and blared its way on down the street, followed by a trail of exasperated drivers.

'We might as well move on,' she said. 'The God-botherers won't gather much of a crowd in working hours. We might find better pickings further up the road. You have to think like a dipper. So we want crowds and we want tourists.'

Earlier, she had explained to him that with all the tourists in town, the middle of London was a honeypot for enterprising performers and vendors, and for coney-catchers, propsmen, rampers and buzzers.

She'd have to teach him the jargon sooner or later. For now, poor Boswell hadn't a clue what he was looking for. He'd told her earlier that in his day (as far as he knew) criminals hung around in what they called mobs, and wore trilby hats and lurid ties and had names like Roger the Razors or Morrie the Cosh. Some of them still do, she had replied.

Boswell slung his jacket over his shoulder. 'Can we walk on the shady side?' he pleaded.

They wove through slow-moving traffic. Boswell almost stepped in some manure.

'I'm amazed at the number of horses still being used,' he said.

'Why?' yelled Jenny over an altercation between two cab-drivers. 'People here can breed horses easier than they can make motor-cars. Besides, England can grow hay and oats far more cheaply than petrol. And the tourists adore the nags.'

'I say, there's a question . . .' exclaimed Boswell. 'Have any animals ever been resurrected?'

Jenny laughed. 'You hear stories from the country-side of farmers who say they have herds of retread cattle or sheep. But that's usually a cover for the fact that they've stolen them from their neighbours.'

Her radio hissed and spat. She bowed into a doorway to hear the message properly. The duty-sergeant. 'We've got a missing person report,' he said. 'You're in the vicinity and everyone else is busy. Can you check it for us?'

'Wilco,' she said, and took the details.

'We're to go to Covent Garden,' she said. 'To look for a missing parson.'

'Missing person?'

'No, parson.'

'Oh.'

They started walking. 'I say, Constable Pearson, I—'

'No, this is too formal,' she said, 'call me Jenny.'

'Well in that case, you must call me Guy.'

*

'We'll cut through Soho,' said Jenny, leading him off Oxford Street and into a side-street. In Boswell's time, Soho had been a rather louche and bohemian place, full of pubs and drinking-dens that stayed open all day and which had been patronized by artists, writers, poets and fast women. Now the place seemed the same. Unlike Oxford Street, where most of the buildings were new and ugly, houses and offices in Soho had either survived the Atom War or been repaired sympathetically. It still seemed rather racy, though. There were a lot of pubs and cheap restaurants boasting that they served 'traditional English food' or 'finest French-style cuisine'. A lot of cheap boarding-houses, too.

'Bedroom of the West End,' said Jenny as they walked. 'Lots of tourists stay here, as do people working in the theatres and music-halls. Well, the music-halls are dying out nowadays. Most people prefer the cinema or staying at home to watch television.'

WDC 'call me Jenny' Pearson was of average size, a little overweight and a great sport. She was funny in a sort of sardonic way that Boswell had found in few women before now, except perhaps with a few of the cleverer WAAFs, women who had some sort of role other than just looking pretty or rearing children. She had marched him around her patch, from one public gathering-place to another, providing commentary and amusing footnotes on the sights and people they were likely to encounter.

Deep in his soul, his psyche or whatever it was called, the women question was troubling him immensely.

No, the whole place was too damnably confusing. So

much was familiar and so much was not. Here the past, the future and what until less than a fortnight ago he had understood as the present, were all mixed up.

On the side of a terrace of buildings was an advertisement, a picture of a strapping girl in white holding a tennis-racquet in one hand and a glass of Eiffel Tower brand lemonade in the other. It could have been produced in 1938 as easily as 2008.

'The trade mark's very big,' said Jenny. 'Know why?'

'I'm sorry?'

'You were looking at the advertisement. The picture of the Eiffel Tower – which did not actually survive the Atom War, by the way. Paris was hit just as badly as London. The trade mark on the advert is quite big, and there are very few words. It's because a lot of people can't read, but they can recognize the trade mark. The advert is using pictures, not words, to sell lemonade.'

He looked at her. 'Sorry,' she said. 'Just thought you might be interested.'

'No, please, this is all most instructive,' he smiled. She smiled back.

Oh hell.

He admired Jenny Pearson.

There was nothing particularly strange about that; she was bright and lively, around his age and not unattractive. But the very fact that he was entertaining romantic fantasies about someone other than Pamela struck him as beastly. It was as though Pamela had died, not him, as though it was he who should be observing a decent period of mourning.

Was Pamela mourning him? He still felt as though he had only died two weeks ago; on another world somewhere else, Pamela was entering her second week without him. But here, he was more than half a century away.

He hoped Pamela had got over him quickly and found a decent chap to take his place.

Now here was another advert for one of these television jobbies from a company calling itself Rediffusion.

'Not a very big trade mark on that one, though,' he observed to Jenny.

'That's because if you're illiterate you probably can't afford one.'

There was another problem. Even if he forgot all about Pamela, if he did not bother to quiz the Public Record Office about her, even if Pamela had never existed, was Jenny Pearson of the right class?

Whaaatt!? What ludicrous notion was that? He must be going mad.

No, no. It was just that Jenny had no particular accent. She certainly didn't talk like a factory girl. But then she didn't talk like a girl who'd been to a decent school either. Boswell had always assumed that he would end up marrying a girl from a respectable family (whatever that meant).

He didn't want to marry Jenny Pearson. Dash it all, he probably wouldn't even get around to asking her out. She probably had a boyfriend or fiancé already.

But what if he wanted to? How would he know if she was from a respectable family? But then so many people here had no family at all. What on earth did a girl of the right type look like, in Heaven's name?

Oh, it was just too hot to try and cope with all this!

'Now then,' said Jenny amid the noise and heat of what he assumed was Charing Cross Road, 'let me tell you all about Covent Garden . . .'

Scipio walked past the rebuilt British Museum, crossed Gower Street and headed across Bedford Square, wondering if he should be doing this. Back when he had been a working detective rather than a paper-pusher, Inky Weems had been one of his best sources, a man with as many eyes as Argus. He might be able to provide some illumination for the business of the Russell Square murder, or rather the chest of money in the basement.

He looked at his watch. Five minutes to midday. Almost opening time. Not that the sort of places that Inky Weems habituated observed the licensing laws.

Numps had said Haseldich had engaged him to retrieve the chest of money from under the floorboards of Lilley's house. He had a feeling that merchant wasn't keeping the best part of £10,000 in gold and silver in his cellar to cheat the tax-man. When he had tried to quiz Mother Heycock as to what she knew last night, the old baggage had tried to turn on the charm, then tried to lend him the favours of one of her girls, and then she had just got plain frightened. She did not know why Numps and the kid had run to her brothel for sanctuary, but he would bet a month's wages that they were looking for a mobster to cache them. Where there were strumpets, there were spoonies, ponces and mobs. Always would be.

He turned off Bedford Square into a grimy side-street of three- and four-storey flats; charvering cribs for workers of the bettering sort. The grandly named Berners Mews had been jerry-built twenty years ago, but had never found favour with people of fashion. Put it a few hundred yards to the east and it would be in the Holy Land rookery, which was where it belonged.

London had always been a patchwork of rich, middling and poor districts, all hugger-mugger to one another, and yet the poor seemed to tolerate their lot, while only the most enterprising criminals preyed on the rich. Most of them just robbed and thieved from their immediate neighbours.

The Jack in the Green. The leering face of a pagan woodland spirit looked down from a sign over the main door to the alehouse. There was already quite a racket coming from the inside.

He opened the door to be faced with a crush of shouting men, most of them middle-aged or elderly, all with their backs to him.

He pushed his way through the crowd, trying not to let the smell overcome him. Stale beer, sweat, unwashed bodies and cotton and woollen clothes, onion-breath, bad teeth and tobacco. Lots and lots of tobacco.

The noise grew as overwhelming as the smell as the men yelled or waved coins in the air. Nobody took the slightest notice of him. The fight must be a very interesting one indeed.

There was plenty of room at the bar, as the action was all at the other end of the room. He leaned up by the beer pumps and fished out his cigarette-case, helping himself to one of a small pile of lucifers that had been left in the indentation of a brick for the convenience of customers.

Nobody was there to serve him. Presumably the landlord would be at the centre of things in order to ensure he took his due share of the wagers. All very illegal. Yet another good reason for getting abroad rather than hanging around in the station. He wouldn't close the place down, but the management of the Jack in the Green would owe him a favour.

More shouting. Someone was working the crowd, taking the bets. All coins, no notes. Nothing fancy about this place. Some of the men there he knew. One or two small-time crooks, a lot of faces who might be on the lay, and even more who were no more than a week's rent away from criminality. A man who was a notorious scaldrum stood on a stool yelling at the top of his voice. Later he would cover himself in sores made of candle-wax, or plaster of Paris, and beg tourists for small change. Close by him was Legless Arnold, a man who had lost both legs in the Feudal Wars and who now propelled himself around on a little wheeled trolley and made a rough living from selling matches and cigarettes on the streets. Legless shot around the edges of the crowd, propelling his trolley with a stick, trying to find the best view.

Legless Arnold could have had a proper wheelchair from the Health Service, the man who acted the scaldrum could have a labouring job with regular pay. All the men here – there did not appear to be a single woman – could settle down and make secure lives for themselves and their families (if they had any), but they chose not to. Some were hereborns, but most, probably, were retreads whose previous lives had been every bit as wasted, and while some paid lip-service to the God who had given them a second chance at life, all had reverted to their old ways.

People never really change at all. It was hard enough, Scipio knew, even to change the ways of children. He and Kitty had been asked to foster enough of them, and to turn even a delinquent six-year-old into a useful human being is the devil's own work, so what chance do you stand with an adult?

The crowd gradually fell silent and tense. Then one or two spoken and even whispered encouragements: 'Look lively there, my boy!' . . . 'Go to it, my son!' . . . 'Come on! Finish 'im off!' . . .

Then a huge shout from some, groans and disgusted oaths from others. Somewhere in the middle of it, a tall man held up a struggling ball of orange-brown feathers and grinned in triumph. Most of his front teeth were missing.

'The victor ludorum, gentlemen. The bantam champion claims another victim!'

Cock-fighting was illegal, but tolerated. There was a great deal the police had to tolerate because there were far more pressing matters to attend to. Some animal-loving charities campaigned for it to be stopped, but frankly they were only going to stop people being cruel to animals once people had been stopped from being cruel to people.

The crowd around the fight started to break up. The landlord appeared in front of Scipio and gave him an enquiring look, half hate, half obsequiousness. It was sometimes hard to be a rozzer when you had such a distinctive mug.

Matteradamn. 'Balloon juice,' he ordered.

A man appeared somewhere around his waist. There was a little flurry as he clambered up on to a stool.

'God give you good winning, Inspector Africanus,' said Inky Weems.

'Good day to you, Inky,' said Scipio.

Inky Weems was just under 4 feet tall and aged anything between forty and sixty. Whether he was a hereborn, a native or a retread was anyone's guess. Some said he'd been a monk in the Middle Ages, or a Victorian circus-acrobat, or a gypsy horse-whisperer. Inky did nothing to discourage any of the speculation.

'Can I stand you a noonchin, Inky?'

'That's very kind of you, Inspector. Don't mind if I do. Brandy, if you please.'

Inky had a reedy voice and an exaggerated sense of his own dignity. Not the sort of aggressive defiance you get with ordinarily small men who feel that nature has dealt them a mug's hand. It was simply that Inky knew his worth, could not care what people thought of his looks, but felt sometimes that folks needed reminding that he had a useful part to play in the world. As always, he was dressed immaculately in a tailored pinstripe suit with brocade weskit. His greying brown hair was slicked back with a strongly perfumed brilliantine. Inky was a great ladies' man and enjoyed some popularity with the fair sex on account of the rumours that the Lord had recompensed his modest stature with the largest cock in London. If it didn't make women enthusiastic for him, it at least made them curious.

The landlord handed Inky a brandy, and Scipio his glass of tonic water. In this heat, it would have been nice to have a bit of ice in it. Even a dump like the Jack in the Green must have a fridge.

'Let us sit down and have a chat, Inky,' said Scipio, paying the landlord two tanners.

They took their drinks and found an empty bench in a quiet corner. Inky pulled an enormous white handkerchief from his breast pocket and dusted the seat before perching himself on it.

Scipio took his lighter and a pack of ten Great Zimbabwes from his trouser pocket, took one out and lit it. Then he pushed packet and lighter across the table. Inky sipped fastidiously at his drink, in no hurry for a smoke.

'So how are you, Inspector?'

'I am well, thank you. And you?'

'Oh, you know. Getting by.'

As a policeman, you could either be infuriated by the hall of mirrors mystery that was Inky Weems, or you could simply accept that some things were probably not worth knowing. What he did know was that Inky knew everything that was going on in Westminster and surrounding boroughs, he spoke fifteen different flavours of criminal cant and he had a mind like a card-index. Inky dressed well, ate well and probably supported three mistresses, all this without formal employment, because a lot of people found him useful. He also worked as a screever, writing letters for the unlettered and helping them deal with the state bureaucracy. Inky was probably not above the occasional bit of forgery.

Sergeant O'Rourke had once described Inky as a 'backstreet accountant'.

'And how are the family, Inspector? Did I see your

boy blowing his horn on the television the other week?'

'You did,' said Scipio, unable to hide his pride. His son John Zachary played the trumpet, piano and electric guitar and now led his own quintet, leading nice young boys and girls mildly astray with songs that hinted at teenage rebellion and illicit sexual relations. John Zachary and other musicians like him had been condemned by bishops and conservative newspapers. Well, that was just older generations resenting the pleasures of the young. These kids hadn't been through the hell of the Atom War and the Feudal Wars like their parents, and they had every right to have their fun while the going was good. It might not always be.

'Is he making a lot of poppy at that, then?'

Scipio shrugged. John had more money that most young men of his age.

Inky took the packet of cigarettes, opened it, took one out and at the same time effortlessly palmed the 10 shilling note that Scipio had hidden in it as a sweetener.

'So what brings you to this den of iniquity, Inspector?' he asked as he lit up.

'Cove name of Haseldich. Murdered yesterday in a big house in Russell Square belonging to a man named Lilley. We know who did it, but I want to know why there should be a large chest filled with money in the basement of Lilley's house.'

Inky shook his head. 'Sorry, Inspector. It's news to me. Lilley, you say? Never heard of him.'

Scipio reached into his pocket and took out another packet of fags. He had already secreted a pound note in this one.

'Have another cigarette, Inky.'

'I've not finished this one yet.'

'Take them for later. Take the entire packet. It's a packet of twenty.' Meaning the number of shillings in it, of course.

'Inspector, I can't help you. I know nothing.'

'Bollocks, Inky.'

Weems looked about him and lowered his head. 'Quarter flash, Inspector. Kingsman dimber-damber. I'll not coney this shadow.'

Which was to say: be very careful, an extremely powerful mobster is involved and I want nothing to do with it. Inky had been speaking in south London cant, one of the underworld languages that the criminal fraternity used when they did not wish to be understood by outsiders. Scipio had himself achieved a degree of fluency in most cants.

He shook his head and drew on his cigarette, watching Inky, who looked shifty and frightened.

'Are we being observed, Inky?' he said quietly.

'A famous policeman, aye, and one with a most unusual hue of skin at that, comes into a low dive like this and he asks if we're being watched.'

'Do I want to find out more about this, Inky? Or is it a matter as don't concern me?'

Inky looked miserable. It was answer enough. Whatever was going on went a sight beyond normal mobbery.

'Is this a political?' he asked.

'It's bleeding political, theological and criminal all mixed up, mate,' muttered Inky bitterly. 'I've said enough.'

He drained his glass, stubbed his cigarette out and

pushed the packet with the pound note in back to Scipio. He hopped off the bench and made to leave.

'I'm sorry, Inspector,' he said, turning jolly, loud enough to be heard by a few of the men around, 'I don't know anything about any forged pound notes. Truly I don't. You know me better than that. Give my regards to all my good friends at Bow Street nick. Cheerio.'

As Inky passed, Scipio grabbed him by his sleeve. The man's head was low enough that Scipio didn't have to lean down to talk to him.

'What forged pound notes?'

'Nothing,' whispered Inky. 'I just don't want these cullies here to know what you were really asking me about. For your sake as well as mine.'

'Inky,' he murmured. 'You will talk to me about this. If not now, then later. I shall not leave you alone.'

Inky pulled himself free. 'I know my rights, Inspector. If you're not arresting me, let me go.'

Should he arrest him? He did not have a car to run him in with. They would have to walk to the station. It would look too obvious.

Inky brushed the sleeve of his jacket and in doing so contrived to drop the packet of cigarettes that Scipio had given him earlier. He bent down to pick it up, making a great deal of fuss over it.

'Inky—'

'Yes, yes, I know. Be at the Globe Theatre in an hour's time,' he sighed as he stood up again, taking great care to show his back to everyone. Then more loudly, 'Good day to you.'

Inky waddled away smiling and jerking his thumb over his shoulder towards Scipio, doubtless making faces that said 'stupid flatfoot' to everyone he passed.

Scipio, aware that maybe fifty pairs of eyes were looking at him, finished off his tonic water, mentally plotting the best-shaded and tree-lined route to the Globe Theatre. The sun outside would be fierce.

As a boy, Guy Boswell had once been taken to Covent Garden by his Uncle Cecil, a market gardener. He remembered a bustling place full of shouting Cockneys, the streets thick with mud and vegetable stalks. Here it was rather different.

'In the eighteenth century,' Jenny explained as they walked along, 'this place was notorious as a haunt of prostitutes, a place where rakes, swells and plungers went to be fleeced by pimps, card-sharps and whores. A lot of these people, having suffered untimely deaths and been reborn, have come back here.'

They passed a pair of middle-aged men in suits and trilby hats. Most uncomfortable in this weather, thought Boswell.

'Most of the folk on the street appear perfectly respectable to me.'

'Certainly,' she smiled. 'It's not Gin Lane. It's not even the Holy Land rookery,' she added, wincing as she looked at her bandaged thumb. 'That's the secret, though. The criminal classes keep the place well regulated because it's best for business. It's the hint of danger that makes the money. Most of the people who frequent the bawdy-houses and bars here are folk of the moneyed or middling sort. Tourists, businessmen, civil servants, that sort of thing.'

'Civil servants!? Surely not! I'm sure that men in

bowler hats never visited houses of ill-repute in my day.'

'Oh, didn't they?' she laughed.

To Boswell's astonishment, she linked her arm through his. He looked at her and reddened.

'Sorry, but it's best this way,' she said. 'It's all right, you don't have to give me spooney looks or anything. In fact, I'd rather you didn't.'

Boswell shrugged and did as he was told.

'It's very difficult for a woman to walk through Covent Garden unnoticed,' she said. 'If we look like a normal couple people are less likely to look at us. Otherwise, a handsome cove like you, and a lone woman like me will attract glances.'

'And we don't want that?'

'Certainly not.'

'I don't understand,' said Boswell as they passed a public house where someone was playing 'Knees Up Mother Brown' on an ill-tuned piano. 'We're on the doorstep of Whitehall. Now you can tell me that every red-tape wallah in town is dashing off to places like Lickpenny Nan Heycock's ... er ... establishment every evening, but surely the Government finds this intolerable.'

Jenny shrugged and rapidly turned him to look in the window of a draper's shop. 'Oh now look, Henry, wouldn't those cushions look simply *divine* in our new parlour?'

What?

'Whatever you say, my dear,' he said, playing along and not knowing why. 'Although you know that I cannot afford them this month, my precious.'

Still looking in the window at the silk-covered cushions embroidered with a floral pattern, she pouted. 'Oh but Henry, you promised me . . .'

'My sweet, you know I can refuse you nothing. We shall buy them after my next pay-day.'

She twisted him around and they resumed their course.

'May I ask what—?'

'No,' she said brightly, 'you mayn't. Not just yet.'

Oh God, here it came again. Here he was, walking along with a young woman whom, let us be honest, he found rather attractive. She had her arm through his and they were acting like a young married couple. Yet he couldn't enjoy it because, with his Ma and Guv'nor and Pamela grieving for him back in 1940, it wouldn't be decent.

'A couple of faces passed us,' she said. 'I know them, they know me, but I thought it best they didn't notice us.'

'Faces?'

'Criminals. Well-known mobsters of this parish.'

'Are we going to follow them?'

'No. We have to investigate the case of the missing parson, remember?'

'So why were we hiding from these, er, faces?'

'It's better to have and not need than need and not have.'

'I beg your pardon?'

'There's no advantage to us in being observed, and probably no advantage in not being observed either. But there might be. Besides, you and I both need to practise our anonymity.'

'Oh,' he said, not understanding at all. He could not, however, help suspecting that she was flirting with him.

Perhaps this really is Heaven, he thought.

'To reply to your earlier question,' she said, 'the existence of this latter-day Sodom troubles many in Government. Religious leaders like it even less. The Bulls would like the place cleaned up, the whores branded, the mollies pilloried and stoned and the pimps and procuresses hanged. The irony is this; we have good reason to believe that the Bulls, these very same zealots who so loudly proclaim that they want Covent Garden all fit and godly, are actually running a number of rackets here. They are making money from all this immorality. We've been able to prove nothing so far, of course.'

'But . . . how can they get away with such hypocrisy?'

'Lord knows.'

They turned into Long Acre. A few yards further down, Jenny led him into a sunless little side-street.

One of the Reverend Harry Seymour's neighbours had telephoned Bow Street to say that he had been missing for a few days. The caller, a woman who had not wished to leave her name, had been quite frightened. She had been around to the Reverend's house to see if he was all right after he missed Divine Service one morning. She got no answer at the door, looked in a window and saw the room in disarray.

Seymour's house was a substantial, ramshackle thing which may have been originally built in Georgian times, but which had been patched up in various eras since.

They sauntered up the front steps. Jenny pointed to the three bottles of milk next to the front door. The sun had curdled them all. Boswell pressed the bell.

Over the radio the duty sergeant had told Jenny that Harry Seymour had no living. Instead he worked with the fallen of Covent Garden, rescuing those he could from a life of vice and trying to straighten their lives out, find them honest work and bring them to the Lord. He might well get cudgelled on a dark night by an angry ponce, but his disappearance without trace seemed uncalled-for.

Boswell pushed the bell again, then leaned over and looked through the window into what appeared to be the drawing-room. As the sergeant's anonymous informant had said, there was every indication of an affray. A couple of tatty, dusty-looking armchairs had been tipped over. A large black-and-white print of two men being burned at the stake (Latimer and Ridley?) was hanging lop-sided on the far wall and in the middle of the carpet was some sort of mess, possibly vomit. He beckoned Jenny take a look while he pushed open the letterbox and looked through. In the hallway, a coat-stand had been knocked over. He pushed the bell again.

'Let's look inside,' said Jenny, going back down the steps. Boswell followed. Halfway down the street, they found a narrow alley.

At the end of the alley was a lane running along the back of the houses. They picked their way through bags of rubbish counting off the numbers as they went.

A black-painted wooden gate led to Seymour's back yard. It wasn't locked or bolted and Boswell let himself in while Jenny radioed news of what they were doing back to the station.

Before he was even into the yard he could see that the back door of the house wasn't locked either. It had been smashed in, and now hung inwards supported only by its twisted bottom hinge.

If the door had been bashed down like that, the culprits probably hadn't been too concerned that the whole neighbourhood might see and hear them.

Boswell felt more like a detective all the time.

Through the door was the kitchen. A saucepan of what appeared to be porridge sat, quite cold, on top of a gas cooker covered in brown stains. There were a few smashed cups and plates on the floor, the table and on a dresser.

It appeared that Seymour had been disturbed while at breakfast. Unless he was so sincere about some vow of poverty that he dined on porridge too.

Seymour was apparently a bachelor whose income didn't stretch to a housekeeper or even a weekly visit from a char. Perhaps he gave it all to a charity for fallen women or something.

Boswell walked through the kitchen into the hall, bare floorboards creaking. In the sitting-room he had earlier glimpsed through the window he saw that what he had suspected was vomit on the balding carpet was porridge, as though someone had hurled a bowl of the stuff at someone else.

'Porridge!' said Jenny's voice beside him. 'I thought it was puke. Same thing, really. You look upstairs, I'll check the rest of this floor and see if there's a cellar.'

The floor of the main bedroom was covered with

cracked and grubby linoleum. There was a greying mat beside the big unmade brass bed. The room looked as though it had not been disturbed. There was a chest of drawers, a wardrobe and a dressing-table on which a wristwatch and a pair of cufflinks lay unclaimed.

Boswell carried out a desultory search through the drawers. It didn't seem decent to grub into a fellow's personal affairs like this.

It was useless anyway. There was nothing but clean, simple and several-times-laundered clothes. Boswell didn't really have a feel for fashions here. Some people dressed sort of in the style of the times they had come from, while some young men went for the Edwardian look – straw hats and blazers – or tights and big, puffy shirts. Most, though, dressed as Boswell himself was attired, in plain, sensible suits and ties, just as they had done in the mid-twentieth century. Most women's clothes seemed to be of the same provenance. He had seen a few wearing trousers, but most wore skirts or dresses. Their hemlines didn't appear to have got any lower since 1940.

The Reverend Harry Seymour was clearly one who preferred the nondescript fashions of Boswell's previous time. He had a couple of dark suits and several plain white shirts. The loudest item he possessed was a bottle-green tie, though most of the time he obviously wore ecclesiastical collars.

In the bottom of the wardrobe he found an old biscuit-tin full of official documents and letters – correspondence with his employer, bank statements, a few old gas bills.

Boswell sat down on the floor and quickly rifled

through the papers. Seymour, they told him, was not, and never had been, a wealthy man.

Jenny passed by outside the door. 'Nothing down there,' she said. 'I'll look around upstairs.'

Boswell put the last of the papers back into the tin and replaced the lid. From his position on the floor, he noticed that under the bed was a book and a chamber pot. Boswell stood and went to investigate.

The po' was (mercifully) empty. Close by it was an old leather-bound book, as if laid on the floor as the bed's occupant was turned in for the night.

Foxe's Boke of Martyrs announced the fly-leaf. John Foxe's account of the sufferings of die-hard Protestants under Bloody Mary had been favoured reading of many folks in the sixteenth and seventeenth centuries. Boswell didn't know a lot about books, but this might be a first edition, or pretty near it. He had looked through a bookshop window this morning and seen nothing but cheap Penguin-style paperback novels, most of them detective stories or trashy romances or adventure yarns set in the Wild West. There were a few other bloodthirsty-looking action-adventure tales of derring-do set during the Feudal Wars, or stories of intrepid individuals travelling to the chaos of mainland Europe in search of British retreads from old wars, but for the most part the reading-matter of the masses didn't appear too different from his own time.

But *Foxe's Boke* was different. And this fine leather-bound book was the first even slightly valuable thing he had seen in Seymour's house.

Jenny appeared at the door. 'Nothing at all,' she said. 'None of the other rooms on this floor or above seem to be in use. Just a couple of mildewed mattresses and some cardboard boxes full of junk and old newspapers.'

Boswell nodded, leafing through *Foxe's Boke*. 'I'd say whoever broke in was after the house's occupant, and not his possessions. His watch is still on the table. And this book might be worth a few shillings.'

A piece of ruled paper of the sort you'd tear from an exercise book fell from Foxe on to the bedspread. Boswell picked it up. Jenny read it aloud as he held it:

Lord God, deliver me out of this miserable and wretched life, and take me amongst Thy Chosen; howbeit, not my will but Thy will be done. Lord I commit my spirit to Thee. O! Lord, Thou knowest how happy it were for me to be with Thee: yet, for Thy Chosen's sake, send me life and health, that I may truly serve Thee. O! My Lord God, defend this realm from Papistry, and maintain Thy true religion, that I and my people may praise Thy holy name, for Thy son Jesus Christ's sake. Amen.

'Is this evidence?' asked Boswell, thrusting the paper into her hand, and stubbing her bandaged thumb as he did so.

Jenny winced. 'Shit!' she said.

Boswell apologized and pushed the paper into the pocket of his trousers.

She forgave him. 'Let's see if the neighbours know anything,' she said. 'Someone must have heard the back door being bashed down.'

Ladies weren't supposed to use words like the one

Jenny had uttered as he hurt her thumb. This must make her working class.

In the back lane outside, Jenny tousled up Boswell's hair and told him to hitch up his trousers to expose his socks and ankles.

'Look stupid,' she said, 'and leave all the speaking to me. We'll likely find out more if they don't realize we're rozzers.'

'Let's imagine,' she said, 'here's the young dodger, keen as mustard to save souls and work among the fallen. His bishop is delighted to allow him to do this because it's a dirty job that nobody else wants.'

Boswell agreed. 'Seymour would never be seen around the close in Barchester, would he?'

'No,' laughed Jenny.

So, thought Boswell, she can read. Or had she just seen versions of Trollope stories in the cinema, or on the television jobbie?

They went up the steps of the house next door to Seymour's. There was a heavy brass knocker on the door, which Jenny tapped timidly.

After a minute, the door was answered by a fat, sweating, wheezing man wearing a stained white vest and grubby khaki trousers.

'Yer, whodjewant?' he said. He was in his fifties, and had lost most of his hair. A scar ran from the crown of his head to just above his right eye.

'Oh, pardon me fer troublin' you, sir,' said Jenny in thickest Mummerset, 'my name is Jessie Sternwaller, an' this yer's my husband Elihu, an' we just come in from Gloucestershire county this mornin'. On the train, it was. We been lookin' for my cousin. I knows he lives somewhere in this street, but I don't know which 'ouse, only you see we an't neither've us got the readin' and writin', and when he sends us 'is letters, it's usually our Peg as reads 'em out to us, only we got to find 'im 'cos we lended some money off 'im a couple o'years back and now I wants to pay 'im back. We Sternwallers always pays our way . . .'

Boswell gave his best cheesey grin and rocked from one foot to another. 'Well, wossyer cousin's name?' asked the man.

'Oh thank you kindly, sir,' said Jenny. 'I knew someone'd help us. Only our Peg says city folk are so unfriendly, but I told 'er, I said, Peg, we'm all God's creatures, in't us? . . .'

'His name?' asked the man impatiently.

'Seymour, the Reverend 'arry Seymour, sir.'

Scarface's reaction was very instructive. He hauled in his massive stomach, and grew a few inches taller. 'Never 'eard of him,' he said curtly, 'you must have the wrong street.' He tried to push the door shut, but Jenny's foot was in the way.

'I said I've got some money for 'im,' she said. 'An' I'm sure it's this street 'ee lives in. Quite a lot of money, it is. It's very important that I get it to him. I could give you some. I could maybe leave it with you to give to 'im when you see 'im.'

'I don't know nuffink. Now get your foot out of my flamin' door and piss orff!'

Jenny removed her foot. The door slammed.

'Do you think he believed your acting?' said Boswell as they descended the steps.

'I shall ignore your insult for now,' she said, nose in the air and feigning offence. 'My acting was never at issue. What matters was how frightened he was. If he's anything to judge by, we'll not get anything out of any of the others. Come on, it's lunchtime. I'll radio in what we've found and then we can get a sandwich at a place round the corner.'

In the portico of the Globe Theatre a bored-looking young woman sat behind a glass screen at the ticket booth. Scipio flashed her his warrant card and took her shrug for permission to pass through.

The Globe Theatre was, it was commonly under-stood, only an approximate facsimile of the original in which many of Shakespeare's plays had been per-formed. It had been built ten years before on the South Bank, near the site of the old Royal Festival Hall, which had been so damaged in the Atom War that it had not been judged worth repairing. The facsimile Globe had been built by a private joint-stock company and did a reasonable business presenting Shakespeare in its original English, or in bowdlerized and shortened versions for the edification of schoolchildren and tourists alike. The National Shakespeare Company, however, preferred to stick to its home-base in Stratford-upon-Avon, or to tour to prestigious regional theatres. The Globe, it was understood, was something the NSC found *infra dig*.

Before the Atom War the National Shakespeare Company had been the *Royal* Shakespeare Company. The previous monarch was gone, and none of her surviving family had as good a title to the throne as the man who had once been king, a monarch who had no cause to love Shakespeare on account of one particular play.

One heard stories, though. Scipio had it on good authority that while His Majesty could not lend the company his patronage without looking foolish, he found the whole thing mighty amusing, and enjoyed impersonating the actor in the film, made a few years before the Atom War, of *Richard III*.

Scipio made his way up the wooden stairs to the top-floor gallery. Might as well have the best view. Inky Weems had been very scared. He probably would not show at all.

He emerged into daylight again. The top gallery was broad and went three-quarters of the way round the building, which was octagonal and open to the air in the middle. Down below was the stage and wooden benches arranged in front of it. There were benches here in the gallery, too.

There was nobody about. On the blackboard outside it had said that the next performance (*The Merry Wives of Windsor*) would be at 3 p.m.

The sun shone into his face. For comfort and discretion he made his way around to a point directly opposite the stage. Here he was in shadow. He pushed a bench long enough to seat three people hard up against the wood-panelled back wall and sat down. On the way across the Waterloo Bridge he had bought the day's first edition of the *Standard*, and pulled it out of his pocket.

The Haseldich murder was a small item on the second page. That was good, he supposed. There was a murder every couple of days somewhere in London, but August was traditionally a quiet month for news, and the story might just as well have taken up the whole front page. Instead, the paper was preoccupied with the remarkable story of how a pair of six-year-old girls – twin sisters – who had both perished in a house-fire during the reign of King George III had both come up in Barking within an hour of one another. The girls were a very fetching pair of little poppets and the newspaper had photographed them in pretty dresses, with ribbons for their blonde hair.

There seemed to be no pattern at all as to when retreads would rematerialize. If a man died in, say, 1600, you couldn't tell when he would be reborn. So for twins to show up more or less simultaneously was a remarkable event. Of course, just because you died prematurely in the past didn't necessarily mean you would be reborn at all. The *Daily Herald* had for years been running a popular sweepstake on which famous historical character would be reborn when. Curiously enough, the two that most people wanted to bet on were Mary, Queen of Scots, and Anne Boleyn. Neither of them had been reborn yet. Perhaps they never would be.

'Funny business, that twins thing, isn't it?' said a voice beside him.

'Indeed,' said Scipio, folding his paper and pushing it into his pocket.

Inky Weems clambered on to the bench beside him, his little legs dangling several inches from the floor. His brilliantined hair glistened in the heat and he smelt strongly of tobacco and expensive Cologne.

'You know, it wouldn't surprise me in the slightest if some sly hack has made it all up and then sold the paper a poke. You get the two squeakers, see, who were like as not born in the Bermondsey lying-in hospital no more than six years back, you teach them their lines and tell 'em they can have the run of Mr Hamley's toy shop if they get it right. Yerss, that ten-bob note you punted me earlier says it's a lay. Some flash cull is trying to lambert the newspaper.'

'It is a compelling story, with a pretty picture. In a case like this, the newspaper would *want* to be lamberted.'

Inky sniffed and nodded. 'Aye, you could well be right, Inspector. You usually are.'

'Want a fag?'

'Don't mind if I do. I noticed as how you had a pack of Great Zimbabwes earlier on. I don't much go for your African tobacco, but I'm sure there's something else of interest in the packet.'

'My pleasure.' He handed Inky the packet with the pound note in.

This time, Inky was not so surreptitious. He opened the packet, put a cigarette in his mouth and took out the banknote to admire the elaborately-detailed picture of the King's head on it.

'You know,' he said, 'if I was in government, I'd urge His Majesty – whom God protect – to grow himself a beard, or at least something in the way of face-fungus. Nice big 'tache and some mutton-chop side-whiskers would do the trick.'

'How so?'

'Look at him. Sixty years old, but with a smooth clean

face like he was half that age.' It was true enough. King Richard's features on the note were bland, a few wrinkles around the eyes, some lines on the forehead and around his long, rounded chin.

'Easy to draw,' said Inky. 'If he had a load of beard these fellows would be a lot harder to forge. Not, I hasten to add, Inspector, that I would ever get involved in anything so nefarious myself.'

'Perish the thought.'

'But I know a man who does. Has a print shop not two miles from where we're sitting. Made up the plates himself. Beautiful work they are, too. It'd almost be a crime to turn him in.'

'But of course your acute sense of civic duty compels you to give me the name and address of this foul spifflicator.'

Inky laughed bitterly and looked up at Scipio. 'I'm offering you a bargain, Inspector. I'll give you the name of a man who's drenched the East End in lousy sovs if you leave me alone.'

'Sorry, Inky, it is too hot to play games. You're the best snout—' Inky winced. The word wasn't one to enhance his self-worth. 'Sorry, Inky, you are the best . . . source of information I know. You are very good at what you do. And what I see is this: Inky Weems, a man who ploughs his own straight course through this confusing world is, for the first time in his life, frightened to give me something.'

'You're not wrong there, Inspector.'

'See it my way, Inky. I have lived here for many, many years. I was among the earliest retreads. When the country collapsed into misrule and anarchy, I served with some distinction in the Feudal Wars. My wife believes, and she is probably correct, that I could now enjoy a position of great dignity in the Civil Service or the armed forces, perhaps even in government.'

'I am sure that Mrs Africanus is correct in that matter,' said Inky, producing a gold Dunhill cigarette lighter and applying fire to his Zimbabwe.

'But you see, Inky, having in my last life been a slave, and having worked very hard after I was reborn to ensure that Monmouth and his motley rabble of Protestant roundheads and malcontented aristocrats never enslaved anyone ever again, I have an over-developed sense of right and wrong.'

'Everyone knows you for a righteous man, Inspector. That Africanus, they say, no bleeding sense of humour at all, but straight as an arrow, they say. A hard man, but a fair one.'

Scipio could not help sniggering at this.

'Please don't mock me, Inspector,' said Inky, a pained look on his face. 'Not when I'm telling the truth.'

Scipio patted him on the back. 'I apologize. What I am saying is that anything that frightens a man like you, a man who lives on his wits like no other, must be something very wrong. And my sense of duty means that I have to confront that wrong. What is going on, Inky?'

Inky looked at the ground, and fidgeted with his cigarette with his pudgy fingers. His nails, Scipio noticed, had been recently manicured. He said nothing, but one could almost hear the wheels and gears grinding in his head as he wrestled with his decision.

'It's the Bulls. The Antient and Honourable Order of

the Sons of John Bull.' He spat the words out angrily.

'And?'

'And I don't know. They're plotting something. Something big. The word is that Haseldich, the cove who was squelched, was a follower. He was entrusted by Lilley, the man who owns the house he was killed in, to go and get the money out to pay off various people. Lilley is the Bulls' treasurer.'

'Where did you hear all this?'

'The word is out. Someone gets murdered it gives folks something to talk about. And as you well know, the Bulls are at least as criminal as they are religious. Somewhere they got the idea that the best way to make money in order to make us all more godly, they have to put the squeeze on criminal activity.'

'Tell me, do they squeeze bawdy-houses in Covent Garden?'

'Certainly. And a lot else besides. Their pastor in that parish is one Jacob Malahide, a very vicious man.'

Inky swore quietly and threw his cigarette-end on the floor. He hopped off the bench to stamp it out with his foot.

'Do we know what it is they are plotting?'

Inky shook his head. He moved forward and leaned on the wooden railing overlooking the stage. 'Something big is all I know. The dimber-damber is a man named Saltonstall. Calls himself Elder Saltonstall. I've seen him a couple of times, the sort of cove you can never fathom. He whores and drinks and curses like a dragoon, but his knees are horny from hours of praying. You could say he was a hypocrite, but he's more complicated than that. I hear his current trug is a girl at

Mother Heycock's stew in the Garden. You should know her. Everyone calls her Lickpenny Nan. I don't know the name of the girl Saltonstall is seeing there, though.'

'This plot of theirs. Is it political?'

Inky turned towards Scipio, leaning the top of his back against the rail which would have been waist-height on any regular man. 'I don't know. They've been putting out a lot of broadsides and flyers lately saying that the time is come to restore England to the paths of righteousness, that a special person will be coming. A new King Josiah.'

'Destroyer of the idols,' said Scipio. 'Chap in the Old Testament who took the Israelites away from the path of worshipping statues as I recall. Popular with old-style Protestants who say that Catholicism is idolatry.'

In Scipio's previous life, Lady Suffolk had seen to it that her lap-dog was well schooled in the Christian faith.

'You know your scripture better than I do,' said Inky, taking out another cigarette and lighting it nervously. 'Talking of scripture, there's something else which might be of use in your investigations. You ever hear of a sky-pilot name of Seymour, works over the Garden way, tries to save fallen women, help junkies and alcoholics?'

'Yes,' said Scipio. 'A curate at St Martin's, is he not?'

'The very same. Only puts in the occasional churchy appearance. Spends the rest of his time trying to help folks, or save the fallen. Serious young laddie, very intense. Out of his depth, if you ask me.'

'So anyway?'

'So anyway, he's gone missing. A few days now. The word is that the Bulls had him. They've taken him, kidnapped him. Nobody knows why. I mean, if he'd been annoying them, they'd have roughed him up and left him in a gutter somewhere. But instead, they've taken him. Looks like he has something, or knows something, that they want quite a lot.'

'I'll tell you something else,' continued Inky, 'and this really is the limit of what I know. There's word they're bringing in a man from the United States. Some manner of expert. Probably one of them weird Yank Puritans.'

'An assassin? A bomber?'

Inky shrugged. 'Don't know, Inspector. It doesn't take a genius to figure it out, though. They plan to stir up trouble, maybe murder some folk and try and raise the mob for the Protestant cause. They know they can't raise the Army – or the Police – and there's only a handful of lunatics in Parliament as subscribe to their ideas, and then only on the QT, so they're likely to try and start riot and rebellion.'

Inky clambered back on to the bench. This time, he sat closer to Scipio, as if for protection.

'Thanks, Inky. Now tell me, why have you told me all this? You are a clever man. You could have avoided my questions, told me you knew nothing. I would not have believed you, but there would have been little I could do to press the information from you.'

'Inspector, I'm not a church-going man, but I count myself as at least a passing Christian, aye, and a Protestant one at that. Like yourself I died young, and when one wakes up here, one does get the feeling that the Almighty is giving one a second chance. Now I am certainly a sinner, and this is certainly a sinful world. It's not perfect, but it's as good as it's likely to get. If the Bulls take charge, everything will turn to shit.'

Scipio closed his eyes. He had to think. How would he deal with this? He would have to report it to the Superintendent, certainly. But this was a plot. The Bulls had done nothing criminal so far, apart from their routine mob activity. Well, he would have to give them a hard time. He and Sergeant O'Rourke would do a little research, ask around, then pull every last rozzer in Bow Street off their usual work and harass every known Bull in the area, then . . .

There was a hissing sound, followed by a thud and the sound of splintering wood beside him. Inky let out a little yelp.

Scipio opened his eyes. The shaft of the arrow was still shuddering though it pinned Inky Weems to the wooden wall behind them.

He pulled his pistol out from inside his jacket and dropped to the floor, trying to work out where the arrow had come from.

Another arrow thudded into the floor a few inches from his head. A cloth-yard. Just like at Agincourt.

He glimpsed the sun glinting off the steel tip of another shaft as it was being nocked.

Straight across. In the opposite gallery.

He thumbed the safety off his Browning 9-mm automatic and squeezed off two shots in the archer's general direction. Try and get his head down, then work out what to do.

Only now did he notice that Inky was screaming,

pinned to the wall by the arrow running through his shoulder.

Sitting target.

He fired another shot at the assassin and scrambled over to where Inky hung. His feet were a good 3 inches off the floor.

Painful. Really, really painful.

Despite himself, Scipio winced.

He picked up the bench they had been sitting on, holding it upright for the little cover it provided for himself and Inky as another arrow flew past him, hammering into the wall a few inches from Inky's head.

Goose-feathers in the back of it. Very traditional.

'This will hurt like buggery, Inky,' he said, letting go of the bench for a moment, hoping it would stand upright for a few moments. With his left arm, he grabbed Inky around the waist and jerked him forward.

'Awwwwww ffuuuuuuccckkk!' screamed Inky. His breath smelled of Parma violets.

'A little longer, Inky . . .' he said. There was just enough space behind Inky now. Hoping that the steel tip of the arrow was embedded deep in the wood, he smashed the butt of his pistol down behind Inky where the shaft should be.

'Jeezus!' said Inky, who was now hyperventilating as the arrow through his shoulder was pushed suddenly downwards.

It broke.

Scipio swept Inky up with both arms and laid him down on the ground as quickly as he could.

Something heavy hit his back. Damn, thought Scipio, he's got me as well. He turned and realized it was just the wooden bench he had stood upright to try and shield himself and Inky. The steel tip of an arrow designed to slice its way into a quarter inch of plate armour protruded through it, humming like an angry wasp.

He crouched on the floor again and laid the bench, seat facing outwards, along the length of Inky's body. Inky was breathing deeply in pain and fear and muttering something as he went. The Paternoster.

Scipio scrambled along the floor to another bench, pushed it over and hid behind it for a while to take stock.

Chummy was on the same floor as them, about 30 yards away. Scipio should be able to work his way towards him, shooting as he went, to keep his head down and stop him from trying to fire off any more shafts.

Tall cove, cropped blond hair, blue eyes, big lips. Would have been a pretty boy without the big blond moustache. Very athletic, very well built. Looked like an actor out of one of those Californian porno films the Customs people were always impounding. Unusual clothes. Leather jacket with lots of pockets. Denim bell-bottom trousers. Possibly foreign (but why use a long-bow, a weapon that needs so much practice?), probably some sort of professional.

Damn!

Something thumped in his face. There was a crackle of splintering wood and he recoiled. Blood. Big splashes of blood falling on the wooden floor.

He had been hit. In the face. In the cheek. Under his left eye.

Blood splashing to the floor.

No, okay, he was all right. The arrow wasn't sticking into him.

It had hammered its way through the upturned bench he was lying behind and scratched him next to his nose. Badly.

He hoped he wouldn't need stitches.

You've ruddy ruined my looks, pal, he thought. You'll pay for that. Small children would be even more frightened of him than ever if he had a scar.

Grasping his gun with both hands, and cursing his not-getting-any-younger bones to do as they were told, he rolled along the floor away from the bench and scrambled inelegantly to a kneeling position, pointing his gun in the archer's direction . . .

. . . Only to see the back of the bastard as he ran off down the stairs. He fired once, twice, and again, the racket of his gun cannoning off the theatre's wooden walls again and again like billiard balls.

He'd missed. As the fug of gunshot noises cleared from his head, he could hear the swine's feet clattering evenly down the wooden stairs.

I've got to have you, cully.

There were three sets of stairs leading down from this upper gallery, and he had taken the one directly opposite. Stopping only to check that Inky was doing okay – he was not, but he would live – he raced down the staircase behind him, hoping to catch up with the man.

Out past the ticket-booth he ran, past a couple of tourists clutching programmes for the theatre and loudly wondering what all the noise was about, out into the large concrete apron in front of the theatre looking on to the Thames.

The longbow and a bundle of arrows held together with an elastic band had been dumped on the ground where a couple of small boys were eyeing them with interest. Anguished shouts from adults to get away from them as soon as the black man with a bleeding face and a dirty great pistol in his hand appeared.

Chummy was about 200 yards in front of him now. Yes, very fit indeed. The bastard was young and kept himself in shape.

Scipio ran, too many people in his way. Lunchtime. Everyone was coming out of their offices to eat their sandwiches in the sun by the river. Tourists, too.

'Stop! Police!' Usually a useless thing to shout, in the forlorn hope that some public-spirited citizen would get involved and try and drop the villain with a rugby tackle, or even just a casually-outstretched foot. It wasn't much to ask, was it? But no, they never did. Nobody wanted to get involved.

He was losing his man, haring away towards the New Blackfriars Bridge.

Chummy was too fast. Scipio was too old, smoked too many cigarettes.

Damn his wizened, dried-up, useless old body!

He was too far away to shoot at.

Too many people around anyway. The wrong person might get hurt.

Damn!

THINGS REMEMBERED (2)

MAJOR SCIPIO AFRICANUS, FIFTH MECHANIZED REGIMENT, COALITION ARMY 1ST CORPS

ATHELNEY ISLAND, SOMERSET; SATURDAY, 25 FEBRUARY 1978, 0645 HOURS

Scipio, wearing trousers and undershirt, poked his head through the tent-flaps. The snow was melting, but the day was still and cold as a card-sharp's heart, the only sound being the murmur of men and the cawing of a few rooks. Mist rose from the ditches and marshes all around, while the sun's pale disc strained through the twigs of a pollarded willow tree beyond his jeep.

He turned back inside, sat on his cot, pulled on his boots and laced them.

He took the white enamel bowl from the trestle table, went outside and crouched, trying to keep his knees from contacting the mud beneath, scrabbling handfuls of slushy snow into the bowl.

The camp was quiet. Three divisions of the Army of Wessex had rallied on Athelney from their dispersals at the end of January and then left again, sneaking off silently under the mists that clung to the soggy ground, the will-o'-the-wisps that supposedly haunted Sedgemoor.

General Lawrence wanted to give the Roundheads

the impression that he, like them, would keep his forces cooped up in winter quarters until spring. He had no such intention.

Scipio strode over to the stone farm-building that was serving as the cookhouse, nodded to the few men breakfasting at the wooden benches outside. Inside the steaming room, the smell of baking bread and the clattering of pots and pans exuded welcome and comfort. Perhaps he would become a baker when the Wars ended. That way, he need never be cold again.

He handed his bowl of snow to a cook, who traded it for a perfunctory salute. The man placed it on top of one of the big iron ovens and returned with a mug of coffee and a fresh bread roll. Scipio leaned against the wall and breakfasted.

The few troops left on Athelney would move soon. General Lawrence was secretly moving his army into the shadow of the Mendip Hills. There he could make a sudden strike for Bristol or Bath, and then Monmouth's headquarters at Oxford. Or he could swing east, straight at London.

There was now little danger the Roundheads would know exactly what the Army of Wessex was doing. They were almost beaten. They had been driven completely from Wales, Scotland and the north of England, shutting themselves into a few towns and cities, or perching atop hills to shake their fists. Any patrols they sent out for reconnaissance were likely to be slaughtered by clubmen, bands of country folk who had long become sick of the wars, and of soldiers seizing their hard-won provisions.

He sipped the hot coffee. At first he had hated the stuff. Now he thought it the best beverage the earth had to offer, and gave silent thanks to the Yank President, Mr – not King, or Lord, just ordinary Mister – Jimmy Carter, without whose coffee and jeeps and guns and ammunition and helicopters and advisers . . .

Without Mr Carter the Wars would not be ending in a year or sooner. Without Mr Carter, England would fall into the hands of a man who wanted to be king with untrammelled powers, supported by a band of religious firebrands whose idea of godly governance was to flog poor whores or run red-hot spikes through the tongues of blasphemers, who would set themselves above Catholics, Jews, Socialists, Democrats, agnostics and atheists, over all men and women with the wit or desire to find their own path to the salvation of their souls.

'What's happening, Bro'?' said a voice at the door.

'Major Bro' to you, you Yank peasant,' smiled Scipio.

Jayzee breezed past him wearing only shorts and demanded coffee.

Master Sergeant John Zachary Washington – Jayzee to his 'buddies' – was another gift from Mr President Carter, one of a few hundred advisers that the Americans had sent to General Lawrence. He was also one of the few other black men that Scipio had met in this life.

'So what's the scuttlebutt, Major Bro'?' said Jayzee, tearing a bread-roll apart with his teeth.

'You claim to be the greatest captain since Alexander. Why not enlighten me?' said Scipio. There was supposed to be a world of difference between their ranks, but Yank advisers tended to be conscious of their importance. Besides, Scipio was twenty-five. Jayzee was thirty, and though he joked he was 'full of shit', he knew so much Scipio did not.

'Reckon us and all the other Mechanos will be outside Oxford tomorrow, with the footsloggers following on,' said Jayzee, 'assuming that's where James the Bastard is, and assuming the weather stays cold and dry enough to stop the ground turning to mud.'

Jayzee was a retread himself. He had died of influenza in New York city in 1919 and had reappeared in that city shortly after the Atom War. By the time the American government had restored order there, Jayzee had decided on a military career and had been a full-time soldier for thirteen years.

'What makes you so sure we will move today?'

Jayzee shrugged. 'It's been days since most of the others moved out. They must be in position now. We could all be ready to take Oxford by tomorrow morning. That's a Sunday. We can sneak up on the them while they're all in church praying to sweet Jesus to save their righteous asses.'

Jayzee had been with them two years. Scipio had first met him when he was teaching the men to drive. He had even taught Scipio, which had led to Scipio's appointment as driver to General Lawrence before the latter gave him an officer's commission in the Fifth Mechanized. ('That's 'cause General Lawrence don't want to die in another motor accident, Bro',' Jayzee had said. 'It's only a shame you ain't Monmouth's driver, then we could all go home.')

Lieutenant Fraser, one of General Lawrence's gallopers, stomped into the room and saluted him crisply.

'General's compliments, sir! Would all officers assemble at the General's quarters for briefing at 0900, sir! The General further requests that your unit be prepared to move by 1100, sir!'

Scipio returned the salute.

'What did I tell you, Major Bro'?' said Jayzee as young Fraser marched out stiffly. 'Jeez, I'll never understand the way some of you English confuse soldiering with having a bad back.'

The cook handed Scipio his bowl of snow. Jayzee dipped his finger into it. 'Sir, please, sir, would the Major do me the honour of letting the Yank have his luke-warm shaving water when sir is finished with it, sir?'

'Very well,' said Scipio. 'Would you please tell everyone to be ready for inspection at ten-hundred. And tell them to ensure all weapons are cleaned and tested.' Scipio was acting C/O of the Regiment while Colonel Maitland recovered from pneumonia.

Jayzee said, 'Yes, sir!' without any sarcasm or irony.

Scipio went into the hard morning air to shave with the help of the wing-mirror on his jeep.

The officers sat in wooden and canvas chairs in the gloomy wooden barn that served for meetings. They smoked and chattered, speculating on the content of the covered map standing on an easel in front of them.

Some armchair strategists and Yank advisers condemned Lawrence's choice of Athelney as the site for his headquarters. They called it sentimental and strategically unsound, the conceit of an archaeologist (Lawrence's original calling), not a soldier. The South-west, they said, was of small importance compared to the Midlands, the North and, the greatest prize of all, London.

But Lawrence's choice of Athelney had been a combination of romance and cold deliberation. Years before, the flatlands of Somerset had been well drained, but the Atom War and the Feudal Wars and other disruptions turned much of the Levels to water and marsh, particularly in winter. The region resembled its condition in the time of King Alfred the Great, who had sought refuge on Athelney centuries beforehand, and from where he had directed the liberation of his kingdom from the Danes and laid the foundations of England itself.

Most people in England knew the story of Alfred. The Coalition radio stations and propaganda pamphlets dropped from the air made the comparisons for those who had not already done so for themselves.

When the Roundheads were victorious, it was an inaccessible fastness. Now, with the marshes being drained once more, and the ground hard enough to take motor vehicles, it would be the point from which final victory would be achieved.

The rhythmic thumping of a helicopter grew louder. Men stomped out their cigarettes in anticipation of the General's arrival. For many months, he had spent most of his time elsewhere, clearing the last enemy pockets from the Midlands.

The Huey's engines roared outside, the draught from its blades penetrated holes in the barn's walls, ruffling papers and animating straw and dust.

Then Lawrence was there, almost unnoticed. They

stood to attention in a muddle of scraping chairs and stamping feet.

A small, fastidious man with big, girlish lips, Lawrence looked more like a vicar than a soldier, smiling and nodding nervously to the burly war-hardened men around him.

Lieutenant Fraser uncovered the map. Lawrence mouthed a thank-you, straightened and turned his clear blue eyes towards his audience.

'Oxford, gentlemen. Town of glittering spires. My home town, as a matter of fact. Not,' he smiled, 'that that has anything to do with my decision.'

Most of the men in the room smiled and nodded.

'We shall move up all our mechanized and armoured columns tonight and try and take the enemy unawares tomorrow. I have reliable information that his Grace the Duke himself is in residence, and though he has not invited us to tea on the lawn, I should like us to breakfast with him. Whether he desires our company or not.'

Lawrence was never the same quantity to any two men. In some he inspired respect or even fear (they said he had a demon in him); in others he triggered love. For many of Scipio's so-called brother officers, especially those of nineteenth and twentieth-century begetting, Lawrence was a talisman, a tangible link with the forever-lost paradise of their own privileged back-grounds. Lawrence epitomized gentility and gracious living, libraries full of recondite volumes, cricket games, long indulgent summers and tea on the lawn with cucumber sandwiches thin as the blade of a safety-razor.

Many in this army – and perhaps in the other one as well – expressed their craving for peace by idealizing the past. Last summer, the Regiment had stopped for a fifteen-minute brew-up and smoker in a deserted Wiltshire village. It was early evening, and the air was heavy with the scent of various flowers gone wild. He had wandered along the road to stretch his legs and found one of his subalterns leaning on a wall, crying like a child. When Scipio asked him what was wrong, the man shook his head and pointed to the upstairs window of the stone-built house behind him, where through a broken window, the evening sun lit up the gilt on a harp against the room's interior darkness.

Scipio had understood.

'If we succeed,' Lawrence was saying, 'we capture their headquarters, which will give the Roundheads and their supporters a terrible mental shock. We might even take Monmouth himself. If we succeed in the next few days, we stand a good chance of finishing the war; it may not be necessary to fight for London.'

They all nodded thoughtfully. Fighting for London street by street, house by house, was a ghastly prospect.

'Now this is what we'll do . . .'

'Major Africanus,' smiled Lawrence when all the others had left the barn, 'still doing your own driving, are you?'

'Yes, General.'

'Extraordinary,' said Lawrence, shaking his head.

'General, your briefing did not mention—'

'—What you and your Mechanoes will be getting up to,' said Lawrence. 'Don't worry. I've got a rotten job for you. Needs a man who can improvise and think quickly. Turn it down if you like.'

Lawrence settled on the steel-framed canvas chair next to Scipio. 'I think,' he said, 'we can probably take Oxford without your help. The fight's gone out of most of them. So I think I can spare you to capture Bristol.'

'With just one regiment? I had four hundred and thirty-two men paraded fit for duty this morning—'

'One of the reasons for our success,' said Lawrence, rubbing his hands into each other and looking at the floor, 'is we have a better intelligence system than the enemy. We have a pretty good idea of what they're up to everywhere. The population of Bristol is close to starvation. The countryside around the city is hostile to them, and people's back gardens don't grow enough. On top of all this, there are a few thousand prisoners in Bristol. If the population and garrison are starving, can you imagine what it must be like for prisoners?'

Scipio could imagine.

'Capturing Bristol will not win the war for us,' said Lawrence. 'Normally, we would pass it by, but if we can take it easily, we will be relieving a lot of misery at little cost to ourselves. Isn't that worthwhile?'

'Yes, General.' People who were starving or freezing to death were perhaps more likely to contemplate suicide than they would have done in the last world, though few actually went through with it. As the brigade padre always said, if we can't treat one another decently in this world, can there really be any hope the next is any better?

'No heroics, though,' said Lawrence. 'I'm only contemplating this because the garrison is supposed to be in a pretty desperate shape. If you can force the city by *coup de main*, then we'll be very happy. But if you meet any serious opposition, you are to withdraw immediately. As you can see, I am allowing us to be a little sentimental, but not too sentimental.'

Scipio knew Bristol. In his last life he had lived in the Great House at Henbury, a few miles away.

The great city of Bristol was the light and the shadow of their lives, a huge, sprawling, noisy port where merchants got rich on slaves and sugar, and the poor drank and pissed their money and miseries away in stinking dockside alehouses.

'Well, Major, do you want the job?'

'Yes, General.'

'I said no heroism.'

'Yes, General.'

'Lieutenant Fraser will give you maps and street-plans. Will you need anything else?'

'A brace of Huey gunships, General.'

'You can have one. Anything else?'

'A generator, an audio-tape machine and some loudspeakers, please.'

Extract from *The Dashing Mechano*, by John Wilmot, Second Earl of Rochester, produced for BBC Television, first screened as a Sunday Play in October 1996.

Lord Rochester's play is based on an incident towards the end of the English Feudal Wars, when, in February 1978, a single regiment of Coalition troops under the command of Major Scipio Africanus captured the city of Bristol, freeing several thousand starving prisoners, one of whom he later took to wife.

Evening, exterior. The fighting is over and Chalky *(West Country),* Spud *(Irish) and* Bert *(Cockney), three private soldiers of the Fifth Mechanized Regiment, are sitting around a campfire. They have just finished their rations and are now smoking cigarettes. Each is drinking a bottle of plundered sherry.*

SPUD: Sure, that was a good day's work now, wasn't it?

CHALKY: S'right. A whole city taken, and not a scratch on any of us.

BERT: That reminds me. You cullies owes me a pack of fags each.

SPUD: Right you are, so. I'll pay you next week, butty.

CHALKY: Arr, me too. I'll sort you come pay-day, Bert.

BERT: (*firmly*) No. That's bad joss, that is. You bet me you wouldn't come out of this show in one piece. You should pay up at once. It's not just a matter of me wanting my winnings. It's that you've got to honour fate when fate's been good to you, see?

SPUD: Aye, I can't argue with you there. (*Takes pack of cigarettes from his breast pocket and throws it to* BERT)

CHALKY: (*Doing likewise*) Reckon the Major had as much to do with it as fate, mind. I casn't think of any other beaks who could fix it to take a whole city with just four hundred and summat Mechanos.

BERT: Cor! Hark at you! That's why I made the bet with you. Ol' Bert knew the Major would see us all right. He cares about us, he does.

SPUD: He cares about everyone. Did youse bowsies notice we didn't burst any Roundhead snot either? Not one of them. Took the whole city peacefully.

CHALKY: Ahhh, that's not quite true, shipmate. I was down the middle of town when the enemy beak surrendered. All very proper-job, it was. But then a sniper up in an upstairs window started popping off at us. The Major soon fixed 'ee, though.

SPUD: What did he do?

CHALKY: He asks Bert here to pass him the platoon bazooka, then strides out into the open where he's a sitting duck for this bastard, puts an HE shell up the spout and, cool as you like, points it at the window and blows this bloody great hole approximately in the place where the contact is. End of story.

BERT: Cullions of steel, that bloke. And smart with it, too. You know he had us bring them big loudspeakers and a generator when we was driving up? You know what they were for? For making the sounds of tanks and trucks and all sorts of other noises like there's ten thousand swaddies getting ready for the kill. He left four men of B Company to the south of the city last night playing that racket to make 'em think there's a huge Coalition army about to come in that way, an' all the time, we're taking a big detour to come in from exactly the other way.

SPUD: The best fighting man I ever served under, excepting General Lawrence himself, of course. I know he's a hard case, and not one for joking or even smiling much, but he's a decent, God-fearing skin is the Major. Like his rule about liberating stuff. If he knew we'd commandeered this sherry-wine, he'd have us on jankers for a year.

CHALKY: Arr. An' he'd be gurt right, too. I reckon we want to be hempstered for drinking this nobby muck. Give I a mug of natch any day. (*Takes manly swig from bottle*) . . . Look out!

(SCIPIO *and* KITTY *walk past, arms linked.* CHALKY, BERT *and* SPUD *leap up and salute, endeavouring to conceal the bottles behind their backs.*)

SCIPIO: (*gazing at* KITTY) Good evening, gentlemen. What are you drinking, there?

BERT: It's sherry-wine, sir. Bristol is famous for it.

SCIPIO: (*gazing at* KITTY) So it is. May I?

BERT: We've got an unopened bottle here, Major. (*Picks up bottle from ground and hands to* SCIPIO). Have it with our compliments. And on behalf of my colleagues I would like to make so bold as to congratulate the Major on a brilliant operation.

SCIPIO: (*gazing at* KITTY) Why thank you, Bert. Bought it in a shop, did you?

BERT: Err. Yes, that's right, sir.

SCIPIO: (*gazing at* KITTY) Marvellous. It is most gratifying to see life in the city returning to its normal business so rapidly, most gratifying. Thank you gentlemen.

(SCIPIO *and* KITTY *walk away*)

CHALKY: Lawks! Bought it? Never thought he'd fall for a stupid line like that. He must be going soft in the head.

BERT: He's just in love, that's all.

CHALKY: So who's his donah, then? She must be one of the locals.

BERT: One of the prisoners, so I hear. The Round-heads had loads of folks, men, women, children an' all, all cooped up in a football stadium. Some were loyal to the Coalition, but I think most of 'em were just there 'cos the Roundheads didn't like the look of 'em. By taking this city, we have liberated 'em.

SPUD: Now isn't that grand?

BERT: Yeah. They was made for each other, really, wasn't they?

CHALKY: How's that? You mean 'cos they're both blackamoors?

BERT: Stands to reason, dunnit? You and me wouldn't fancy one of them black women, any more than he'd fancy a white woman.

CHALKY: I can think of plenty of white women fancy him. Everywhere we've been, he's always had the offer of a warm bed for the night.

SPUD: Ah, no, though. That's not because he's black, it's because he's a beak, an officer.

BERT: No. What about that sergeant? The Yank military adviser he's always got next to 'im. He's black, too. He gets plenty of offers. Now you name me any woman of any colour who'd want to swive a white sergeant.

CHALKY: Ah, but that's not because he's a moor, or because he's a sergeant. It's because he's a Yank, see? Shagging a Yank is the nearest most women are going to get to actually going to America, innit?

III

WEDNESDAY, 20 AUGUST 2008

I wander thro' each charter'd street,
Near where the charter'd Thames does flow,
And mark in every face I meet
Marks of weakness, marks of woe.
      – William Blake, *London*

Jacob Malahide's electric torch flickered. He turned it off, then on again; the beam grew stronger, but after he had walked for a few seconds more, it pulsed, then died once more.

He stood still in the darkness of the tunnel.

In the blackness, he was aware for the first time of how many different noises there were Underground. Somewhere ahead of him, water dripped from the ceiling to a pool on the floor. Around his feet, rats scrabbled and chirruped. In the distance – before or behind him he could not tell – the roars and murmurs which always haunted the tunnels.

He had been Underground less than twenty-four hours, but already he hated it. Hell might be like this.

He had to walk about ½ a mile, then take the tunnel forking to his right. Further on, he would find the others. Even without his light, he could do it.

There was no need to be afeared.

He wouldn't have had to be here so soon if the chavie and the spack hadn't come looking for his help at Heycock's. If they hadn't stolen the Order's money, then led the rozzers to him, he could still be above ground. As it was, Elder Saltonstall had said that now the peelers were curious about him, it'd be best to join the others Underground.

The tunnel had once been part of the Underground Railway. It had been built long after Malahide's death, but was mostly unused since the Atom War. London County Council sometimes proposed restarting it, or some of it, but always failed for want of the money and the navvies.

Malahide stepped over one of the rails running through the centre of the tunnel, and groped for the wall on his right.

He would feel his way along to the place where he had to turn. There might be some life in his torch yet, but he would save it.

He began to shuffle slowly forward, arms held out in front in case there was something in the way. In places, the tunnel floor would be strewn with rubbish or masonry, or the rails were broken. In other places there were pot-holes.

Or the mortal remains of the dead.

Underground was said to be choked with corpses, skeletons with clothes and strips of flesh hanging from their cold, damp bones.

Many of the tunnels had fallen through in the wars, or from want of maintenance. Others had been flooded, though the London County Council spent a lot of money trying to keep them pumped dry to stop them damaging the foundations of buildings up above.

Most folk did not dare venture into the Underground. But others made it their home, like the bands of rampsmen who would dash up into the streets, prop their victims, then run back with their loot to their secret lairs and warrens Underground, where the police could not – or dared not – follow.

Malahide flashed the torch on; in the guttering beam he could see for only a few yards ahead. There seemed to be no obstruction. He quickened his pace a little.

There were others who just went Underground for shelter because it was cheaper than paying rent. Some retreads were actually reborn in the tunnels, and wandered them, thinking themselves in Purgatory.

Some tunnel-dwellers lived in the remains of the long carriages which had once moved through the tunnels, powered by electricity. You heard tales of vast palaces some had built down here, but that was probably just idle talk.

A cold breeze blew up behind him. There was a low wailing noise in the distance. The hairs on the back of his neck stood on end. It would be simple for a cove who knew the tunnels, was accustomed to walking through them without torches or lamps, to slip up behind him and wallop him out cold with a neddy.

Malahide quickened his pace, rubbing his fingers on the side of the wall, feeling the rail to his left with his leg.

Perhaps there were ghosts here. If there was any need for ghosts in a world where the dead returned to life, they would be Underground.

In the alehouses and ordinaries, around the hearths in netherskens, people told one another tales of the souls of the dead moving through the perfect darkness of the tunnels under London. You heard fewer tales of ghosts now that darkness up above had been banished by electric lights and the television. But sometimes old lags and young braggarts told of the eerie things they claimed to have seen.

When the Atom War started, many Londoners took to the tunnels, thinking they might afford safety from the bombs and the missiles. They did not, and folks said that the noises were the moans and screams of the tormented souls of all the thousands who died in the Atom War and of the radiation plague shortly thereafter.

Was it his imagining, or had the rats scratching and squeaking around his feet run away? He stopped. There was only the distant rumbling sound. It was probably just the noise of traffic in the street, or machinery in a factory up above.

One old woman had told him of seeing lights dancing through the tunnel, like the candles and tapers carried by revellers at some night-time summer rout at the Eagle Pleasure Gardens. Not souls, these flames dancing in the dark, not ghosts of anything human.

The lights were the Pest Maidens. The Angels of Plague.

Superstitious nonsense, it was. Like all superstition, it was probably Popish.

He stubbed his foot against something hard and stumbled forward. He scraped his hand on the wall, but managed to stop his fall by grabbing for the rail with his left hand. He turned his torch on the obstacle, but no light came. He probed at it with his foot. It seemed to be a small mound of rubble. Delicately, he clambered over it.

The floor on the other side seemed as smooth as before. He walked on, now a little faster than before, telling himself his eyes were growing accustomed to the gloom.

The Pest Maidens . . .

The rumbling behind him grew slightly louder, and changed to a lower pitch.

The wind. That was what it would be. He didn't know what manner of day it was up above. It was probably the wind entering the tunnels from several different directions, and blowing through them, playing them like vast organ-pipes.

The Pest Maidens appeared as little lights, orange or red or blue. They carried death from one victim to another. When they had completed their work, they emerged from the mouth of the corpse and travelled on their way, seeking a new body to enter.

The plague – the olden plague, the disease that killed thousands in the Middle Ages and in epidemics that swept London every few years thereafter – was a killer of the poor. It was the oiks' disease, the one that carried off honest working folk. It didn't touch the well fed, the well-to-do. The plague could well be the work of Catholics. Aye, if there was anything to the Pest Maiden story, it was like as not some sort of Romish sorcery.

The noise behind him grew louder, as though a huge beast was approaching him at speed. Malahide's right hand felt cold and sticky, whether with blood or sweat he could not tell.

He would have licked it to find out, but there was no time.

The hair on his head was now standing upright.

He had not brought a gun with him. He preferred his chiv.

He put his left hand to his back, and drew the knife from his belt.

A gust of cold air slapped him on the back. His trousers flapped against his leg.

The sound died down. Something more even and rhythmical remained.

Like a voice, muttering something over and again.

It was a voice. A woman's voice. Talking Latin.

His chest tightened, his balls rode up into his body. His head was dizzy for not breathing out.

He turned and looked behind him.

Nothing. No lights, no voices, no dancing skeletons, no Pest Maidens.

He breathed out, screwed his eyes shut, tried to calm himself.

The woman's voice was back, now louder.

He opened his eyes. A few feet behind him, a few feet above his head, was a small blue flame.

Jacob Malahide turned to try and run. He tripped on something and fell. He heard his knife clattering to the ground. He cushioned his fall with both hands. The torch in his left came to life once more, illuminating the face of a human skull, leering toothlessly inches from his own face.

GUY BOSWELL'S DIARY
WEDNESDAY, 20 AUGUST 2008

As I was about to go home this evening, Uncle Seamus (Sergeant O'Rourke) suggested to me that I ought to be keeping a diary. I told him I was and he said it was as well, since I had landed myself in the middle of a most interesting case which just might form an interesting chapter in my memoirs when, forty years hence, I retire from the Metropolitan Police heaped with civic honours.

I'm not sure I want to be a policeman for that long.

This afternoon, WDC Jenny Pearson and I were stooging about on the streets, acting as guardians of the public when Uncle Seamus pulled up in an unmarked car and told us both to get in.

All very hush-hush, says he, and drives us off, pulling up outside a big house in Baker Street. He told us go on in and go downstairs while he parked the car.

Beside the front door was a brass plaque announcing that this was the registered office of the Acme Import Co. Ltd, but the building appeared to be empty. In we went. Down no less than four flights of stairs we found a steel door with Constable Glyndwr standing at it clutching his frightful automatic shotgun and, with his funny moustaches, looking like a one-man barbarian horde.

'Local civil defence offices,' said Uncle S. appearing behind us and showing us into a huge room that was wonderfully cool after the heat on the streets. All over the walls there were huge maps of London and the South-east, diagrams of guns, posters telling you how to use gas-masks, that sort of thing. Along one wall was a narrow table with half a dozen different-coloured telephones on. There were a couple of filing-cabinets, a sink in one corner with a table beside it with an electric kettle, half a pint of milk, a few filthy tin mugs and a bag

of sugar. In the middle of the room was an immense table with all sorts of charts and bits of paper on it. There were chairs of every shape and size around the place and immense quantities of buff files and manila folders and bits of paper. The whole place had an overpowering reek of stale fag-smoke.

'Welcome to our little nest,' said Inspector Africanus, who presided over this subterranean kingdom from an upright chair at one corner of the table. In one hand he had a pint-pot of tea, in another a bundle of index-cards and one of his African cigarettes. On his face, just under his left eye, was a sizeable lump of sticking-plaster from where he got nicked by an arrow yesterday.

The Inspector bade us sit down while Glyndwr came in and busied himself making tea. Uncle Seamus produced a packet of thin arrowroot biscuits from somewhere.

'Smoke 'em if you've got 'em,' growled the Inspector. I got out my packet of Players Navy Cut, but when I caught poor Jenny looking appalled, I thought better of it. She doesn't smoke, and doesn't much like the smell of other people's smoke, so . . .

Glyndwr delivered the mugs of tea to one and all and sat down.

'Well then,' said the Inspector. 'I suppose you're wondering.'

Rather!

He explained that he, Uncle Seamus, Glyndwr, Jenny and myself are to be part of a very hush-hush operation, which is why we are to be based at this secret location underneath Baker Street. The building is owned by the government, and is one of a number of *local ops rooms for running things in time of war or civil emergency (fire, flood, earthquake, riot, that sort of thing). Apparently it's been here since the Hitler War and from the look of the place hasn't been used much since then.*

'We know that they, the Bulls, the Upright Men, are, or were, plotting some manner of mischief,' said the Inspector. 'It may be that they have already committed it and we are yet to taste its fruits. We know that the murder of Richard Haseldich and the loss of the treasure-chest may have thwarted or frustrated their plotting. We know that I was being followed when I went to see Inky.'

As if on cue, this immaculately dressed dwarf emerged from behind a curtain in a far corner of the room. There were a couple of camp-beds there and he had been resting. Inky had his arm in a sling. He really ought to be in hospital, but Inspector Africanus invited him to come and live under Baker Street with him for his own safety. Inky sleeps a lot because he's taking all sorts of pills for the pain of his wound. He pushed a chair over to the sink, climbed up and set about making himself a mug of chah.

The Inspector continued. Nobody has a clue who the would-be assassin was. A forensic examination of his longbow yielded nothing of interest. It was of a kind that any one of thousands of people who had lived between Plantagenet and Tudor times could have made from yew, catgut, goose-feathers and steel arrowheads that you can buy even in Woolworths. What with archery practice having been compulsory for every male of military age every Sunday for 400 years, it's still a very popular sport. There are national championships, with the finals shown on the television every autumn.

'I reckon,' said Inky, climbing on to a chair with his mug of tea to join us, 'that cully might have been this "specialist" I heard about, the cove they were supposed to be bringing in from the United States.'

'Possibly,' said the Inspector, 'but to the best of my knowledge archery is not a popular pastime among the Yanks.'

'Unless you count the redskins,' said Uncle Seamus.

'Do the American Indians manufacture their bows from yew? Do they shoot cloth-yard arrows with goose-feather flights?' asked the Inspector. Nobody had a ready answer.

Anyway, we have to find this chap, whoever he is, because he is part of the mystery of the chest of money in the basement. Then, the Inspector told us that the Reverend Harry Seymour, the missing vicar that Jenny and I were making inquiries about yesterday, might be part of the mystery as well.

This morning, the Inspector had a meeting with Commissioner Carpenter, who is chief of the Metropolitan and City of London Police. They decided that the best course would be to bring in every Upright Man – member of the John Bull Society – they could find for questioning. This might not solve the mystery of what they're up to, but it might disrupt whatever devilment they're planning. Commissioner Carpenter then telephoned the Home Secretary himself, who agreed that nothing must be allowed to disrupt Accession Day, and who offered us the use of this secret hideout. The Home Secretary wishes to demonstrate to the world that

Britain is now fit to take her rightful place in the world as a modern, civilized and democratic nation. All police forces throughout the country have been alerted and told to be on the lookout for bombs. Extra troops are being brought into the capital. But none of these measures can be sure of frustrating their knavery. That is up to us.

'The Commissioner accords us his unconditional support – for the time being,' said the Inspector. 'He has offered me unlimited resources. I told him that all I require, for now, is you four. And Inky, of course.

'You Boswell, because I know you are on our side, and because you are my 'prentice. So you have to do as you are told.

'You, Pearson, because you are the best pad in the force.'

'You, Glyndwr, because you frighten the wits out of me, so you ought to have a similar effect on the enemy. Besides, you are a sodomite. What do the Upright Men want to do with she-shirts?'

Glyndwr shrugged as if to say, 'Let them come for me, I'm ready!' Glyndwr a homosexual!? I never suspected that for a moment! And him so big and masculine in appearance, too! Just fancy!

'Burning, boss,' said O'Rourke. 'Or is it stoning? I think it depends which one of them you're listening to.'

Under that gruff exterior, Glyndwr is actually a rather nice man. I was later told that he lives with a gentleman-friend and the latter's bedridden mother and looks after the pair of them like any responsible head of household. He himself was telling me about how he wants to make a model of my Hurricane in *copper or brass. Apparently he does this for people he likes. Jenny Pearson told me that the day she was promoted to the Detective Branch he gave her a little rose he had made from copper. 'Beautiful, but hard. Right hard,' he said to her as he presented it. Until then, she said, she thought he'd hated her.*

'And I require you, O'Rourke, for your wisdom, experience and creative way with reasoning.

'You may be wondering why I asked you to meet me here. The reason is a distasteful one, but one which we must all confront. It is this; there may be several members of the force who sympathize with the Bulls, or perhaps even be ardent in support of them . . .'

What a rum lot these Bulls are!

He must have passed out. When he opened his eyes once more, a blue light flickered in front of his face.

Beside it was a piece of cardboard, with writing on it. Jacob Malahide was illiterate.

'Alms,' said a voice from above the sign. 'Alms for a poor penitent.'

He pushed himself upwards with his arms, then stood. The owner of the light and the card was dressed in rags and, from what he could see by the dim light, was a woman.

A lot of the Underground-dwellers were medievals, particularly from the time of the Black Death plague. They were drawn to this dark, cold place where many had died of the later radiation plague.

'You fucking Papist! You frightened the wits out of me! I've a good mind to speed you on your way to hell!' said Malahide. He knelt, his hand fumbling on the ground around him, trying to find his chiv.

There was a Popish sect of monks and nuns, mostly medievals, that made its members spend years living underground, never seeing the sun. They carried lanterns of blue glass, so what illumination they had – if they could scrounge the candles from anyone – was as faint as possible. They were not supposed to speak, except to ask for food or candles, or other needs.

Malahide's hand settled on something hard. He picked it up, then, realizing it was a bone from the skeleton he had fallen on, not his knife-handle, dropped it. 'Go on! Go to the Devil, you witless fucking ghoul!' he shouted.

It was penance for the sins they had committed in their last lives. Their friends would sometimes leave food for them at points of entry to Underground, but usually they had to feed themselves.

The woman's approach explained why the rats had all disappeared. They had run for their lives.

When the penitents emerged, maddened by darkness and lack of proper nourishment, the Papists venerated them as near-saints. The Underground ramp-gangs did not harm them. Indeed, to have a penitent living near you was seen as a blessing, a mark of grace.

He could not find his chiv, nor the useless torch. He would take the lantern of the mad crone and use it to find them. He turned upwards, only to see the blue light was gliding away, off in the direction from which he had come. The woman must be walking along the top of one of the rails.

He stood upright, groped for the wall, and walked on, feeling for the skeleton with his foot and stepping over it.

For several minutes, he could still hear the woman canting in Latin and English, asking her God to save the world from avarice, usury, worldliness, adultery, blasphemy, falsehood, luxury and irreligion.

GUY BOSWELL'S DIARY
WEDNESDAY, 20 AUGUST 2008

It's going to take me years to understand this place. Perhaps I never will.

So there we were in this underground ops room which we have borrowed to see out this case. What's wrong with working from Bow Street Station, like normal coppers? Because the John Bull Society might be watching us, and because, whisper who dares, certain police officers based at the station might be sympathetic to the Bulls. Jenny told me that quite a few rozzers are all for the Bulls' hell and damnation act, and think they should close every brothel and Catholic church, eject all women from paid employment and shoot every felon stone dead on the streets.

On the surface of it, the John Bull Society sounds so demented, such an insane cause, that you could hardly believe it has any supporters at all. But there's too much history here. History from people's past lives, and the history of this world since the time I died.

So . . . 1939–45, the Hitler War, which Britain won, with the help of Russia and America, but which left the country bankrupt and exhausted. Britain was gradually pulling back to a state of prosperity when, in 1962, the Americans and Russians, having long since stopped being allies, went to war, and in the ensuing exchange of immensely powerful bombs, obliterated much of Britain, Europe, Russia, parts of Asia and a lot of the eastern half of the United States. People died in their millions as a result of the bombings, or later from the after-effects of the bombs, what people here called the radiation plague.

That's when people who died prematurely in the past started coming back. Just materializing out of nowhere, usually near where they had died, for reasons which science cannot properly explain. In Britain, because the place was such a mess, the country collapsed into anarchy for several years. Eventually, you got the formation of gangs of bandits, or people grouping together for mutual protection – the feudal system all over again. Some of these gangs and groups, and the warlords that led them, started thinking about philosophy and politics round the campfire of long winter evenings. By the early 1970s, there were two loose federations; one of them Protestant and authoritarian, people who believed that they had been given a second chance at life to atone for their previous sins and get it right this time. The other faction, which became known as the Coalition, was less clear-cut in its views, but was more democratic and less inclined to religious dogma. If the Coalition was disadvantaged by its lack of clear ideology, it did have the huge advantage of material and military help from the Americans, who had scarcely recovered their own country, but who judged it strategically important to bring Britain back to a state of civilization as fast as possible.

The Feudal Wars finally ended with Coalition victory in 1978 and the Liberal Settlement, whereby Great

Britain and Northern Ireland is governed by a two-chamber parliament elected by everyone over twenty-one who can read and write, no feudal privileges of any sort, and a king who is just a figurehead. Apparently, the constituent assembly that drafted the Liberal Settlement, which is for all practical purposes a written constitution, had a huge row over whether or not women should be allowed the vote. In the end, the clause allowing female suffrage only got through by a single vote.

In the space of forty years there were two catastrophic wars followed by years of anarchy and low-level conflict, topped off by a rerun of the English Civil War. No progress in science or medicine, precious few great works of art or literature, just poverty, suffering and loss. After all that, people must have been relieved to have stability and peace finally. And so they were – most of them. But some of the Protestant die-hards, a lot of whom weren't even here during the Feudal Wars, hanker for what they call the Good Old Cause. Block-headed bigots, for the most part, they hate the Liberal Settlement, they hate all these Catholic medievals on the streets (the hatred is, of course, abundantly recipro-cated), hate the Catholic churches. They seem to believe that by making the country as Protestant as possible they will usher in a marvellous new era, perhaps even the return of Christ himself to live among the Godly. They will quote you Bible passages in support of their claims.

Blithering idiots, say I. Why can't they leave well enough alone?

All this was explained to me in baby-talk in our

underground cavern while Jenny and I waded through several files on known criminals who have used the long-bow as a weapon (there were plenty, but none matched the Inspector's description of our man).

Okay then, I said to Uncle Seamus, isn't this a matter for the Secret Service? The cloak and dagger boys ought to be dealing with this, surely? He just smiled and said there was no secret service. The Liberal Settlement was most emphatic on that point. Die-hard Puritans and Democrats alike all agree the state has no business spying on its citizens and so there is no secret service. To retreads, secret service equals secret police, the sort of thing they used to have in less enlightened Continental tyrannies. To people from my time, I suppose the idea conjures up images of the Gestapo, too.

So what are they up to? We don't know. Murder and inconvenience to the public, most likely. They're probably not influential enough to overthrow the State, but they might be able to raise the mob. The Inspector looked over at me while someone at the other end of the phone was keeping him waiting. 'The Bulls are trying to create an atmosphere of hysteria and apprehensiveness among the oiks – Boswell, you will please take note that rozzers are not supposed to call people oiks.' It's the standard pejorative for the lower classes. In this world you're either a nob or an oik.

Nice to see the English class-system has been simplified!

We may presume that they will try and stage marches during the Accession Day parades. They may well also try and plant bombs, or assassinate prominent public figures. Apparently they have planted bombs before, *usually in Jewish synagogues or Catholic churches. And a young Bull rejoicing in the name of Arise Hampson (a retread seventeenth-century Puritan) was just the other day convicted of killing two children in Manchester and trying to make it look like some bizarre Jewish ritual slaughter. He will almost certainly be hanged for this.*

How many Bulls are there? Sorry, we haven't a clue. If we had a secret service, then perhaps we would know. But we don't. Uncle Seamus reckons there are hundreds of active supporters in London, and tens of thousands of sympathizers.

Do they have any influential supporters, such as members of parliament? Nobody who'd admit to it, apparently. This is because they're regarded as the lunatic fringe, rather like Mosley and his Blackshirts in my day. Except that where Mosley got his money from Mussolini, the Bulls make their money from extortion, prostitution, drugs and illegal gaming. Nice people!

So why haven't they been rounded up and flung into the chokey before now? Because it's difficult to catch them red-handed, or amass evidence against them. People are too afraid of them to testify against them in court.

Inspector Africanus telephoned various other police stations around London, telling them to arrest so-and-so, or keep an eye on someone else. By the early evening, all these stations were calling him back saying that the various individuals they were supposed to be bringing in for questioning couldn't be found. All the Upright Men in London, it seems, have gone to ground.

'What a revoltin' development,' Jenny Pearson said in a funny American voice.

At 9 p.m. the Inspector told us all to go home and get some rest and get back in again by seven tomorrow morning. He and Inky were going to stay there and wait by the phones in case of further developments.

Sir Digby asked me yesterday to invite the Inspector over for dinner tomorrow evening. He is most eager to meet my boss, the celebrated thief-taker. I imagined the Inspector would say he was far too busy at the moment, but he said he would be delighted to come. A bit like Sir Francis Drake finishing his game of bowls, I suppose.

Jacob Malahide pulled out his wiper and blew his nose. The snot was heavily streaked with black soot from the petrol-driven generator making the electricity to run the lights and the radio.

Sometimes they shut off the generator, to save petrol and to let the draughts coming through the tunnels clear the air.

There were about forty of them camped here beneath the streets of London. Somewhere up above them was the Tottenham Court Road.

Moving in here had been in the plan, though Malahide had had to come down earlier than anticipated to steer clear of the rozzers.

This freezing, damp hole in the ground was the place from which England would be reconquered from Satan. Babylon would have hard work of it to find them here, and they could travel around the city, appearing overground in a thousand different places, then disappear once more as easy as a trollop could pick a boy's pocket.

They were in what had once been a port for the Underground trains. The rails ran along in a trough to one side of them, and they were encamped on a broad, flat part of the room. Behind them were other rooms and staircases, but Elder Lilley insisted they all stay within sight of one another, lest they be attacked by rozzers or rampsmen. The others had already driven off a ramp gang. With the flash American weapons that Ethan Miller had brought in with him, it had been a walkover.

Malahide stood up and rubbed his arse, which had been numbed by the cold, hard floor. Around him, men sat or lay on the mattresses they had brought with them. They chattered in low voices, or smoked pipes and cigarettes, only adding to the thick, unbreathable atmosphere. Some, those who had found places under the few light-bulbs, read their scriptures.

All were sound Protestant men, ready to do what must be done for the return of the Lord. A few, like Ethan Miller, were hereborns, but most were retreads from the seventeenth and eighteenth centuries. Those who had fought against Charles I and his evil Papist advisers in the Civil War were especially ardent for the cause. Many of the New Model Army who had survived the Civil War had been convinced at the time that the Lord was about to return in judgement there and then.

Each man had left his work and family to be here. Each had his task to perform in the coming days. A small army, waiting for the command to go into action. Waiting for the elders to pass on their instructions from the Almighty himself . . .

Malahide walked along the platform. Towards the far end, two men worked the printing-machine they had brought for making the leaflets and broadsides which Elder Saltonstall had said were so important to their success. Earlier, Malahide had been to the surface to give bundles of leaflets to Brethren to hand around. They had to be careful. The rozzers seemed to be looking for every known Upright Man in London.

The next time, he would carry spare batteries for the torch. Aye, and a pistol.

Near the press, beside where Elder Saltonstall sat, Seymour lay on a mattress, his hands bound in front of him. From all he had heard of him in his last life, he had imagined that Seymour would be the sickly kind, but he was nothing of the sort. He was a tough, stern-looking youngster in his late twenties. Easily as tough as his father.

Not everyone here knew who Seymour really was, and Malahide was under strict orders not to tell. Seymour himself had shown no inclination to reveal his true name, and made it plain that though he was a convinced Protestant, he wanted nothing to do with the Society's plans.

Well, they had him all secure here now. He had no choice.

Jacob Malahide knew how to bend Seymour to doing God's will, if the elders would but let him try. The man was obstinate enough, but nobody could hold out for ever. He was acquainted with the man from his interfering in Covent Garden, and from taking him from his house the other morning. At first he had resisted and rained curses down on them, then, when he knew they had him, he had turned sullen.

Ethan Miller sat next to Seymour, surrounded by half a dozen guns, or parts of guns. 'Okay there, Brother Jacob?' he said. Malahide nodded.

219

Malahide was not sure of Miller. The man was from a place called Georgia in the United States, and was still on his first life. Miller was expert in the use of guns and explosives, and said he was a good Christian. But Malahide knew the elders had had to promise to pay him a shedload of tin for coming to help. If he was a good Christian man, why did he need quid pro quo? Miller was not to be trusted. How could a man who was not a retread truly understand the great mystery of God's purpose in giving people a second chance to lead a more righteous life?

Well, some of the money buried in Lilley's house was supposed to pay Ethan Miller. When Miller had done his work he would find there was nothing to pay him with.

But by then, no free-born Englishman would have any need of money.

'Hey, Jacob take a look at this,' said Miller, jerking his head backwards. 'The poster. Behind me.'

Inside a wooden frame, with a thick covering of dust and smuts, there was a picture of a man in white robes standing in a yellow landscape. Sand?

'If I was superstitious, my friend, I should say that was a pretty bad omen, don't you think?'

Malahide shook his head.

'Oh I see,' said Miller. 'You can't read, can you? It's an advertisement. It's been here since before the Atom War. It's for a movie. Lawrence of Arabia. It's about Lawrence's adventures in his first life. Like I said, a bad sign if you're superstitious, Lawrence, the architect of the Liberal Settlement looking over us like that.'

'On the contrary, Brother Miller. It means he is

looking on, but he is helpless to prevent us from doing the Lord's work.' Jacob Malahide was pleased with himself. Just because a man cannot read does not mean he is without wit.

Elders Lilley and Saltonstall arrived and marched into one of the small rooms at the back of the platform for a private parley.

Malahide cadged a cigarette from one of the Brethren. It was thought unseemly for a true Upright Man to take tobacco, but many did so.

Elder Saltonstall's voice grew louder behind the thin door. 'What on Earth possessed you, man? Are you insane? You know how much of our work hangs on the Yank! And you sent Miller out after the blackbird policeman to *kill* him? Why did you not simply send a letter to the Metropolitan Police giving full account of our designs?'

'What of it?' said Lilley in return. 'It helps our cause to engender fear and disruption.'

'Can you not see the risk!' said Saltonstall. 'You had Miller put himself at risk of captivity. If he had been caught, we should now be in difficulties. Furthermore, Babylon now knows that we are about great work. Were it not for your adventuring, they should simply have a murder and a disappearance.'

'I sought the Lord's guidance while I was unable to seek yours,' said Lilley. 'The Almighty made it clear to me the police are not wholly stupid. The police-man was meeting an informer. Miller was right to try and kill them both. They might yet frustrate our designs.'

'So they might. And I cannot fathom why Miller

decided to try and despatch them with a longbow. Such foolishness!'

'Miller assures me that he is an expert with the English longbow and that he has practised at the butts for many years. He says it was an appropriate weapon in the circumstances as using a gun would attract more attention. It would make more noise and it would be hard to conceal. A man can walk through London with a longbow and attract no notice at all. Archery is the pastime of thousands.'

'I think it best for you to remain here. Do not return to your house,' Saltonstall said at length, 'the rozzers will be seeking us both. Go up for your preaching engagements only. Take some men with you. Ensure you are not followed. Or arrested.'

The door opened. Malahide instinctively took a step sideways. The two elders strode out, looking like thunder.

'Brethren,' said Elder Saltonstall, 'hear me for a moment . . .' In the gloom, men stood, or put down what they had been doing, and gathered around. Seymour and Miller ignored them, the latter preoccupied with a screwdriver and a small piece of machinery. Seymour lay on his side.

'As some of you may know,' said Saltonstall, 'we have suffered a reverse of late. A great portion of the money which has been tithed to the Order in recent years was stolen from us.'

Some of the men murmured.

'We had taken the tithes,' said the Elder, 'and converted them into gold and silver, for all but a fool can apprehend that in the times of tribulation to come, the paper money of the Liberal Settlement will only be fit for us to wipe our arses with.'

Some laughed, others said 'Amen!'

'The only money of lasting value is the gold, silver and precious stones God alone can create, not the worthless paper scrip that man creates. Our plans have of necessity been altered. Elder Lilley and myself, Brother Malahide and some of the others among you, have been ordered here more early than we had wished, but with God's will we shall still triumph.'

'To work, then,' said Lilley. 'Brother Miller, if you please.'

Miller grinned, and leapt to his feet without the use of his arms. He scooped up a small black box the size of a telephone.

'Plastic explosive,' he said, throwing it into the air and catching it once more. 'I've made a dozen of these little babies, infernal machines, you might say. They can be operated by radio from here. All you have to do, brothers, is plant them around the town.'

Malahide cursed quietly to himself. More tramping around the tunnels braving ramp gangs and mad Popish crones with blue lamps.

'I shall tell you where to place them,' said Elder Lilley.

Seymour coughed loudly.

'Patience, brethren,' said Saltonstall smiling. 'In three days' time, it will be Accession Day. The day on which all our plans come to fruition. We shall not need to remain here a moment longer. We will soon by the grace of God, emerge from this stinking gloom into the brightness of his everlasting light. Now let us pray . . .'

THINGS REMEMBERED (3)

DETECTIVE SERGEANT SCIPIO AFRICANUS

HENBURY CHURCHYARD, NEAR BRISTOL, AUGUST 1995

He left the others in a nearby field. Kitty had spread out a rug and opened the picnic-basket and was distributing sandwiches, tomatoes, boiled eggs and chicken-limbs. The ravenous brood fell on the food as though they had never eaten before.

He had taken a cheese sandwich and wandered off alone.

The church had fallen into disuse, the graveyard overgrown, the stones were all weathered and broken.

They had seven children, three of their own and four adopted. There had been no hope of taking a holiday this year on his modest salary, but then he had bumped into one of his veterans in the street. Veterans you met often enough. The officers would politely ask how he was doing, slap him on the back and then roar off in their big cars, or dip through the doorways of their ministries or clubs, never inviting him in. They had all done very nicely for themselves. The other ranks were different; they really were interested (though one or two made their excuses and disappeared when they found he was a rozzer), and were keen to tell him how they were getting along. Such a one had been Ernest 'Chalky' White, a small, thick-sinewed cove who had been in one of the rifle companies of the Fifth Mechanized.

He barely remembered the man, who had accosted him in the street a month ago. Said he was up in London on business. Now he ran a very successful building firm in Bristol, and invited – insisted – Scipio and his family avail themselves of his holiday-house in Weston-Super-Mare. ('Bit o' sea-air'll do thee and your nippers a power of good. I would think it a great honour, sir, if you would make my house your own. Me an' all the lads, we owes you, sir. For lookin' arter us so well, aye, an' for makin' men of us.')

Nonsense, but honest, heartfelt nonsense. The two of them had stood in the street for an hour talking about what their comrades were up to. That evening he had gone home and heard on the radio about General Lawrence. After the Russians destroyed Tel Aviv during the Atom War, Israel had been overrun by her Arab neighbours. Lawrence, who had many friends among the Arabs, had gone out to the Middle East to try to help make some sort of settlement, but had failed. He had stayed on there anyway and resumed his previous calling as an archaeologist. But of course with retreads popping up all over the place who might have been characters out of the Bible, there were a lot of religious zealots out there of every description. Depending on which version of the story you believed, Lawrence had been shot by Jewish fanatics objecting to his digging in a particular place, or he was shot by an American

Protestant fundamentalist in an argument over . . . well, over nothing important.

Lawrence dead. It was three months ago now, and he still could not believe it. Many others had the same problem. He remembered how even Glyndwr had been in tears at the station the morning after.

So then . . . where was he to start looking for his grave? He knew that it would be here somewhere, but did not know exactly where. The graveyard was not big, but the weeds and grass were so abundant he could spend the afternoon here and find nothing.

He decided to search systematically, starting with the path towards the main door of the church.

So they had all come to Weston for a week. Chalky's house was an enormous thing on a hill overlooking the sea. Chalky had left a cook and a servant to look after them. The kids were having a wonderful time, building sandcastles on the beach, devouring the enormous meals that Mrs Boucher cooked for them, and being fussed over by everyone they met. The African family was a curiosity everywhere it went. Scipio and Kitty were treated with varying degrees of contempt, mistrust and (generally) kindness, but everyone took a shine to the children. Women would congratulate them (often rather patronizingly) on how well presented the kids were, how well behaved, how simply *adorable*. When they got home, their piggy-banks would bulge with all the tanners and threepenny-bits that had been bestowed on them by doting old biddies. When they had to go back the day after tomorrow, the younger ones would cry bitter tears. Ah well, as hard knocks went, there could be worse.

He moved the grass around one stone aside with his foot. The occupant had died in eighteen something-or-other.

It had been Kitty's idea to take the bus to Bristol, and then to Henbury. She had wanted to show the children something of their parents' earlier lives. The city that he had freed from the Roundheads, the place where she herself had been held captive until her knight had come to her rescue. They had spent a couple of hours looking around the city, which seemed industrious but dull, before Kitty had spotted a bus bound for Henbury. She had insisted that they get on it.

Henbury itself was a shadow of the village it had once been. Most of the houses were unoccupied, though all the fields were evidently being worked. There were quite a few cows around, too. It was good land, but the population, as with so much of England, was much smaller than it had once been.

He crouched and pushed aside the grass in front of another grey stone. The inscription was almost completely weathered away, but the date was wrong.

Someone was behind him. He turned. John Zachary, his eldest son, an angry and intelligent seventeen-year-old, stood there, unsure of himself.

'Hello,' he said.

'Hi there,' John nodded in greeting.

The boy had been awkward and left out of things so far. Too old to build sandcastles, too unsure of himself to be chasing girls along the seafront at Weston, too clever to be content while he was becoming a man, impatient with everything. He was only standing here now because his mother had told him to. Relations between father and son were difficult, communication almost impossible.

'So whatcha doin' here?' he asked. John and his friends were obsessed with everything American. They especially loved the cop and thriller films from Hollywood, especially the violent, cynical stuff that had come out in the last few years to take the place of the happy, escapist fantasies that had been made to help people forget the miseries of recent decades. A few months ago he had taken John to the local Gaumont to see a thing called *Shaft*. It was one of his periodic, doomed attempts to open a channel of communication to his son. The film starred a cove named Will Smith as a shrewd, nattily dressed private detective in the booming, corrupt city of New York, now being rebuilt after its destruction in the Atom War. John had clearly loved it, not least because the hero was black. Scipio had hated it, thinking it mindless and silly. They had walked home again afterwards in silence.

'Looking for my grave.'

John shook his head in disdain. 'Say what?' John and his pals used a lot of American expressions. It was not affectation, but it sounded queer all the same.

'Son . . .' he searched for an answer. None came. 'I am buggered if I know.'

John smiled, then burst out laughing. It was probably the first time he had ever heard his father swear.

'You want some help?'

'Be my guest.'

John turned to the stone next to him, to the right of the path, and stamped down some nettles with his foot. Scipio moved on to the next one.

'Father,' said John a moment later. 'I think we got somethin' here.'

The stone was worn, but you could still clearly make out the words on it. John read: 'HERE Lieth the Body of SCIPIO AFRICANUS Negro Servant to ye Right Honourable Charles William Earl of Suffolk and Bradon who died ye 21st December 1720 Aged 18 Years.'

There was more. His nibs had had the masons carve:

> I who was Born a PAGAN and a SLAVE
> Now Sweetly Sleep a CHRISTIAN in my Grave
> What tho my hue was dark my SAVIORS sight
> Shall Change this darkness into radiant light
> Such grace to me my Lord on earth has given
> To recommend me to my Lord in heaven
> Whose glorious second coming here I wait
> With saints and Angels Him to celebrate

Scipio smiled and shook his head.

'What's so funny, Father? This is the scene of a crime. It's nauseating!'

'How so, son?'

'Well, they took you like they took millions. They took a child from his home in Africa, enslaved him, gave him a new name that was some lousy joke from their own white man's history, and then forced you to become a Christian. Don't that made you angry? It makes me madder than I can say.'

Scipio's first instinct was to correct the boy's lazy grammar, to explain how those who could not or would not use language properly rendered themselves power-less. Instead, he took off his jacket and spread it on the

229

ground, hitched up his trousers and sat down.

'I was treated in the same way as they would have treated a lap-dog, which is to say with affection and condescension, but as a dog nonetheless. If they had despised me completely, they would not have gone to the expense of this comparatively grand memorial.'

John took off his own jacket, dropped it to the ground and sat next to him. 'Why'd you keep that name?'

'Because I do not remember my original one. What else should I call myself? Fred Smith? I carry my joke-name as a badge, John. It tells me who I am and from whence I come. You carry it as well.'

'Don't you think it's shameful?'

Do you think it shameful, John? Are you ashamed of your father?

'John, if I knew the name I was given by my parents in Africa, I would use it. But I do not, and I doubt any of us shall ever find it out. So changing our name to anything else would be shameful. I was a slave – oh, they gave me a notional freedom before I died, but I was a slave for all that – and in this life I fought in a war that I hope means no one in this country will ever be enslaved again. I have fought, many would say honourably, to prevent slavery in this country. But I cannot and will not deny the fact of my slavery.'

'So tell me, do you hate the people who enslaved us?'

'Us?'

'Yes, Dad, us. Our people.'

Dad? The boy uses the word almost affectionately. This is too confusing.

'No, I do not hate them. They were acting according to their nature. You cannot hate the cat for hunting mice and birds. You cannot hate the big fish that eats smaller ones. These people were money-loving men who managed to convince themselves that enslaving fellow human beings was a proper and fair thing to do. There are people like that in every land at every time. Aye, they live in Africa, too. It ain't useful to hate 'em. Distrust them, be on your guard against them, watch them like hawks, and fight them if you have to, but don't hate, John. Hate will eat you up and destroy your health and happiness – it will enslave you – just as surely as a merchant with a gun and a whip will.'

John nodded. 'I can see that. I understand, yeah.'

'An American I once knew told me that when I was younger. An American of African descent – your mother and I have spoken to you of him before, because we named you in his honour. He said the most important thing is to be proud of what you are. That is American thinking, of course. The Englishman would say that the best thing is to be pleased with yourself.'

John looked him direct in the eye. It startled Scipio to realize how the boy usually avoided looking at him straight. Now the look was eager, greedy even. 'How do you do that? Be proud or pleased, I mean.'

'By ensuring that you always do what is right, no matter how unpleasant or inconvenient it is. By looking at yourself in the mirror each morning and asking if this is a man whom you can respect. That is how Jayzee put it. But as I say, my thinking is more English. Each morning as I shave I venture a smile at the man in the mirror. If he smiles back, then things are well enough with me.'

'So *that's* when you smile! I figured you must do it sometime.'

Scipio gently cuffed the lad's head. 'Insolent whelp! I'll have you know that back in the days before tobacco turned my teeth yellow, the ladies would frequently comment upon the winning nature of my smile.'

'This guy Jayzee, he sounds like a good man.'

'He is. He was my comrade in the Feudal Wars, then he returned to America where he gave up soldiering and became a musician. Do you know what jazz is?'

John laughed and shook his head. 'The man asks me if I know what jazz is!'

'You are familiar with this jazz nonsense then?'

'It matters to me about as much as life itself.'

'Oh. I am sorry. Truly I am.'

He leaned forward to fumble in the pocket of his jacket for cigarettes and matches. Suddenly, getting a great big hit of smoke into his lungs felt like the most important thing in the world, as though a little tube of tobacco-filled paper would somehow save him from drowning in guilt.

'Sometimes,' he said, pulling out his silver cigarette-case and a box of Swans, 'I get so bound up in the job, and all the rest of the family that I fail to notice things.'

'Give us a smoke, Dad . . .'

'You are too young,' he said, but offered John a cigarette anyway. 'They will ruin your health,' he added, striking a match and offering it to him before lighting his own.

'Thanks,' said John, puffing out smoke-rings. This was far from his first cigarette.

'Do not let your mother see you smoking.'

Of course he should have known that jazz music was John's great passion. Often enough he had come in late from work to hear the transistor radio on in his room late at night, the only time of day when the BBC Home Service or Light Programme would cater for such a small audience. Of course he should have noticed the boy leaving the house on Saturday afternoons with his trumpet to go and practise with his friends. He had merely assumed that John was in an orchestra, or the church temperance band, or something. And he was supposed to be a rozzer, an observer.

'This friend of yours,' said John. 'I've just realized. He's John Z. Washington, isn't he?'

'Yes. You know of him?'

'Dad, the man is a genius! He's one of the greatest pianists who ever lived! Wow! All these years I never thought to ask about him. I just heard you and Mother mention him occasionally, and I was thinking he was just a soldier. Gee! I really should talk to you more.'

'No, son. I should talk to you more.'

'So tell me about him. Do you ever hear from him?'

'Certainly. We exchange letters and Christmas cards. In his last letter he said he was becoming very prosperous. He said that he was now being insulted in places where the average Negro could never hope to be insulted.'

'John Z. Washington,' said John, shaking his head in wonder. 'Well, you're going to have to ask the guy to send me some of his records. I hear them on the radio, but you can't buy them here, or if you can you need to be a millionaire.'

'I have several already,' said Scipio. 'He sends them

to me, but I do not listen to them as I own I neither like nor understand the music. They are yours for the taking.'

'Really? Do you have the latest one? It's called 'A Night in Tunisia' – Charlie Parker tune made famous by Dizzy Gillespie. Washington's cover of it is the greatest thing you ever heard!'

'I have never heard of these people. Tell me more about them.'

'First thing you have to know, Dad, is that they're Americans. But they're *African* Americans. That matters. It matters to them and to me. It also matters,' he pointed towards Scipio's grave with the butt of his cigarette, 'to that guy down there. I want to be like Parker and Gillespie and Washington, but I want to make African *British* music.'

'Go on . . .' said Scipio. 'Tell me more.'

IV

THURSDAY, 21 AUGUST 2008

If all the good people were clever,
And all clever people were good,
The world would be nicer than ever
We thought that it possibly could.
– Dame Elizabeth Wordsworth, *Good and Clever*, 1890

Scipio sipped at his brandy and puffed on a very fine cheroot as he looked at his watch. Just after ten. He would have to get back to Baker Street before midnight to let Uncle Seamus get some sleep.

He could happily stay here half the night and get pleasantly hammered on Sir Digby's wine, but, he ruefully reflected, he was getting old. Back in the 1980s and even the 1990s, he could knock back four or five bottles of sack in an evening and still be fit (just) for duty the following morning.

Old Sir Digby seemed a decent enough cove, and had seemed genuinely flattered that the celebrated Inspector Scipio had 'deigned to grace his humble table'.

There had been nothing humble about it, unless you counted the modest number of people here. At the head of the table sat Sir Digby, with Scipio next to him. Next to Sir Digby on the other side was Miss Athene Rutherford, a remarkable old bird who was, he understood, something big in the Women's Royal Voluntary Service and who shared some or other of Sir Digby's scientific enthusiasms. Next to Scipio sat Lady Lovejoy and opposite her was Boswell, eager to please as ever. The Lovejoys' daughter and her companion had eaten with them, but then excused themselves to go and watch something on the television.

'And what about public hangings, Inspector, what-what? Do you not believe it would serve as a better disincentive to wickedness if the criminal classes were every week to witness the ostentatious annihilation of one or two of their number? What say you?'

Sir Digby Lovejoy was one of those sprightly old (old? He probably only had a couple of years on Scipio) coves who was interested in everything. He and Miss Rutherford had spent the entire evening grilling him on every conceivable matter.

'Dead against 'em,' he said.

'But Inspector,' said Lady Lovejoy. 'Would you not agree that justice must be seen to be done? Will not the lower orders benefit from the example of seeing the ultimate penalty being exacted from criminals?'

Lower orders? He had the measure of her Ladyship. High Victorian, muscular Christian, wogs-start-at-Calais type. Unpleasant side made up for by a powerful sense of duty and propriety. Probably capable of kindness, though not to the likes of him. He'd seen the look on her face when Boswell had brought him in earlier. She did not much relish the notion of sharing her table with a thief-taker. Her husband, on the other hand, had been the epitome of civility.

'Lady Lovejoy,' he said slowly. 'I have in my time attended two public hangings. The first, that of the Duke of Monmouth, I believe was a political necessity. People needed to see that the leader of the Roundhead faction in the Feudal Wars was truly dead in order to ensure the peace. The second hanging, which occurred many years ago, before it was decided to hold them within the privacy of prison precincts, was a most instructive occasion. I was by then a Sergeant of Detective Police – I had joined at this rank in consideration of my service in the wars – and the older officer who accompanied me advised me that at the moment of execution, I should not watch the felon, but rather look at the faces of those witnessing the event. It was most instructive. The pleasure which the mob, aye, and educated folk too, derive from public executions ain't wholesome. Public hangings make savages' – here he directed his eyes at Lady Lovejoy – 'of all of us.'

The dinner had been pleasantly untraditional. Given that it was August, they had simply helped themselves to a salmagundi and assorted cold plates. There had been jugs of delicious white wine from Australia and New Zealand, some excellent fruit pies and tarts and iced cream.

'So you are opposed to public executions as they are incompatible with human dignity, eh?'

'Yes, Sir Digby, though that would not be my primary reason.'

It was a very handsome house, too. A Victorian villa with plenty of rooms and enough of its own grounds for a huge lawn, tennis courts and more. The old bloke had made his money years back in government contracts for booklets, pamphlets and comics about personal and public hygiene. The dining-room was large, with two immense bay windows looking out on to well-tended flowerbeds.

'Then why, in Heaven's name, man?'

'Because hangings bring out enormous crowds, and where you get crowds you get crime, and where you get crime, I get paperwork, which I greatly resent. When the eyes of everyone in a jostling crowd are fixed on the criminal being turned off, pickpockets can make hay. Where the felon is especially popular or especially reviled, the crowd competes for the best position, or throws refuse, and is generally unruly. It all creates work for us poor rozzers, Sir Digby. So if we are going to hang 'em – and I can think of a very few cases where hanging ever served any useful purpose – then do it in private, say I.'

He had half expected the womenfolk to retire after the meal had finished, leaving the chaps to their drink and good-fellowship, but it had become quite clear that this was one practice that Lady Lovejoy would not tolerate.

'Tell me, Inspector,' said Miss Rutherford, 'do you or your colleagues ever have much cause to go Underground?'

'I am sorry?'

Miss Rutherford was a heavily built (not really fat) woman in her late fifties. She wore bulky, shapeless clothes and had one of those blue rinse hairstyles that women of a certain age liked. She was ruthless, eccentric and brooked no nonsense of any sort, which presumably made her very good at whatever it was she did to help people through the WRVS.

Dirty hands, too. Deeply ingrained oil, or soot or something. Mechanic's hands.

'Inspector, as I am sure you know, there are two Londons, that which exists overground, at pavement level and above, and that which exists Underground. The population, I own, is not as large Underground, but it is considerable.'

He realized now that he had heard of Miss Rutherford before, but had never met her. 'You are the leader of that famous gang of fearless ladies who travel around beneath our streets looking for newly arrived retreads and rescuing them.'

'At your service, Inspector.'

'Have you had any interesting cases recently?'

'Why, they're all interesting! What most people fail to realize is exactly how much of underground London there is. There's the old sewer-trams – the Underground Railway – then there are the sewers and electrical workings, not to mention all the shelters that the Government built to protect people from air-raids during the Hitler War. Some of those, such as the ones at Clapham or Tottenham Court Road are big enough to hold eight thousand people. And there are all manner of other, smaller works as well, you know.'

'Indeed,' he said non-committally, thinking of his own current home in a civil defence bunker under Baker Street and how he should be getting back there soon. He had only come here in the first place for the change of scenery. Sometimes, one could worry away at a case and come up with no answers. It often helped to go off and do something else. Then sometimes – just sometimes – the answer would be staring you in the face when you got back on the job.

He permitted one of the servants to pour him one last glass of brandy. Any more and his head would be no good for anything.

Kitty and the kids had gone away to visit one of her friends in Bognor for the week. This was the one week of the year he could have arrived home completely stotious every night and she wouldn't have been there to nag him about it.

Oh well.

Another servant came in with a taper and lit the candles on the five sets of silver candelabra which ran the length of the dining-table.

'Truly, Boswell, you should try it,' Sir Digby was saying. 'How else do you think that schoolmasters live so long? Aye, or what about the Roman Catholic nuns? Eh? Eh? They live a plaguey long time, don't they?'

Sir Digby had earlier been telling them all about his belief that one might prolong one's life by daily inhaling the breath of virgins. The start of dinner had been delayed while he had insisted upon drinking in the exhalations of the Misses Lovejoy and Bright (who both looked fearfully embarrassed) for a full five minutes.

Sir Digby's daughter and her friend might well be virgins, but given their startling good looks and easy sociability, Scipio would not have bet more than a groat upon it. Nowadays, women could get these pills which made conception all but impossible. They were only supposed to be available to married women, but in practice, doctors, like coppers, had better things to do with their time than regulate the morals of others. Once women could control precisely when they had children, they would be less dependent on men than before and the world would be a very different place. Probably a better one.

'It seems a very, ah, plausible thesis, Sir Digby,' replied Boswell, trying to restrain himself from laughing.

'Now then, Boswell,' said Sir Digby, raising his voice a little to silence everyone else's chatter. 'You have been here a couple of weeks now. I would be most interested to hear your beliefs as to why you are here. Why were all of us – you, the Inspector, Miss Rutherford, my dear lady wife and myself – why were we and millions of others reborn, what-what?'

Miss Rutherford caught Scipio's eye and winked, then made a slight nod in Lady Lovejoy's direction, as though to say, 'We're going to have some fireworks in a moment.'

Boswell looked a little flustered. He knew his host was a man of science (albeit of a bizarre seventeenth-century flavour – no twentieth-century scientist would give a moment's thought to the alleged life-enhancing properties of virgins' breath), but he also knew that his hostess was a devout Anglican. He was in a spot.

'I believe it possible Sir Digby,' he ventured, 'to reconcile the accounts of Christians who say we are given a second chance at a more righteous life, and the views of men of learning who say there is an empirical explanation. Why should religion and science be incompatible?'

'Ha!' barked Miss Rutherford. 'You're a true diplomatist, young man. Should go into politics.'

'You see,' said Sir Digby, 'religion and science might be compatible, but not here they ain't. Not in our England of 2008. Religion and science here are mortal enemies. On the one side, superstition, credulity, intolerance; on the other, empirical observation, rationalism and a belief in the perfectibility of the world.'

'Did not Saint Augustine say that Christians must believe in the perfectibility of man?' asked Scipio. Scientists could be just as bigoted and intolerant as God-botherers. Yes, people throughout history had killed in the name of their gods, but it had taken scientists to devise atom bombs.

'Yes, Inspector,' said Lady Lovejoy, 'Christians do believe that human nature under God can be brought to perfection. If one does not believe such a thing, then one might as well give up living. You will please forgive my husband. He has taken a few glasses of wine and now that he has an audience he has decided to clamber on to his hobby-horse.'

Sir Digby bowed his head towards his wife and said, 'Neigh!'

Scipio could read individuals, but couples were much harder. It was possible that Sir Digby and his wife hated one another, but equally likely that they were locked by bonds of love and interdependence. The truth was likely somewhere between the two.

'Radiation, Boswell, radiation is the agency of our rebirth,' said Sir Digby, lighting himself a cheroot from one of the candles on the table. 'Tell me, Inspector, your last life was in eighteenth-century Bristol. Did you ever visit the nearby resort of Bath?'

'Yes, several times.'

'And why did this small city become such a popular resort, Inspector?'

'Why, for the waters of course. People believed – still

believe – that by drinking or bathing in the mineral waters from deep below the city, they can cure all manner of ailments.'

'Precisely,' said Sir Digby. 'The waters spring up from deep in the ground, they taste sulphurous and vile, and for want of decent public sanitation people nowadays account them pestilential. And yet since the long-distant day on which they cured King Bladud of his leprosy, people have gone to Bath for their health. Are you aware, Inspector, Mr Boswell, that the waters are radioactive?'

'I was not,' said Boswell.

'Well!' said Sir Digby, 'D'ye not see it, man? Men considered the waters beneficial to health. In a like manner, I am certain, the great effusion of radiation during the Atom War, caused the reappearance of the dead from previous ages.'

'A fascinating thesis, Sir Digby,' said Boswell evenly.

Sir Digby expounded at the gallop. 'There is invisible atomic activity all around us. We retreads, those who have already died and return here with our memories of our past lives intact, we are almost immune to the radiation sickness caused by the Atom War. It is also important to note that no retread has arrived here over the age of fifty-five. We enter this world only if we died in the last before our time – of violence, or disease, or childbirth. But, note, few retreads are infants. Heavens, man, the place would be awash with babes if all those who died arrived here!'

'A most pertinent observation,' interrupted Lady Lovejoy sarcastically. 'What should we do with them all?'

'Why we should have to eat 'em!' roared Miss Rutherford.

'No,' continued Sir Digby, ignoring the hilarity around him, 'those who come here have died before the full maturity of their years, and must have been capable of reasoning that this was so. I believe that when someone dies prematurely, the brain releases electronically and atomically charged particles, invisible, minuscule fragments of matter carrying part of the personality.'

'Or the soul, dear,' said Lady Lovejoy indulgently.

'Or the soul, if you will,' conceded Sir Digby. 'These particles I call egons. My proposition is that the egons settle somewhere close to the site of death – in the ground, the walls or in a tree, for example.'

'Perhaps even in the floorboards, dear?' observed Lady Lovejoy.

'Yes, indeed, why not the floorboards, what-what?'

'Our birth and rebirth are the work of the Almighty, and there's an end to it,' said her Ladyship. 'In his infinite mercy, he takes those whose lives were cut short and gives them a second chance. We must all live a more righteous and godly life than before. Because who knows when he will return in all his glory?'

'Medieval superstition!' said Sir Digby. 'Leave it to the Papists and the John Bull Society! Have you noticed, Inspector, how these two different groupings of people whose views are virtually identical, do so loathe one another?'

Scipio had noticed. 'Tell me, Lady Lovejoy,' he said. 'Do you sympathize with the John Bull Society's aims?'

He sensed his hostess stiffen beside him. 'Certainly not, Inspector! These people are criminals and Roundheads. They know as much of divine mercy as I know of trigonometry. Which is plaguey little.'

'I meant no offence . . .'

'None taken, Inspector. But you must know that the great majority of patriotic English Anglicans consider the so-called Upright Men neither upright nor Christian.'

'Can we stick to the point here?' said Sir Digby slightly irritably. 'I was telling the Inspector and Mr Boswell about my theory as to how we have come to be reborn. Miss Rutherford here is helping me in my researches.'

Miss Rutherford smiled, nodded, and glanced her eyes heavenwards. She patently enjoyed indulging the old boy. 'My ladies and I occasionally take Sir Digby and his scientific instruments with us on our underground expeditions; we seek out retreads, he seeks his precious egons. He says there is less noise and distraction Underground.'

'Inspector, are you familiar with the magnetic tape-recorder?' said Sir Digby.

'Certainly.'

'Well then, you will know that if you speak into such a machine, your speech is registered on magnetic tape. Then you can simply depress a switch and the sound is played back to you, a perfect and accurate reproduction of your voice. If one can do that, then why might it not be possible that there is a means of storing souls, to be accessed again whenever nature decrees it?'

'Wicked atheism!' snorted Lady Lovejoy.

'Madam, as I have told you in our private conversations several times, I do not seek for one moment to deny God,' said Sir Digby. 'I merely suggest that he plays no direct part in rebirth. Consider . . . It is beyond dispute that when a retread arrives, he or she absorbs some of the matter roundabout. Some soil and grass in a field, the moisture in the air, aye, even fragments of carpet and even furniture if indoors. All of us who have ever witnessed the arrival of a retread can testify to this, and to the heat given off by the process. We must presume that the matter which disappears on the retread's arrival is used to compose the retread's new body. Now sir, if the Almighty was bringing us back, why should he, being as he is the source of all potency in the Universe, need to scrape up clods with which to manufacture us? It is a natural process, ladies and gentlemen.'

The company sat silently for a moment, considering Sir Digby's seemingly irrefutable thesis.

'So, Sir Digby,' asked Boswell, 'what is the mechanism whereby retreads are summoned back? According to the police manual around a hundred and fifty a day appear in London alone, but there is no apparent pattern to it. One cannot predict when any particular individual will appear, if at all.'

'One suspects that sooner or later they will all come back,' said Sir Digby. 'Since the Atom War forty-six years ago, close to three millions of us have reappeared in the city. We have no way of telling how many will appear eventually because we have no reliable record of how many folk died before their time—'

' "The days of our years are threescore and ten . . ." ' said Lady Lovejoy, quoting Psalm 90, verse 10. Just about the best-known line from the Bible, if you assumed that the Almighty intended you to live to seventy and had made you a retread for that purpose.

'—But for the entire area governed by the London County Council, perhaps there will eventually be a total of six or even ten millions. But in answer to your earlier question, Mr Boswell, I do not know what it is that sets the rebirth of any given individual in motion. That is obviously one of the matters which I am investigating.'

Lady Lovejoy cut in. 'Are you familiar, Inspector, Mr Boswell, with Chapter Eleven of Genesis? Its moral is that men who try to build Towers of Babel so that they may pry into Heaven will come to a bad end.'

'That may be,' intervened Miss Rutherford. 'But I would rather seek to challenge Sir Digby by observing that his views are at radical variance with those of the physicists in California, with their talk of resonances and parallel universes.'

'The Californian physicists,' said Sir Digby, 'are at liberty to construct the truth which best suits their ideas. You see, ladies and gentlemen, every age produces its own truth. Antiquarians tell us that in ancient times, men smeared themselves in woad and tried to propitiate their pagan deities to ensure a good harvest. Then, in the Middle Ages, they believed the world flat and credited unquestioningly the existence of a just but vengeful God who would judge them according to the lives they had led. Then came the Puritans, who said that their fate was predestined. Then Sir Isaac Newton – in my last life, I knew the man for a blithering idiot in much of what he did – established rules which the physical world always obeyed, and so did man try to understand the world by reason rather than religion.

Our truth about the laws and shape of the Universe is a fascinating, elusive thing that shifts constantly, like a beautiful flirtatious girl with a handsome dowry.'

Sir Digby sniggered to himself and slurped noisily on his drink before continuing. 'Now these Californian physicists fashion one hypothesis upon another for the diversion of one another and the edification of no one. They prattle in their arcane mathematical cant, they build valve-machines the size of houses to perform immense calculations. But for what purpose? What good' – he thumped the table – 'comes of it?'

The old gentleman looked all of them in the eye, one by one, to challenge any who would rush to defend the reputations of the American scientists. 'These are the same men, by God,' he said more slowly, 'who before 1962 claimed that the power of the atom would be a great boon, that they would yoke it and create unlimited and cheap energy to benefit all. And what was the result of this vile sorcery? It destroyed them and all around them in a conflagration which the very fires of hell itself could not imitate. So who the devil are these men of science to claim that their truth has any more value than that of Aristotle, or the Anglicans – aye, or of the Papists – or the truth which I have made for myself?'

'But surely, Sir Digby,' said Boswell, 'these twentieth-century scientists were the agency of our rebirth? Should we not be grateful for that at least?'

'A happy accident,' snapped Sir Digby, 'which was never in their designs. The radioactivity and egons catalysed our rebirth. The physicists merely destroyed the world which had loved them so much, trusted them so, and afforded them such privileges. I merely share my truth with you, ladies and gentlemen. I am no papal inquisitor, I do not wish to tyrannize you with my dogma. You are at liberty to accept it or reject it as your reason and your consciences direct. I simply share it because 'tis an adequate engine for me, and so may work for you, too. And in due course I hope to use empirical means to establish its truth. Inspector, your glass is empty. Have some more.'

'Thank you, Sir Digby, but I must return to my work.'

THINGS REMEMBERED (4)

JENNY PEARSON, JUNE 1992

'Mummy, I'm home!'

'Hello dear. Wipe your feet and come and sit down. Pour yourself a cup of tea. There should be some left in the pot.'

'Thank you.'

'So, tell me, what did you do in school today?'

'We did spelling and geography, and at dinnertime we played Feudal Wars.'

'Gracious, couldn't you think of anything nicer? Like the Black Death plague perhaps?'

'That's silly. If you played Black Death all you'd do is all fall down dead.'

'But in your games you're never really dead, are you? With the pestilence you all fall down and then you can get up again. The only difference is that with the real thing, it takes a bit longer to come back. With the Feudal Wars, the dead don't come back. Not ever.'

'I don't understand . . .'

'Never mind, you will soon enough. Do you want the scrapings from this bowl?'

'Yes, please! Gosh! You're making a chocolate cake?'

'That's right, dear.'

'But it's only a Tuesday!'

'All chocolate's off the rations now. I've decided that

you, your father and I are going to eat chocolate until we get sick of it.'

'Mummy . . . am I a Catholic or a Protestant?'

'You are a Protestant. Why do you ask?'

'Because when we were playing the Feudal Wars, Obedience Cattermole said that if I was a Protestant I had to be a Roundhead.'

'That's not true, girl. This family is Church of England, though I can't say we get to church as often as we should do. But you can tell Obedience Cattermole that your father is a Protestant and he fought for the Coalition.'

'Why did he fight for the Coalition?'

'Because he didn't think it was right the Duke of Monmouth be made the King and have all the power for himself. He didn't think it was right that Monmouth and his noblemen should be allowed to tell everyone else what to do. Your father believed that the country should be governed by the Houses of Parliament elected by every adult who can read and write. He also said that General Lawrence was a good man who wanted nothing for himself – you could tell that by what Lawrence did in his previous life. And you can tell Obedience Cattermole that your father also fought for the Coalition because he reckoned that neither Monmouth nor anyone else had any business telling the rest of us what they should believe about God. Your father says we should not make windows into other people's souls, and the Almighty gives us all the freedom to choose our own roads to Heaven or Hell.'

'Obedience Cattermole says Catholics all go to Hell.'

'Then I feel very sorry for Obedience Cattermole.'

'Why?'

'Because his poor young mind is being poisoned by religion. What if he discovers his best friend at school is a Papist? What if he falls in love with a Catholic girl when he is older? Listen, girl, you're not really old enough to understand yet, but one day you shall. We live in a very small country. Your father and I saw a lot of terrible things when we were younger, and all we want now is peace and quiet. For people to live and let live. Why, Mrs. Beck across the road is a Papist, and as you know you couldn't wish for a better, kinder neighbour. I'll tell you this, girl, and you can ask your father when he gets home from work, he'll tell you the same thing. Never ever ever get mixed up with people who tell you that they know God's will. It will only lead you into trouble.'

'Obedience Cattermole says he would rather cut his hand off than be friendly with Papists.'

'Obedience Cattermole seems to say a lot of things. And you seem to listen to him, too. Is he your boyfriend?'

'Eeeuuuuurggh no! Nobody likes Obedience Cattermole. Except Lucy Pickett. But she's such a girlie. She likes everyone.'

FEBRUARY 2003

Detective Sergeant O'Rourke pulled the car up behind three other squad cars.

They had raced through the streets with the bell on the front ringing . . . Was every day like this?

She had assumed that on her first day at work she would be pounding a beat with a uniformed officer.

Instead, Inspector Africanus had assigned her to the big Irish Detective Sergeant, saying that a week or two in his company would teach her more than her three months at the Police College.

'Follow me, girl,' said the Sergeant as he opened his door. 'Don't so much as scratch your nose unless I say so.'

They had parked outside a large tenement-block, five-storey council cribs built around a rectangular court-yard. Up ahead of them, two police cars blocked the arched entrance to the yard. Armed officers in flak-jackets crouched behind cars covering the entrance.

Her first day at work and she was already at the scene of what at the Police College they called a 'major incident'!

Across the road, hundreds of people – men in working clothes, women in aprons, scruffy kids – stood silently. Most had probably been evacuated from the flats around the incident.

She got out of the passenger door. Up ahead, other policemen and women stood around smoking, chatting, fidgeting, loading shotguns and rifles, awaiting orders. Some would occasionally crouch down to pass behind the cars which blocked the entrance to the courtyard.

The Sergeant led her around to the back of the car. He opened the boot and pulled out two flak-jackets.

The boot smelled of oil. Strapped inside, next to the spare tyre, a single-barrelled pump-action shotgun caught the glint of the harsh winter sun. Beneath it was a long suitcase which contained a short-magazine Lee-Enfield rifle, 200 rounds of .303 ammunition, and, carefully wrapped in soft cloth, a telescopic sight.

Guns, guns, guns. Half her training at Hendon had been about guns. She had joined the police force to help people, not shoot them.

She took off her belt, with its holstered pistol, and laid it on top of the spare tyre.

The Sergeant held the jacket behind her like a lady's mantle. She slipped her arms through the holes and meekly thanked him.

'I'll tell you something,' said the Sergeant quietly behind her. 'I'm not a great one for the weapons. But a lot of the other fellas are. And they don't like to see women constables with them. So you might as well know that if you strut around showing off your side-arm, you'll annoy a lot of them. Doesn't bother me if you vex them or not, but I thought you'd like to know what goes through their heads.'

He took her huge Browning pistol from its holster, and pushed the little button on the grip to drop the magazine into his left hand, checked it and pushed it back in again.

'You see,' he continued, gently putting the gun into the pouch sewn into the flak-jacket, 'fellas get funny about guns. They're the repositories of honour and masculinity. A bit like the medieval knight and his sword, I suppose.'

He turned her around by her shoulders to face him and began to lace up the front of the jacket for her. 'And to see women with guns diminishes their manhood. The way I see it is that if you need a piece of machinery to be a man, then you're not much of a man at all . . . There, you'll do.'

Inspector Africanus walked up to them, hands in the

pockets of his overcoat. He wore no protection. He nodded to her.

'What's happening, sir?' said O'Rourke.

'Religious fanatic. He shot and killed three prostitutes in the West End last night,' said the Inspector. It was the first time she had heard him speak. Slightly to her surprise, he had a deep, rich and very nobby accent.

O'Rourke shook his head in disgust. 'Think he's gone karzi?'

'I cannot tell,' said the Inspector. 'He has holed himself up in one of the flats inside. Three floors up. No hostages. He is believed to have an M-16 automatic rifle and a pistol. Quantity of ammunition unknown. He has not barricaded the windows yet, so we shall endeavour to flush him out with tear-gas the moment it gets here.'

The Sergeant nodded. 'No sense in taking risks.'

The Inspector walked on to organize the road-block.

'What's a karzi, Sarge?' she asked as O'Rourke struggled with his jacket.

'A kamikaze,' he said, 'is a Japanese word for a soldier who wants to die. We use the word for people as want to go out in a little self-made Armageddon of their own. Usually people who think dyin' doesn't matter because they'll wake up again in another Heaven somewhere else.'

'Gosh,' she said, 'do we have to deal with a lot of those?'

The Sergeant struggled to free the shotgun from its straps. 'Thankfully, no,' he said. 'But maybe now you understand why rozzers always have to carry bloody guns. There's thousands of the things in circulation out there since the Feudal Wars, and if you're in a corner faced by someone with a firearm, or even just a half-brick, you must entertain the possibility that he doesn't care a fig for his life, and so won't be too concerned about yours either. So forget what you learned at Hendon about the Use of Weapons Regulations. Just aim for the chest, blow the poor eejit away and let God be the judge of him.'

She shivered.

'Ah, don't upset yourself,' he smiled. 'It doesn't happen very often. And if you do have to use your gun, remember it's not just to protect yourself. It's for the good of your fellow-officers, and of the rest of the community.'

The Inspector reappeared. 'You two go round the side. You'll find a fire escape,' he said to O'Rourke. 'I expect him to do a runner once we lob the gas in. We have all the other exits and fire escapes covered, but according to the janitor he might make it to that particular one if he batters a couple of doors down.'

They stood at the foot of the fire escape. This side of the building looked over a large expanse of grassy waste-land garnished with all manner of plastic and metal rubbish, from rusty prams to a burned-out lorry. It would be heaven for the local kids, though right now they had more interesting things to watch.

Sergeant O'Rourke half leaned, half sat on the lorry's bonnet, shotgun across his lap, smoking a cigarette. His radio stood on the ground by his feet.

Jenny paced and fidgeted and kept looking at the top of the steel steps leading from the building's top storey.

She had to keep moving to keep warm, she told

herself. The harsh winter sunlight did not intrude here in the tenement's shadow.

The radio crackled. The Inspector's voice announced that the first tear-gas shells had been fired.

Almost immediately, the door at the top of the steps burst open.

The next thing she saw was a pair of black-clad legs.

Feet clattered down the steel steps.

She unholstered her pistol, and winced a little as her left hand grasped the gun's freezing metal and forced back the slide.

The first round was chambered.

The feet reached the bottom flight of steps.

She spread her legs slightly, found her balance and grasped the gun firmly with both hands, pointing to the suspect's chest.

He was young, still had spots on his face, and a moustache. He wore a black coat and breeches and across his chest he held an ugly American M-16 rifle.

His name was Obedience Cattermole. She had been at primary school with him. He was the class herbert. The one who was never allowed out to play after school because his father made him read his scripture. The one who never got chosen for any of the teams. The one that everybody picked on.

He looked at her. She couldn't tell if he recognized her.

There were dark shadows under his eyes and blood-stains on his coat.

'Put the gun down, Obedience,' she said.

The blood was dried. Probably not his own.

She let down her own pistol, to prove she was no

threat to him. 'Put the gun on the step beside you, Obedience. Everything will be all right. I promise.'

He shook his head, muttered something about being on God's work.

He raised his rifle, pointing it at her head.

She tried to lift her own gun. She had to shoot him, or he would kill her. She had to.

Her finger closed on the trigger.

Her hands were shaking.

Obedience Cattermole's chest seemed caved in, as though something had created a vacuum inside which it could no longer resist. He flopped forward and thumped and clattered down the steps.

He came to rest at her feet, quite dead.

Sergeant O'Rourke was at her side. 'Who's your friend?' he asked, pointing his still-smoking shotgun at Cattermole's head.

'I went to school with . . .' She could say no more. She turned away, wanting both to cry and throw up.

'Poor stupid young bloody fool,' O'Rourke sighed behind her.

She had cried on her first day at school, too.

V

FRIDAY, 22 AUGUST 2008

If England were what England seems
An' not the England of our dreams
But only putty, brass an' paint
'Ow quick we'd drop 'er. But she ain't.
– Rudyard Kipling, *The Return*

NEWS of GREAT IMPORT to ALL TRUE BELIEVERS in the GLORY of THE LORD. This day, our Brother Inky Weems was STRUCK DOWN by the ANGER OF THE LORD and he is now SUFFERING the TORMENTS of ETERNAL DAMNATION. Inky Weems is now CRYING OUT to the LORD from the DEEPEST PITS OF HELL where he BURNS, where he is TORTURED WITHOUT END and SCREAMS in his UNBEARABLE AGONY. Weems was CONSIGNED TO HELL for CON-SORTING with THE DARK ONE. In his PRIDE and ARROGANCE he thought fit to BETRAY his brethren to BABYLON for THREE GOLD PIECES. And the LORD, on seeing this, did DESPATCH him with a GREAT THUNDERBOLT. NOW LET US PRAY.

Oh Lord, thou knowest I am but a weak and humble sinner, and that I need your strength that I may lead a righteous life. I beseech you Lord especially that you may see fit to lend your strength to me, thy servant, that I may never fall to Satan's

*wiles and that I may never, in the manner of the
wretched Inky Weems, indulge the sin of pride, or
bear false witness against my brethren, who are
elect and the true believers. I pray also, Lord, as
always, that though we are not fit to receive you,
your imminent return in great majesty may not be
too long delayed and that you will give all true
believers the courage and wisdom to prepare a path
of righteousness for your return. AMEN!!*

Boswell folded the handbill and gave it back to Jenny,
who sat next to him. She pushed it into one of her
pockets. She had her shoulder-bag but as there was a
radio in it, she was not about to open it. Not here.

They had found the broadside announcing Weems'
fictitious fate lying in the gutter as they were getting out
of her car.

A pack of lies, of course. Inky Weems was very much
alive and residing underground at Baker Street, where
he made himself useful by making cups of tea and
offering the Inspector little tit-bits of information about
various criminal culls here and there.

Boswell had been mildly surprised to learn Jenny
Pearson owned a car, a tiny British-built thing that went
around quite smoothly. Glyndwr had followed them in
an unmarked Humber and would wait outside for them.

He, Jenny and about nine hundred others had come
here to the Isle of Dogs to listen to Elder Oliver
Saltonstall, thought to be one of the principal leaders of
the Antient and Honourable Order of the Sons of John
Bull.

The meeting had been advertised for several days

beforehand. Initially, the Inspector had thought to use the occasion to arrest every leading Bull that turned up. But to do so, they would have had to go in mob-handed, and the political consequences of a major riot (with the possibility of lots of shooting as well) were too ghastly to contemplate, Boswell gathered.

So instead, he and Jenny were here in mufti, trying to gather some sort of idea as to what they were up to.

It was his first visit to the East End of London since his arrival. The Docklands had been comprehensively levelled in the Atom War and were now an area of new factories and warehouses. The port itself was becoming more and more busy as Britain began to trade with the wider world once again. Politicians, Jenny told him, described the East End as one of the sites of the New Britain's 'economic miracle'.

Among all this activity, the Bulls had built a meeting-hall. Presumably the land had once been cheap; certainly the building – called the Industrial Mission – looked cheap inside and out. Most of its walls and ceiling appeared to be built of corrugated metal, with very little brick or stone in its construction.

It put him in mind of an enormous Nissen hut. There were only a few windows in the roof, the rest of the lighting coming from a few strip-lights. Puritans liked their buildings nice and simple, didn't they? The less you have in the way of fuss and frills, the easier it is to concentrate on your religion.

The room was filled with row after row of different types of chairs and benches. Men, mostly workers by the look of their clothing, came in quietly, some greeting one another, others looking for friends and acquaintances, as though they were turning up at a union meeting.

There were only a few women, none of them with the appearance of the labouring classes. Not all of them were sour matrons with pinched faces, either, though some had the abstracted look of opium addicts.

They had sat in the car outside until the last minute because, as Jenny explained, they did not wish to end up being ushered to a seat at the front, a place from which escape might be difficult.

They had been welcomed by two ushers, both men in black with exceptionally short hair. The first had a crushing handshake and an overwhelming good-fellowship. The other was hard as plate armour, staring them over coldly. Both he and Jenny had tried to dress as soberly as possible for the occasion, but it was clear that in Boswell's case at least, a grey suit was not sober enough. As soon as he got his first month's pay, he would have to expand his wardrobe.

They sat down in the back row.

A man dressed in black appeared behind a wooden lectern at a podium at the front of the stage. The congregation fell silent.

'Good evening and God be with you, Brethren,' said the man, who turned out to have a mouthful of teeth as ravaged as the stones in a Dickensian graveyard. 'Elder Saltonstall will be with us in a moment. Before he speaks, he has asked us to think on this reading from Chapter 37 of the Book of Ezekiel . . .

'The hand of the Lord was upon me, and carried me out in the spirit of the Lord, and set me down in the midst of the valley which was full of bones, and caused me to pass by them round about: and, behold, there were very many in the open valley; and, lo, they were very dry.

'And he said unto me, Son of man, can these bones live? And I answered, O Lord God, thou knowest . . .'

Jenny had had the presence of mind to bring along a copy of the Authorized Version. Like many of the others around them, she had turned to Ezekiel to follow the text. She pushed the book between them, so he could pretend to read with her.

'. . . Thus saith the Lord God unto these bones. Behold, I will cause breath to enter into you, and ye shall live: and I will lay sinews upon you, and will bring up flesh upon you, and cover you with skin, and put breath in you, and ye shall live; and ye shall know that I am the Lord.

'So I prophesied as I was commanded: and as I prophesied, there was a noise, and behold a shaking, and the bones came together, bone to his bone . . .'

Beneath the book, Jenny had tucked her thigh against his. What on earth did that mean? Was this some sort of come-on, or was it a perfectly normal way for people to behave here?

'. . . And when I beheld, lo, the sinews and the flesh came upon them, and the skin covered them above, but there was no breath in them.

'Then he said unto me, Prophesy unto the wind, prophesy, son of man, and say to the wind, Thus saith the Lord God. Come from the four winds, O breath, and breathe upon these slain, that they may live.

'So I prophesied as he commanded me, and the breath came into them . . . And they lived, an exceeding great army!'

The reader bowed slightly to the still silent congregation and left.

Moments later, a tall thin man strode to the lectern. He wore a long, close-fitting black coat, with breeches and stockings beneath, rather than the trousers favoured by most of the men here.

Some of the audience stood, as though out of respect, but others waved them down.

The long-haired preacher had no books or notes with him, and stood to the side of the lectern so that he was fully visible.

He stood quite still, hands clasped in front of him, looking at the floor in silent prayer.

If he had been wearing one of those tall hats with a buckle at the front he would have looked like everyone's idea of something out of the Barebones Parliament. This must be Elder Saltonstall.

'Brethren,' he said at last. 'Even a babe can explain the meaning of Chapter 37 of the Book of Ezekiel. I entreat you to listen silently, prayerfully, while I bring you a great and wondrous message. Great news for all who live righteously . . .'

Long pause.

'Just as the Lord raised up the great army of the Israelites, just as he gave life and sinew to the slain, so has he raised us, and our fathers, and our children. The Lord has given us new life so that we, too, may be as a mighty army to prepare the way of his coming . . .'

Another pause.

'And brethren. The moment of his coming is nigh. The righteous shall rule England by this time next week!'

*

Someone in the distance shouted, 'Action!'

Scipio understood this to mean that he should be as quiet as possible as he threaded his way over cables and between unused pieces of equipment.

In front of him was a brightly lit stage. The backdrop was painted to resemble the stone walls of a castle, and a man and a woman in cod-medieval costumes acted away in front of it.

The man sat in a chair, while the girl made various ineffectual plays to seduce him. Scipio did not recognize the actor.

The young woman was Dorcas Chubb, who until but a few days ago had been a dollymop at Mother Heycock's brothel in Covent Garden.

Between Scipio and the stage were cameras, more lights, a few busy technicians and several dozen people standing around doing nothing.

Dorcas made a heroic effort to rouse the man's ardour, but was evidently failing. She looked to the audience, stamped her foot, then smiled, lifting her finger, as though struck by a foolproof idea. She turned to her swain and, facing away from the cameras, pulled open her bodice to expose her breasts to him.

'. . . Aaannnd cut!' said one of the people hanging around at the front. 'Dorcas, darling,' he said, 'you're an absolute treasure. Who's your agent?'

Dorcas turned, still packing her ample charms away, and smiled.

'Thank you, Mr Chatterton,' she said. 'I don't actually have—'

A man in a peruke sitting in a canvas chair close to Mr Chatterton cleared his throat.

'Ooooh, I see,' said Mr Chatterton. 'Well, you take my advice, dearie, you get yourself an agent and you won't need to do his Lordship any more favours.'

A few people around them laughed, and in moments the set was swamped in the hubbub and clatter of people preparing to film the next scene.

Scipio reckoned it safe to approach the man in the peruke without disturbing the work in hand. He had never been to Broadcasting House before and he had to own he found it a little intimidating.

His quarry was still seated. Next to him was an empty chair on the back whereof was the legend 'MR CHATTERTON'. On the occupied chair, in rather smaller lettering, was 'JOHN WILMOT, EARL ROCHESTER, BARON WILMOT OF ADDERBURY IN ENGLAND & VISCOUNT WILMOT OF ATHLONE IN IRELAND'.

Rochester sat serenely, leaning his chin on his stout, gold-topped cane. He wore a baggy white shirt and tight pantaloons.

Scipio sat himself in Mr Chatterton's chair while the latter was talking to the actor.

''Tis a pity we did not find her earlier, don't you think, Mechano?' said Rochester, without turning his head.

'Who?'

'The girl. I could have woven her into the whole script, had her come in and out like a parlour-maid. It would have made passing good comedy, but alas much of the principal photography is already done.'

'Your Lordship is scripting this teleplay?'

'I am, Mechano, and Chatterton directs. Chatterton is

an old woman, of course, but there is a manner of comradeship between us. We both whore our genius for recognition and riches.'

'What is the subject of this teleplay?'

Rochester let out a little snort, still staring ahead into some far distant place. Even though he had led two dissolute lives and was now ageing, his handsomeness was almost feminine; his eyes were deep and distant, his lips thick and sensual.

He stood. 'It is to be called *Carry on Courting* and its setting is the court of the King of far-away Sexmania. The *Radio Times* will in due course describe it as a bawdy romantic comedy. Within the BBC, plays of this sort are known as "crap". Tom and the crew will now film the scene in which Prince Wee-Wee visits the astrologer Alexander Bendo to discover the most fortuitous time to declare his love for the fair Lady Swivea. The worthy Bendo will say the wretch shall only have the hand of the maid with the aid of spells and potions, which, for a small consideration, he shall prepare. For Bendo recognizes that cupidity is the truest handmaiden to Cupid . . .'

Rochester sighed. 'Look at poor Tom.' Chatterton was gazing through the lens of a huge camera, discussing some technical matter with a man with a tape-measure.

'He could have been a great poet, a great playwright. Instead, the old buffle-head directs Saturday Night Specials . . . Aye, and I write 'em. But I can deceive myself I am a true artist yet by hammering out an occasional verse.'

Rochester led Scipio away from the stage, occasionally smiling and nodding to various workers.

Though he understood the scientific and mechanical principles of the television, and though he had seen an episode of his own life spectacularly misrepresented by Rochester on it, Scipio still found the whole business impossibly magical. 'I had always imagined that working at the BBC would have rewards beyond the merely financial,' he said.

'It does not, Mechano. It is drudgery and frustration. I thank the gods I am only an occasional employee. We are at the moment – Marlowe, Chatterton and I – engaged in writing another comedy; some producer considered it an act of great inspiration to bring us three together. But comedies for the British Broadcasting Corporation shall never attain the dignity of art. There is scant opportunity for meditation on truth, or the uplifting of the spirit, or ennobling the dignity of man. What we do, we do for the diversion of the oiks, the plebs, the basest people . . .'

They had reached an office partitioned from the studio by a large glass window. Rochester turned to him as he opened the door. 'And the base people, Mechano, are scum. No matter in what age they were begotten, they do not desire art. They desire lewdness, pratfalls and jokes about pig-turds. And that is what we give 'em.'

The office was furnished with a large formica-topped table, a few battered chairs and a filing-cabinet. Rochester pulled open its top drawer and took out a bottle of South African sack and a pair of substantial tumblers.

'Working with two men of such auspicious repute must be interesting,' said Scipio, accepting a glass.

'I suppose so,' said Rochester. 'It is diverting to watch how retreads of renown cope with their unexpected reprieve. Marlowe is a man of dark humours who would rather give himself over wholly to art, but without money life is too dull. So he compromises, and it maddens him. Chatterton is different. Consider . . . In his last life, young Tom comes up to town from his native Bristol. He starves in a loft, unloved, unrecognized by the world, and so takes poison. But in place of his much-craved oblivion, he finds himself here in Arcadia where everyone of any learning who trod the earth since his death thinks him a very genius. That, my dear Mechano, is heavy baggage for the poor squit. It is many years now that he was minded to throw that baggage away and accept the tawdry recognition that this world can offer him. I, on the other hand, awake here, fully cured of the pox, naked and bearing nothing save my reputation as a coward, a fornicator, a drunkard. I have everything to play for, yet I, too, find myself engaged in this nonsense . . .'

Scipio sipped on his wine. It was very pleasant.

'Indeed,' he said, sitting down at the table. 'One's reputation can be a bother. Consider the case of the man who coined the term "rake-hell". Such is his renown as a dissolute that the most fashionable confessor of his day takes it on himself to secure the rake's death-bed conversion.'

Rochester sat and slurped his wine. For a moment, he said nothing, but looked at Scipio through heavy, suspicious eyelids.

'Indeed. Your cleric would be like the young woman who fancies she can cure a pansy with her feminine charms.'

'Ah,' said Scipio disputatiously, 'but posterity thinks that the good cleric, a Doctor of Divinity, no less, did succeed. Our poor rake-hell is there in his bed, the pox draining away the last of his squandered life, surrounded by vicars and bishops and God-wot else . . .'

'His family, Mechano, the poor unfortunate would have his family around him as he expired . . .' Rochester smiled for the first time. It was a charming smile, the smile of a seducer, an intriguer. A leader.

'Yes,' said Scipio, 'our poor rake's family would be present. According to the confessor, Dr Gilbert Burnet, the rake's conversion was so abundant, his lamentation of his past wickedness so complete, that he took the sacraments and then persuaded his wife to renounce her Catholic religion.'

Rochester's face set hard.

'After the rake's death on the twenty-seventh of July 1680,' continued Scipio, 'his repentances were much broadcast and rejoiced over. One of the rake's later biographers – a Catholic – likened this to some final victory of the Puritans over the Cavaliers, the triumph of the Protestant religion over the Catholicism of previous generations.'

Rochester drained his glass and set it on the table before him. 'The Puritans say that this new life gives us a second chance to follow a righteous path. The rake might say 'tis a second chance to seek new pleasures.'

Scipio nodded. 'The rake would work hard at his raking. Even into his fourth decade. I am reminded of one of the rake's own verses:

He'll still drudge on in tasteless vice,
As if he sinn'd for exercise.

Rochester took a packet of hand-rolled Fribourg and Treyer filters and a lighter from one of the folds of his shirt. 'I wrote it of someone else, Mechano,' he said, offering Scipio the packet.

Scipio accepted cigarette and light and leaned back in his chair.

He blew smoke towards the ceiling, deliberately keeping his peace. Rochester was a more complicated individual than his writings and pranks suggested.

'Inspector,' said Rochester, clearing his throat, 'to what should I account the pleasure of this visit?'

Unless Rochester took Scipio for a complete wooden-top, he knew damn well what this visit was about.

'Your Lordship has already made a story of one episode in my life. Now I have another story for you. It concerns a murder, the attempted murder of a humble and diligent Inspector of Police, and the disappearance of a cleric.'

Rochester smiled and held out the bottle. Scipio covered his glass with his hand. 'This does not sound like an area to inspire me. Clerics and murder are more in Marlowe's line.'

'I think also,' said Scipio, 'that the Bulls will feature in the story, though I am not sure of their precise role.'

'I should think that the Bulls are the villains,' smiled Rochester pleasantly, filling his glass. 'Fanatics, zealots replete with the sense of being God's especial pre-occupation, sure of their place in Heaven if they but do his work . . .' He drank.

Rochester had no cause to love the Bulls. Given the opportunity, they would probably burn the scripts and the film of his plays in public. Some would burn Rochester himself and piously claim it was the man's only chance of getting to Heaven.

'Your Lordship takes his dislike of the Bulls into deeds as well as words,' said Scipio. 'Or so it seems to me.'

Rochester raised an eyebrow and half smiled.

'When I spoke with the neighbours of the missing Reverend Harry Seymour, I discovered, when the poor frightened souls could be persuaded to speak to me, that your Lordship had been enquiring after the Reverend also.'

Rochester shrugged. 'Harry Seymour is a cousin of mine. In truth, he is a great-great-great uncle, but I call all my relations cousins. You know that many here seek out their kinfolk. They like to enlist one another's help with money or influence, misliking the trouble the state takes to meet their needs. A man in my position finds he has several distant relations, an affinity which I don't much want. Thanks to my writings I am of some means financially, but the more ignorant of these relatives, both forebears and descendants, imagine me more important than I am. Some of them are ruffians, some of them I like to help. Such a one is Harry Seymour.'

Scipio shook his head. 'A writer of fictions should be able to do better than that. Have you ever been fluttered? It is the police word for use of the polygraph, the lie-detector machine. Your Lordship would find it most instructive . . . I believe that your Lordship admires virtue in others, but I cannot conceive of how a man like Harry

Seymour would wish to have anything to do with a rake. And what need has he of your money or influence?'

Rochester smiled unnervingly and nodded.

'Seymour is not your kinsman,' said Scipio, 'or if he is, that is not the cause of your interest in him. This morning I also paid another visit to Mother Heycock's establishment. She would tell me nothing the other night because she was so frightened. I have sharp work upon me though, and I threatened her with all manner of trouble if she did not co-operate. Among other things, she informed me that yesterday morning, you visited her and took away the girl Dorcas Chubb. You paid Mother Heycock a handsome sum of money to release the girl from her obligations to the madam. What is it about her that interests you so?'

'She expressed an interest in a career in television. I can help her. She has star quality. She has the making of an actress.'

Scipio banged the table. 'Stop playing games with me, man! Dorcas Chubb is Elder Saltonstall's trug of choice. Heycock told me that you interrogated her and Dorcas about Saltonstall's movements. You only visited the whorehouse with your pretended saint in order to spy out the land. You and your cronies have been seen watching Bull meetings. Now, I do not know what the Bulls are up to, but I know that you know more about this than I do. Now speak . . .'

'No,' said Rochester, driving the cork back into his wine-bottle. He looked at his wristwatch. 'Come, my dashing Mechano. I wish you to meet a close friend of mine. He speaks far more eloquently than I.'

*

Jenny's head moved a little closer to his. 'Look at his cheeks,' she muttered.

Boswell looked first at the distant speck of the speaker's face, and then at the screen behind him. Elder Saltonstall was a little blue around the chin (probably from punishing himself with a blunt cut-throat razor), but he could see nothing remarkable.

'Look about you,' said Saltonstall. 'The world is in its dotage. War, famine and pestilence stalk much of the Earth, while here, in God's chosen land, a Popish murderer of children sits upon the throne . . .'

There did seem something a little odd about his cheeks, though. Dark patches on each one.

'And while Christian men and women are supposed to bow down before this abomination and call it King, the real power in the land is held by secret cabals, Brethren, evil men plotting devilry, plotting the foul violation of the souls of the righteous . . .'

His voice grew louder, more passionate. Even at this distance, you could see the glistening little diamonds of sweat gathering at his brow and temples.

'The nobs, Brethren, we call them the nobs, the big nobs, the big wigs, the men with the money and the power . . . The ones who sit in Parliament, Papists, and the would-be Papists of the so-called Church of England, and the Jews, sitting there in Parliament daily contriving new ways of oppressing God's people, while we must toil for their enrichment.'

Some of the men around them nodded agreement. Boswell decided it would be best to nod as well.

'But they do not know the great secret which the Almighty has revealed to the Upright Men. My brothers and sisters, I bring you wondrous news. There will imminently arise a new Josiah in England, a great king who will destroy the idols, who will be the scourge of the pagans who blight our land with their depravities.

'Remember how it was written in the Book of Judges: how he put down the idolatrous priests, those that burned incense unto Baal, to the sun, and to the moon, and to the planets, and to all the host of heaven. And he broke down the houses of the sodomites that were by the house of the Lord. And he slew all the priests of the high places that were there upon the altars, and burned men's bones upon them, and returned to Jerusalem . . . Brethren, just as good King Josiah laboured to cleanse the land of Judah of idolatry, so it shall be in England. The new Josiah who is promised us shall destroy the Popish churches, the Jewish synagogues, and even the so-called Church of England. The established church is but a harlot in the service of the nobs, the Jews, the Papists and the rich, who conspire together to steep our land in GREED, IDOLATRY and SODOMY!'

Someone in the congregation said 'Amen!' Others took up the word. Saltonstall, the sweat running from his brow on to the mysterious dark patches on his cheeks, raised his right hand for silence.

Now he smiled. 'Brethren,' he said, 'in my last life, some men spoke of the Fifth Monarchy, the end of the corrupt order of things, and the ushering-in of a new order, one in which Christ would return in person to reign over the righteous until the end of time.'

'The wise men and the astrologers said that the end of the world would be heralded by a series of signs and wonders. They spoke of the conversion of the Jews as one such sign. Already we know that our Josiah is coming to tear down their synagogues.'

'Another sign we were to see would be the defeat of the Turk. What could be simpler? When King Josiah returns to England, he shall raise a mighty army which will go on crusade to the Holy Land and liberate it from the Egyptians. Then, Brethren, then . . .'

Saltonstall closed his eyes and smiled.

'What's this about Egyptians?' hissed Boswell to Jenny.

'They overran the state of Israel in 1965,' she muttered.

'The state of where?'

A man in the row in front of them turned and shushed at them.

'Then, Brethren,' said Saltonstall, 'having freed the Holy Land from the infidel, we shall await the return of the greatest retread of them all.'

Some in the audience gasped, some smiled and nodded.

'There shall the righteous gather, at the foot of Mount Calvary, to wait . . .'

Silence.

The crowd broke into spontaneous shouts of 'Amen!' and 'Hallelujah!'.

It was a fascinating idea, thought Boswell, for Christ to be resurrected along with everyone else. Most of the people in the audience here probably had no idea where Palestine was.

'And so good King Josiah shall yield his throne,' smiled Saltonstall, nodding as the shouting died down, 'to the only true king. He will reform the laws, he will

raise the humble, he will humble the great. No more
painful childbirth, Brethren, no more premature death,
no want nor poverty, and all things shall be held in
common, for there will be no need of private property
among the saints. Brethren, there shall be no blessing
which the righteous shall want. It is written, in the
Book of Amos: Behold, the days come, sayeth the Lord,
that the ploughman shall overtake the reaper, and the
treader of grapes him that soweth seed; and the
mountains shall drop sweet wine, and all the hills shall
melt. And I will bring again the captivity of my people
of Israel, and they shall build the waste cities and
inhabit them; and they shall plant vineyards and drink
the wine thereof; they shall also make gardens, and eat
the fruit of them.'

More 'Amens' and 'Hallelujahs' from around the
room. The gathering of the faithful fell slowly silent to
contemplate the joyful lives they would lead after the
second coming. The man next to Boswell was humming
something to himself. Others rocked their heads back
and forth.

It was as crazy as a Nuremburg Rally.

Elder Saltonstall gradually erased the village idiot
smile from his own face and looked stern again.

'The great days whereof I speak are within our grasp,
Brethren,' he said. 'But we may yet find ourselves
frustrated' – cries of 'No!' and 'For shame!' – 'We must
let nothing stand in the way of our righteous cause. We
must prepare the way for his coming, we must prepare
also a path for King Josiah . . .'

Here comes the bill, thought Boswell.

'We must all obey our pastors and elders. We must be

prepared to sacrifice ourselves for the greater good.' Saltonstall was getting red in the face again. 'We must be as a mighty host rising up when our leaders say the day is come . . . We must be ready to do the Lord's work by smiting the ungodly and destroying their idols.'

Men stood, waved their hands in the air, shouted their preparedness to join in the smiting. Boswell thought he had best do likewise.

Elder Saltonstall looked out over them, nodding slightly, approvingly. Then he raised the flats of his hands. Silence came quickly.

Boswell sat down. 'There is one idol,' said Saltonstall, 'the greatest and most dangerous idol of them all, a graven thing we must all fear, a thing which may yet be the frustration of our just cause . . .'

A man in a black three-piece suit walked down the centre aisle towards Saltonstall. He carried what appeared to be a large wooden box.

'It is the foul spawn of Satan, the devil's wile masquerading as the invention of man, and it enslaves the minds of the people and enfeebles their bodies just as surely as Pharaoh bound the Israelites.'

What, wondered Boswell impatiently. What was this wonderful thing, and where could he get some, or was the preacher going to give them the obligatory five minutes on the evils of drink?

'An engenderer of effeminacy, of viciousness and irreligion, the pedlar of all lies, it is a whore and a dissembler . . .'

The man in the black suit had reached the front. He placed his box on the stage in front of Saltonstall.

It was a television set.

'The Papists and the Jewish nobs, and their lap-dogs and jackals in the established church want you to debase your virtue and squander your strength by watching the television . . .'

Oho, thought Boswell, now we're getting to the nub of it. If the likes of my Lord Rochester are writing lewd plays and the television news programmes are telling the truth (assuming they are telling the truth!), no wonder the Upright Men hate it.

'. . . They would have you believe the filthy lies, the foul calumnies they pass off as news. They want you drugged into vice and the sin of Onan by their lewd plays and their American Hollywood films . . .'

And I bet you watch it all the same, thought Boswell. Just like we couldn't resist listening to Lord Haw-Haw from time to time back at the station. Boswell was fascinated by the television, though he could not see what was actually sinful about the BBC. He had watched a great deal of television at the reception centre, and could see nothing lewd and vicious about programmes following a year in the life of a stoat, or the reading and writing lessons, or the newsreels, or Shakespeare plays, and American cowboy films, some of which had been old even in 1940.

Saltonstall had taken a long, heavy stick of the sort you imagined Dickensian villains carried.

'It is written in Deuteronomy,' said Saltonstall, 'ye shall destroy their altars, and break down their images, and cut down their groves, and burn their graven images with fire . . .' Holding the cudgel with both hands, he fetched the top of the TV an almighty wallop. There was a confetti-burst of tiny glass splinters as the cathode-ray tube exploded outwards towards the congregation with a rather satisfying *crump*.

'Isaiah 30,' said Saltonstall. 'Ye shall defile also the covering of thy graven images of silver, and the ornament of thy molten images of gold; thou shalt cast them away as a menstruous cloth; thou shalt say unto it, GET THEE HENCE!!'

Most in the hall were on their feet now, cheering Saltonstall on in his destruction, clapping or stamping their feet. Again and again, he slammed the stick into the hapless box of valves and circuits, putting all his strength into executing the television set, signalling to the faithful that acts of violence would not only be necessary but sanctioned in the pursuit of the millennium.

It was hard work. His face was turning red, nowhere redder than on his cheeks, where the letters S and L were now quite visible.

Rochester ushered Scipio out of a side door from the building and into a narrow back-street where his carriage awaited. It was one of the horseless variety, a Rolls-Royce, but unlike any Roller Scipio had ever seen.

The bodywork was that of an early model, a Silver Ghost, say, with an enclosed passenger compartment to the rear of a driver's seat which was open to the warm summer air. But it had been decorated in a fashion that could be described as lavish, or perhaps merely grotesque.

Rochester's chauffeur, a young man dressed in sober suit and tie, stood stiffly to attention, holding the passenger door open.

It took Scipio a moment to realize that Rochester's chauffeur was the boy who had been at Lickpenny Nan Heycock's on Monday night. The one who was supposedly Saint Ethelbright.

He had little time to reflect upon this, as he was too preoccupied by the car. It would have been slightly less of an outrage had it been horse-drawn.

The vehicle bore a superficial likeness to one of the royal state carriages, used for displaying visiting dignitaries through the streets. The windows were of darkened glass so one could not see inside it very well. The roof was covered in gilded plaster (or plastic) nymphs, satyrs and muses cavorting about, like something from the Palace of Versailles, though considerably more lubricious. The passenger door featured an intricate coat-of-arms and on the bonnet was a painting of two entwined naked bodies of indeterminate gender, who were clearly engaged in business of an urgent and intimate nature.

'Aretine,' said Rochester. 'They've been copied from Aretine's postures. I know a little man who can do the most deliciously obscene pictures with a device called an airbrush . . .'

Scipio took a closer look at the bonnet. 'In truth,' said Rochester, 'Aretine, or Pietro Aretino, only wrote the lewd verses to go with the pictures, but I cannot remember the name of the cove who created them.'

'The artist's name was Giulio Romano,' replied Scipio. 'Italian renaissance pornographer. Every so often I find myself arresting or cautioning someone on obscenity charges for printing or distributing the pictures. Modern pornography leaves less to the imagination, but many retreads prefer Romano's old-fashioned filth.'

Rochester smiled. Though the pictures were certainly suggestive of sexual congress, they were not really explicit enough to reliably secure a conviction.

'Come,' said Rochester, beckoning him into the back of the car.

There was a bulge under Ethelbright's shoulder too big for even a dozen wallets. It looked more like a large pistol. It betokened that my Lord Rochester had more enemies than merely the National Viewers' and Listeners' Association.

The carriage seats were vast leather things. On a panel in front of them, behind the driver, was inset a shelf of bottles and glasses.

'And you, Mechano, what of your soul? We have spent a deal of time discussing my death-bed musings, and the manner in which I repent now, but are you a religious man?' Rochester spoke with his chin resting on the top of his cane.

Scipio shrugged. 'I have not had the benefit of drinking the sweet milk of the Christian religion at my mother's breast,' he said. Being with Rochester made him feel obliged to act all sardonic and worldly. 'For all I can remember, I was born into a society which worshipped the sun, or jungle animals, and all manner of graven things. From reading books and watching the television I gain the impression that mankind might be better served by worship of the sun and the Earth.'

The car pulled out into traffic and almost immediately had to stop at a zebra crossing. People gawped in astonishment or disgust at Rochester's conveyance.

'But you became a Christian, Mechano,' he said. 'You underwent a conversion.'

'I did not come to Christianity by my own intellect,' said Scipio. 'I was taught to read the Bible and as a child was brought to accept that Christianity is as much part of the order of things as sunshine, rain and indigestion.'

'And now?' asked Rochester.

They were still stationary at the crossing. A gang of young mashers in big shirts and tight trousers passed them by and cheered the car. Scipio sank down in the seat a little until he remembered that while he could see them, they could not see him through the special glass. If Rochester was wasting his time, he would throw the ruddy book at him for this humiliation.

'And now?' he said. 'I do not know if there is or isn't a God, but I do know that if we do not treat each other with love and respect then we are doomed.'

Rochester's horseless embarrassment pulled off from the crossing at last.

'Where are we going, my Lord?'

Rochester ignored the question. He was looking out of the window, admiring a group of young Japanese women – office ladies – who were being hurried along the street to the next attraction on their tour itinerary.

'Your great failing, Mechano,' said Rochester, 'is that you refuse to be of one party or another. The brave major who liberated Bristol should know which side he is on. He should stop pretending that the Feudal Wars are over and forgotten.'

'Do not patronize me, Rochester! If more of us forgot the blasted Feudal Wars, perhaps we would be in a better state now!' he snapped.

Everything was growing clearer. Rochester the Cavalier, Rochester the rake, Rochester the writer of bawdy plays and poems, Rochester the man who had surrendered to the Puritans on his death-bed, Rochester who had even been persuaded to command his own dear wife – the only woman he had ever truly loved – to forsake her religion . . . Rochester loathed the Upright Men.

'I can think of nothing more pleasant than the sight of a healthy young woman in short skirt and black stockings,' said Rochester, looking at the Japanese girls. 'People say 'tis sluttish, but I think not.'

There would be no more short skirts and black stockings if the Bulls took over.

Rochester would be a prominent man in the Sealed Knot, the secret society committed to defending the Liberal Settlement and the Acts of Accession and Toleration against all who threatened them. He already knew from the tattoo he had seen on Saint Ethelbright's chest that the young man was a member. Like all secret societies, Scipio thought it a schoolboy conceit, and probably nothing more significant than a drinking club for men who wished occasionally to flee their wives and children for good-fellowship.

He had lost count of the number of times he had been invited to join. He did not doubt that if he had joined, he would now be a Chief Superintendent of Police at the very least.

The car turned up into Whitehall.

Scipio was intrigued, despite all his prejudice about the Knot, whom he judged little better than the Bulls. Old men fighting old fights, and suffocating the natural idealism of the young with their hoary, threadbare hatreds.

'I have only been here some ten years,' said Rochester, still looking out of the window, 'but I listened to all the history and anecdotes of the wars, the plagues and suffering that went before. And I see the problem as clear as if it were a wart on my prick. It is that you people, the rozzers, and those in the ministries and offices along here, became abstracted, isolated. You all became too preoccupied with your big motor-cars, with eating in curry-houses or Frenchified restaurants, and swiving one another's wives, and reading lewd books and magazines.'

'Your Lordship surely does not speak of me,' said Scipio. 'That is a more apt description of yourself.'

'After a fashion, Mechano,' said Rochester, turning to him. 'Like the people in Whitehall, you are a nob. You have only a limited comprehension of the oiks, all those who by virtue of humble birth, mean education or simple stupidity, lack a voice in the society. You only know the felons among them. You cannot see what takes root in the hearts and souls of the rest. They are honest, sober, hard-working men, for the most part. And some of them hate the established order so much – aye, and love God too, after their fashion – that they judge no sacrifice too great if it prepares the way of Christ's return.

'Now, you see, you need poor clapped-out old rake-hell Rochester to tell you what they're about. Because they fascinate me; I don disguises and watch them as a professor watches beetles. Because I hate them so, I find I love them too. They mesmerize me.'

The car turned off Whitehall, into a narrow street.

'Tell me, Mechano,' said Rochester, 'do you know why they want Harry Seymour?'

'No. That is what I am trying to ask you.'

'I now know all about Seymour. Gleaning this intelligence required a great deal of threats and bribes on the part of several of my friends,' said Rochester. 'Why do you think the Upright Men might need his co-operation?'

'Perhaps he knows something of use to them, or has something they desire. Perhaps he is dear to someone they wish to influence or blackmail.'

'No, Inspector,' said Rochester, shaking his head.

'So?' said Scipio.

'They want him because of *who* he is.'

'What? A little come-to-Jesus mission priest?'

'No, Mechano, because of who he used to be. Think on it.'

Who he used to be? The records accounted Seymour a mere lad when he died in the mid-sixteenth century, son of a cleric in Spitalfields. Unless . . .

He suddenly felt as though a towel soaked in cold water was being drawn upwards along his naked back.

'Good grief!'

'Quite,' said Rochester. 'Now whether it suits you or no, Mechano, we are of the same party. I was expecting your visit today and accordingly I made an appointment with the old man. 'Tis a pity he will not permit me through the main gate in this car, but I suppose the secrecy does no harm.'

The car turned sharply, going through a narrow entrance set into a high wall. Just inside, a wooden barrier was lifted by a tall man in red tunic and bearskin. Next to him, two corporals of the Coldstream Guards presented arms and snapped to attention.

They were going through one of the back entrances to Buckingham Palace.

'You are most welcome, Brother,' said the Bull, proffering a quill pen. The little man wore a worsted suit and wire-rimmed spectacles, and though both she and Guy stood before him, he ignored her. Women did not rate much above farm animals in the Bulls' outlook.

Saltonstall's destruction of the TV set had been the signal for all manner of intemperance on the part of what had until then been a disciplined and restrained congregation. She and Guy had joined the hymn-singing, the shouting and chanting, and waving of uplifted arms, calling down the curse of the Almighty on the Liberal Settlement and its vile Popish king.

Guy had taken to it with such gusto she almost feared he might go native.

Now the faithful were filing out of the hall, smiling, chattering, shaking hands, clapping one another on the back.

The man at the door had spotted them for newcomers and invited them to join.

Joining was less conspicuous than refusing to join.

The Solemn Covenant pledged members of the Order to do all in their power, to the point of sacrificing life itself, to ensure the building of a righteous and holy kingdom in England in preparation for the return of the greatest king of all.

'Is there a problem, Brother?' asked the little clerk

sharply, as Guy's hand hesitated over the sheet of paper.

'No,' said Guy, 'I'm just reading it through properly, er, Brother.' He signed with a small flourish.

'And will you sign for your wife?' asked the clerk.

She looked downwards, trying to act modest and demure. I'm only a little woman. I've got no brain at all. All I want is to bear babies, preferably sons. Men make all the decisions in my life.

'She is not yet my wife,' said Guy. 'Though we are betrothed.'

The weight of the queue of impatient converts bore down on her as heavily as the vast amount of shapeless clothing she wore.

The clerk beckoned to one of the stocky ushers who stood quietly and observantly along the sides of the room.

An usher appeared before them and inclined his ear to the clerk, who whispered something. She could hear none of it.

The Solemn Covenant to Endeavour a Reformation According to the Word of God, which would separate the precious from the vile, and which was said by one wag to comprise exactly 666 words, lay in front of the clerk.

'The brother here will see if it is possible for Elder Saltonstall to spare you some of his time. He likes to speak with young men and women to offer guidance on the holy estate of matrimony,' said the clerk. 'Go with him.'

Going would be less conspicuous than refusing.

She didn't like this one little bit.

Guy took her hand and squeezed it a little. 'Come, my dear,' he said. 'This will be a great honour for us. Something to tell our children about.'

She smiled sweetly.

The usher was well over 6 feet tall and had enormous shoulders. He wore a plain black jacket and trousers. Against his right thigh she could make out the faint bulge of some sort of neddy, lead pipe, or a leather sheath filled with sand, perhaps. His hair was cropped very short and his forehead was non-existent. He did not have the appearance of one versed in the more intellectually demanding aspects of theology.

Wordlessly, he led them down the side of the room towards the stage.

The further they progressed from the door, the more empty the hall was. Their footsteps echoed off the high roof.

Suddenly, there were more footsteps behind them. Heavy steps, men's steps. Four men, maybe five.

She wanted to look behind, but dared not. She was supposed to be a modest little Christian seeking spiritual guidance. She would have no reason to look around. Like Lot's wife, it might be her ruin.

Ahead of them was the stage. She bore her eyes furiously into it, trying to fathom a reflection of what was behind them, whether there was any cause for fear.

The usher led them towards a small door at the side of the stage. Saltonstall would be in his dressing-room, or vestry, or whatever it was Upright Men dwelt in before and after services. He would now be at prayer, or saying grace over a glass of water, or sodomizing a schoolboy, or something.

The stage door opened. Five men, who could all have been close relatives of their usher, emerged. Two of them openly carried pump-action shotguns.

She tucked her hand casually into her right-hand jacket pocket. Here, and not in her handbag, was where she had put her peach. She palmed the little farthing-sized radio beacon and, passing her hand across her face as if to stifle a nervous cough, put it in her mouth.

The steps behind them grew louder. Guy did not appear at all concerned.

Perhaps she just needed a holiday. Perhaps she was just nervous after having nearly had her thumb bitten off the other day.

The men who had emerged from the stage door did not appear to be going anywhere. They slouched around, not talking.

They were all looking at her and Guy with great interest.

The men made way for them. The usher stopped, stood to one side and gestured them through the open door.

The door closed behind them.

The room was bare and simple. A low ceiling, a couple of strip-lights, a full length mirror. The unpainted brick walls were decorated with colour posters of scenes from Britain's wild places; pictures of mountains, rivers, forests, animals, each with a biblical quote about the Lord of Creation, or the miracle of life. Sunday School pictures.

Elder Saltonstall sat at a table, eating a boiled egg. Two others stood behind him, one an identikit short-haired, black suited bravo.

The other one pointed a submachine-gun at them.

'Constable Pearson, Constable Boswell,' said Salton-stall. 'Please be good enough to put your hands in the air and fall to your knees. In that posture you will be more easily managed. You will also find it the position most appropriate for offering up a final prayer before your death.'

Scipio's head was spinning as Rochester led the way along a lengthy red-carpeted corridor lined with gilt-framed landscape paintings. 'But why are we to meet the King?' he said. 'My business is with my superiors, and the Police Commissioner.'

'The Bulls are playing a cunning game, Mechano,' said Rochester. 'We are trying to frustrate a plot against the King. Queen Dick is the only man in England whom we may be certain we can trust.'

At the end of the corridor there was a high double-door attended by an elderly man in a purple silk tailcoat frogged with gold and silver thread. He wore yellow breeches, white silk stockings and a powdered wig. His dress bore an uncomfortable resemblance to that which Scipio had worn in his previous life.

Suddenly, Scipio felt very hot. He ran his finger between neck and collar.

The servant opened the door. They passed through into a library with modern double-glazed windows looking on to an inner courtyard.

The room was empty. It was surprisingly simple for a royal apartment. Buck House had suffered innumerable indignities during the wars, and had been compre-hensively refurbished after Richard came to the throne.

The walls were lined with bookshelves containing old and modern volumes. There were a few small desks in the corners, and a large circular table in the middle with a few chairs around it. A vase of flowers and several notebooks stood on the table.

Rochester wandered to one of the windows and stared out absently. Scipio sat at the big table and examined the work in progress on it. There were several ring-bound books filled with printed or hand-drawn groups of statistics on causes of death, arranged by profession, age or date of birth.

In the years since he had been crowned, Richard had been dubbed Queen Dick by those who thought he had little influence and no power. He appeared a mere adornment to the Liberal Settlement, an eccentric curiosity; even his court ceremonial was the creation of a government commission of psychologists and advertising experts who had devised an elaborate set of false traditions. The short-term intention of this was to make the British feel more comfortable in the world, though it singularly failed to impress most Scots, who paid the King but grudging loyalty. The longer aim was to attract overseas tourists. This had succeeded; when finally the message sank in in the United States, Scandinavia, the Far East, India, Canada, Australia and New Zealand that you could visit England without being shot at by feudal secessionists or religious fanatics, they started to come in stupendous numbers. To the allures of peace were added those of cheap food, drink and hotel accommodation. The erratic nature of what businessmen called 'customer care' augmented rather than diminished the charm of a country where you could meet people who had lived hundreds of years ago and who might even be your own ancestors.

But Scipio, who could read newspapers and official statements between the lines, knew Dick for a clever and influential man. He must have been in order to settle himself on the throne in the first place. No king in English history had a worse reputation than Richard III on account of his alleged implication in the murder of his nephews in the Tower of London. And yet he had managed to parley his way back to the throne, and even into the affections of most of his subjects. Richard had been reborn towards the end of the Feudal Wars and immediately set about acquiring a faction of armed men around him in North Yorkshire. Here, carefully styling himself Richard, Duke of Gloucester, rather than using his royal title, he had fought for the Coalition cause. The story went that the price Richard had demanded for his fealty to General Lawrence had been a promise of the throne when the war was won. The promise had been kept, but the monarch's powers had been shorn to nothing, and most people were content.

The library doors opened, and Scipio leapt to his feet, all ready to bow, worrying about whether or not he was appropriately dressed.

Two of the purple flunkeys entered, but no king. They set about a little light dusting and tidying up.

Dick never mentioned religion. When it was suggested that he might build himself a private chapel at the Palace, he had refused. Dick spent most of his days in charitable good works, or parrying the dozens of aristocrats who petitioned him each week to restore their former fortunes, or at least provide them with a comfortable sinecure consistent with their status. He had even learned BBC English, the better to promote communication among his subjects.

In the course of his service to the well-being of his people, he had survived numerous assassination attempts, some by Protestants, some by various of his own in-laws and relatives (for he had assembled a mighty collection of enemies during his first career) and only one by a documented lunatic. Dick was one of the few retreads who genuinely endeavoured to live a better life this time around. He had not yet murdered anyone. At least not to Scipio's knowledge.

The two flunkies left as wordlessly as they had arrived.

Dick had married a Protestant commoner. Queen Martha was a short, modest and altogether inconspicuous woman who had died of the sweating sickness during Elizabeth's reign. The union had been blessed (or complicated) by children, and the absurd compromise had been reached whereby Prince Edward had been raised a Catholic, whereas Princess Cicely was an Anglican. In practice, the Princess's upbringing was so High Anglican as to be Catholic in all but name.

Several times it had been suggested that Richard should declare himself head of the Church of England, as had previously been the monarch's position.

Richard had refused to discuss the matter. It was said that he considered a church following the Pope in Rome (or, since the Atom War, San Francisco) was an international church, the whole of Christendom united. Besides, the King becoming an Anglican would solve none of the doctrinal arguments that had set most Protestants at each other's throats.

The doors opened again. A small man wearing an immaculate grey suit entered, smoking an expensive cigar.

There was no time to be afraid.

Either they were going to die or they were not. Clear. Simple. Black and white. That part of the job was easy.

There were three men in the room. Saltonstall sat at his desk eating his boiled egg with thick slices of bread and butter. Beside him stood a cull who was a spooney or twang or something from Covent Garden named Jacob Malahide (nasty piece of work!) and a stranger with a blond moustache and hair who closely matched the Inspector's description of the man who had tried to kill him and Inky Weems at the Globe.

There were at least half a dozen armed men outside.

Guy stood beside her with his hands in the air. He seemed calm enough. Not breathing heavily, not sweating or anything.

Probably good, but not necessarily. Everything she knew of Guy Boswell told her that he would be finding the threat of being killed a second time in a couple of weeks as much amusing as frightening.

'Go on then, on to your knees,' said Malahide. 'Do as the Elder says.' He pointed an ugly all-metal machine-gun at them. A Sten gun. Four million or so of them had been manufactured during the Hitler War and had still been around in huge quantities during the Feudal Wars. Nine-millimetre ammunition, tendency for the feed system to block up.

Amazing what you remember from training-school.

The Sten. Not a very reliable weapon, but they couldn't count on Malahide's popp jamming as he was trying to shoot them. That would be too lucky.

Besides, the other man was pointing an altogether more efficient-looking piece at them. An outlandish matt black gun she assumed was a machine-pistol, at the top of which was a cylinder which might have been a telescopic sight, but clearly wasn't.

'I said on your knees, bitch!' said Malahide.

Guy was already kneeling.

On your knees. Hmmm . . . That would make movement a little more difficult. But she had no choice in the matter.

Against us: two armed men and a religious lunatic in a small room, with several other armed men outside.

In our favour: Constable Glyndwr is waiting outside with his customary arsenal. But he doesn't know we're in trouble.

She got down to her knees. If she did not, then Malahide or Saltonstall or the other cove would hit her, and that would stop her from thinking clearly.

She and Guy had no weapons. They had decided not to bring any just in case they were searched. If they had been discovered coming into a Bull meeting-house bearing pistols they would have been in more trouble than the guns could have got them out of.

As it was, of course, they now were in trouble.

Think, girl, think. In our favour . . .

In her mouth, wedged between her back teeth and cheek was a peach. No use in this situation, but if everything was hopeless she could at least try to slap it on to one of these men before they killed her so the Inspector could track them down.

She had her keys in a pocket, along with a couple of paper tissues.

She had a radio in her shoulder-bag. Switched off. In the bag were also a small penknife, a nail-file, purse, stick of chewing-gum and a few other bits and pieces which were unlikely to be of any use.

The same shoulder-bag that Malahide was tearing from her.

Bastard.

He opened it and spilt its contents on to the floor. He stamped on the radio, cracking but not smashing its plastic casing. It would probably be useless.

'Let's not leave anything lying around, Brother Jacob,' said the tall blond man. He had a strong accent. American? Northern Irish? 'Put it all back in the bag. We'll dispose of it when we dispose of these two.'

Malahide gave blondy a dirty look, but did as the man suggested.

Interesting.

Elder Saltonstall, oblivious to his lieutenants' mutual loathing, sat at his desk and carried on eating his boiled egg.

'We should whack them outside. Somewhere quiet,' said blondy. American, definitely American, but from one of the Southern states, by the sound of him.

'We got something to show them first, Brother Ethan,' said Malahide. Blondy's name was Ethan. She filed it away for later, when she might be able to match the name with known American troublemakers.

Who was she trying to fool? They were finished. They were going to die.

No, no, no! It was her duty to the Metropolitan Police not to die, but to survive and bring these men to justice.

Not only these men, but she had also to find whoever had betrayed them. Someone must have told the Bulls that she and Guy were coming here. These men knew their names, dammit. She had not been recognized as a detective constable who pounded the streets. She had been greeted by name, and so had Guy. Someone had sold them.

Keep cool. Don't get angry.

She glanced at Guy. He knelt beside her wearing a blank expression, then caught her glance and returned it, winking.

Good.

Malahide whistled. The door burst open and some of the culls outside pushed the torn and lifeless form of Constable Glyndwr through it.

King Richard III of England and King Richard I of Scotland was indeed hunchbacked, though only slightly, and almost certainly in consequence of his age.

Rochester bowed floridly, Scipio bowed stiffly from the waist.

The king waved his hand impatiently. 'No need for any of that chickenshit writing-with-feathers nonsense when we're alone,' he growled in nobby BBC spiced with a trace of a northern English. 'Sit down. Smoke if you want. I'm damn well going to.'

The king collapsed into one of the chairs around the big table in a white cloud of cigar-smoke.

'So,' he said. 'You are Inspector Scipio Africanus.'

'Yes, sire,' said Scipio, uncertain if 'sire' was the correct form.

'Bloody stupid name, isn't it?'

Scipio was taken aback. 'Many of your Majesty's subjects have stupid names,' he said.

The King nodded, and gathered some of the books and papers from the table. 'D'you know what I've been studying recently?'

'I cannot begin to imagine, sire,' said Scipio.

'Oh!' said the King, 'I smell sarcasm there, Inspector! Well done! I like your style, man. Don't take any crap from me. I'm only the fucking King after all.' Richard broke into a giggle, and resumed arranging his papers.

'American academics,' said the King, examining a table of figures, 'love to visit and pay court. They sit and enquire of this or that episode in my past, but I know there's only one question they really want answered. Being Americans, they are forward, and they eventually find the gall to ask about the business.'

'Business, sire?'

'Yeahhh,' he drawled. 'You know. The nephews business. The princes. The sprogs in the Tower whose assassination I am widely accused of organizing . . . So anyway, when the forward Yanks ask me about the poor truncated squits, do you know how I reply, Mr Scipio? I cackle and turn all malevolent like the actor in the old film of Shakespeare's play and I say . . . NOT TELLING!'

Scipio realized that his jaw had dropped somewhat in the last minute or two.

Had Richard murdered the young King Edward V and

his brother? Had he caused them to be murdered? No one would ever know for sure unless . . .

'Has your Majesty not considered the possibility that the boys will one day be reborn? And that they will then be able to bear witness before all as to what befell them?'

'Of course I've considered the possibility, man! I go to bed each night sweating over when the brats will turn up and tell on me. Then again, Inspector, how do you know they have not already been reborn, and that I have not commissioned their murder a second time?'

The King smiled, then giggled, and then puffed on his cigar once more.

'Will you be receiving an old-age pension after your retirement, Mr Scipio?'

'Umm, yes, sire.'

'Good. I'm sure you deserve it. I won't get a pension myself. In fact, I own nothing. This old stew of a palace, all the paintings, carpets and other flummery is just my lodgings. I am as naked as the newest-arrived retread. So you see, Inspector, I have to provide for my old age lest I get sacked from my present employment, or lest they force me to retire. I am sixty-five next year, you know. And at my age you cannot simply sign on at the Labour Exchange can you? They'd ask, 'What sort of work can you do?', and I'd reply, 'Oh, you know, the usual, constitutional ruling, a little light tyranny, murdering my siblings and in-laws' . . . No, it won't do. And that, Inspector, is why I shall not yet tell the true story of the precious fucking princes in the Tower. Should I be made redundant, I shall have to sell my memoirs to support me in my old age.'

'Your Majesty should write his memoirs regardless,' said Scipio. 'You would have many interesting tales to tell, and I feel certain you have a most compelling prose-style.'

'Bollocks,' said the King. 'Writing is the most dreadful chore. I've been hammering away at the memoirs on my typewriter for years. But the chapter about the princes is handwritten, and entrusted to a very safe place.'

Rochester, who had been standing at the window, now came and sat with them at the table. The king ignored him.

'Mr African,' said His Majesty, 'do you know why Britain is so prosperous at the moment? Do you know why the country has recovered from the devastation of three catastrophic wars within a few decades?'

'Because we are at peace, sire. Because there is order, and the rule of law.'

'Well yes, yes, obviously it helps that we're not all trying to kill one another,' he said, waving his cigar impatiently. 'But the principal reason we now enjoy prosperity which is greater than we had even before the Atom War is because we have a young population. The wars killed the frail and elderly first, and our population is constantly being added to by a high birth-rate and the return to life of people who are, for the main part, in excellent fettle. We have to support comparatively few elderly people, and few invalids, Mr Scipio. In the past, these people would have been cared for by their families, but here there are many without families. And we do not want the elderly and the infirm begging on the streets, do we?'

'Certainly not, sire,' said Scipio. 'There are too many beggars already.'

'So we shall need a system of old age pensions paid by the State to those unable to support themselves,' said the King, pointing to his pile of books and papers. 'That is what I am studying.'

'Is that not the business of the Government, sire?'

'Government!?' snorted the king. 'Government!? Politicians never think beyond the next election. This is a matter which has to be thought out carefully. That is why I have engaged several experts to help me. We shall draw up a secret report, make our recommendations, I shall try to bully the politicians into accepting it, I shall have my people talk to the press and the television, start people talking about it. And do you know what will happen next, Mr Scipio?'

'No sire.'

'Some lying toerag of a politician will announce that they're bringing in state pensions, and claim it was his idea all along, the bastard. So the poor old widow Bessy Bloggs sits there warming herself by her little electric fire, her belly full of, full of, full of . . . widow-food, and she'll bless the Right Honourable Neville Nobcheese, Minister of Dissembling, Cozening and Jobbery, for her pension, and not spare a thought for the King who has worked so hard to cleanse his vile reputation as a killer of babes by striving for the welfare of his subjects down the years! I'm putting all that in my ruddy memoirs, too, you see if I don't!'

Glyndwr was dead.

'Well, that was a nice piece of theatre, Brother Jacob,'

sneered Brother Ethan. 'There'll be bloodstains throughout the building. And what on earth did your people do
to him? Go at him with razor-blades? What would be so
terrible about a nice clean kill? Huh?'

Glyndwr was dead.

Elder Saltonstall waved his hand impatiently. 'It
matters not, Brother Miller. It is enough that the man
was on Satan's business and is now dead. We may leave
the bloodstains. In two days' time the godly shall rule
the country.'

Glyndwr was dead. The big, rough ruthless man who
should have been a village blacksmith, Glyndwr who
had given her a lovely, intricate rose he had crafted
from copper the day she joined the Detective Branch,
grunting, 'Beautiful, but hard . . .'

'Amen,' said Brother Ethan Miller.

Glyndwr was dead, lying behind her and Guy where
he had been thrown like a sack of coal.

'Turn around,' said Malahide. 'Look at him. Turn. Go
on!'

Glyndwr was dead.

Still on her knees, she turned. Glyndwr, the big, crazy
Welshman, built like a tank, the man you could always
count on to look after you, was dead. No longer able to
save them or himself.

Someone had betrayed them.

Beside her, she heard Guy whisper, 'Oh my God!' in
appalled disgust.

Glyndwr had had his throat cut. Someone who didn't
have the bottom to face him head-on had come up
behind him and slit his throat. And then they had
riddled him with bullets for good measure.

'You lousy murdering filth!' she wailed. 'He was a better man than any of you cowardly swine!'

Glyndwr was dead.

Glyndwr, the man who could always get them out of trouble.

Glyndwr the walking arsenal.

'Very touching,' said Saltonstall's voice behind her. 'But we really must be about our business now.'

'Oh Glyndwr,' she screamed, 'what have they done to you!' She fell on Glyndwr's legs and hugged him around the ankles. 'How could they do this, my love!'

A little play-acting to alert Guy. Glyndwr had never been any *woman*'s love, and Guy knew it.

'You never deserved this Glyndwr! We could always count on you to get us out of trouble.'

. . . And sure enough, just where it always was, was the short-barrelled 9-mm Beretta pistol Glyndwr always kept taped around his left ankle for extreme emergencies.

Thank you, Glyndwr, thank you, you big, strange, difficult man. Thank you one last time.

Still hugging him, with her head to the spot where the gun was, she worked it loose with her right hand and thumbed the safety. She brought her left over to it to cock it.

'Oh come on, bitch!' said Malahide behind her.

Brother Ethan Miller first. He was the dangerous one, the cool one, and the one with the better gun.

Slowly, she knelt upright, keeping her hand on the pistol beneath Glyndwr's bloodied trousers, wanting to get her arm extended as far as possible.

She took a deep breath, twisted, and as fast as she

could, swung the pistol towards where Miller stood and, aiming for his midriff, fired.

With the King smiling broadly, Scipio was unable to tell if he was serious. Covering one's true opinions and intentions was probably an important component of being what they called a constitutional monarch.

A liveried servant entered and coughed gently. 'The Right Honourable Mr Alfred Bradlaw,' said the flunkey, in a strangulated nob accent.

'Here's one of the scoundrels now. Show him in, show him in,' said the King. 'At least I can half trust Bradlaw as he comes from the same part of the world as I.'

The Home Secretary, Alfred Bradlaw, was a native. Born in North Yorkshire in the 1950s, he had survived the Atom War, plagues and the Feudal Wars. In between, he had become leader of the Yorkshire coal-miners' union, and so entered politics. Although Bradlaw was not a retread, he acted like one, cultivating the dress and manners of a Victorian or Edwardian working man. He was a Methodist lay-preacher, and liked nothing better than to be filmed by the television in his shirtsleeves and flat cap cutting down trees, breaking rocks or some similar act of plain-speaking, no-nonsense destruction. At election times, Alf, as he was simply known, was reckoned worth fifty seats for the Labour Party all on his own.

Alf stood at the door, shot off a faintly embarrassed bow and entered.

'Home Secretary,' said the King, 'do sit down. This is Inspector Scipio Africanus. You know my Lord Rochester, of course.'

Alf nodded to Scipio and Rochester and sat next to the King. Prominent in the temperance movement, Alf regularly spoke out on the evils of whoring, gambling and irreligion. Scipio had imagined that Alf would barely be able to suppress his disgust at being in the same hemisphere as the Earl of Rochester, but he happily accepted a cigarette from Rochester's proffered packet.

'Well then, Rochester,' said the King, addressing him for the first time, 'what tasty little tit-bits of sedition and subversion have you and your boy-scouts uncovered this time?'

'Methinks,' said Rochester, drawing heavily on his cigarette, ''tis what gold prospectors call the mother-lode, sire. My view, and the Inspector here concurs, is that the Bulls are plotting rebellion. They presumably hope to raise the mob, and their own supporters, in open revolt against the Government, probably on Accession Day or during the week of Saint Bartholomew's fair.'

Scipio nodded. 'Or they may be playing a longer hand, planning to undermine the stability of the State and the confidence of the people.'

'Aye, and the tourist trade,' said Bradlaw, 'damn their eyes. Just when you think you've got everything going nicely, along come these idiots to bugger everything up.'

'Do you think,' said the King, 'that they plan to assassinate me? . . . Now that's a stupid question, ain't it?'

'It seems highly probable, sire,' said Scipio. 'We believe they have a pretender to put forward in Your Majesty's place.'

'Bloody Nora!' said Bradlaw. 'Who've they got?'

'King Edward the Sixth,' said Rochester.

'You what?' gasped Bradlaw.

The King smirked.

Bradlaw frowned. 'Henry the Eighth's son?'

'Correct,' said Rochester. 'He has been here for some years, but assumed the identity of one Harry Seymour, an Anglican vicar. He named himself Harry for his father, and Seymour for his mother Jane. He succeeded his father, but perished at an early age of the tuberculosis. He was very learned, and always ardent for the Protestant cause.'

'The worst kind,' snorted the King.

'How certain are you of all this, Rochester?' said Bradlaw. 'What evidence do you have?'

'I would wager my estates on it. The Bulls have recently begun to prophesy the arrival in England of a new King Josiah, a ruler who will cast down idols and prepare the way for the return of the Lord. In his own day Edward was known as Josiah because during his reign a lot of statues and other Popish things were pulled down. Remember that his father Henry was a Catholic at heart who simply desired the Church be governed from England, not Rome. Edward fell under the influence of reforming clerics and was far more radical.'

The King stood up. Bradlaw and Rochester stood, too, some court deference which Scipio was unfamiliar with. He leapt up a moment after them.

The King paced up and down the room, leaving the others standing.

'Why was this Edward not recognized at the

reception centre, or when he came up?' said the King.

Scipio said, 'I imagine he was recognized, but that a Bull sympathizer succeeded in concealing his identity and contriving a new one. He would have been instructed to keep silent for his own sake and that of the Protestant cause. The Bulls have been waiting for the right moment to pitch him into the game.'

The King's pacing accelerated. 'Yes, yes, that's possible.'

'Your Majesty should also be advised,' added Rochester, 'that he may well no longer wish to serve the Bulls' cause. We are of the view that Edward, like your majesty's pious cousin King Charles the First, has no desire for the throne.'

Charles I, executed by beheading in 1649, had reappeared at Whitehall, his head fully attached to his body, ten years ago. He was the only well-known monarch apart from William Rufus and Richard III to have thus far been reborn. Charles had realized – or had been persuaded – that his active participation in public life could have disastrous consequences. His virtual Catholicism and belief in his own divine right to rule had already caused one civil war. So now he lived a life of piety at a Catholic monastery on a Scottish island.

'The Bulls appear to have been obliged to kidnap Seymour from his house in Covent Garden,' said Rochester. 'Perhaps he is happy simply caring for the lost souls of that place. Perhaps he believes it is God's will that your Majesty be king because he was the first to be resurrected.'

'Zealots and hotheads,' spat Bradlaw. 'In my experience their interpretation of the will of the Almighty is usually pretty selective. They take that as suits 'em and explain away that as don't.'

The King stopped dead. 'Sod it,' he said. 'I do so detest wearing that bullet-proof armour on public engagements. Especially in this confounded hot weather.' He strode back to his chair and sat down. The others followed his example.

'Your Majesty would be best advised to cancel all his public engagements until this nonsense has been dealt with,' said Bradlaw.

The King turned and looked Bradlaw in the eye. 'I'll burn in hell first, so I will, Mr Home Secretary. Cancel my engagements indeed! Why, that's as good as conceding defeat to them.'

Bradlaw said, 'Sire, your courage is an inspiration to us all, but I am sure I speak for the Prime Minister as well as myself when I implore you to—'

'Pig-nuts!' snapped the King. 'I don't give a fig for what you think, Bradlaw! Nor for the opinions of your Mr Gordon Brown, that po-faced Presbyterian Machiavelli. This is nothing to do with courage since in truth I am cur-whimpering terrified. That's not what's at issue. I may not rule this country, but I have reigned over it for over thirty years. I will not see all my work overturned now, do you understand?'

Bradlaw took a deep breath, 'Sire, we cannot afford to—'

'You cannot afford to have your king abdicate to live in a sixpence-a-week nethersken. Your Labour Party – aye, and the Whigs, Conservatives and Liberals – cannot afford the publication of my candid memoirs. And you may be sure I'd publish a month before a general election. Everything, and I mean *everything* will proceed as normal! I will brook no opposition on this, Bradlaw, even if you and every other minister kisses our royal and anointed arse!'

Ethan Miller yelped and said, 'Shit!'

Beside her, Guy moved in a blur.

At his desk, Saltonstall simply said, 'Oh!'

Miller crumpled to the ground, but did not let go of his gun. A thin filament of red light burst from the cylinder on the top of its barrel and touched the wall opposite.

The men outside would come in at any moment.

No, they might assume that the gunshot was the sound of Guy or her being killed.

Guy, she realized, had taken Malahide in a rugger tackle.

Malahide was on the floor, Guy was on top of him, wrestling him for possession of the Sten gun.

Saltonstall sat at his desk. He might have a weapon somewhere.

She walked over to Miller, who sat on the floor, more interested in the blood seeping from his leg than in using his gun.

All piss and wind. They usually were.

She had missed his stomach and shot him in the leg instead. The wound did not look at all serious. Just a scratch.

She pushed the Beretta to Miller's head. He got the message and offered up his gun.

Guy stood up, holding Malahide's Sten gun, grinning like a Saxon farmer tasting his first chocolate bar. 'Jolly good show, partner.'

'Don't thank me, thank Glyndwr. And it's not over yet. Cover these two. Malahide, Miller, lie on the floor please, with your palms flat on the ground. Elder Saltonstall, please keep your hands on your desk.'

Miller and Malahide slowly, resentfully, did as they were told.

Saltonstall sat and smiled.

You don't faze me, you mad bastard. He might be insane enough to want to die.

Miller's exotic machine-pistol had a leather strap hanging from its stock. She slung it on her shoulder. She picked up her handbag and tried the radio. It was useless.

'Telephone?' she asked of Saltonstall.

The man shrugged.

'Invention of the Devil? Telecommunications the spawn of Satan?'

Saltonstall shrugged and smiled again.

There were at least half a dozen heavily armed men out there, not to mention three temporarily disarmed ones in here who would give a great deal to see to it that she and Guy died horribly. They needed to get out of here, and to do that they needed help.

'Cover him as well,' she said to Guy, nodding towards Saltonstall. 'I'll search these two.'

She knelt by Miller first, holding her gun to his face with her right hand, patting him up and down with her left.

Nothing. A handkerchief, a set of brass knuckles and some loose change, some of it American.

'You from the States, then?' she said pleasantly.

'Fuck you,' he said.

She went to Malahide to repeat the procedure, trying not to look at the blood-sodden corpse of Glyndwr next to him. She knelt with her back to Saltonstall and coughed delicately into her hand. As she did so, she spat out the tiny radio beacon she had earlier put in her mouth.

She patted Malahide down. There was an ivory-handled knife tucked into the waistband of his trousers. This she pocketed.

The rest of Malahide's possessions – battery-powered torch, a few Bull handbills, cigarettes and a lighter, a few coins, yielded no information.

'What's the torch for, cully?'

'Go fuck yourself, Papist whore,' he muttered, matter-of-factly.

He could want a torch for all manner of things. All the same, it seemed curious to carry one in daylight.

She unscrewed the top of the torch with some difficulty. She dropped its two batteries out on to Malahide's back. There was nothing of any interest hidden inside it.

She slowly became aware that Malahide, who had turned his head from her, was mumbling under his breath. At first she thought he was praying. Then she realized he was cursing her. '. . . Papist bitch . . . filthy slut . . . bet you can't get enough priest-cock . . . fucking love it . . .'

She considered kicking him, but decided she was above that kind of thing. Like a lot of retread males, Malahide had a problem with women.

She felt in the last of his pockets. There was nothing except fluff there. She left the peach in it.

'We're arresting Elder Saltonstall,' she announced as she stood up, 'and taking him for questioning.'

Saltonstall shrugged. Guy nodded.

She moved closer to Guy. 'We'll go out through the hall and the main door,' she said quietly. 'I'll keep an eye on the Elder. You cover anyone who tries to follow us. Be careful with that thing. If you have to fire it, try and keep it to short bursts or you'll lose your aim and be out of ammunition in no time. Keep looking around in every direction. Don't forget to look upwards, too.'

'Wilco,' said Guy.

She'd not offer anything better than evens they'd come out of this alive. All turned on Saltonstall's willingness to go meekly.

'Stand up,' she said to him. 'Nice and slowly.'

Saltonstall stood, his arms hung limp at his sides.

She wished she had a pair of handcuffs.

There was a desk-lamp on the floor, in among the detritus of the Elder's supper. It had a few feet of plastic-coated flex. She moved behind Saltonstall and, jamming the gun into his spine with her left hand, she wrenched the thing from its wall-socket. She handed Guy her gun and took Malahide's knife from the pocket in her long skirt.

She cut the flex from the lamp and used it to bind Saltonstall's hands behind his back as tight as she could manage.

'You'll not get out of here alive,' he said loudly. 'In a few moments you'll be speeding on your way to Hell.'

'I think not, Upright Man,' she spat into his ear. 'You see I really am a Papist. My faith is every bit as strong as yours. Death holds no fear either for me or for my colleague. So forget all this schlenter about which of us is the most pious and get on with the job.' She yanked the last knot on the flex tight.

She wasn't a Papist at all, but talking like one might stoke up some fear in him.

She held out her hand. Guy placed her gun into it.

She bent down and picked up her bag with its useless radio.

'You go first,' she said to Saltonstall, and nudged him forward around the fallen table towards the door. 'If your chums outside try sandbagging us, you'll die first.'

They formed their procession just inside the door. Saltonstall first, then her holding the pistol in his back, then Guy and his machinegun facing back into the room to ensure Malahide and Miller didn't rise just yet.

'Now when I push you forwards,' she said to Saltonstall, 'take ten steps out into the hall. Remember they need you. Fail me and you fail God,' she ad libbed.

Her car was parked 100 yards or so from the main entrance to the hall. The roads around here would be fairly quiet now. If the Bulls didn't know it was hers, if they hadn't disabled it, they were clean away.

Even if they could not use the car, they would at least be out in the open. There was a chance of running for it, or of reaching the first house or shop with a telephone wire coming from it. They could call Bow Street or whoever was on duty at their secret lurk in Baker Street.

Even though someone had warned the Bulls they were coming.

And if she ever got out of this in one piece, whoever the traitor was would go down for a million years.

'We're coming out!' she shouted. 'Don't try anything

or this heretic scum gets it in the head. And don't think we give a damn about what happens to us after that just as long as we take some of you to Hell with us,' she yelled, adding 'Prod bastards,' for good effect.

She pushed Saltonstall forward. He was all very matter-of-fact.

At the threshold, he turned his face right and left as though about to cross a busy street. The letters branded into his cheeks burned redder than ever.

Saltonstall stepped forward, the blackness of his Puritan's coat, breeches and stockings contrasting with the harsh light of the hall ahead of him.

He took nine more paces, looking straight ahead.

'Stop there!' she said from her position of comparative safety inside the doorway. 'Turn to face me.'

Saltonstall obeyed.

She was about to step out, to take up position behind him, when she noticed the open door had a keyhole in it.

The door was open wide, almost touching the inside wall.

'Key,' she said to Guy, nodding at the door beside her.

He understood. Without taking either gun or gaze from the two Upright Men lying on the floor, he used his left hand to pull back the door, reach around it and emerge with a key.

She smiled at him.

'I'm coming out now,' she said loudly. 'My partner has a machine-gun trained on the Elder . . .'

She took a deep breath and smartly strode out, slipping behind the Elder, facing the door where Guy now stood alone.

To either side of the door, ten men, most of them

armed with shotguns or Sten guns, pressed close in against the wall. A few of them looked at the floor, frightened. But most looked at her with faces which spoke eloquently of what they wished to do to her.

'Drop your weapons,' she said. 'Or the Elder dies for the Good Old Cause one more time.'

She was sounding like the villain in a second-rate cowboy film!

The Bulls, all young and fit, all wearing sober suits, muttered among themselves.

She heard the word 'bluff', turned her gun towards the ceiling and fired, close to Saltonstall's ear.

The shot crashed around the hall, reverberating again and again.

'Do it!' screamed Malahide from inside the office. 'Do as she says. We must not let her imperil our plans.'

Each man slowly and gently laid his weapon on the floor.

'Come out, Guy,' she said. 'Beside me. Keep an eye behind.'

He stepped out smartly.

When he was beside her, with his machine gun trained on the Bulls, she motioned them to go through the door into the dressing room where their two comrades still lay.

The leading ones to either side hesitated, then slouched into the room.

Guy rushed forward, reached in, pulled the door closed, then pushed his key into the lock and turned it.

Most of the chairs in the hall were still laid out in neat rows, but someone had begun stacking them at the sides of the hall.

Guy slung the Sten gun over his shoulder and took a pile of ten or so chairs and put them against the door. He repeated this three times.

Then he picked up each of the weapons from the floor, ejected cartridges and pulled out clips and put them in his pockets.

'Let's go!' she said.

Guy took one last stack of chairs and tumbled it forward, scattering them in front of the door. It might buy them a few more seconds when the Bulls burst through the door.

They had seen no other doors or windows to the little dressing-room. She hoped there were no hidden exits.

There was still no one else around. 'If you cry out,' she told Saltonstall, 'you will die. You will have failed.'

They walked smartly towards the main door, through it and into the evening light. Guy tucked the machine-pistol into his jacket. She opened her shoulder-bag, threw out the broken radio and put the pistol into it.

She still had Miller's fancy black gun slung over her shoulder. It was no use to her. She wouldn't know what to do with it. She took it and examined it. There was a long box in front of the grip, the magazine presumably. She thumbed a catch at the top of the magazine and it came loose. She pocketed it and threw the rest of the gun on the floor.

'Let's go,' she said.

The hall was among small factories and warehouses. There were few people around; it was evening and tomorrow was a public holiday.

They turned left and made for where her car was

parked. An elderly man in flat cap and stifling overcoat wished them good evening.

Two bored-looking security guards in smart uniforms passed them on the other side of the wide and traffic-free road. One saluted Elder Saltonstall, not noticing his hands were bound, or that a woman appeared to be keeping her hand in a shoulder-bag which was permanently held against his back.

Her car, a white L-reg Mini Cooper, waited 50 yards ahead. The bigger Humber that Glyndwr had come in was around somewhere, but she could not see it.

'*Damn*!!'

Guy was on the ground, sprawled straddling the kerb and the pavement.

'Tripped,' he said. 'Actually, I think our friend the Elder here stuck his foot out, and . . .' He stood up, then collapsed again, with a sprained or broken ankle.

She bent down to try and give him a hand, get his arm over her.

This was the moment Saltonstall chose to bend forward and stumble back towards the building, his hands still bound behind him.

There was a commotion from the door of the meeting room. The caged Bulls had burst free and were now after them.

'Go!' said Boswell. 'Get out of here! There's no sense in the both of us being killed. Damn!'

He was right. But you are not supposed to desert your partner.

Saltonstall was falling safely into the arms of one of the big men at the door as the others hesitated.

'Jenny, for pity's sake, leave now!' said Boswell from

the ground. 'You can't take me!'

The Bulls, reassured their leader was all right, were turning towards them. One was taking aim with a shotgun.

Boswell rolled over on the ground and pointed his machine-pistol at the men. He tried pulling the trigger.

Nothing happened.

'It's jammed. Away with you! You must report what has happened. It's your duty!'

She knew he was right.

'We'll get you back, I swear it,' she said.

'Yes, yes,' he said from the ground, pretending to draw a bead on the Bulls with his useless gun.

She ran towards her car and jammed the keys into the driver's door, never looking back.

Her hand shook.

The door was open.

She got in, jammed the key into the ignition and turned it.

The engine started.

She put it into first and let off the handbrake.

She eased up the clutch, gave it plenty of gas. The car moved forward.

She looked back. A group of small black figures was behind her, arms and legs working furiously, like angry insects . . .

The car shot forwards.

In the mirror, she saw a dozen black-suited men, a swarm of furious insects. Jacob Malahide was in front, carrying an old-style double-barrelled shotgun.

Her foot jammed into the floor.

Second gear.

The men were running.

Third gear. The engine screamed.

The Bulls were getting closer.

Fourth.

There was a distant bang.

Then another.

The clock said she was doing 45 m.p.h.

The car jerked. Something spattered against the back like hailstones. The car jerked again.

In the mirror, the back window frosted over, then fell down like a dropped towel.

She was getting further and further away from the insects. Malahide, the lead insect, had broken open his gun to feed in more cartridges.

She shot through a red light at the crossroads taking her out of the estate.

THINGS REMEMBERED (5)

PILOT OFFICER GUY BOSWELL, 171 SQUADRON
RAF BIGGIN HILL, SUNDAY 18 AUGUST, 1940

Fliers' kit moved in a blur of grey-blue, brown and orange.

Everyone had a personal ritual to try and ensure good luck and good hunting. Old Dougal Templeton, the Squadron Leader, made a point of kicking Neville, something that was getting increasingly difficult as the dog learned to associate the order to scramble with imminent pain. Bunny Williams got his nickname from the rabbit's foot he would pull from his pocket and throw into the air. Both Prune Warren and Stinker Higgitt touched the swastika on the slice of Heinkel they had nailed inside the door of the hut.

Boswell's ritual was much more pragmatic. 'Don't forget your leg-straps. Don't forget your leg-straps. Don't forget your leg-straps,' he recited to himself like some Indian holy man as he ran to his Hurricane pulling on his jacket and Mae West. He swiped up his helmet and goggles and yanked them on. 'Don't forget your leg-straps.'

The ground-crew started the engine as Boswell pulled on his parachute from where he had carefully laid it and its straps out on the aircraft's tailplane.

He clambered into the cockpit, strapped himself in

and plugged in the R/T jack. He pulled his glasshouse back and forth a few times to make sure it was working properly. Nothing worse than finding yourself locked into a burning aircraft.

He gave the erk the thumbs-up.

Moments later the squadron was tearing off the ground and making angels.

Down below to his starboard were four cyclists in a country lane. They'd dropped their bikes and were shading their eyes to get a better view of the Hurricanes. Beyond them, a man and a woman stood in the kitchen garden of a farmhouse, waving. A group of kids by a stream jumped up and down, yelling silent and doubtless bloodthirsty cheers. It was like a scene from a newsreel.

The squadron formed up with each section – Green, Blue, Yellow and Red – flying in a vee of three aircraft each. Yellow Section wove around above the rest in case any bandits tried to clobber them from on high. Boswell flew with Red Section, led by Templeton himself.

Over the R/T the ops room twats pointed them south-east. It was bombers, large formation. They'd have Messerschmitts above for escorts, but Group would be vectoring in Spitfires from somewhere else to see them off. At least, that was the plan.

They made contact less than five minutes later, exactly where the twats said they'd be. Stinker saw them first, calling everyone's attention to the swarm of black dots in the middle of the clear blue sky off to the south. There were too many of them, too far away to count, like a horde of midges over a Scottish loch.

Things Unborn

The Old Man called the 'Tally Ho!' to let the Ground Controller know the Boches were in sight, then ordered his squadron to open up to full throttle and charge bald-headed at them.

Boswell watched them getting bigger. Heinkel IIIs. They seemed to sit still in the air.

That meant they were heading straight for one another, closing at 7 miles a minute.

The most important role of the Hurricanes, the Old Man never tired of telling his pilots, was not necessarily to shoot down bombers (though there was no harm in that, by Jove), it was to break their formation. That way, a lot fewer of the swine would be able to drop their bombs on target, and once they were deprived of the mutual protection of their defensive armament, they could be shot to smithereens at leisure. This was why the Old Man was keen on flying straight into their faces. It took a bit of nerve, but was no more dangerous than squaring up to them from any other angle. And it put the fear of God up them.

Boswell picked his target. He flexed his thumb over the firing-button as he closed.

In the corner of his eye another bomber jinked up and down to avoid having to look Templeton or Stinker in the eye.

Momentarily, the sun glinted off the glass nose of his Heinkel like the flare from a Very pistol.

The nose-gunner opened up, nervously popping red tracers uselessly wide.

The silvery shark's nose of the Jerry moved into the graticules of his gunsight.

He eased his thumb into the tit.

His aircraft shuddered a little as his eight .303 machine-guns opened up. He gave it two seconds.

The bullets tore open the Heinkel's crystal snout, then its remaining glass suddenly shocked red with a blot of blood.

'Lord!' gasped Boswell, still driving straight for the Heinkel. Again he fired, wanting to put the machine out of its misery, before yanking the stick backwards to avoid colliding with it. Passing over where it should have been, he saw it was already heading for the ground, trailing a smudge of black and white smoke.

'Good show, Guy,' said someone. 'The beers are on you tonight. I'll vouch for you on that one.' Boswell nodded to himself as he put his craft into a U-turn to come back into the scrap and bag himself another.

'Silence on the R/T,' snarled Templeton. 'Nice kill, Boswell. Come on, you shower, let's get some more of the blighters . . .'

'Messerschmitts!' yelled Popeye Crewe from Yellow Section. Boswell paid no attention. Surely he had a few seconds' grace to concentrate on the job in hand.

He was now coming at the jittery German formation from above and behind. If you ignored their big, sensually-curved wings, the Heinkels looked like oversized mackerel from this angle.

'Boswell! Behind you!' someone shouted. Still mesmerized by the Heinkel whose tailplane was just moving into his gunsight, Boswell fired, probably ineffectively, and peeled away.

Too late. Half a dozen bullets banged into the armour plating behind his seat. In the mirror he saw a 109 hanging on to his tail, its wing guns spitting poison. There was no way his machine could turn and meet the more manoeuvrable German. Boswell pushed the stick forward as far as it would go and went into a steep dive, the only thing that might give him some speed on the Hun.

In seconds, the plane roared and shuddered like some furious primeval monster. The needle touched 400, faster than God or Sidney Camm had ever intended a Hurricane to move.

The 109 was still after him as he levelled out, hoping to use the momentum of the dive to take his aircraft into a fast turn, get behind the Jerry and take a shot at him.

Coming around, he saw the 109 had better things to worry about; Stinker was behind him, plugging 303s up his arse like there was no tomorrow.

Stinker's Hurricane and the Jerry plunged downward towards the green and yellow patchwork of the Home Counties below. In moments, they had disappeared from view completely.

He decided not to follow, looking upwards to try and find his way back to the main battle.

The sky was completely empty.

This had happened to him before. You left a scrap for just a moment and it disappeared. He had no idea where everyone else would be. The last time, he had asked the rest of the squadron where they were over the R/T before realizing what a dotty question it was.

He pulled out his hankie, wiped some of the sweat from his face and looked at his watch. He had been aloft for less than fifteen minutes. Aside from a few bullets up the jacksie there didn't appear to be any damage; all the controls responded, and he had plenty of fuel and ammunition left. He turned towards the coast to stooge around for Jerry stragglers.

As soon as he turned his Hurricane he spotted a series of tiny flashes and blooms of sooty smoke over to the east. A stick of oil bombs. There didn't appear to be any town nearby, and no airfield he knew of. By the look of it, a wounded Hun was jettisoning to lose weight, trying to make it back across the Channel.

Once more, Boswell's aircraft screamed in complaint as he put it into a dive.

Whoever had dropped the bombs would be out to sea by now.

In a moment, his judgement was rewarded when he spotted a Dornier flying across the Channel at about 8,000 feet, gradually losing height all the time. Its cockpit was badly shot up, and there was a wispy trail of coolant coming from her port engine.

Boswell eased it into his sights. Its crew hadn't even noticed him yet.

There was a blinding flash and a deafening explosion in the left side of the cockpit, somewhere behind the instrument panel. Then a numbing blow to his arm.

In the mirror he saw behind him a brace of 109s. They'd come at him out of the sun.

He pulled the stick backwards, clutching it to his belly to try and gain height, then swing around and get as far inland as possible.

He could never outrun or out-climb the 109s, but he needed the height if he had to bale out. If he ran inland there was a good chance the 109s might have to break off and go home. They didn't have enough fuel to stay over England for long.

In the mirror he saw a Messerschmitt right behind him, its wingtips sparking venom.

He was soaked in petrol.

The bandits had punched a hole in the reserve tank in front of the instrument panel. There were 45 gallons in there and now it was hosing out all over him.

The stick went slack and the Hurricane flipped over and over into a spin. The cracks and spatterings of German bullets went on and on and on.

He turned off the fuel and opened out the throttle to empty the carburettor to try and lessen the danger of fire. Petrol was slopping around the cockpit, his clothes were soaking. Just one little spark and he'd brew up like a dried-out Christmas tree.

The engine coughed to a stop, the prop slowed until it was just turning over in the slipstream. He switched off the ignition. He pushed the stick forward and worked the rudder-bars to try and pull out of the spin. The stick wouldn't respond properly.

With his own engine cut, he clearly heard the hum of the Daimler Benz engine coming at him from behind. In the mirror he saw a 109's vicious black and yellow prop spinner, looking like some oversized wasp.

He watched almost dispassionately as the Jerry's wing shuddered. He jerked forward as the bullets slammed into the plane somewhere behind him.

The whole world turned crimson.

Something hit him on the side of the head.

His aircraft was spinning downwards again. There was a bright red haze in the cockpit and the stench of petrol was making him nauseous. Through the red mist the altimeter read 5,000 feet. His head was aching, his left arm and right leg hurt.

There was something he was supposed to do, but he couldn't think what it was.

The right side of his face was numb, as though it had been walloped with the flat of a cricket bat. He touched his finger to it gently. There was a huge, ragged gash in his cheek, all the way from ear to mouth. His oxygen mask had been torn off and was flapping about in the breeze on one side. The lower half of the flesh on his cheek and jaw was flapping on the other side.

The red fog in the cockpit was his own blood.

It was pouring out, then being whipped up and turned to spray by the wind tearing through all the bullet holes in the glass of his canopy.

The canopy. That's right. That's what he had to do. He remembered now. He had to open the greenhouse, get the hell out of here and use his parachute.

He tried to open the canopy.

It wouldn't budge.

He could not move the canopy.

He could not move his legs to kick anything.

The pain and the noise disappeared as he became aware that there was red mist being whipped up from his abdomen, too.

A number of bullets had gone through the middle of him. One had smashed through his spine. Though he had felt no pain, and couldn't see everything through his jacket and Mae West, he now knew and understood that he had been virtually cut in half.

The ground was getting closer. No matter, the crate

would like as not brew up in a moment or two. It was evens as to which would get him first — terra firma or combustion.

He wished he had a cigarette, wished he could sit back, relax, put his feet up and enjoy his death properly. He had imagined that if he were to spend his last moments in the cockpit, it would be in some desperate panicky struggle to open the canopy, or get out, or douse flames. Instead, he felt terribly cool and detached.

Part of him was awfully sad; this was dashed rotten luck, for him, for Pamela, for Mother, the Guv'nor. But it was exciting, too; this was the ultimate fairground ride, and at the end of it lay the answer to the Big Question.

He reached up with his good arm — hard work, for some reason — and rubbed the red mist from the windscreen.

Fields, trees, corn, a road, a small lorry moving along it.

Shouldn't be too long now.

If there was an afterlife, all well and fine. If there wasn't, if he was just consigned to some kind of oblivion, well that was all right. If he was not conscious, then he couldn't possibly be bothered about the fact that he didn't exist, could he?

He'd told this to the Padre only last night. The Padre didn't like it one bit. Said it was barrack-room lawyer's logic.

It would be a field. A ploughed field. He could see the furrows of fine black soil. It would be soft, dried and warmed by the sun.

The warm blackness embraced Guy Boswell.

VI

SATURDAY, 23 AUGUST 2008

It may be we are meant to mark with our riot and our rest
God's scorn for all men governing. It may be beer is best.
But we are the people of England; and we have not spoken
yet.
Smile at us, pay us, pass us. But do not quite forget.
– G.K. Chesterton, The Secret People

This is the BBC Home Service and here are the news headlines at seven a.m. on Saturday the twenty-third of August 2008.

We are receiving reports of an explosion in St James's Park, London. Police do not as yet know its cause. There are no reports of any casualties, and it is not expected to disrupt any of today's Accession Day events.

The London Guild of Hoteliers and Innkeepers has reported a record number of bookings for the month of August. This year, all available statistics indicate that Britain will have a record number of overseas visitors, particularly from the United States and Britain's former dominions in Canada, Australasia and Southern Africa. This year has also seen larger than ever numbers of tourists from Japan and the Far East. Tourist industry representatives believe that this will be the busiest week of the year, with many visitors coming to London for the Accession Day celebrations. The Home Secretary, the Right Honourable Mr Alfred Bradlaw, says that he anticipates no difficulty in keeping order among the crowds which are expected in London today. People are being warned to beware of pickpockets, particularly if they visit the St Bartholomew Fair, which also begins today. Mr Bradlaw added that the tourists were welcome and valued guests who had it in their power to bring unparalleled prosperity to Great Britain.

President Collins of the Irish Republic has joined the country's Prime Minister, Miss Claire Hayes, in calling on Irish citizens who have emigrated to Britain to consider returning home. The Irish economy is currently suffering from an acute labour shortage in its booming electronics industries. Although the country was unharmed in the Atom War, its agricultural economy and dependence on imported manufactures minimized its economic growth for much of the last century and many Irish nationals emigrated to Britain in search of work. In recent years, the boom in Irish and foreign-owned companies manufacturing and assembling electrical, electronic and optical goods has led to an increased demand for workers which the arrival of retreads is insufficient to resolve. President Collins said he is also keen to encourage workers from Ulster, particularly Protestants, to come and work in the Republic as it would improve understanding between the two communities.

Scipio turned the transistor radio off, threw a teabag into the mug of boiling water and mashed at it with a spoon which had been chained to the table. There was no milk. He spooned two heaps of sugar into the mug and stirred it, then took it over to the curtained-off corner of the room where Pearson had been trying (and failing, almost certainly) to sleep.

He pulled back the curtain to find her lying fully clothed, with Inky sat on a canvas chair next to her.

'Breakfast,' he said. 'I fear this will have to suffice until O'Rourke comes back with the groceries.'

'Thanks, chief,' she said, taking the mug. Her eyes were red and there were bloodstains on her clothes. Glyndwr's blood. Otherwise, she looked a lot more composed than any other rozzer would be.

He crouched down beside her and offered her and Inky a cigarette.

Inky took one, she refused. He nodded at Inky to leave them alone for a moment. Inky took the hint.

'I'm just going to visit the little boys' room,' he said.

Scipio put the cigarette pack back in his jacket and sat down beside her on the chair Inky had been on.

'Shall we fetch you a doctor? A sedative pill might help a little.'

'I'll be all right thanks, sir,' she said weakly.

'Pearson, you know me well enough now to realize that I am parsimonious in bestowing praise. But I want you to know that what you did yesterday evening was amazing work. To keep your wits about you in the way you did and to escape in one piece like that was admirable in the extreme.'

She shook her head. 'I failed, sir. We all did. Glyndwr is dead, Boswell probably dead as well, and we are not a bit closer to foiling whatever devilment the Upright Men are about. All I did was save my own hide.'

'No, Pearson. It was no fault of yours that Glyndwr was killed, and as for Boswell, it was tripping over that let him down. You almost succeeded in saving him, you brought us back the names of three of the principal conspirators, and you managed to place a peach on one of the Bulls. That we have been unable to get a signal from it is hardly your fault. And you have succeeded in saving one of the best police officers it has ever been my privilege to work with. Umm, by that I mean yourself.'

'You flatter me, boss.'

'No, Pearson, I do not. I have never flattered anyone in this life.'

She sighed and lay back. She pointed to two posters pinned to the wall beside her. One was a faded and torn silkscreen print of a bit of rolling English countryside. A propaganda picture from the time of the Hitler War. 'YOUR BRITAIN – FIGHT FOR IT NOW', said the caption underneath. Beside it was a smaller picture, a map of the London Underground, the system of tunnels where trains had once run, carrying Londoners about their daily business and pleasures.

'I didn't sleep much last night,' she said. 'I spent a long time looking at those things. I suppose I'm in shock or something, but there was a time I really believed that if I stared at the wall for long enough I'd be able to make sense of all this.'

He patted her on the shoulder and smiled.

The game was up. Whatever the Bulls were about, it was too late to stop them. Now all he could do was salvage what he could from this mess.

Could he salvage Pearson? Could he make her strong? Could he prevent her from having nightmares for years to come about Glyndwr's corpse or Boswell lying on the ground demanding that she desert him?

'Do you believe in God, sir?'

'Do you?'

'I'm a rozzer. I believe what I see, though I sometimes allow a little intuition.'

'There's your answer. Me too, Pearson. The best coppers are all agnostics.'

'I can't understand these people at all. It just doesn't make any sense.'

'That is why the only really interesting thing in this world is people, Pearson. I am fifty-two years old and every day I will encounter some act of startling human stupidity, or wickedness, or kindness, or selflessness. My capacity for being amazed is as powerful as ever.'

'Who set us up, sir? Who told the Bulls that we were going to their meeting? Who is responsible for Glyndwr's death? And Boswell's?'

He shook his head. That was the hardest thing to cope with. At best, it had been one of the few people in the Home Office or the Met who knew what they were doing. Perhaps they had organized for this place to be bugged. At worst, it was someone they knew well. Whoever it was, he (or she) would be caught. He would see to that.

Beyond the curtain, the sound of O'Rourke coming in with some food.

'Well, we can have a decent fry for breakfast at the least,' he said.

'Begging the Detective Sergeant's pardon an' all,' said Inky, 'but your cooking is horrible. Everything swimming in grease and lard. Now why don't you let me do breakfast for us?'

'I'm easy,' said O'Rourke. 'Are you sure you can do it with only one hand?'

'Just leave it to me, Sergeant. It's the least I can do to

repay your hospitality. I take it I can trust you to do us all some strong coffees? I don't think any of us got much sleep and it's going to be a whoreson long day.'

'Come and have some breakfast,' Scipio said to Pearson.

She shook her head. 'I'm not hungry, sir.'

When Scipio had joined the Police Service, there were precious few women officers, and he still did not know quite the best way to deal with them. Were they honorary men, or were they different?

Matteradamn. 'Pearson,' he said, 'I cannot be hard on you after the hell you have been through, but I suggest that you have something to eat. There is a possibility, however slim, that we might be able to be of some service today. In order to do that, you will need some sustenance and a heavy dose of caffeine.'

She smiled weakly and got off the bed. 'A hot bath and a change of clothes would be a lot better.'

'I fear I cannot help you there.'

They had acquired a primus stove and a large frying pan which had been placed on one corner of the big table in the middle of the room. Here Inky busied himself with eggs, bacon, tomatoes and bread. Over in the corner, O'Rourke made coffee.

Scipio and Pearson sat at the table, Pearson nursing the mug of black tea he had made her earlier.

Late into the night, the four of them had sat or paced, chain-smoking, drinking coffee, worrying at the problem from various angles, to no avail. Just before three, he had ordered them all to get some sleep.

And now there had been an explosion in St James's Park, a few hundred yards from the Palace. Scipio had confirmed by phoning Bow Street that it was almost certainly a bomb.

Alf Bradlaw himself had rung shortly afterwards. He was nervous. He had every right to be. There was now no doubt the Bulls were going to try something today; assassinate the King, probably; excite the mob and proclaim the former Edward VI king once more, probably. And Lord only knew how many more bombs they were going to let off. Bradlaw had spelled it out: 'Even if they do not succeed in raising the mob and killing the King, they'll disrupt bloody everything, they'll kill innocent people and they'll louse up the tourist industry for a couple of years. They have well and truly pissed on my chips, Inspector . . . The only good thing is it'll stop the Liberals whining about free trade. Them poncey gits are so frit of the Puritans that the PM's just got them to sign on the dotted to keep us in power through to the election.'

'It's going to be another hot day out there,' said O'Rourke.

Scipio could imagine. Here they were, cooped up in this hole under the ground while up above the light would already be white. Crisp air, passing motor traffic, the clatter of horses' hooves, the cooing of pigeons, the banter and cries of people starting about what promised to be a profitable day's business.

He felt tired and sick, but dared not show it. The loss of Glyndwr, the likely loss of Boswell, his failure to resolve this case . . . all this and the fact that someone must have betrayed Glyndwr, Boswell and Pearson to the Bulls, bore down on him like a half-ton of bricks.

Worst of all, he was still fighting the same battle he

thought had been won years ago. This time, he was fighting it alone.

No, it was no good.

'We have lost it,' he said to Pearson and O'Rourke. 'After breakfast, you two can go home. Get some rest. Inky, you can lie low here as long as you need to. If you are worried about reprisals from the Bulls, I will arrange for you to be moved somewhere else in the country. We will forge a new identity for you.'

Inky grinned and held up the blunt knife he was trying to slice tomatoes with. 'No disrespect, Inspector, but if Inky wants a new identity, Inky will cook it up a sight better than any rozzer can.'

'What'll you do, sir?' asked O'Rourke.

'The only remaining thing I can do. I shall join the King and should the need arise, I shall . . .'

'Ah now,' said O'Rourke. 'There's no need to talk that way. Besides, the King already has plenty of detectives to protect him.'

'None that have ever seen his likely assassin face-to-face,' said Scipio.

'True enough. I'll come with you then,' said O'Rourke.

'Me too,' said Pearson. 'I got a better look at this Ethan Miller than any of you.'

'Please yourselves,' said Scipio. 'What is his Majesty's itinerary?' he asked O'Rourke.

'First, the Lord Mayor's Parade. He'll be watching from an upper window of the Mansion House.'

'He's probably safe there,' said Scipio. 'They'll have searched the building thoroughly for bombs, and he'll be behind bulletproof glass for most of that.'

'Next,' said O'Rourke, 'he takes a barge to Chelsea to open the new Pensioners' Hospital there. Then back by boat and car to the Palace for lunch, then he troops the Colours, inspects a new armoured regiment, salutes a flypast by the Air Force, then goes to a banquet with the Prime Minister at the Guildhall in the evening . . .'

'All told, plenty of opportunities to throw bombs and shoot at him,' said Scipio. 'Very well, after the splendid feast which Inky is forging for us, we shall go and join him at the Mansion House.'

'While we're waiting,' said O'Rourke, 'I'll go and get the car ready and bring it round to the front of the building. There'll be no problem parking it there this early.'

'No,' said Scipio, 'Let us walk. With all the crowds and traffic, it will be quicker.'

The bacon and fat began to sizzle in the frying-pan. Scipio stood up and went to the door. Next to the light switches was a button which turned on the extractor-fans – very necessary in this airless room. 'I am sorry, Pearson,' he said, turning, 'but I fear I have to have a cigarette . . .'

She was no longer sitting at the table. Under the harsh strip-lights, her shape behind the thin curtain in the sleeping corner was visible.

He walked over, unwilling to pull the curtain aside lest she was on some private business.

'Are you all right, Pearson?'

No answer.

'Help me with this loaf of bread, will you?' Inky said to O'Rourke.

'Pearson, is anything the matter?'

No answer.

Oh hell, the poor girl was going to pieces on him. Well, he could not blame her.

He pulled the curtain aside. Pearson stood by the bed, staring at the wall. At the propaganda poster and the fancy coloured lines of the Underground map.

'Pearson?'

'We're walking, sir. You said there was no sense in taking the car because of the traffic. I've been looking at this wall half the night and the answer was staring at me all the time. The sewer-trams, the Underground. That's where the Bulls' lurk is, sir. That's where they're hiding.'

Boswell was pretty sure the man lying on a palliasse next to him was Seymour, though in the poor light he couldn't be absolutely certain.

He had tried whispering to him a couple of times, but the chap was too busy coughing and wheezing and praying. The Bulls took slightly more notice of Seymour than they did of him, and when they did it was with a queer mixture of respect, contempt and outright curiosity. They seemed a little in awe of him. It made sense. The man was a former King of England who evidently didn't fall in with whatever plans they had for him.

He had problems enough of his own. His ankle hurt like buggery. Normally he would be earnestly hoping it hadn't been broken, but that wasn't the half of it.

He had expected to be dead by now, but the Bulls had a lot of other business on their minds and reasoned that a living man, even one with a broken ankle, would be less cumbersome than a corpse.

Besides, they had been very keen to find out what the police knew of them, what Jenny and he had found out at the meeting, and where she would have gone when she made her escape.

He had been pushed down a hole in the ground, and had been made to hobble along what he realized was the London Underground for what seemed like miles to this place, a dimly lit station platform where the air was thick with petrol-exhaust.

Close by, Ethan Miller, the one with all the guns and the electrical gubbins, spoke to Malahide.

'Okay, Brother Jacob,' Boswell clearly heard him say, 'I've labelled each one of these switches. There's a little picture of a square for Leicester Square, a cross for Charing Cross and so on. All you have to do is listen to the BBC commentary through the day on the Home Service on this transistor radio and judge when's the best time to let 'em rip.'

Brother Jacob nodded and smiled. Malahide didn't hate Miller so much now that he had seen all the fuss the tall American had made when he was grazed in the leg by a little bullet. Miller was a blowhard. Malahide was the hard man here.

Around them there were three or four dozen men busy with a printing press, bundles of leaflets, with ugly-looking guns and the ammunition for them. There was plenty of praying going on as well.

They had questioned Boswell about how much the police knew of the Bulls' plans. They had roughed him up quite a bit. Brother Jacob Malahide had been the worst of the lot, laying about him with his fists and his boots, and threatening him with a knife.

He couldn't lie comfortably, not with his hands tied behind his back. Not with the bruises and what were probably a couple of busted ribs. Even so, it was the blasted ankle that hurt the most.

'Seymour,' said Malahide. 'Brother Seymour, even. You will please sit up and remove your shirt and undershirt.'

Seymour did as he was bid. Malahide held one of those new-fangled ballpoint pens which Boswell had initially thought was made of glass and which wrote with black grease instead of ink.

If he ever got out of this, if he ever mended, he would love, just *love* to meet Brother Malahide in a dark alley somewhere and slosh the living daylights out of him.

Malahide was drawing something on Seymour's back, giving him some sort of tattoo. Maybe the black grease didn't wash off.

Boswell hadn't talked.

He held on to that. Whenever the pain and discomfort were getting to him, he reminded himself that he hadn't told them anything. Aside from what he realized was already a powerful loyalty to the police, to the Inspector and to the Liberal Settlement, he had seen, in the only moment of ice-cold lucidity to interrupt his ordeal, that if he told the Bulls what he knew of their plans, he would cease to be of any use to them. Brother Jacob and his fellow stormtroopers would finish him off.

Keeping his trap shut was his only chance, however slim, of staying alive.

(But what if he died? Would he simply end up in

another strange world like this one? He had wondered when the beating was at its worst. Then it occurred to him that he had gone to Hell, and that he would spend all eternity going from one world to another and being killed horribly each time.)

It was a cross. Brother Jacob was drawing a big black crucifix on Seymour's right shoulder-blade, all the while quietly cursing the fellow's coughing for spoiling his artistry.

Through the distractions of his aches and agonies, Boswell had looked for means of escape. His wrists and legs were firmly bound; he had tried working his wrists free, but to no avail. To move his ankles only turned pain to agony. Besides, there were too many people around to try anything. On the credit side of the account, there were plenty of sharp or potentially useful objects down here. Lots of guns, knives, tools, bits of rubbish, machinery, broken glass and so on.

He wouldn't be able to run very far or very fast on this ankle, though.

Malahide summoned Saltonstall over to inspect his work on Seymour's back. 'Good,' said the holy man. 'That should be visible over a distance. It's trickery, but necessary. It might win over a few wavering souls in the mob.'

Seymour was bid to put his shirt back on.

'Psst!' Boswell whispered to Seymour. 'What's all that about, then?'

Seymour looked at him for the first time. 'A mark of God,' he said. 'A sign from the Almighty that I am to usher in the millennium. There was a time when every would-be Messiah had the mark of the cross . . .'

'Are you a Messiah?'

'No,' said Seymour angrily. 'And I call on you, stranger, to witness the vile blasphemy committed by these men who claim to be men of God, these villains who would use my bloodline to further their lust for earthly power.'

'Whoa!' said Boswell quietly. 'If I live, I shall be your witness, but you must tell me their plans. What's this about a bloodline?'

'I am the Reverend Harry Seymour,' he said, lying down on his mattress. 'In my last life, I was a more exaulted person. I was King Edward the Sixth. Much longed-for son of King Henry the Eighth, for the want whereof my father divorced his first wife, hacked off the head of his second, and condemned the third to die in childbirth. I am the engine of the English Reformation. But for me, these godly knaves might have been content to be Papists, or conventional heretics.'

He fell silent.

'Rum old thing, religion,' said Boswell, trying to keep up the conversation. He wanted to say he'd never met a king before, but thought he'd better keep his mind on the job. 'I'm C of E myself, though I'm not a great church-goer these days. Still, this rebirth business makes you think, doesn't it? I mean, I've only been here a couple of weeks, and I don't know what to make of it all.'

Seymour – King Edward – sighed and turned towards him. 'The Lord renews us that we may renew our commitment to him. That is why I do not wish to be king. I am as ardent for the Protestant cause as any man here, but these are not godly men, my friend. They are knaves, driven by hate and greed. And they will try and gull the base people into giving them dominion over them. I want none of it. The Lord has made it plain to me my calling is not to rule. I can do more of his work in a single day trying to save sinners and help the desperate as a humble priest than I would in a whole lifetime as a paper king putting an imprimatur to the edicts of Brothers Saltonstall and Lilley. Doubtless they will style themselves Lords Protector. No, let me revise that. Saltonstall will style himself Lord Protector and he will have Lilley killed at some point. And the agent of Lilley's death will be Jacob Malahide or the American, Mr Miller.'

'I don't understand,' said Boswell. 'If you're so dead set against their plans, why are they bothering with you?'

Seymour said nothing.

Boswell realized Malahide was standing over them.

'We want him,' said Malahide, 'because he is King Josiah. His Majesty here died young, but a lot of good Protestant folk couldn't believe it. They said as King Josiah would come back one day to return England to the true faith.'

'Oh,' said Boswell. 'Then why not use a pretender, a Simnel or a Warbeck?'

'Because,' said Malahide, kicking him in the small of the back, 'that would be deceiving folks, wouldn't it? Besides, there's a few people here as would recognize him.'

Malahide grabbed Seymour by the arm, pulled him upright and led him further along the platform. Boswell had wondered if it was possible for him and Seymour to lie back to back and loosen one another's bonds, but now he'd have to go back to the drawing board.

'Bring him over here,' commanded the Elder, as Jacob Malahide led Seymour – King Josiah, as they would all have to learn to call him – towards the centre of the platform.

Jacob Malahide had not seen the sun rise this morning. None of them had. The wireless had said it would be sunny.

Elder Saltonstall summoned all to gather around him. Today would be the day, the day of the struggle to which they had all dedicated so much work, so much prayer and planning.

Somehow Malahide didn't associate sunshine with days on which the course of history was changed. History got changed in winters, or in rain and thunderstorms. Not that he would see much of it. Malahide's part in the great day was to remain Underground and throw the switches on the bombs Ethan Miller had made. He had already detonated one of them. He had not heard the explosion, but the report on the radio had indicated a satisfactory enough result. Jacob Malahide would remain here the rest of the day, listening to the BBC and the police and ambulance radio on a transistor and use his judgement as to the best time to let off each bomb. At the end of the day, he would emerge from the ghost-ridden gloom of Underground into the bright sunshine of a new and godly world.

'Brethren,' said Elder Saltonstall, 'our plans are now ready for execution. Every man among us knows his role. Elder Lilley is now in the north once more, trying to raise the people against the Liberal Settlement by telling them of the foul deeds perpetrated by the Jews. Here in London, though, is our work. Throughout the day, Brother Jacob here will set off explosive devices to sow confusion and discord among the unrighteous. Brother Ethan Miller here,' he indicated Miller, who now held another of his outlandish guns, a thing with a wide tube beneath its barrel, 'will strike at the usurper Richard.'

'Amen!!' said one or two of the others. Some of them smiled and clapped one another on the back, while Malahide himself nodded grimly. So be it.

'A few of you accompany Brother Miller. Brother Andrews here, because he knows how to drive the machine Miller will be using,' continued Saltonstall. 'A few of you will hand out leaflets saying the Millennium is at hand, King Josiah's return is upon us, and the bombs are the work of our enemies. Most of you will accompany me to Vauxhall for Bartle's Fair.'

They looked at one another all quizzical-like. What business had they at the fair? Malahide knew. The fair was where the mob would be. Few tourists would dare venture there for fear of dippers and rampsmen. Only true Englishmen went to Bartle.

'At the fair,' said Elder Saltonstall. 'I shall bring the message to all true Protestant Englishmen, aye, and any Papists as wish to abjure their error. When news reaches us of the death of the usurper-king, I shall proclaim Josiah, I shall show the crowds the mark of godliness on his back, and then, by the grace of God, the mob will be moved to follow us. London shall be ours before nightfall. The country will be ours before the week is out.'

'What of the Army?' said one of the brethren.

'What of them?' shrugged Saltonstall. 'At the most there are ten thousand soldiers in London, and perhaps a similar number of police. Remember – just because a man wears the King's uniform for pay does not mean he is ready to die for the King. Many are God-fearing men who will not shoot their brethren. Besides, what are ten thousand against so many of us?

'Brethren,' he said, 'let us pray together this one last time. Let us beseech the Almighty to guide our bombs and bullets to his purpose, let us ask for his strength.'

When the prayer had finished, as men gathered up their belongings and weapons, Malahide asked Elder Saltonstall what was to be done with the rozzer they had captured the previous night.

'Kill him.'

Jenny padded up and down the room, trying to force answers from a mind distracted by fatigue and worry. It was like trying to do the cryptic crossword in one of the big newspapers, except that if she didn't get the answers, people would die. Ten more minutes of this and she would be a useless hysteric.

'I've found some more detailed maps of the Underground,' said Inky, jumping down from a chair which he had stood next to a filing cabinet with the words 'CIVIL DEFENCE' stencil-painted on it. In his arms he cradled a ring-bound book and a couple of folded charts. The Inspector took them from him and laid them out on the big table.

Breakfast would have to wait.

'It all fits into place real snug-like,' said Inky. 'Using

the tunnels permits them to move around the city without being seen or caught. Second, they need somewhere quiet as a ken for the bombs, the assassinations . . . Where did the signal for the peach Constable Pearson put on Malahide disappear to last night?'

'Here,' said the Inspector, pointing to a red pin that they had stuck into a street-map on the wall.

'Bob's your uncle, Inspector,' said Inky. 'Right where the old Stepney station used to be. And that bomb this morning went off near the old St James's Park station . . .'

'Bombs,' said the Inspector, his eyes widening. He straightened and went to the red telephone, the one with the direct line to the Commissioner.

Someone at the other end answered almost immediately. The Inspector spoke quietly, warning that other bombs might explode close to the disused Underground rail stations.

At first, she had felt elated at the breakthrough, but now tiredness and depression overcame her again. So the Upright Men were using the Underground. So what? From what she could see there were dozens and dozens of miles of tunnels. Then there was the sewer system as well, not to mention a sizeable network of secret government underground tunnels and bomb-shelters from the time of the Hitler War and the Atom War.

'Right,' said the Inspector, replacing the telephone receiver. 'A question. Should we bother trying to run the Bulls to ground, or should we continue with the original plan and fall on any bombs thrown at his Majesty?'

'His Majesty,' said Jenny, 'has plenty of guards as it is.

We'd be better employed underground. You never know what we might find,' she said, thinking of Guy.

'Sure them tunnels run for miles and miles,' said O'Rourke. 'What chance do we have of finding anything? It's as like as not we'd come up against floods, or heaps of fallen-in dirt and masonry we can't get through.'

The Inspector nodded.

'But isn't it a chance worth taking?' said Jenny. 'Down there, we just might be able to find some of them, perhaps stop them letting off any more bombs. Inky, you know everyone in town; are you acquainted with anyone who could guide us through the Underground? Someone who knows the tunnels, where the floods and cave-ins are?'

Inky pondered briefly, then shook his head. 'To be honest, the Underground isn't the kind of place where self-respecting culls go to. It's full of desperate scumbags and religious maniacs and madmen.'

The Inspector had picked up the receiver on one of the black telephones and was dialling furiously.

The rattle of the extractor-fan was the only sound in the room.

'Ah, hello,' he said at length. 'I am trying to contact Miss Rutherford. Miss Athene Rutherford . . . Yes . . . Oh, I see. Of course. Thank you.'

He put the phone down. 'Pearson,' he said, 'I can only think of one person who could help us. Her name is Miss Athene Rutherford. She is a prominent member of the City of London Women's Royal Voluntary Service. You will find her with the rest of her colleagues preparing to march in the Lord Mayor's Parade. Go and find her at once. Take a radio so we can arrange an RV once you have found her.'

'Wilco, sir.'

The pavement was thick with people, tourists in silly Hawaiian-patterned shirts poring over maps, lovers with linked arms, families with children trailing helium-filled balloons.

The Lord Mayor's Parade would be assembling along High Holborn. She crossed the street at a Belisha beacon and cut into Chancery Park.

The park was already full of courting couples, families, groups of friends, even a few people already spreading picnics on the grass. It occupied an area which had been flattened in the Atom War, formerly the setting for the Inns of Court and, further down towards the Thames, the Public Record Office.

The rebuilding of the City's administrative and legal structures had taken place in the first flush of optimism following the end of the Feudal Wars. The homes and businesses which had once occupied this area had not been rebuilt, but the Inns of Court had, as had the vast Public Record Office building, with its miles and miles of shelving and card files with government documents, legal papers and birth, marriage and death records.

Each of the buildings in Chancery Park had been constructed in the conventional post-wars style of concrete, steel and glass, but then each had been adorned by teams of specially chosen craftsmen, all retreads, from different periods. It was a sort of symbolic team-effort. The rest of the park, likewise, was laid out in the

Things Unborn

styles of various eras, an Elizabethan knot-garden here, a miniature landscaped park there.

She half-ran across the broad paved area at the front of the PRO, with its huge façade of plate glass and recesses for life-sized painted statues representing people of different trades from different ages. It was supposed to resemble the façade of a medieval cathedral, except the statues represented not saints, but your ancestors.

Buildings like this, and the lush green park in which they were set, were among the things that attracted visitors from countries which were not blessed or cursed with retreads of their own. This morning, it was quiet enough.

She ran.

Along High Holborn, which was now only a broad pathway cutting through Chancery Park, there were thousands of people. Most were obviously spectators, but there were plenty of others in fancy-dress costumes, or uniforms. There were carnival floats, too.

Men and women in armbands walked up and down the road, trying to marshal everyone into their allotted place in the procession before it set off.

She glanced at her watch. The parade was set to move in five minutes. These things were always late. But would they keep the King waiting?

Straight ahead of her a brass band was tuning up, polishing instruments, brushing dust off uniforms. The Salvation Army?

She pulled the silver slice from her bag. But all the parade marshals she had seen a moment ago had disappeared.

She burst through the crowds quietly lining the route. Some cursed her, thinking she was trying to barge in to a prime spot from which she would spoil their view.

Behind the brass band was a huge float, its top got up to look like the interior of one of those gloomy north-country pubs. Along the top of the float was an elaborately painted sign announcing this to be the entry of the Worshipful Company of Television Retailers and Repairmen.

Here, people were not quietly lining the route, but were mobbing the float itself. The TV men had won the first prize for their entry in last year's parade and, as one of the most wealthy and powerful guilds in the City, were determined to repeat their success this year. She had read something in the *Standard* about how they planned to bring the entire cast of *Coronation Street*, a continuing drama about the lives of working folk in a city in the north of England, to the parade.

'Look, there's Theophilus Gillroy!' said a woman next to her as she pushed her way through.

'Don't be soft,' said the woman's companion. 'That's not his real name. His real name's Salathiel Pavey. Died in the eighteenth century. Used to be a great actor until he got on that television nonsense . . .'

'I knew that,' trailed off the voice behind her.

Still no sign of anyone with a white armband.

It was easier to get past the other floats, devoid as they were of celebrity interest. Each year, the guilds and companies would try to out-do each other in the finery of their livery, or in the elaborateness of their procession-floats. It was a matter of honour, both for them and for the Lord Mayor. The City of London had been holding these parades on Accession Day for the last twenty years. It was a way of proving the City's loyalty to the Liberal Settlement, but also a means of reminding the Government of the importance, the influence and the wealth of the City.

She collided with a small man with a white beard who was talking urgently into a walkie-talkie.

And a white armband.

'Police,' she said, pushing her warrant card into his face. 'I must find the WRVS. It's very urgent.'

The man shrugged and jerked his thumb backwards. They were behind him.

The City of London WRVS would not, of course, have a float. They simply marched. There was a small knot of about forty women, mostly middle-aged and older, in heavy brown uniforms and broad-brimmed felt hats. They were between the St John Ambulance Service and the Boy Scouts, which must have reflected the official estimation of their place in the order of things.

The speedometer next to the steering-wheel read 30 m.p.h., though it felt as if they were travelling a lot faster.

Ahead of them stretched a few yards of illuminated tunnel, but beyond that, and behind them, a velvet, infinite darkness.

'Of course, a lot of the tunnels further out of the Great Wen have fallen in, or flooded. The London County Council try to keep the central tunnels shored up, if only to stop the buildings above falling into them,' said Miss Rutherford. 'But they do keep this area near the Thames reasonably free of flooding. It's to stop the water undermining the foundations of other buildings, and causing other problems. But it's also because they hope to get the old sewer trams moving again one day. Just as soon as they can all get the Metropolitan Board of Works to pay for it, of course. Some hope! You people really should investigate the activities of the Board of Works. There's enough money there sticking to people's fingers in a single year to reopen the whole Northern Line. Still, mustn't grumble; it means that I and few hundred other folks have the tunnels to ourselves. It's a smashing adventure, it really is.'

Jenny sat next to Miss Rutherford inside the cabin of one of her Underground cars. The old lady kept her hand firmly on the steering wheel – though there seemed to be little steering to be done – and craned her neck forward peering into the tunnel ahead.

'It's astonishing how many different people there are down here. There are all those curious little medievals, of course, the penitents and scapegoats, down here to live a hermit's life, or carry away their sins. Then there are the sturdy beggars and the criminals of course. Never have any trouble with them. I just turn on the siren and the blue light. That terrifies most of them out of their wits, although every so often one of them takes a pot-shot at you with a pointed stick or suchlike. So I always travel inside this cabin. It wouldn't be bullet-proof of course.'

'What if you get caught outside?'

'Oh, I have the carving-knife in my handbag,' she laughed.

Miss Rutherford's vehicle was an adapted motor-car. She said it had once been referred to as a 'bubble car', because of its shape, but this one had been somewhat modified. It was now mounted on a long wooden platform atop four rail wheels, two of which were driven by the car's engine. The cabin of the car, which opened at the front, was towards the forward part of the wooden platform. At the rear were two stretchers, two jerry-cans of petrol, a first-aid kit and a directional searchlight powered by a huge battery which had originally belonged to a milk-float. More illumination was provided by the car's own headlamps, plus the flashing blue light which, when accompanied by the siren, would have scared the bejesus out of anyone in the Underground's closed, eerie, spaces. There was one of these vehicles available to Miss Rutherford on the various separate levels of the remaining Underground system.

'Of course, it's tricky to go around backwards in this thing, which you have to do some of the time. But it's better than walking, what? Naturally, there are a few places where you have to get out and go by shanks's pony, such as when you're transferring from one line to another. They removed most of the old trains a few years back, to try and discourage people from living down here. Board of Works cut 'em up for scrap metal, but there are still a few lying around.'

Jenny looked out of the tiny rear window to check the Inspector was still there standing at the back. All she could make out was his shape against the lights reflecting off the walls. Miss Rutherford had offered him her leather flying-helmet to wear, explaining she never went Underground without one because of the filth down here. ('My dear Inspector, have you any idea how much a blue rinse costs these days?') She had appeared quite relieved when the Inspector refused the offer, and had buckled it on herself.

As a woman of some modest independent means, and as a stalwart of the Women's Royal Voluntary Service, Miss Rutherford devoted most of her time to travelling the Underground in her converted bubble-cars, searching for newly arrived retreads, of which there were quite a few Underground. Here in the cold and dark, deprived of food and shelter, many could die not long after arrival, unless of course they were taken in by many of the criminal gangs who lived down here. So she carried out a complete circuit of the accessible areas of the Underground every few days, picking up anyone who needed assistance, and bringing them to the nearest reception centre. Some, of course, were beyond rescue. Some went feral. Others were convinced they had arrived in Hell or Purgatory.

'Most of the time,' explained Miss Rutherford, 'I just bowl around as fast as these old girls will take me. It's the old business of the retreads coming up near to where they died. I've been through all the available records, and so I know where to look for the major concentrations.'

Miss Rutherford based this particular bubble car at the old King's Cross station, parked inside a ship's container to prevent theft. She had led Jenny and the Inspector through a couple of padlocked steel doors and down some flights of stairs, all by torchlight. As they were going down, Sergeant O'Rourke had radioed from the safe house where he and Inky were holding the fort to say a bomb had gone off at Notting Hill.

Things Unborn

This time there had been casualties.

Miss Rutherford had been brisk. ' Inspector,' she had said, 'I am of course delighted to be of assistance. I only hope we can help you get to these murdering blackguards before they cause any more damage.'

They had climbed aboard and begun their search. The plan was to circumnavigate a line which ran a roughly circular course through central London, and then search all the lines inside this circle. After that they would probably be too late anyway.

So far they had seen nothing of the remotest interest, although Miss Rutherford's commentary would have been fascinating if Jenny was not being eaten up from the inside by anxiety.

Miss Rutherford explained how she reckoned on picking up two retreads a month, a few of whom had been wandering Underground for days. Some of them still sent her Christmas cards.

She pointed out areas she referred to as 'hot spots', the places where one disaster or another had occurred involving multiple deaths, and where – if she had not been on more urgent business this time – she would normally slow down to take a careful look. Most ghoulish of all was her description of a collapse in the tunnel back in Victorian times which had trapped dozens of navvies. 'The poor beggars ended up eating one another. Can you imagine that?'

'Why do you call these areas hot spots?' Jenny asked.

'Force of habit. According to my metaphysician friend Sir Digby Lovejoy, these are also supposed to be areas of high radioactivity. I often take him on trips down here. He has a theory that the essence of a human being is contained in a collection of subatomic particles which he calls egons. He believes that when a person dies before their time, a recording of their physical and conscious being is lodged in the ground, or the trees, or whatever, in the form of egons. The Atom War and the consequent release of radiation has in some way catalysed the egons into re-forming their owners, perfect physical replicas with all their memories up to the time of death complete.

'We've had the most enormous fun running around the tunnels, me in here, him out on the back with his Geiger counter trying to establish if there are any appreciable concentrations of radioactivity in those places where I have found new arrivals.'

'And have you established any connection?' asked Jenny.

'No. None whatsoever. But you see, the point is not that my friend's theory is true, the point is, he is content with it. It's like a battered but comfortable old armchair that makes his life tolerable and dismisses awkward questions. Besides, it is a theory which has never harmed anyone, which is more than can be said for these blithering fools who claim the Lord has chosen them especially for resurrection so's they can tell the rest of us how to think and behave.'

'What do you believe?' asked Jenny.

'Me? What I believe don't signify, my dear. I prefer to just get on with things. Too much fuss and bother in the world. Are you a retread?'

'No.'

'Ah well, there you are. I am, you see. Died in the Second World War. Dashed rotten luck really. Sitting by the window in a café when a doodlebug pancaked the next street along. Got cut to pieces by the flying plate-glass. Must have been a frightful mess. Now, in my first life I never bothered much about where I came from. Left all that to the sky-pilots. So did most people. You just get on with it, don't you? Now here, everyone's got a different answer to the great big question. They say they're here to settle up accounts with the Almighty, or because of egons, or because of resonances or what-have-you. It's all a blooming great tombola isn't it? Why bother yourself with it at all? Life's hard enough as it is, you take it from me, my dear. You just concentrate on keeping yourself as content as possible at all times, keep everything simple as you can, try and help others when you get the chance. That's Doctor Rutherford's solution.'

Miss Rutherford changed gear downwards and slowed the car. 'We have completed our tour of the Circle Line. We are about to pull into Liverpool Street station. I suggest we now do the Central Line.'

She led Jenny and the Inspector across dark, dusty, litter-strewn caverns. All three of them carried powerful battery lamps, but none of it stopped Jenny feeling frightened and overawed by the huge amount of work that had built these cathedrals under Londoners' feet. It was a reminder of the life, the energy, that had been in the city before the Atom War.

'Oh bother!' said Miss Rutherford as she led them on to another platform. Jenny and the Inspector directed their lamps towards the rails. The steel hangar where her vehicle should have been had had a vast hole punched in its side. Its metal twisted inwards.

'Well that wasn't done with any slingshot was it?' said the Inspector.

'Looks like explosive to me, Inspector,' said Miss Rutherford. 'Someone was awfully keen to find out what was inside. Not that there's anything of any use in there now.'

'Looks like we're on the right line then,' said Jenny.

'Well, there's nothing else for it,' said Miss Rutherford, climbing into the well where the rails ran. 'Just let me get my hands on these wretched vandals. Come along, you two. We'll head west to start with. Pass me my handbag, would you, my dear?'

'The next one along is Tottenham Court Road,' announced Miss Rutherford.

Walking through the Underground tunnels was a far different business from proceeding in the comparative style of the cabin of a bubble car. The poor light made the rest of Jenny's senses more acute. Despite the lamps they had, she kept banging her shins on the rails, or on pieces of debris. The tunnels were surprisingly rich in foul or stale smells; a sewer leaking in here, the decaying corpse of a small animal there, a residue of lubricating oil or burned rubber . . . But most of all the tunnels were full of faint sounds, strange echoes and breezes, and what seemed to be distant screams. Miss Rutherford said it was just the wind.

Usually.

They had got nowhere. They were now standing under Chancery Park, across which she had raced in search of Miss Rutherford earlier this morning. The Inspector looked grim. He was probably thinking he would have been better off staying up at the top protecting the King.

'Shh!' said Miss Rutherford, lifting the ear-flaps of her flying-helmet. 'That is definitely not a usual tunnel noise.'

They listened. Jenny heard nothing.

'Put your lights out for a moment,' said Miss Rutherford.

Jenny and the Inspector switched off their lamps and looked ahead.

They stayed silent for a few moments. Miss Rutherford sniffed the air like a connoisseur of fine wines.

'There's someone burning petrol down here,' she announced. 'Can you hear the engine?'

They couldn't.

'It doesn't seem to be getting any closer or further away.'

'A generator,' said Jenny. All the big procession floats she had passed that morning were towing generators to power the loudspeakers for their music.

'It may be,' said the Inspector. 'They would want it for the light. Okay, line astern everyone. I shall lead. Miss Rutherford, you take the middle. Pearson, you're at the end. Keep looking back from time to time.'

They turned their lights on again and walked on a few hundred yards. The sound of the petrol engine grew more distinct.

'Lights out,' whispered the Inspector. 'Pearson, follow me. Miss Rutherford, I would be grateful if you would wait back here a while. I would not wish you to come to any harm.'

Miss Rutherford snorted, but did as she was asked.

Jenny opened her bag and took out her gun.

'What have you got?' asked the Inspector quietly.

'A thirty-eight.'

'Stuff that,' he said. 'Here, I brought a spare.' He handed her one of those he-man 9-mm automatics. 'It is loaded with hollow-points. I found them among Glyndwr's things. You will not tell on me, will you?' he smiled.

Hollow-point bullets were against regulations.

She took the gun. The pain in her thumb, which had almost receded in the last day or two, returned at once.

'And now, the Lord Mayor himself passes his Majesty in the great gilded coach which was commissioned by the City of London corporation seven years ago. It is drawn by a magnificent team of six black horses . . . It is a little-known fact that while he is within the boundaries of the City, the Lord Mayor takes precedence over all the rest of the nobility of England. The only ceremonial authority he recognizes is that of his Majesty the King himself . . .

Jacob Malahide pulled on his fifth cigarette in the last hour. The man on the wireless was commentating on the Lord Mayor's Parade, which would soon finish. He looked to the set of switches for the bombs and wished there was one near the Mansion House, from where the King was watching. Letting one of Ethan Miller's infernal devices off near there would corpse or cabbage quite a few of those braying tourists who came to gawk and sneer.

It wouldn't have paid off, Elder Saltonstall had said.

Malahide had to admit the Elder's reasoning was sound. If, he said, you let off bombs too close to the King, you risk driving him to earth. He'll go and cower behind ten thousand soldiers deep in the atomic shelter at Buckingham Palace. They needed to keep Queen Dick up in the fresh air long enough to send him to Hell.

The rozzer they caught last night leaned against the wall a few yards away, groaning with his pains and aches. Malahide eyed the complicated gun Miller had given him, wondering if he should squelch the plod now.

He would have done it a lot sooner, but even with the lights on, he didn't much fancy being down here all on his tod with only a stiffie for company. All the business of Pest Maidens and meeting the penitent in the tunnel the other day had given him the willies. All these medieval Papists down here had made Underground a whoreson, ungodly place.

It would soon be time to let off more bombs. When the parade was over, he would turn the switch labelled with a little picture of a newspaper. Fleet Street would fill up with people leaving the parade and he would send a few of them to Hell.

He stubbed the fag and stood up.

The hair on the back of his neck stood on end.

Something was not right. Something in the air had changed. He looked at the trussed-up plod, who was wincing, his eyes closed.

He listened. Something was wrong, damn it, something in the sound, the smell of the place.

He picked up Miller's gun and scurried over to the generator. He turned off all the lights except for the one at the far end of the platform. The lights flickered and died. He lifted the gun to his shoulder and turned a little switch on the sight at the top and looked through it.

The dim view through the sight grew gradually clearer.

Jacob Malahide could see in the dark.

Scipio cursed. They had been spotted. Why else would whoever was on the platform douse the lights, but leave the generator and transistor radio on?

He moved slowly, carefully along the track, which was now parallel with the end of the platform at Tottenham Court Road Underground station.

He had told Pearson to stay a good 10 yards or so behind him. They did not know how many Bulls they were up against here, and he did not relish the idea of someone throwing a stick of dynamite or a grenade into the rail-channel.

Somewhere up on the platform, someone was groaning, quietly cursing.

On the wireless, crowds were cheering something in the parade.

Scipio took advantage of these distractions to move a little further forward. He stretched his arms out in front of him, gun in right hand, lamp in left. He could switch the light on, shoot, and switch it off again in an instant, he hoped.

'What the blue blazes is going on now?' said the groaning voice.

Boswell.

A blood-red filament of light lanced out of the

darkness in the direction of Boswell's voice.

A laser-beam.

Pearson had said something about this American, Ethan Miller, having had some fabulous newfangled gun when she and Boswell had been caught at the Bulls' meeting.

There was a muzzle-flash from the source of the laser. The shot crashed and reverberated around the tunnel, a bullet ricocheted off the platform.

Scipio turned towards the flash, turned on his lamp. Jacob Malahide stood in an archway leading off the platform holding a rifle with an immense telescopic sight of some sort.

Scipio fired once, twice, and again.

The laser turned towards him. He turned off his lamp, ducked back among the rails and stumbled forward as fast as he could.

Two shots smashed into the darkness, cracking into the ceramic tiles behind him. Another lamp came on. Pearson's. He looked up. Malahide was caught in her light for a split second. She fired. Malahide ducked back behind his archway. She turned off her light again.

The echo of the gunshots seemed to travel off on down the tunnel.

'Boswell! How many?' he shouted, then scurried forward once more so that Malahide would not fix his sight on his voice.

'Just the one. Look sharp there, sir. I'm dashed uncomfortable here,' said Boswell.

By the shadows thrown out by the single light at the far

end of the platform, Jenny could just make out the form of the Inspector a few yards ahead.

He lay between the rails. There was no sign of Malahide's laser-beam. Maybe he had run for it.

Over on the platform, just a few yards from her, Guy moaned in pain or discomfort. But at least he was alive. He'd just have to suffer until they'd made sure the coast was clear.

The burning in her stomach seemed to diminish at the thought that Guy was still alive.

Eurydice had come to the Underworld to reclaim her Orpheus! She smiled at the thought, then shook her head. Maybe she was on the verge of hysteria.

Christ! Did this mean she was sweet on Boswell?

Not now, girl, not now!

She edged her way along beside the rails to the Inspector.

'I'm going to try and work my way around behind him,' he muttered, trying to keep his voice lower than the generator and the commentator on the Home Service. 'You stay along here and keep him occupied. I might want to douse that light down there in a minute. Without it, his night-scope is useless. It needs some sort of external light to work. It is one of these newfangled things. It gives out a tiny glimmer of light if you do not hold it hard against your eye, so it is possible he might give himself away. And remember, we need to take him alive.'

Well, that all seemed perfectly straightforward.

Her stomach gurgled a little. Even with her ears ringing after all the gunfire, even with the radio commentator's wittering about the ancient traditions of the City of London, even with the irritating rattle of the generator, it seemed deafening.

It was only fear, she told herself. Only fear. If she ever got out of this nonsense in one piece, she was resigning. Or asking for a desk job, at the very least.

The Inspector crawled away.

The laser shot out again, over her head. To hell with the Inspector's 9-mm, she thought, tucking it into her jacket. She took her little .38 from her bag.

The laser was over the Inspector. She fired three shots rapidly in its general direction, not intending to hit Malahide, just keep him from looking out while the Inspector circled round.

The filament of red light sought her out. She crouched down by the rails once more and scurried back a few yards. She felt like a tin duck in the shooting gallery at a funfair.

'Oh, do get on with it, please!' groaned Guy.

Crouching by the rails, Scipio approached the one remaining electric light. If he tried getting up on to the platform, it would reveal him. Even without it, Malahide would probably spot him with his night-scope.

'Sod it,' he thought, and shot out the light.

He clambered up on to the platform and rolled as fast as he could across it. His body connected with some-thing solid. It was a wall. Definitely a wall.

He felt his way along it. From what he had been able to make out in the gloom, there was a passageway running parallel to the platform, and it was in one of the entries to this passage that Malahide had been standing.

He was sure there was another one somewhere along here.

Unless there was any other source of light down here, Malahide was now blind. His scope would be useless. What was going through his mind? What was he doing?

Further back along the platform, a beam of white light suddenly leapt up towards the tunnel's ceiling.

Pearson had turned on her lamp down by the rails and had pointed it upwards.

Sure enough, Malahide's laser sight fixed on it. But it did not have a target to shoot at. Malahide was staying put where he was.

Several yards from her light, Pearson's gun and the tiniest possible portion of the top of her head emerged over the parapet and fired three rapid shots towards the laser.

Malahide's gun did not respond. The laser shone impassively across the dark, empty space.

He had left it there as a decoy!

Scipio felt his way along the wall.

Suddenly there was no more wall. He must be at one of the entrances to the other passageway. He pressed his back against the wall and willed his breath to quieten.

There was no sound apart from the transistor, and Boswell's complainings and gruntings had stopped.

He held his gun and lamp together, once more at arm's length, swung around to face into the arch through to the other passage. When facing full in to it, he turned the lamp on.

Nothing. He killed the light again and dashed through.

Further along, Malahide's gun was motionless at about waist level. He had left it on top of some boxes or something. Was this just to cover his escape?

He turned his lamp on once more, illuminating the whole of the passage. It was empty. In the distance, the vague outline of a staircase. He quickly turned the light off again.

He crept back towards the archway to the platform. Pearson's lamp was still on down in the rail-well.

He could risk shining his lamp on the platform. He had a solid looking wall to duck behind . . .

Again he extended both arms, pointing at the furthest extreme of the platform, the place where he and Pearson had entered.

He turned on the lamp and quickly swept it along the length of the—

Malahide was standing with his back to him, pointing a pistol straight down towards the rails, towards . . .

'Pearson!!' he yelled, firing once, twice, again.

Malahide turned towards him. In the glare of Scipio's lamp, the lines on his face gave him a look of fiendish malevolence, something not of this world.

Malahide turned his gun towards Scipio, but sluggishly, without anger or enthusiasm. Then his arm dropped.

Still standing, Malahide looked downwards. He put his hand into his leather jacket and felt his stomach. Quickly, his hand came out again, smeared in something dark and glistening.

Then he crumpled to the ground.

'And so, as this great procession reaches a close, and as

*the Lord Mayor joins his Majesty at the window of the
Mansion House, now fully and magnificently restored
following its near-destruction almost fifty years ago, to
wave to the cheering crowds . . .'*

'No, leave it turned on,' said the Inspector, as Jenny's
finger poised over the transistor.

The Inspector had found the light-switch. The whole
area was now illuminated as bright as day.

So were poor Guy's wounds. He looked as though he
had been through the mangle several times. She had
untied him and fussed over him a little, dabbing at the
bruises on his face with her hankie, but he said he was
just glad to be free of the ropes. He stood gingerly,
favouring his twisted ankle, and was prodding and
groping at various parts of himself, trying to assess his
injuries.

Now they all examined the box which, Guy said, was
Malahide's concern. It had an antenna and twelve little
switches, two of which had been turned downwards,
setting off bombs.

'Well,' said the Inspector, 'the least we can say is we
have prevented the deaths of several dozen innocent
people. That is worth a day's pay in itself.'

He took out his radio. 'O'Rourke, come in. Are you
there, O'Rourke? Come in, O'Rourke.'

No reply. The signal probably wouldn't carry too well
this deep under the earth.

O'Rourke came in.

He walked through one of the archways holding a
Sten gun.

'Now then,' he said cheerfully. 'I had hoped it

wouldn't come to this, but that's the luck of the draw for you, isn't it? Inspector, Jenny, take your pistols out and put them on the floor, nice and slowly, please. And the radios, too.'

'O'Rourke, what the—' said the Inspector.

'I'm not fooling around,' he snarled. 'Just do it.'

Jenny placed her .38 on the ground. The Inspector put down his Browning.

She still had the Inspector's spare Browning in her jacket.

'Now, backs to the wall, all three of you,' he said.

They did as ordered. He moved round to face them.

'The radios,' he said.

The Inspector put his radio gently on the floor. She reached towards her bag.

'Just throw the whole bag, if you please,' said O'Rourke.

She tossed it to his feet. He scooped it up with one hand, keeping his eye on them. He took out her radio, dropped it to the floor and stamped on it. Then he smashed his foot down on the Inspector's radio.

'That's not quite everything, is it?' he said. 'Jenny, your jacket is bulging like a Papist's drawers on May Day. Take it out, nice and slowly.'

'I say, Sergeant O'Rourke, do you mind if I sit down, only my ankle is killing me . . .' said Guy.

'Stay as you are,' said O'Rourke. 'Either your ankle kills you, or I do. Jenny, carry on, please . . .'

She took the gun from inside her jacket, crouched down and laid it on the floor.

'To me,' he said.

With her toe, she flicked it along the ground towards him.

The Inspector shook his head. 'Don't we get an explanation, O'Rourke?'

O'Rourke shrugged. 'What's to explain?' he said in a broad Cockney accent. 'God's purpose needs no explanation. I've been with the Order for years. Meanwhile, good old Uncle Seamus is a rozzer. After all, who's going to suspect an Irish Catholic of being a Bull? Except that I'm not an Irish Catholic. I'm an English Protestant who knows that the Pope is the Antichrist and the Liberal Settlement is a godless abomination. And I long for the day when this land is once more ruled in the same way as it was in the days of Britain's greatness. And I wouldn't mind using my old name again. Mills, James Mills, at your service.'

'You treacherous bastard,' said the Inspector. 'How many good people have been killed because of you? There's Glyndwr to start with. You'll hang for this, O'Rourke. I swear.'

'You're not in a position to swear anything,' said O'Rourke. 'Enough of this jawing. This isn't a film and I'm not about to explain everything.' He cocked his gun and took two steps back, the better to spray the three of them.

A small brown blur moved behind O'Rourke. The top of a head wearing a flying helmet.

Jenny fought to avert her eyes in case her gaze alerted him.

To late. He half-turned and the little woman rose up from the platform's edge wielding what appeared to be a small sword.

She plunged it into his side.

For a quarter of a second, O'Rourke looked startled, then tried to bring his gun to bear on her. The Inspector rushed him, pushing him off the platform's edge, past Miss Rutherford, and on to the rails.

Jenny leapt forward and picked up her .38. In a moment she was standing next to the Inspector and Miss Rutherford. O'Rourke was sprawled, astride the rails, his machinegun lying yards away.

'Shit!' said O'Rourke.

'Miss Rutherford, I am very much in your debt,' said Scipio.

'Stuff and nonsense, Inspector. Just doing my duty as a taxpayer. Now get about your business while I attend to this young man,' she indicated Boswell, and opened her immense handbag to pull out a bandage and a hip-flask.

'What about him?' said Pearson, pointing to O'Rourke, who still lay on the rails, panting, staring at the long knife that Miss Rutherford had stuck into him.

Scipio sighed. 'I don't suppose there's any chance of his bleeding to death in the next hour or so.'

'I shouldn't think so, Inspector,' said Miss Rutherford. 'Not as long as he leaves my trusty bayonet in there. If he pulls it out, I imagine most of his innards will come tumbling after.'

O'Rourke had exposed himself as a traitor. He had ceased to be an asset to the Bulls.

If he had taken that risk, it must mean that there was still time to stop them trying to kill the King.

Scipio looked at his watch. It was 11.15.

The King would be leaving the Mansion House. He would be driven through the streets in a bullet-proof car to a landing stage on the Victoria Embankment. There, he would get on to the Royal Barge at 11.30 to head for Chelsea . . .

The Bulls probably couldn't get him while he was in his car. It would be hard to get anywhere near the barge.

They would try to take a shot or throw a bomb at him when he was transferring from the car to the boat. In about fourteen minutes' time.

'Pearson,' he said. 'I have to leave you in charge here. If anyone comes to vex you, shoot to kill. And put your bloody spud-gun away and use the Browning and the hollow-point shells. That way, you only ever have to shoot someone once.'

'Wilco, sir.'

'And keep a close eye on these two . . .'

O'Rourke was still lying where they had left him, but Malahide was gone.

'Malahide!' said Pearson. 'Where's he got to? He must have slipped away in all the excitement a moment ago . . . Shall I go after him?'

Malahide had taken a gut-shot with a hollow-point bullet that would have fragmented inside him. He would likely have massive internal bleeding. He would soon be in extreme pain. Unless he got to a hospital soon, it was unlikely that he would live more than an hour at the most. Certainly he would be in agony by then.

'No,' said Scipio. 'The most important thing is to remain here and ensure nobody lets any more of those bombs off. Put some cuffs on O'Rourke. I am going back up to the land of the living. There's a fraction of a chance of stopping this attempt on the King's life. I'll get help sent down to you here as soon as possible . . . Miss Rutherford, can you tell me how I can get out of here?'

Following Miss Rutherford's directions as to the quickest way out of the tube station, Scipio had had to bash his way through a chipboard partition, and another one of wriggly tin. Now his left hand was bleeding from a 2-inch gash in the palm.

He emerged into harsh, glaring daylight.

The King would get out of his armoured car in seven minutes.

Scipio turned into Charing Cross Road and wondered what to do next.

Find a rozzer with a radio?

No time.

The street was busy. Passers-by were looking at him from the corners of their eyes, giving the crazy man a wide berth.

The air was still, thick and heavy. He loosened his tie, slung his jacket over his shoulder and began running towards Leicester Square and the river.

Six minutes.

He could hire a cab, or commandeer a car.

It would never get through the traffic in time.

He ran across the junction with Old Compton Street, and saw the answer. A young dark-haired man was pulling on his crash-helmet, preparing to mount a huge Norton motorcycle.

He ran up to the biker, saying, 'Police. I need your bike. Now.'

The man looked at him as though he was a lunatic. A man in grimy clothes with a bloody hand . . . Scipio threw his jacket at the man. 'Warrant card is in the wallet. Take it all as security . . .'

He pushed the startled man away and climbed astride the bike. The key was in the lock.

He kicked it into action, and in moments roared into the traffic. He slalomed between buses, cars, cyclists, horse-cabs and carts, barely hearing the angry shouts and honking horns over the engine.

The needle on the speedo touched 70. With a flick of the wrist he was doing 75, 80, 85 . . .

Down Charing Cross Road, straight through red lights, he skirted Trafalgar Square, scattering pigeons, then powered through a group of schoolchildren at a Belisha beacon.

One minute.

There was a tiny side-street ahead which led straight to the riverside. He decided to follow it rather than lose precious seconds detouring down Northumberland Avenue.

It was blocked. A brewer's dray was unloading. There was no pavement, no way he could get the bike through.

He skidded the bike to a halt, and tumbled off, rolling to his feet. He ran, squeezing past the dray.

Ahead was a huge throng of people, craning necks, waving Union Jacks, some of them cheering and applauding.

He barged through, and came up solid against an unyielding, sinewy wall of red-jacketed soldiers.

'Let me through!' he shouted at the swaddy who blocked his immediate path. The soldier ignored him.

'I am a policeman. Someone is about to make an attempt on the life of the King. You must let met through!'

The redcoat looked wide-eyed at him, taking him for a lunatic, but not daring dismiss him without higher authority. He glanced sideways, looking for a superior officer.

It was all the opportunity Scipio needed. He rammed his shoulder between the man and his neighbour.

'Oi! Come back, you!' said a voice behind him.

In front was a line of black Rollers and Austin Princesses. He squeezed his way between two of them. A couple of dark-suited detectives stood at the top of the steps to the landing stage where the King would be about to step on to his barge.

He rushed towards them, shouting, 'Police!'

Somewhere from the side came the drone of a helicopter. Probably the Met's own wokka.

The detectives moved to block his way.

'Police!' he yelled again.

The helicopter was white, a blue stripe along its middle. It flew low along the course of the river.

Civilian aircraft were not allowed over this part of London.

The detectives grabbed at him.

The side door of the wokka was wide open. A man was leaning out, holding something.

'No!' said Scipio. He fell forward and caught the security-men off-balance. All three of them tumbled down the steps.

The King stood towards the side of the stage, surrounded by nervous black-suited men, and assorted dignitaries in ceremonial clothes that dazzled against the grey-painted wood of the stage.

'The African!' said the King. 'What is it?'

Scipio didn't have time to stand up.

He clambered to his knees and grabbed the King around the waist.

The pitch of the wokka's engine was unchanging. It hovered a few yards away. Ethan Miller, the man who had tried to kill him and Inky Weeks at the Globe Theatre, leaned through the door, holding a gun with a wide barrel.

Scipio put his head against the King's arse.

Above them, something popped.

He struggled to get some purchase with his feet.

Around him, men were shouting, pulling out guns.

A cloud of grey vapour enveloped the whole area.

Scipio pushed with all his might, scrabbling his feet along the floor towards the water.

The King fell in. Scipio scrambled in after him, as above them the world turned yellow, then orange.

Scipio got his arms around the King's chest and struggled to move the pair of them away from the landing stage.

Above there were two more explosions, screams, the roar of the chopper's engine, the rattle of machine-guns.

When they were a few yards from immediate danger, he risked letting the pair of them above the surface to breathe.

The landing-stage was on fire, the water around it burned, too.

Miller had used an aerosol-grenade, intended to

douse a wide area in a cloud of vaporised petrol before it ignited.

Bullets splattered into the water in front of his eyes. The helicopter hovered within spitting-range and the blond assassin was firing at them with a machine-gun.

Scipio took a deep breath and pushed the King's head under the water, then ducked under himself. Above them the helicopter roared, churning the water with rotor-blades and bullets like a huge whisk.

Could the King swim? Could he suggest the pair of them move to somewhere more safe?

He could see nothing in the filthy Thames water.

The bullets stopped.

The noise of the engine changed pitch.

He needed air. He dragged the King upwards once more.

They broke the surface, gasping for breath.

Redcoats and rozzers lined the wall overlooking the river, firing rifles, machine-guns and pistols over their heads towards the helicopter. Others were flapping jackets and other garments on men with burning clothes.

Scipio waved and shouted.

So did the King.

Thanks be to God.

Two dozen pairs of hands had hefted them out of the water, though his Majesty enjoyed the attention of considerably more of them.

Richard III stood by the water, dripping wet, but looking none the worse. He waved to the soldiers and the few courageous civilians standing around and graciously acknowledged their cheers.

'Well, Mr African,' he said, 'my bullet-proof waistcoat wouldn't have saved me from that, would it? I am greatly indebted to you.'

Men talked urgently into radios. In the distance, sirens blared and bells rang. The landing stage still burned. Police launches buzzed around it like moths to a light, looking for injured people in the water.

'Where did the helicopter go?' asked Scipio.

'Over the river,' said a young Guards officer from beneath a huge bearskin. 'I don't think they intended to stay around for so long. We winged it. It was trailing smoke, moving slowly. It'll have to ditch soon.'

The King clapped him on the back. 'If there's ever anything I can do, African . . .'

In a few minutes' time, every rozzer in the south of England would be looking out for a white helicopter with a blue horizontal stripe. The Met's own chopper and the RAF would be seeking it. If it landed in London, it would be surrounded by plods and tommies in moments.

There was only one place where it could ditch with any hope of its occupants getting away.

'Tell the police to get down to Tottenham Court Road Underground station now. Send an ambulance and some army bomb-disposal officers as well,' he said to the guardsman. 'Two of my officers are there and one of them is injured. They are holding a very important prisoner, who is also injured. They will also find a device intended to trigger bombs across London. Tell them I am going to Bartle. That is where the helicopter will land.'

The guardsman saluted. Scipio stood and rushed to find his commandeered motorbike.

He was in the Vauxhall Gardens almost as soon as he was across Vauxhall Bridge.

He dropped the bike, deciding to carry on on foot.

Almost at once he was assaulted by the noises and smells of the fair. Between here and the Oval cricket ground there were hundreds of stalls and attractions.

'Old Saint Bartle' was for the English, for Londoners and folks up from the country. The guidebooks did not discourage foreigners from visiting, but observed that men should have a care for their wallets, women for their handbags. The police were not particularly welcome here.

Bartle, a fair which had taken place annually for centuries (though it was originally held at Smithfield), was for cozening and cajoling a credulous public into parting with their hard-won money in exchange for worthless trifles, quack medicines and tawdry finery.

Scipio passed tents dedicated to prize-fights, freak-shows, astrologers and ball-gazers, palmists and conjurors, strip-teasers and miracle-plays. There were jugglers, tumblers, fire-eaters, dancers, jesters, hurdy-gurdies and musicians of every sort, all of them circled by small to middling crowds.

There were preachers, praters and barrack-room politicians, sellers of almanacks, squibs and broad-sides, devotional and seditious literature, illustrated books about popular television shows such as *Coronation Street* and *Eastenders*, books and magazines about beat musicians, colour prints and posters of beat stars, actors and football players, records and legal and illegal music cassettes.

On he walked, past halls of mirrors, mechanical rides, beer and cider tents, burger and sausage, pie and mash, fish and chip, eel and whelk stalls. There were booths for hiring workers – farm labourers, servants, navvies and merchant seamen, all fronted by booming costermen promising an easy life and good wages, escape from your present troubles, from debts and unhappy marriage.

The only person he saw who was doing a poor business advertised himself as Painless Williams, tooth-puller. Painless was obviously a recent retread trying to ply his former trade. He would very quickly learn that every retread knew that modern dentistry was far, far better.

The ground was thick with litter, but a leaflet caught his eye. He bent to pick it up.

King JOSIAH will return to England THIS DAY. Now is the time for all ENGLISHMEN to RISE UP and join the ranks of the RIGHTEOUS who will STRIKE DOWN the ungodly and RULE A THOUSAND YEARS.
Expect the MIRACLE at BARTLE'S FAIR.

He looked up. The bullet-ridden helicopter stood on an empty patch of ground. A few people gawked at it, but of Miller and the pilot there was no sign.

He approached it casually. There were a few bloodstains inside.

There were also small splashes of blood in the hard-baked clay and the yellowing grass leading away from the stricken machine.

He did not have a radio. He did not even have a gun with him.

The splashes led towards an open-air prize-fight ring, a raised platform bounded by a rope rail. It was empty. A blackboard in the middle of it announced that the next contest would be at 2.30 p.m.

On the far side of the ring there was a helter-skelter, the tallest thing in the vicinity, a magnificent red and yellow striped tower topped with a fluttering Union Jack. A sign over the entrance-booth announced it as 'ALEXANDER BENDO'S MAGNIFICENT HELTER-SKELTER. ONLY 2d A GO!'

Alexander Bendo? Where had he heard that name before?

He wandered up to the booth. It was curtained off, closed. Why would a fairground ride be closed at such a potentially profitable time?

He walked around the back of the booth and gently parted the curtains to take a peep. As he did so, two pairs of fiercely strong arms grabbed him and pulled him in.

'The Dashing Mechano is most welcome!' The Earl of Rochester greeted him cheerfully. 'I believe you've met my friend Ethelbright.'

Ethelbright, the skinny youngster who was not a saint, smiled cheerfully. It was the first time Scipio had seen him smile.

He had never heard Ethelbright speak either, except a few words of Anglo and Latin to the retread who had turned up at Mother Heycock's brothel.

Rochester and Ethelbright were up to no good. They wore working men's clothes, tatty corduroys, flat caps and denim jackets.

Rochester cradled an SMLE with a telescopic sight on it, as though it were a baby.

'We have been listening to the Home Service. We have heard all about your exploits back on the Embankment. I shall have to write another play about you. It shall be the greatest work of my life, a masterpiece. But I have to warn you, Mechano, it shall end in your tragic and miserable death should you attempt to interfere with my business this afternoon.'

'What is going on, Rochester?'

'In both my lives I have always tried to live by the precept that I shall try everything at least one time except celibacy, sobriety and accountancy. I have never yet been a murderer. That is something I plan to rectify.'

'You shall not escape the consequences.'

It was the first time he had seen Rochester grow angry. 'And what, Mechano, do you fancy the consequences of letting these lunatics live will be? Saltonstall is imminently going to get into that pug-stage and start prating. He is an Upright Man, a person of standing with the mob, who are all around us. If he succeeds in rousing them, what will follow will be riot and mayhem at best, civil war at worst. These are the dispossessed, the pawns of history, Mechano. Oh, their bellies are full, and they are easily cured of the pox or of toothache, but there is a part of all of them that loathes the Liberal Settlement because they are no part of it. The Protestants among them scratch their heads and wonder why a Papist is on the throne, and why they must have their letters to have the vote . . . It is your privilege to judge me as you like. If you mark me an unscrupulous rake, so be it. But I am telling you, Mechano, that I am prepared to die – aye, and to kill – to see to it that bigotry, superstition and stupidity do not triumph. You have saved his Majesty's royal hide, you have played your part. Now it is time for Rochester to enter stage left.'

Ethelbright took hold of Scipio's arms. He had a length of rope.

In the distance, over the music and bustle of the fair, came a small cheer. A man's voice began to prate.

'They will tear you into small pieces and eat you raw, Rochester,' he said, as he was being bound.

'We have improvised an escape-plan. I shall shoot from the top of this helter-skelter, then slide down it. The bottom of the slide is obscured from public view and leads to a hay-cart which we have backed up to it. Ethelbright will whip up the horses while you and I hide in the straw and make a slow, but hopefully secure, escape. Come, it is time.'

They passed through a wooden doorway and into the middle of the helter-skelter. Rochester bowed and bade Scipio be the first to go up the wooden spiral staircase.

'How did you know they would be here?'

'Deduction, Mechano, the business of detective police. They were bound to go where the mob is, and the mob entire is spending its Saturday at Bartle. From there it was a mere matter of spying out where precisely they would be, and hiring a few stout labourers to erect Bendo's Magnificent Helter-Skelter.'

At the top of the tower was room enough for both men

to stand. The view over the prize-ring was excellent. Saltonstall stood alone in the middle, arms outstretched, explaining how the Millennium was upon them. There was no sign of Seymour, though a couple of dozen sober-dressed men with either very long or very short hair lined the ground around the platform. Even at this distance, Scipio could be sure that the bulges in their jackets were weapons.

Below was a growing crowd, at least five thousand strong already.

'We are dead,' he muttered. 'Lynched.'

'Oh cheer up, Mechano,' said Rochester, screwing an extension on to the muzzle of the gun. A noise-suppressor. 'Now sit down and enjoy the spectacle. And if you budge without my approbation, do not doubt that I shall put one of these brutish little exploding bullets between your eyes.'

Scipio sat. Over the rail, he could see the stage below. Saltonstall roared and damned the politicians across the Thames for taking the working man's wages in taxes to pay for their whoring and sodomising and drinking, and to keep Queen Dick in luxury.

'He must know by now that Dick is still alive,' muttered Rochester. 'This is his last play. He hopes to trump us with King Josiah.'

Rochester pulled the flat cap around on his head, so that the peak faced backwards. He picked up the rifle and rested it on the rail. 'Best to fix him now, before he stokes up their ardour any more, before he conjures up King Josiah.'

'You are not going to kill Seymour?'

'Why should I? Seymour intends no ill to anyone . . .

When I shoot, throw yourself belly-first on to the slide, Mechano,' said Rochester, steadying the rifle and squinting into its telescopic sight.

He was too far away to kick Rochester. If he rushed him, Rochester would slot him.

And to be honest, did he really want to risk his life to save that of the man who had killed one of his comrades, tried to kill two others, subverted his trusted sergeant, had let off bombs in London with no regard for innocent casualties, tried to kill him and the King?

Scipio sighed. Assassination had become England's principal medium of political and religious discourse. What a gopping filthy state they had got into! Rochester was about to put another bullet into the rule of law, God curse him!

Rochester rocked back slightly. Below, Saltonstall jerked a little, his outstretched arms lost their fluidity, became rigid. Then his gore flicked out of his chest, spattering over the greying canvas of the boxing-ring.

He flopped to the floor like a rag doll.

'Come, Mechano,' said Rochester, moving to the top of the slide. Down below, the crowd was beginning to buzz. As yet, only one voice was screaming.

Scipio shook his head. He had had enough running for one day, enough of assassins and complicated weapons. His hands were tied. Nobody would suspect him of being the killer. He wanted to have nothing to do with Rochester.

Rochester shrugged, slung the gun over his shoulder and dived headfirst down the helter-skelter to his waiting hay-cart.

Scipio stood, and made his way down the stairs.

Outside, people spoke excitedly of what had happened as, upon the platform, several of the Bull guards attended to Saltonstall.

'He's dead,' said the man in front of him.

'No he's not,' said an elderly woman. 'The advertisements said we were to expect a miracle.'

'Yaa, it's all done with sheep's guts, innit?' said a man. 'He's just pretending. He'll get up in a minute and make out that God has made him a retread again.'

A few yards away, a pair of young lovers shared an apple. The boy was cutting slices off it with a pocket-knife.

Scipio walked over to him and asked him to cut the ropes behind his back. The man obliged smilingly. He didn't even ask any questions. Men with their hands tied behind their backs were not such an uncommon sight at Saint Bartle.

They carried Saltonstall off stage.

Ethan Miller clambered into the ring and immediately began shouting. 'Brethren,' he shouted, 'you have all borne witness to what has just taken place. The politicians and the Catholics and the Jews have just fatally wounded Elder Saltonstall.'

Boos and hisses from the crowd, cries of 'For shame!'

'What you've all got to do now is rise up!' The louder he shouted, the more noticeable his odd Yank accent became.

'You must march on Parliament, march on Buckingham Palace and overthrow the satanists and whoremongers who sit in government over you . . .'

A foreigner . . .

Scipio casually wandered into the middle of the silent, bemused crowd.

'For I say unto you,' said Miller, using a verbal flourish that just did not fit, 'that the Millennium is here. King Josiah is here. The thousand-year rule of the righteous is at hand if you only but use your power, use your God-given strength to seize power . . .'

'And what are you doing while all this is going on?' Scipio shouted as loud as he could.

People around him laughed.

'You must rise up! Rise up!'

Scipio cupped his hands to his mouth and roared in his best East-Endese: 'Vat's vot my missus says every Sat'dy night!'

Raucous laughter all around.

'No, no, you don't get it, do you?' yelled Miller. 'You English, you must understand that you are being governed by the Pope, by Jews and big business. They are conspiring against you. You English must free yourselves. You are slaves to these evil men . . .'

'That's it,' said a strapping young man in a butcher's apron beside Scipio. 'That's enough of that!' he shouted. 'Are we going to stand here as free-born Englishmen and be insulted by this bloody foreigner?'

The butcher's 'prentice strode forward and leapt on to the platform holding up his fists like a good 'un. Around Scipio, everyone cheered as the lad landed Miller a beautiful right hook.

Scipio cheered.

Scipio raised his head to the sky and began singing 'God Save the King'. Others joined in. By the time they were sending him victorious, most of the crowd was singing along, the butcher's boy was giving Miller a right spanking and all the other Bulls, their resolve lost, were melting away.

Jacob Malahide fought the pain in his guts, trying to keep his mind on the business at hand.

The business at hand was getting to Heaven.

He had struggled through the tunnels, come into the daylight, and got here. He didn't remember how. Something to do with a frightened cab-driver and his chiv.

The King lived. He did not know how he knew that either.

The King, someone had said, was going to Bartle.

One of the Brethren had come out of the haze. Frightened, he was, scared. Too weak to do the Lord's work.

Back in the tunnel, Jacob Malahide had seen Hell. Jacob Malahide's Hell was not an inferno. Hell was cold. It was the Stone Room at Newgate Prison. Hell was being all alone in that damp with two bottles of gatter and a candle, knowing you were to be turned off the next day, knowing the multitude who had come to see you cry cockles would curse you and curse the hangman for not getting on with it.

He had taken the Brother's gun. The Brother was relieved to be free of it.

His guts boiled, yet he was cold, so cold.

The cold cleared his mind some. He knew two things. He knew he had been a sinner, that God's light had never shone on him. He knew that his only way of getting to Heaven was to do God's work, to complete what Ethan Miller and Elder Saltonstall had failed to do.

Placing Miller under arrest was a straightforward matter. He had two lovely shiners, a broken nose and ears that by evening would resemble cauliflowers.

There was still some fight left in him, but there was more fight in Scipio, and that was the end of it.

At the fair's edge, on this side of Vauxhall Bridge, he met a police constable, borrowed handcuffs and a radio. He was about to call for a car, when he saw the procession coming towards them, led by a magnificently dressed line of red-coated guardsmen.

The King was coming to the fair.

Scipio cursed quietly. There were still plenty of Bulls with guns around.

He handed Miller over to the constable and awaited His Majesty.

His Majesty was on foot, surrounded by a few ragged-looking detectives. He was coming to prove to everyone with eyes that he was still alive, that despite anything that Bull preachers and handbills might be saying, he was breathing and cursing yet.

He had changed into dry clothes, a regular suit with a wing-collar. His jacket was open and showed no evidence of any kind of protection underneath.

A scrawny-looking young man walked past Scipio, heading towards the King.

Scipio lunged and grabbed him before fully realizing who he was.

Seymour, Harry Seymour, King Edward VI, King Josiah . . .

'All right, Josiah?' Scipio asked him.

'The name is Harry Seymour,' he said. 'I wish to see my King.'

Well, that seemed okay.

The King spotted Scipio and waved him over. 'Who's your skinny friend?'

'Your Majesty, let me introduce . . .'

'King Edward the Sixth,' said Rochester, appearing suddenly among them, still wearing his backward cap.

'The name is Harry Seymour, sire,' said Seymour.

'Well, well, well . . .' said the King. 'Grandson of that scum-fuck Henry Tudor, aren't you? How are you off for accommodation, Harry Seymour? If you need a place to stay, I've got a nice suite of rooms in the Tower you can have. Lovely – heh-heh! – soft pillows . . .'

Seymour looked confused.

'Only joking,' said the King. The courtiers and detectives around him laughed loyally. After what they had been through earlier, most of them looked as though they would laugh at anything, and were hating every minute of all this.

And while they were all laughing, a short-haired man with a lined face, his clothes covered in blood, had somehow got among them.

Jacob Malahide pointed a revolver four feet from the King's chest.

The King's detectives pushed him to the ground. Scipio lunged for the gun. It fired.

Scipio found himself lying on the ground, on top of Malahide. The gun had fallen from his hand.

He looked to his side. There was a small mountain of

bodies, men who had thrown themselves on the King to shield him.

'Bloody hell,' said the King's voice. 'Two suits ruined in one day. Do you think you could get your elbow out of my face, Rochester?'

THINGS REMEMBERED (6)

JENNY PEARSON

EALING GRAMMAR SCHOOL FOR GIRLS, OCTOBER 1999

There was a small group of boys – sixth-formers from St Augustine's! – around Lucy at the school gate. She said goodbye to them and joined Jenny.

Now that she was in the O-Level stream, she saw less of Lucy Pickett, who had been her best friend last year. But they lived close to one another, and still walked home together the same way each evening.

They would go along suburban streets; they were quiet enough for a body to hear herself talk and think. And they could compare the houses and dream of the homes they might make one day.

She was a little envious of Lucy, who had blonde hair and blue eyes and whose figure had swollen out in all sorts of good places in the last year or two. Jenny had grown, too, but not in all the right places.

'You remember that Edmund Burnham walked in with us this morning, and offered to carry my satchel?' said Jenny.

'Uh-huh,' drawled Lucy.

'Somehow he managed to slip a three-page love-letter into my English exercise book.'

Lucy nodded. She was experienced with boys, much more than Jenny was. That was one of the things that made her exciting to be with. Boys always came up to talk to her, so sometimes they talked to Jenny as well.

'It's very childish of him, don't you think?'

'Yes,' said Jenny, 'very immature.'

She had thought nothing of the sort. If his action had not ended in catastrophe and humiliation, she would have been delighted. Not because Edmund Burnham was any great catch – some people said he was touched – but because a boy had taken the trouble to write a three-page letter to little plain her.

'It was very embarrassing,' Jenny said. 'I don't think I shall ever forgive him.'

Across the road, Lucy had caught sight of a boy she knew who had left school. He was seventeen, had a job as a milkman, and owned a motorcycle. 'Wotcher, Will!' she waved at him. Will smiled and waved back. Lucy slowed down, hoping he'd cross the road to come and talk to her. Will was number four in Lucy's Hit Parade of Most Dishy Coves of the Parish. (Actually, he might have been number three. Lucy changed her Hit Parade every Thursday, just like the music charts on the Light Programme.)

Will carried on walking. Lucy looked as he walked down the road and sighed theatrically. Jenny took a good look at Will, too. He walked with bandy legs, as though born in a saddle. His arms were long, heavy and muscular.

Will looked like a gorilla.

But he did have a real job and a Triumph moped, and the few times she had spoken to him, he had seemed a decent enough lad. She could see how all those things mattered.

Lucy turned away from Most Dishy Cove of the Parish number four (or three), and they carried on walking.

'Always the flipping same,' said Lucy, shaking her head. 'None of the nice boys want to look at me because I'm a bloody schoolgirl! You know, sometimes I hate my father for making me stay on at school. All I want is to get a job and stop being treated like a flaming kid! Girls aren't supposed to go to school anyway. If you're going to end up getting married, what do you need to be in school for?'

'My mother says I should stay at school,' said Jenny, 'because she says an education means you don't have to be just a housewife if you don't want to.'

Along the quiet roads, the trees had dumped mounds of leaves.

Jenny walked straight through a leaf-hill, threshing them to either side with her feet.

Lucy looked at her slantwise. She didn't say anything, but Jenny could tell that kicking the leaves was immature. It wouldn't do for any of the boys to see them doing this.

They walked on in silence.

'What was embarrassing, anyway?' asked Lucy.

'Hmmm?' said Jenny, who was thinking of Edmund Burnham, comparing him with Will the milkman.

'Edmund Burnham embarrassed you, you said. With the letter.'

'Yes. He put the letter in my English copybook. I didn't know it was there, and we had to give our books in to Miss Carter this morning. I gave her my book and his letter fell out of it. She picked it up and spent half the lesson reading it out loud to the whole class. She said we would look at all his spelling and grammatical mistakes, but she couldn't find any. At the end of the lesson she was telling everyone else in the class that I was' – she imitated the teacher's high, nasal tone, '"very fortunate to be the object of such an eloquent young man's attentions" as he was bound to do well for himself. It was so embarrassing. I just wanted to die.'

Lucy squealed. 'How awful for you! 'Course, that would never happen in our English class. Nobody bothers doing their homework any more. That's for kids.'

2002

They had got up at 4.30 a.m. to catch the Brighton train as far as Reigate, sitting next to their bikes on the floor of the mail waggon with the Ordnance Survey map spread out in front of them.

Strategy was one of Edmund's enthusiasms, and he plotted their route through the back-roads around Dorking with all the lunatic precision of the Schlieffen Plan that he had been learning about in A Level History at St Augustine's.

She wasn't sure that this was a terribly good idea, but knew it was best to keep quiet when Edmund was gripped by one of his enthusiasms.

They had ridden out of Reigate Station at half past six into a glorious summer morning, heavy with the scent of wild flowers and decay.

Along the roads and lanes were derelict houses, or

the ruins of public buildings. The area, her father had told her, had less than a quarter of the population it used to. Much of the land was being farmed, but a lot of it was common or crown land which had either turned to wilderness or was being managed by the Countryside and Agriculture Commission.

They rode through sleepy little villages, some deserted, some not. Wouldn't it be wonderful to live in one of these places? she thought. All that peace and quiet, no grime, not many cars, have a little garden to grow your own vegetables . . .

By mid-morning, Edmund had got them well and truly lost, though it took him another two hours to admit it.

It didn't matter.

They lay on the grass by a small stream, shaded from the fierce afternoon sun by a pair of huge oaks. They had eaten the picnic her mother had packed for them.

'I hope you can cook as good as your Mum,' said Edmund, stretching out on the grass.

In the last few months, both had started to assume that one day they would marry. They never said anything about it openly, never discussed the wedding arrangements, but they always talked as though they would spend their lives together.

She passed him the bottle of Corona as he lit a Passing Cloud. He offered her one, she took it, and caught the box of matches he flipped to her.

Once or twice she had almost yielded to him. She worried about this. She also worried that Edmund didn't seem to press her too hard for sex. All her friends constantly complained of how their boyfriends just wouldn't take no for an answer. Edmund usually took no for an answer with a good grace. Did that mean he was a gentleman, or just that he didn't fancy her that much?

She had sort of spoken to her mother about this. Mum didn't exactly dislike Edmund, but she wasn't mad keen on him either, said that Edmund was too in love with himself to be in love with anyone else very long.

Jenny wasn't sure that was completely true. Edmund was a retread. He'd been working on a farm for a living by the time he was four years old. His drunken father would lay about him and his brothers with a leather belt once or twice a week. He had been eleven when he died of the smallpox. If Edmund was in love with himself, it was because whenever he looked in a mirror, he saw a different person each time. The idea that he could be anything he wanted, do whatever he wished, intoxicated him.

'They're bad for you, you know,' he said, holding up his cigarette. 'They're addictive, make you short of breath, give you a cough and cost a lot.'

'So why do you smoke them?' she asked.

'Why do you?' he said, pointing to her cigarette.

She shrugged. 'Because I'm addicted.'

'Exactly. There are millions of us, all enslaved by tobacco. The man who can invent something to free people of this bondage will become very wealthy.'

He stretched out on his back and took a luxuriant drag on his fag, letting the smoke out in a long, slow stream. Edmund was becoming infected with another enthusiasm.

The list of Edmund's enthusiasms was a long one. He was going to start a company making better, cheaper transistor radios than the Indians. He would study physics to degree level and join the United States National Aeronautics and Space Administration and join their project to put a man on the moon or Mars. He was convinced that retreads were the work of extremely advanced creatures from another planet, and wanted to be among the first to make contact with them. In less fanciful moments, he was going to print greetings-cards with verses on them, or write best-selling detective stories, or learn to play the saxophone, or manufacture aeroplanes cheap enough for every family to own one. His latest obsession was with old records, pop music from before the Atom War, the closer to the beginning of the Atom War, the better. He would ride his bike all around London and the suburbs raiding curiosity shops and jumble-sales to pick up his beloved records. He played them to her in his bedroom when she went to visit (his stepmother insisted they keep the door open to protect Jenny's virtue!). These old records by Joe Brown, Terry Dene, Lonnie Donegan, Billy Fury and the Tornadoes, Johnny Kidd and the Pirates, The Shadows . . . well, some of them were okay, and they often sounded a lot like modern beat groups. Edmund liked them as much as she did, sometimes less, but, he said, they were all working towards something. It was, he said, as though youth music in Britain had been on the edge of some astonishing leap forward just before the Atom War. Jenny didn't really understand what he was grasping for, and perhaps he didn't either.

She ground her cigarette stub into the hard-baked

ground beneath her, lay on her back and closed her eyes.

She would, she decided, give up cigarettes. She'd just confessed to being addicted to them. That would never do.

Only gradually did she become aware that Edmund's hand was on her breast, and that his hot, tobacco-tinged breath was playing along her neck. Another hand was fumbling with the zip on her shorts.

Drowsily, she pulled his mouth on to hers.

Something had happened today, she wasn't quite sure what it was. But it had convinced her that she would own Edmund, if only for a short time.

EPILOGUE

WEDNESDAY, 27 AUGUST 2008

The curfew tolls the knell of parting day,
The lowing herd winds slowly o'er the lea,
The ploughman homeward plods his weary way,
And leaves the world to darkness and to me.
– Thomas Gray, 'Elegy in a Country Churchyard'

Jenny pulled up and parked her Mini behind an old Morris 1100 in a long street of meticulously maintained Victorian semis, prosperous Italianate homes, some of which would once have had servants living in those strange basements, not fully underground, but not wholly above it either.

A lot fewer people had servants these days. Guy Boswell said there were servants at the home of his kinsman Sir Digby Lovejoy, but he fancied that they were probably related to him, and that they were retreads he had taken in from a mixture of kindness and practicality.

The tang of fresh-cut grass carried into the car as she wound her window down. It had rained abundantly during the night, turning yellowing lawns and parks across the city green once more.

The back window, shot out by pursuing Bulls when she had left the Isle of Dogs so quickly, had been repaired at police expense. The paint-job on the back of the car, where it had been scarred by shotgun-pellets, could wait.

She was a few minutes too early.

She turned on the car radio. A young man, American by the sound of him, sang in a raucous voice with a raw, minimal amount of backing. A guitar, a few hand-claps and drums that sounded so dull they might have been cardboard-boxes. He had the 'Summertime Blues' and there was no known cure for them.

Yes, definitely American. He was talking about complaining to his 'congressman'.

'Eddie Cochran, folks,' said the radio presenter, 'with a song he first recorded fifty years ago. Mr Cochran died in a road accident in Wiltshire while he was touring Britain. He was reborn here a few months back.'

Cochran, Cochran, Eddie Cochran . . . She'd heard that name before somewhere.

Then she smiled. Edmund. Edmund sent her a long letter and a single red rose on her birthday every year. Back in May he had reminded her of his enthusiasm for music from the few years before the Atom War, of how he had got together with 'this amazing old bird from Liverpool' named Epstein to start a record company reissuing this old stuff. And then, two days after they had registered the company – E and B Records – 'as though God Himself had willed it', said Edmund, this American boy Cochran had been reborn. Like a lot of foreigners who arrived as retreads, he wasn't in too much of a hurry to return to the home where all the people he had loved would be gone, and they persuaded him into a recording studio.

Perhaps this latest enthusiasm had finally put him on the road to a fortune.

'Good for you, Edmund!' she said out loud.

Two hundred yards away, she saw Guy Boswell coming around the corner, evidently whistling. One hand was in his pocket, the other worked the walking stick like a sprightly squire. He spotted her instantly, even at this distance. He waved and grinned like a cheeky schoolboy.

In a year or less, Guy would be going off on courses and sitting exams. By then, the Inspector had assured her, she would be a sergeant, but Guy would be on the road to becoming a minor potentate in the Civil Service, or a police inspector at the least. He would earn far more than she, he would mix with different people – the rich, the pretentious, the witty, the beautiful . . . people terrified of being ordinary. He would probably marry an heiress or an artist, someone fashionably thin or fashionably fat.

He might as well be going to New Zealand. Or Mars. The Liberal Settlement had always been generous to retreads of the right class.

In the due course of things, she hoped she would find a decent man, settle down and have children.

No, let's be clear about this; she would probably marry Edmund. Edmund had called her 'the great unfinished business of my life'. In his letters he would joke about how he was seeking his fortune in order to be worthy of her hand, but she fancied he meant it. The two of them would meet up once a year or so, in a pub or a restaurant, and talk like old friends, gossiping furiously about the people they both knew, or about her work as a rozzer or about his latest enthusiasm. He would then escort her back to her flat (though Heaven knows he was usually in more need of an escort than she); they would kiss chastely and he would leave.

She did not love Edmund. Yet. When he determined what he was going to do with his life she might do. There was time enough.

Marriage. Children. There would be days on which her own mother and father came to visit their grandchildren, take tea on the lawn and delight in the antics of the youngsters.

On days like that she would have to look over the edge of the abyss.

The inevitable loss of people you love.

To knowingly increase the number of people you care about is far harder than facing down a lunatic with a gun.

Her old schoolfriends didn't know what she knew. They hadn't seen the things she had seen. Most had plunged into marriage and motherhood as though their lives depended on it. They had not yet looked into the abyss. But Jenny Pearson was a rozzer. She was paid £28 a month, plus clothing allowance, to stare over that edge, to look on the fragility of human happiness, every single working day.

Guy opened the passenger-door and climbed in, with some difficulty, beside her. His ankle was in plaster, but was evidently not causing him any more pain. He walked with the aid of a fancy ebony cane he must have borrowed from his host. This he now parked between his knees.

'Had a devil of a job escaping,' he smiled. 'Sir Digby's

lively daughter and her friend have gone off to Bath to spend the rest of the season with some of their old schoolfriends, and Lady Lovejoy decreed that we should have a musical soirée this evening. It was horrible, horrible.'

He broke into a shriek and sang. 'Pale hands I loved, beside the Shalimar . . .'

She burst out laughing. 'Couldn't you have played them some songs from your time?'

'Oh, certainly,' said Guy. 'Back at Biggin Hill, your humble servant was much in demand at mess-parties for his dextrous tickling of the ivories. I don't know what Her Ladyship would have made of my two specialities, though . . .'

'Which are?'

'Well, there's our old favourite, "Bless 'em All", which at least has a non-obscene version. I have also received many compliments for my rendition of "Ain't the Air Force Blooming Awful". Um, except that the done thing is to substitute "blooming" with a far stronger expletive.'

She smiled.

'So what did you tell them?'

He shrugged. 'I'm so in debt to dear old Lady L. that I was sorely tempted to give her some cock-and-bull about going to meet a kinsman I'd traced at the Public Record Office, but that would have been cowardly. I told her I was meeting a colleague.'

'. . . Which was almost as cowardly,' she laughed.

He smiled and shrugged.

After all the drama of Accession Day they had all been given a week's leave. Guy might be off for longer, depending on how his ankle fared. She had tidied her flat, painted a bit of the woodwork, bought a couple of dress-patterns and tomorrow was going to go to Brighton for a long weekend with a couple of friends.

Edmund had telephoned on Monday after reading about her part in the events of Accession Day in the newspaper and about how she had been recommended for the Police Service Medal. He had asked her – no, begged her – to consider a safer job.

She had considered, was still considering, wondering if she was growing addicted to danger in the same way she had once been addicted to cigarettes.

Still wondering. Especially at night. She usually slept okay, but there had been nightmares, frights.

'So what have you been up to?' she asked Guy.

'Oh, taking it easy, trying to get better. And I went to the Public Record Office yesterday. Lady L. was coming into town for some shopping so I got her to drop me off.'

'And?'

'She died last year. Only last year, would you believe? She'd have been 90 years old.'

He must mean his fiancée from his previous life. He had never mentioned her before now, but Jenny had guessed there would be someone.

'Pamela married an Army officer in forty-five. A Scotsman who'd been in one of those cut-throat outfits who had operated behind enemy lines. Quite a hero, to judge by all the letters after his name. He carried her off to the Shetlands, where he owned some land. It saved her life. The Atom War, the Feudal Wars, the whole bloody storm passed them by. I imagine that life was hard, but she had five children and twenty-two grandchildren and probably great-grandchildren as well. She would have been happy, wouldn't she, Jenny?'

Jenny nodded. 'It certainly sounds like it. You should be glad.'

'I am,' he said.

Guy was crying.

'I'm sorry,' he said.

'It's all right. Nothing to be ashamed of.' She reached over and pulled his head to her shoulder. She said nothing while he sobbed.

'It's the best possible outcome,' he said eventually. 'She had a long, happy, fulfilled life. I'd have hated it if she'd just been killed in the Atom War, or spent the rest of her days brooding over me.'

'That's right,' she said, stroking his hair.

'And if she was still alive, I wouldn't know what to do. Would she have wanted to see me? Would I have wanted to see her?'

'Or would her nonagenarian laird have given you the bum's rush like a proper war-hero should?' she said.

Guy pulled away from her, produced a hankie from somewhere and blew his nose loudly. He turned and smiled at her. 'He'd have the best of me, considering the state I'm in.'

She smiled back.

'Oh Jenny, you're a great sport. I don't know what I'd have done without you.'

She placed her right index finger over his lips. 'As a detective constable to an apprentice, I am giving you an order – don't complicate things.'

He smiled again and nodded. 'You're quite right. I am sorry, but I did mean it. I do owe you a great deal.'

'Forget it.'

'Right then, where are you taking me?'

'Food or drink?'

'Drink. Lord, how I need a drink!'

'It's a bit of a drive, but I know a very nice country pub just up the road a bit.'

'Sounds good to me.'

She didn't know where this would lead to, but what the heck? They were on leave, and there wouldn't be much summer left. She started the engine.

She loved men, and loved what she could learn from them. Every man she had been close to made her a better, stronger person, but she needed to grow much stronger yet.

Was she using Guy? Was she just playing with this cove while she waited for Edmund to pop the question?

No, she wasn't using him. She was helping him. She wouldn't – couldn't – own him. At best, they would own one another temporarily. She was getting him on loan before the world embraced him as a favoured, pampered son.

Do we have a bargain, Miss Pearson?

Yes, we do. This could be a disaster, it could be embarrassing and humiliating for all concerned. But probably just a bit of a lark.

It was eight o'clock on a bright, warm evening. The scent of freshly cut grass hung heavy in the air and Jenny Pearson pulled out from the kerb, offering a silent prayer to God, whoever he might be, to thank him that she was alive.

It was a large town-house in Chelsea, one of a block of

five set in a small side-street. His Lordship liked to give the impression that he was a substantial landowner in the country, which might or might not be true.

Somehow, Scipio doubted it. Land in many parts of the countryside was cheap, and Rochester certainly had plenty of tin. His plays for the stage and the television saw to that, but the man was a city-dweller to the marrow.

He jammed his thumb into the brass button at the side of the door, heard the bell ringing inside.

Almost at once, the door was opened by a butler in purple jacket, purple breeches, white silk stockings and powdered wig.

'I need to see Rochester. Now.'

'I am sorry, sir,' said the butler haughtily. 'His Lordship is not at home to visitors at the moment. But if sir would deign to leave his card . . .'

Scipio showed the man his warrant-card and pushed past him.

The hall was very grand. Polished parquet flooring you could see your face in (Rochester probably used it for looking up the skirts of female visitors). Expensive flock wallpaper, a marble staircase.

'Where is he?'

'I must insist, sir, that you leave at once.'

He pushed his card into the flunkey's face a second time. 'Where is he?'

'Downstairs, sir, but—'

'Which way?'

Rochester was probably diverting himself with a woman. Or maybe even a boy.

The butler pointed to a small door at the foot of the

410

staircase. Scipio tried the handle. It was locked.

'You have a key? Get it now.'

He followed the man to a small room beneath the stairs. From a hook on the wall, he took a large bunch of keys.

'Don't dawdle, man. I am eager to apprehend his Lordship in the midst of whatever sin he is engaged in.'

The servant gave him a filthy look. The sort of wrathful stare that could have killed one of the aspidistras growing in large china pots on little tables around the hallway.

The door opened. Scipio found himself descending a narrow, dark wooden staircase.

Suddenly, his nostrils were assaulted by a sweet, pungent smell, slightly oily, vaguely familiar.

At the bottom of the staircase was another door, which he opened . . .

And found a small chapel, richly decked out in all the paraphernalia of the Catholic rite, but big enough to accommodate no more than twenty people. A mass was in progress.

'*Dominus vobiscum,*' said the priest from the altar no more than 10 yards away, ignoring the arrival of the newcomer.

'*Et cum spiritu tuo,*' responded the only other person in the congregation, a man in middle age wearing a plain black modern suit. Rochester.

'*Initium sancti Evangelii secundum Joannem,*' said the priest, a swag-bellied man in his late forties wearing a fantastically-elaborate robe embroidered in dazzling silks and threads of silver and gold.

'*Gloria tibi, Domine,*' responded Rochester, who had

not turned round to see who the newcomer was.

I may as well sit here and wait, thought Scipio. Only now did he notice that sitting at the top corner of the room next to the altar was young Ethelbright, wearing a cassock, acting as altar-boy.

Incense. The powerful smell was incense. That and the smell of whatever nut-oil it was they burned in their lamps.

The priest spoke. '*In principio erat Verbum et Verbum erat apud Deum, et Deus erat Verbum. Hoc erat in principio apud Deum.*' The start of St John's Gospel. 'In the beginning was the Word, and the Word was with God, and the Word was God. The same was in the beginning with God.'

'*Omnia per ipsum facta sunt, et sine ipso factum est nihil quod factum est; in ipso vita erat, et vita erat lux hominum; et lux in tenebris lucet, et tenebrae eam non comprehenderunt.*' 'All things were made by him; and without him was made nothing that was made. In him was life; and the life was the light of men. And the light shone in darkness; and the darkness comprehended it not.'

The Puritans had a point. What was the sense in all this flummery? In a religious service that most folk did not understand the words of. The man could be reading out his grocery-list in Latin and most plain Catholics would cant their responses and get down on one knee.

The priest droned on. So Rochester was a practising Catholic? The great atheist rake of the Restoration era had turned to God, aye and the Catholic God at that. Why was that not even slightly surprising?

A pound of sprouts, a jar of strawberry jam, a quarter

of tea, a bag of sugar, or whatever, went the priest before raising his voice. '*Et Verbum caro factum est!*' 'And the Word was made flesh.'

Ethan Miller was under lock and key. A phone call to the US Embassy had confirmed that back home Miller was as tasty as a grilled kipper, wanted by the authorities in four different states for murder, planting bombs and other nonsense. He had been a member of an extremist Protestant sect that believed that white Anglo-Saxons were one of the twelve tribes of Israel. He would be extradited.

The priest finished speaking. '*Deo gratias*,' said Rochester.

Jacob Malahide was dead, Saltonstall was dead, his side-kick Lilley was arrested and singing like a canary. He had turned king's evidence in the hope of avoiding a capital sentence and had given the names and addresses of dozens of lesser Upright Men. O'Rourke was under lock and key, too. O'Rourke – Uncle Seamus – a traitor. He had been a Bull since the day he joined the force twenty-five years ago. Someone in the Order had been playing a long game, reckoning on the great usefulness of having a trusty in the rozzers. O'Rourke had done his masters proud. He had familiarized himself thoroughly with the police files and the workings of the Public Record Office and proved an indispensable source of intelligence to the Good Old Cause. It was O'Rourke who had alerted them to the arrival of King Edward VI.

Who on earth could you ever trust in this world?

None save God.

The priest, followed by Ethelbright, disappeared

through a door at the side of the altar.

Rochester blessed himself, walked to the end of the short pew, genuflected towards the altar and approached him.

'Still on the job, Mechano?' He seemed unsurprised to see Scipio. 'Well, now you know my big secret.'

'A man as hasty-witted as your Lordship must have many secrets.'

Rochester smiled and sat down beside him. ''Tis the smell of the incense I always feared would give me away. In a moment I shall have to change my clothes and have a shower, then drench myself in Cologne.'

'Why, Rochester?'

'My public face is that of a rake. Aye, and I still sin mightily, and I don't expect you to believe me, but I very much regret that. I am growing old, Mechano. As men age, they become more fearful. Why else would war be a business for clay-brained youths? I find that the Church of Rome, with its timeless rituals, is a source of wisdom and comfort. But I worship in secret because it suits my work.'

'Which work would that be? Your saucy plays, your raking, or your secretive political mischief?'

Rochester grinned his winning smile. 'All of them. Don't worry. Cardinal Campion is a good friend of mine. He is most eager that at some propitious moment I ostentatiously announce my conversion.'

'How does a man call himself a Christian after he has killed another in cold blood? What does your Catholic God think of you perched atop Bendo's helter-skelter calmly shooting Saltonstall?'

Rochester shrugged. 'That I cannot answer. There is no

possibility that you would believe me, but I seek for-
giveness for that and other sins in my every waking hour.'

'You are right, Rochester. I do not believe you. If only
because that would make it even harder for me to
understand. The man should have been arrested and
tried by due process of law.'

'No, Mechano. How were you, a single man, to arrest
him in the midst of that great beslubbering mob? Had I
not ventilated him when I did, who knows how many
different flavours of misery we should be enduring
now? It was necessary. It was an evil that prevented far
greater evil.'

'I should arrest you and charge you with murder.'

Rochester's eyes widened and his shook his head
furiously. 'I beg you not to do that, Mechano.'

'Why?'

'Shall we go upstairs? We can have a drink.'

'No, Rochester, just answer the question. Why can I
not run you down to Bow Street and throw the book at
you?'

Rochester sighed. He took an amber rosary from his
pocket and began to fidget with its beads. 'I am invul-
nerable. You could apprehend me now, and I would be
free within half an hour. No case would ever come to
court. I have more friends than you can possibly
imagine.'

That made sense. The Sealed Knot, the secret society
committed to preserving the Liberal Settlement, was
not without influence. It was not beyond possibility
that even the Vatican had agents in Britain. One heard
rumours, from time to time.

'Of far more importance, Mechano, if you arrest me,

then the only consequence will be that you will be made to look foolish. For the moment, you are a hero. Distinguished in the Feudal Wars, a policeman of great repute, and now the saviour of the King from assassination, the saviour of London from bombs and the saviour of the country from chaos and possible war. You are very valuable to us all, Mechano. But should you annoy the wrong people, they will chew you up and spit you out with no hesitation.'

Of course he had known it. He had come here to arrest Rochester, to clear up the last of the business of recent days. But in the back of his mind he had known all along that it would be impossible.

'Inspector, you are a good man, a rock of moral certainty in a sea of dissembling, selfishness and compromise. More important still, you are a great upholder of the Liberal Settlement. We need you. Join us, Inspector.'

Inspector? Not 'Mechano' any more.

By Christ, he was serious!

'Think about it. Come and see me any time.'

Scipio stood up. 'I do not need to think about it, Rochester. If you think I will join some secret society, if you think I can gaily connive at conspiracy and assassination to keep you and your cronies in fine houses, servants, private chantries and chapels, frenchified food and expensive whores, then you are a much poorer judge of men than I accounted you. I trust – no, Rochester, I earnestly hope – that our paths shall not cross again.'

Out in the street, the air was fresh and clean. The sun was still bright in the early evening sky, but a downpour last night had done the place the power of good. It almost seemed sinful to be smoking in such splendid weather, but he lit a Zimbabwe anyway.

He would walk home along beside the Thames. It was a fair old trudge to Blackfriars but he needed the exercise.

And the fresh air to get the smell of incense, the stink of religion corrupted, out of his clothes.

He would try not to think about Rochester and his conspiring cronies. So the man was immune from prosecution, and Scipio so detested loose ends, but there was nothing to be done.

He would take a couple of days off. Be with the kids a while, do some jobs around the house. A rest would do him good.

The Shoreditch reception centre had telephoned him at the office this afternoon saying they had an eight-year-old African child to place, a kid who'd died of some disease or other there in the eighteenth century, and would he and his wife be interested in fostering the girl? He had given them his home number and told them to talk to Kitty. Kitty would say yes. She always did.

How many children had they fostered or adopted, now? This would be the twenty-first. His own son was a distinguished musician, his daughter was training to be a doctor. Of the retreads, all those who had left home were making their way in the world. Not one had been in trouble with the law (as far as he knew).

That counted for something. He made a difference.

Across the Thames, the lights were starting to come on at the New Battersea funfair. That's what we'll do, he decided as he flicked his fag-end into the river. We'll all go to the fair tomorrow and make a big fuss of our newest arrival.

To hell with walking, he thought, and started to look for a bus-stop.

HISTORICAL NOTE

Most of the slang used by the characters is real and comes from a wide variety of sources, including the rich verbal traditions of the twentieth century British Army and from Eric Partridge's seminal *Dictionary of Slang and Unconventional English*. Other than the latter, I did not read any books specifically for research purposes, though there are dozens which influenced the story. The ones that spring to mind include Graham Greene's biography of Rochester, Peter Linebaugh's *The London Hanged*, Kellow Chesney's hugely entertaining *The Victorian Underworld*, several books by Christopher Hill, Keith Thomas's classic *Religion and the Decline of Magic* and Norman Cohn's remarkable and harrowing *The Pursuit of the Millennium*, which remains the best account there is of what happens when people get their religion and politics all mixed up.

Rochester really existed. An ornament of the court of the Merry Monarch, King Charles II, he was indeed the original rake-hell, and got up to all sorts of decadent devilment. In general, he is not well known because the little historical knowledge the majority of Brits possess is perverted by an education system which filters out the sex and violence. This takes the story out of history, leaving us with a wide array of safe-but-tedious topics, such as crop-rotation, parliamentary reform and Austro-Hungarian foreign policy. Because of this dreary sanitization of school history, every writer who comes across Milord Rochester does so independently in adult life. The writer immediately considers his Lordship to be his/her own personal property and gets very cross on discovering any other author fooling around with him. Having noted a few writers doing this, I myself fell victim to precisely the same folly. So anyway, N., I want you to know you're not a bastard really. It's that swine Rochester who's been cheating on all of us.

Of the other main characters in this story, Lawrence is real (obviously) and so is Richard III. Historical purists would be entirely justified in pointing out that the personality of my Richard bears no resemblance whatever to the real Richard, who was a driven, insecure hardcase given to the kind of hypocrisy that would make a newspaper editor blush. Yes, of course he murdered the princes in the Tower.

Scipio Africanus, a black slave or servant in the household of the Earl of Suffolk, died aged about 18 and was buried at Henbury Churchyard, Bristol, in 1720. If you visit Scipio's grave, you will usually find a bunch of flowers laid on it. I do not know who puts the flowers there; it may be several different people. One assumes that they do this not only in memory of Scipio himself but because his grave is one of the few known burial places in the UK of an African from the period when Christian Englishmen traded in slaves.

All the other main characters are fictitious.

ACKNOWLEDGEMENTS

In one form or another this story has been years in the making, and I need to thank lots of people for their assistance or interest. These include (among many others and in no particular order) Meg Davis, John Jarrold, Kim Newman, Brian Smedley, Alex Dunn, Julian and Carol Dunn, Kate and Lizzy Harvey, Jim Fanning, Rod Jones, David Pringle, Pete and Gina Burilin, Kath Coupland, Tony Curtis, Mark Kenny, Charles McFeeley, Jim Will and Alan Clarke, plus everyone at Venue Publishing, particularly Dave 'Stinker' Higgitt, Robin 'Hippy' Askew, Marc 'Popeye' Crewe, Cris 'Prune' Warren, Dougal 'Fatty' Templeton, Ann Sheldon, Jo Renshaw and Raheela Raza-Syed. Above all, I have to thank my wife Monique, without whom . . .